Soul Shift

2012 and Beyond

Judith Horky

Book Two
of the
EarthShift Series

Crystal Mountain Press
Pagosa Springs, Colorado

Soul Shift — 2012 and Beyond

By Judith Horky

Published 2010

ISBN: 978-0-9711862-1-7

Published by
Crystal Mountain Press
Pagosa Springs, CO 81147

http://www.JudithHorky.com

Printed in the United States of America

Acknowledgments

Once again I must thank so many beings, both visible and invisible, for their support and guidance on the development and completion of ***Soul Shift—2012 and Beyond.*** Indeed, many souls have begun and will continue to shift during this time of increased energy and vibration.

To my wonderful family, who accept and support my endeavors for which I am deeply grateful, I love you all. Special thanks go to Tom Drews for his encouragement and creative assistance, for going the extra mile, and for always being there.

I'm thankful for the many friends who read for me, made suggestions, and held my hand when I most needed it. Big hugs to Jill Barnes, Jeanne Kaiser, Sally Hanson, Jan and Dave Dutton, Renae Karlquist, Katie Hudson, and Sue Martin.

To my frontline editor, Pauline "Sam" Hunneman ... you are amazing. A huge thank you for your guidance, clarity, and dedication. You shared my journey and honored my message.

And to Ann Miller, for your skills in the world of publishing, editing and formatting, your patience, and for all the other professional computer skills I lack, my deep gratitude.

Meredith Young-Sowers, you continue to be my special angel. I so value your friendship. God bless both you and Mentor.

And with all my heart, I thank my husband for allowing me the time and space to "do my thing" and for believing in me ... and most of all, for his deep love. Jim, I love you dearly.

THE FAMILY

Julie and Dave Armstrong: Parents and grandparents, strong and courageous. Spiritual teachers.

Bill Cramer: Julie's oldest son, married to Kathy.
Children, **Joey**, age 4* and **Erica**, age 2*.

Steve Cramer: Julie's second son, married to **Megan**.
Children, (twins) **Jesse** and **Mike**. Age 5*.

Jon Cramer: Julie's youngest son.

Chris Armstrong: Dave's son, married to Ellen.

Jeannie Mathews: Dave's daughter, married to **Jerry.**
Their daughter: **Angela**, born during the EarthShift.

*Ages as of the time of the EarthShift.

Prologue

As before, in accordance with Gabriel's instructions, an enormous bonfire had been built in the meadow. After dark, they'd set it ablaze. Now, the entire family circled around it, struggling at times just to stay on their feet as the violence of the vibrations intensified. But struggle they would, and they would stay. For as long as Jesse and his cousins needed their help, this was where they'd be; these men and women and the children they'd made, joined by blood, by purpose. Joined, most of all, by love.

When Julie and Dave Armstrong had put out the call that *everyone's* energies were needed to help Jesse complete his mission, the family had dropped everything and come instantly to Wind Dancer Ranch.

Julie looked at them now, standing shoulder to shoulder, daughters with their husbands, sons with their wives, young ones clinging to parents, not quite comprehending the enormity of it all, but certainly picking up on the gist of it. She'd never been more proud. And if she hadn't been clinging to Dorado's reassurances and working very hard to be positive, she would have been utterly terrified.

The darkness in the meadow deepened to pitch-black, relieved only by the fire. It didn't matter to the family, now deep in prayer.

But as the minutes ticked down toward midnight, the fire rose up, hotter, brighter, and brighter still, until Dave became aware of it on a conscious level. When he opened his eyes to make sure it was still under control, his gaze was immediately drawn to the peak of Crystal Mountain.

"Oh, my God!" he yelled, horrified. "Look at the mountain! Oh, God, the kids are up there!"

PART ONE

Four years after The EarthShift

The potential possibilities of any child are the most intriguing and stimulating in all creation.

Ray L. Wilbur (1875-1949)

Chapter One

Yes, what a long, strange trip it's been, Julie thought as she waited in the sunlight on the wide, weathered deck for Jesse to answer her call. Breathing in the glorious scents of meadow flowers and pinion pines, and enjoying her view of Crystal Mountain, she thought about the strange and twisted path which had led to her own spirituality. It still seemed improbable—if not impossible—and, she admitted without regret, more the stuff of dime novels or bad poetry than prayer books.

Oh, there'd been plenty of religion in her past. The American branch of the family history began with an Irish immigrant great-grandfather who'd converted from Catholic to Protestant the minute he'd stepped off the boat. Young Bowen Cramer soon discovered that in his family, blood was thicker than water, but not *holy* water.

Bowen's son, Bryan, her jack-of-all-trades grandfather, had been seized in his middle years by a Christian fervor so hot and bright, he'd eventually built his own chapel. He'd raised spirits as well as vegetables, and delivered "The Word" as well the U.S. Mail. He'd told Julie, when she was just a little girl, that "the man on the throne up there watches every move we make, so you'd better be a good girl." Scary stuff.

Oh Gramp, if you could see me now, what would you think? Of this reality. The Fifth Dimension. Flying on spaceships. Traveling with only the power of your mind. Conversing with E.T.s. And angels, for Pete's sake! Archangels, at that! And your great-great-grandson chosen—by Gabriel himself—to have a hand in saving the world.

That thought brought Julie back to the present with a jolt. No matter how great the honor, Gabriel's assignment was a huge responsibility—especially for one so young. As much as Julie and her husband, Dave, had always made it their first priority to provide a strong support system for their family, she knew it was especially important that they be there for Jesse.

Cupping her hands around her mouth, she called again, "Jesse!"

No response.

Since the dinner bell was about the only thing that could bring her grandchildren back from their adventures once they were running loose on the ranch, Julie rang it with enthusiasm.

"Jesse! We need to talk!"

Julie's delightful step-daughter, Jeannie, swung through the screen door with her 4-year-old daughter close on her heels, teddy bear in hand. Julie scooped up the golden-haired Angela for a hug and a snuzzle.

Like her cousin, Angela was also predestined for big things. Her birth—the delivery handled by Gabriel himself—had come only moments before Zero Point; that moment during the Shift, when the darkness had fallen, palpable as a living thing, time had stopped, and the world stood still.

Angela had entered the world with spina bifida, but miraculously healed, literally during the EarthShift. And now, she ran and roughhoused with the best of them, rode her pony, Lily, with abandon, and could melt icicles with her cornflower blue eyes.

A fascinating, sometimes disconcerting, result of the Shift vibrations was that all kids in The Fifth were more mature than their chronological ages. For some, there was an additional piece of cosmic wisdom stemming from the awareness of their past lives. As appealing as this was to Julie's inner *woo-woo girl,* she felt that most of Angela's maturity came from understanding that the same cosmic force which healed her fragile body was the same one which shattered her father's fragile spirit and left him trapped back in The Third.

"Hi, Grandma!" Angela giggled. "What do you want Jesse for?"

"Oh, just a check-in, sweetie. I like to keep track of where my grandchildren are hiding."

"Well, *I'm* right here and I know where *he* is. I'll tell you if I can have a candy," she teased, batting her long lashes.

Julie raised one eyebrow. "Hmmm. Is my sweet granddaughter guilty of extortion? And so soon after breakfast?"

"Did I say 'a candy'?" The blue eyes sparkled. "I meant 'a kiss'."

"I just happen to have an endless supply of kisses!" And leaning in, Julie planted a smacking one on Angela's neck followed by vibrating 'raspberries'. "There! Now, you rascal, where's your cousin?"

"In the barn talking to Misty. He sure likes your horse, Grandma."

"I know. And thank you." *Well,* she thought, *at least, he hasn't translocated to a space ship or another planet ... again.* "How about picking me a bouquet for the dinner table?"

"Okay! I know right where the prettiest flowers are!" Little legs spinning, the young carbon copy of her mother took off across the meadow.

Jeannie collapsed, laughing, into a rocking chair and settled Angela's bear on her lap. "Julie, do kids make you old and gray, or keep you young?"

Julie smiled. "Keep you young. Definitely. And I love every minute with them." She turned and her smile dimmed a bit. "But sometimes, Jeannie, Gabriel's assignment feels so very heavy ... maybe not for an archangel, but certainly for mortals, and kids at that! The kids are growing up beautifully. Amazingly. But when I think of what they have to face ..."

"I know. Raising Angela without her dad just makes things that much harder, especially not knowing whether Jerry will ever make it out of the

Third Dimension and be with us again. It hurts so much. I'd go back for him in a heartbeat, but I don't know if I'm strong enough to pull off the return trip. And Gabriel was very clear, right from her birth, that it's crucial for me to be there for Angela, for her to know she can count on me."

Julie placed a reassuring hand on Jeannie's shoulder. "And in the way of archangels, he was right. And you know that Chris and Ellen and Jon are doing everything they can to find Jerry. Whatever happens, you and Angela need to stick together."

"I know, Julie. Thanks for the reminder."

"You are so very welcome, hon. And now, if you'll excuse me, I'm off to see a boy about a horse."

Julie heard them as she neared the old cedar barn. The doors were wide open, and a shaft of sunlight angled down through the dusty haze. The sweet scent of hay and the familiar smells of horses and leather drew her in, but not wanting to intrude, she hesitated at the door.

"Y'know, Misty," Jesse confided, "I envy you sometimes. As long as you have grass and oats and can run in the fields, you're happy. You don't have to worry about growing up and saving the world and all that stuff."

Julie could sense Misty advising that Jesse lighten up and enjoy being a boy; that maturity and answers would come soon enough. Well pleased, she walked closer and touched his arm.

"Sorry to interrupt, Jesse."

"Oh ... it's okay. I was just talking about some stuff with Misty."

"I know." She rubbed the horse's velvet nose, then slid her hand under Misty's halter to find the mare's favorite scratching place. "And I wanted to talk about some stuff with you. But now, I think it can wait a while. So here's a better idea. Misty needs some exercise. Want to take her out for a run?"

His eyes lit up. "Oh Grandma! Could I?"

Julie urged the habitual curl off his forehead before kissing it. Turning to her horse, she stroked the glossy neck. "Misty, you'll take good care of my very special grandson, won't you?" The horse snorted, and shook her handsome head in assent.

Together, they saddled up, and after a quick adjustment of stirrups, Jesse headed for the hills, careful to warm Misty up with a short walk first. Then, with a wave from Julie, the pair took off at a full gallop, horse and rider melding in a smooth rhythm.

Julie thought that Jesse's trip on this plane had been pretty long and strange, too. A shy, nearly timid little boy, during the Shift he'd grabbed onto his own spirituality with both hands to guide his family through the changes. *Such a strong spirit—no wonder Gabriel chose him.*

Jesse was one of the few souls Julie knew who'd been assigned his own extraterrestrial guide, Dorado; a more visible and hands-on presence than even personal angels. Dorado had overseen Jesse's advanced instruction, taking him to the stars and beyond, and introducing him to beings from other worlds, other times and other dimensions. Jesse had, in Julie's estimation, gotten his spiritual wings the old-fashioned way: He'd earned them.

In the distance, majestic Crystal Mountain glowed; an earthly mountain that hadn't lost the golden aura of Julie's post-Shift vision. She would have to talk to Jesse soon because she could feel the forces building, but for today, "Ride, Jesse, ride," Julie whispered. "Be young and carefree while you can."

The thunder of hoof beats and Jesse's exuberant whoop danced back to her on the breeze.

Chapter Two

Unlike Jesse, his fraternal twin brother, Mike didn't have a problem relaxing, and fishing was his time to escape and contemplate life. He took his self-appointed role as Jesse's protector seriously—maybe too seriously—as Jesse had pointed out just that morning.

"Sometimes you make me feel claustrophobic, Mike." Using *that* tone of voice, Jesse continued, "I love you, bro, but can you please just back off a little? Go fishing. Go hiking. Read a book—or something. I need some space."

"Sure, Jess. I understand."

But he didn't, not really, and his feelings were bruised. Here he was, a warrior, according to Gabriel; and after all, he just wanted to be there to defend his brother and cousins from—well, anything. Sighing, Mike wiggled his line to scare away the little trout poking around the hook. "It's okay," he declared to no one in particular. "Someday something will happen, and he'll be glad I'm there." With that, he let his mind drift off in search of fun memories and was soon focused on his cousin, Joey, a year younger, who lived on the other side of town. *Now take Joey,* Mike thought. *He's fun, always ready for an adventure—not uptight like Jesse. Boy, I sure wish he was here now!*

Such thoughts have great power in the Fifth Dimension, and young Joey, bored with yard work and taking a break under an old oak tree, was soon visualizing Mike. He knew exactly what was going on and focused on his cousin, filling his third eye with Mike's image. It didn't take long to complete the translocation.

"Joey!" shouted Mike, dropping his pole in the creek. "Did I do that?"

"Yeah ... and I'm glad you did! What's goin' on, buddy?"

"Sorry, Joey. Hope you weren't doing anything important."

"Hardly," Joey said, rolling his eyes. "How's the fishing?"

Mike shrugged, not wanting to admit that he had no real desire to catch anything. "Aw, they just tease me most of the time. Can you stay? What d'ya wanna do?" he asked, perking up considerably.

"The folks won't miss me for a while. How about we go get something to eat? Grandma always has some treats stashed in the kitchen. I'll bet we can find 'em."

"Let's go," grinned Mike. Life was getting better by the second.

Julie gave Dave's horse, Orion, a good brushing and released him into the pasture to wait for Misty's return. The hens had obliged with plentiful fresh eggs, and she collected them into a basket before squatting on a little stool to relieve the goat's full udder. Mert was accommodating, and it was pleasant, meditative work. Missing Dave, Julie's mind wandered. He'd been her rock—companion, lover and soulmate in so many lifetimes—and still was. He kept her grounded, on an even keel.

Dave's kids brought tremendous joy and richness to Julie's life, and he loved her sons as his own, so Julie could hardly begrudge his trip to North Carolina just that morning. He'd wanted to check in with his son, Chris, and daughter-in-law, Ellen, whose mission it was to help people still trapped in the Third Dimension.

After the first few forays through the vibrations, Chris and Ellen had become fairly adept at making the trip between dimensions. It was hard work; sometimes heart-breaking, always dangerous and usually frightening. Even so, the rewards were rich and gratifying. Dave had gone to ask them to try again to locate Jeannie's missing husband, Jerry. And if there was any way possible, to bring him back with them. Jeannie was hurting and lonely, and their relationship needed to be resolved—one way or another.

When the milk pail was nearly full, Julie patted Mert's flank, mentally asking her to please not kick it—or put her foot in it, like last time, and her thoughts turned toward her children.

Her middle son, Steve, and his wife, Megan, were comfortably settled in a lovely and comfortable old home in Boulder. Their spiritual awakening had been a revelation, especially to them, guided, as it was, by young Jesse during the EarthShift. In fact, both twins had challenged their parents' reality, and as a result, they had all survived the transition.

Her eldest, Bill, and his wife, Kathy, had moved to Takoma Springs with their two children after the Shift. Joey, a mischievous 9-year-old, had been able to read minds even before the Shift, a gift that had often confounded his parents. Julie knew that he was chomping at the bit to get on with Gabriel's assignment.

Joey's sister, Erica was "an assertive 5-going-on-20-year-old" according to her mom. A strawberry blond with her daddy's gentle blue eyes, Erica appeared quiet and laid back. But let anyone say anything to impugn the power and/or wisdom of the female sex and she became a tigress. *Erica,* thought Julie, *will be a leader of women. Soon enough she'll find her way to the Third Dimension and bring back hordes of repressed and depressed women.*

Jon was Julie's youngest. A tall, handsome man with unruly sandy hair and deep, piercingly blue eyes that could look straight through you. A committed bachelor—for now—he remained a kid at heart, full of energy. He and his mother were spiritual soulmates, always able to connect through the ethers. Since the Shift, it was almost too easy. The mere thought brought him into her third eye. Like now.

"Hey, Mom, what's going on? Everything okay out there in beautiful Colorado?"

"Jon! Sorry, I was just thinking about you. I didn't mean to actually call. But, since we're tuned in, I'm fine. And how are you?"

"You can think about me anytime, Mom. I'm great. Just real busy working with the kids, as you know."

She did know. It was Jon's area of concentration, to help the children who had Fifth Dimensional abilities but had chosen to remain in the Third. These kids used their energy to work on healing their dysfunctional families—a slow and frustrating process, teaching their parents about love and trust—but there was progress. For Jon, it was incredibly rewarding.

"Now that we're connected, I'm thinking I'd like to see you in person and get a Mom fix. Besides, there's someone else there I want to surprise."

Julie opened her heart and mind, and instantly, Jon materialized right before her eyes.

"I do miss having you around, Jon. Thanks for coming." Her voice was muffled in his shirt as he swept her into a bear hug.

"No thanks necessary. Besides, we've got something to do. Come on—and be very quiet." Eyes twinkling, he strode off toward the house with his puzzled mother following in his wake.

"Finding anything, Mike? Anything good?" whispered Joey.

"Not yet. But Grandma's cookie stash has gotta be around here someplace. It was in this drawer last time. Keep looking."

"I am." Joey let out a whistle. "Hey! Look at this! A whole bag! Smells like chocolate chip!" He was half inside the cabinet over the refrigerator.

"Wow! Bring 'em down here! Now that's what I call a snack!"

A Darth Vader voice rumbled up from outside the kitchen window. "I wouldn't eat those if I were you," it growled.

"Did you hear something?" asked Joey, nervously looking around the room.

"Yeah, but there are just girls here. It's just our imaginations. Come on, toss 'em down!"

"I said," the voice warned, "*Do not eat those cookies.*"

Behind Jon, Julie pressed both hands to her mouth, barely able to restrain the giggles.

"Yipes!" Joey looked panicked. "Let's get outta here!" He jumped to the floor and bolted through the door where he was swept up in his uncle's strong arms.

"Uncle Jon! What're *you* doing here?" It slowly sank in. "Hey, was that you?"

Jon answered with a belly laugh.

"You scared me!"

Julie regained enough composure to declare, "The question is Joey, what are *you* doing here? And do your parents know where you are?"

Looking sheepish, he hung his head.

"Shame on you, Joey Cramer! And I expect Mike had something to do with this, too. But, sweetie, you know you need to respect your parents and ask if it's okay when you want to visit," said Julie.

"I know. I'm sorry, Grandma. I'll go home now."

"Oh, no you won't. Not until I get a big hug and you get a cookie. You too, Michael. Okay, guys?"

"Okay!" the boys shouted, flinging their arms around her waist.

"Yes, Uncle Jon," she laughed, not even needing to read his mind. "You may have cookies, too."

High spirits filled the room and cookies filled the tummies as the boys shared their exploits with their uncle who was more than a little envious of his youthful, carefree nephews. At their urging, he shared some of his own experiences in the Third Dimension; some of the joys and, to give them a balanced picture, some of the sorrows.

"Can we go to that place with you so we can help kids, too?" asked Joey.

"You probably will someday, but it's very dangerous, and it's not pretty. There are still wars going on—shootings, poverty and disease. But when you're a little older, and you have a bit more training, and only if your parents give the OK. You have to remember that there's a very real danger of not being able to get back if something goes wrong," Jon warned, "so you've got to know what you're doing."

The boys looked somber. "We're growing up fast," said Mike, puffing out his chest. "We're strong. We'll be ready soon."

"Yeah, I'm afraid you will be, and that's something I prefer not to think about at the moment. In the meantime, I'll bet you'd like to spend some time back at the fishing hole. That is, after you get in touch with your parents, Joey."

With grins on their faces and cookies in their pockets, the boys raced for the door.

Jon smiled as he watched them go, then asked, "Well, Mom, what else can we do for fun?"

Still smiling, she took his hand. "How about a little walk-and-talk? I want to hear more about 'your' kids."

They headed across the meadow to the knoll, where the view of Crystal Mountain was best, Jon's arm around his mother's shoulders. "That mountain never changes. It's always beautiful in that ageless sort of way ... like you!"

She rolled her eyes, then bumped his hip with hers, prompting him quietly, "Now tell me what you didn't want to say in front of the boys."

"It's hard, Mom. There's the good and the bad. I had a major breakthrough with a family last night ... things like that keep me going.

The kids are so happy to connect with someone who understands and can communicate with them on a higher level. But it hurts me to see all the sickness in that dimension when I know it can be healed here. I remember what it was like, seeing the boys and girls in the hospitals at the time of the Shift—throwing away tubes and braces, hair growing back overnight, all the smiles and laughter. I keep praying for more of the same."

"It'll happen, Jon. I know it will," Julie sighed. "Where are you headed now? I mean home or somewhere else?"

"Actually, I'm going to Chris and Ellen's. We're going back into the Third together this time. They want to search for Jerry; try to find out what's going on with him. I want to help."

"Dave is with them now talking about the same thing. Be careful, Jon, and if there's anything I can do from here, just tune me in. And please keep me posted."

He gave her shoulders a squeeze and pressed his face into her hair. "I will if I can, Mom. I promise." He paused. "I love you."

"I love you, too."

The aspen leaves rustled and shimmered in the soft breeze. Crystal Mountain glowed in the distance. And even as Julie watched him and smiled, Jon disappeared into the unknown. Looking again at the mountain, Julie shivered. Even in the Fifth, all moms worry.

Chapter Three

Dave, Chris and Ellen gave Jon a hero's welcome. It had been a long time since they'd been physically together. Sitting around the dining room table, sharing a meal, they caught up on news and talked about plans.

"We've had some success in the Third," said Chris, "but it feels like it's getting harder. There are pockets of people ready to make the transition, and they're so grateful for guidance and reassurance. But others. So many others ..." He shook his head, his eyes reflecting the pain in his heart.

"On our last journey," continued Ellen, "Chris and I got separated. For a while, I wasn't even sure he was still alive." She shuddered, remembering. "There's a huge terrorist underground determined to keep the population as fearful as possible so no one will question their authority—or their morals. For them, it's all about power and control. And they've twisted the concept of a loving Higher Power into something so inherently evil ..." She trailed off. "When we're there too long, our Fifth Dimensional powers start to fade. It's like feeling the life drain right out of you. I've never felt more alone than when my connection to Chris just ... turned off. Not even any static, just silence. And by then, we were so out of sync we were vulnerable to physical injury and emotional stress and all those other pieces of what we used to accept as 'the human condition'." She drew a shaky breath and fought to steady herself. "So what about you, Jon?"

Hearing the details was hard for Dave. He rubbed the gooseflesh prickling along his arms and concluded that as much as he'd like to deny it, having his kids in danger just plain scared him. In his opinion, his son and daughter-in-law were way too sensitive to be working in the endless war zone of the Third Dimension. He remembered Chris as a goofy teenager with a dry, off-the-wall sense of humor whose dark good looks were reminiscent of Tom Cruise; contagious smile, wavy brown hair and green eyes. He hoped some part of that boy could one day return. For now, Chris's background as a cop should stand him in good stead, but the demands for life in the Third were several steps up from crowd control and well on their way to disaster of catastrophic proportions.

Dave slid his eyes left to Ellen. An attorney before the Shift, she was tall and slim, and her straight dark hair and soft brown eyes gave her a sultry, sexy look that hadn't been lost on Chris. Where she got her strength and guts was a mystery to Dave, but he suspected it came from a truly exceptional partnership. Love, devotion, commitment. Theirs was a rich and productive relationship.

Jon cleared his throat, wondering where to begin. "Well, guys, as you know, I did a lot of nighttime out-of-body work with kids in hospitals and orphanages before the Shift. It was pretty great. You should see the young ones light up when they feel that telepathic link and know it's not 'just your imagination.' And now I'm doing follow-up visits. Reassuring them so they know they're not alone." He pulled his chair closer to the table, eyes sparkling. "There was one little girl—Colleen. She's Irish with red hair, big green eyes, pudgy cheeks and freckles. She stole my heart away. I hope I get to see her again under better circumstances." He swallowed hard.

"We understand." Dave squeezed Jon's shoulder. "So I guess the next question is, have any of you seen or heard anything about Jerry? It's been four years, and there's so much he's missing. So much he doesn't know. Jeannie still misses him terribly. She understands that he just freaked out over the baby's condition—not that his deserting them wasn't a huge blow. But he never knew that Angela was healed during the Shift, and

Jeannie believes that if ..." he trailed off. "Dammit, Jeannie still loves him and that's all that matters. Personally, I ... no, never mind." Dave knew full well that total forgiveness was something he'd have to keep working on.

"I remember when Gabriel led us all back to the Third to witness the chaos and Mom saw him wandering the streets," said Jon. "She described him as being scared, and managed to connect enough to tell that his memory of life with Jeannie had been lost—or at least blanked out. I can only imagine how helpless and frustrated you and Mom feel, Dave. So yes, let's talk about combining our efforts to locate Jerry; help him transition if it's possible. If he's meant to stay there, once we've done everything we can, then we'll live with it. And we'll help Jeannie live with it. But right now, we need to find out if there's any hope for him at all."

"Ellen and I are ready to give it another try," said Chris. "Working with you, Jon, might make a big difference. When do you want to go?"

"My bags are packed, so to speak."

"Hey, wait a sec," said Dave. "I want to go with you."

Chris was quick to respond. "Sorry, Dad. That's not going to happen. We have to be able to count on our base here staying strong, and that means that you're staying put.

"... And besides, I am *not* facing Mom's wrath if we let you just take off to the Third!" Jon smiled as he said it, but he was absolutely serious.

Outgunned, Dave sighed, "Okay, okay. But be safe. Be careful. And if there's anything we can do from here, well, we'll be open for you. And you know my prayers and Julie's will be with you every step of the way."

Chris put his arm around him. "We know, Dad. We'll be in touch when we can."

All too quickly the travelers joined hands and disappeared. Suddenly, crushingly alone, Dave took a deep breath and focused on his wife. He was soon wrapped in the comfort of her arms.

* * *

"A penny for your thoughts, honey," said Megan, as she and Steve rocked listlessly on the old-fashioned porch swing. The sunset over the Rocky Mountains was breathtaking, but there was a nagging emptiness wrapped around the evening cool. As much as they were trying to ignore it, they missed Mike and Jesse—even if they had agreed that vacation time at Wind Dancer Ranch was spiritually and emotionally important to the twins.

"Actually, I was just thinking about the mountain cave where we spent the days during the Shift. We didn't know what was happening or even whether we'd survive. I'll never forget that horrendous feeling when Rusty bolted out of my backpack, and I fell off the cliff, and the angel saved my life. The whole thing was something else."

Lying on the top step watching a chipmunk wrestle a pine cone twice its size into a hole under the branches of a barberry, Rusty barked in agreement. He remembered the near miss all too well.

"When we finally left to try and find our way home on foot," Steve continued, "I was pretty worried. If it hadn't been for Jesse, I doubt we would have made it—either home *or* into the Fifth Dimension."

"It was a time for miracles. Remember coming across that abandoned cottage? We were so tired and hungry and scared. I hope the owners, if they ever return, will understand our taking the jar of peanut butter. And that made us so thirsty! Thank goodness for the well out in back. The water was clear and good, and the boys drank so much, I thought they'd burst!"

"Then later, still lost, wondering if we were going to starve to death, trying to keep warm by the fire, and there was all that crashing around in the brush. I thought sure we were going to be attacked." Steve looked inward as he recalled what happened next. "I can still see that mountain lion as he slowly walked up to us. He was so quiet, so beautiful . My heart was beating like a bass drum, but he just dropped the rabbit and calmly walked away." Steve smiled at the memory. "It was amazing—a real life 'Peaceable Kingdom'."

Megan smiled. "Now we know all those 'coincidences' were really the gift of manifesting. And yes, they're engraved in my memory for eternity. *I'll* never forget seeing your mother appear out of nowhere when Jess called her just using his mind. Remember our first experience with translocating? Thank heaven it worked! I'm so thankful she and Jesse were able to get us back to Boulder."

The memories of their awakening were crystal clear and poignant, and Steve brought Megan's hand to his lips. "We're so blessed, Meg, and we've overcome so much. Life is much better when it's lived in love and trust instead of fear. I think we're doing really well at it." He paused. "At least until I think about what the kids will be facing someday." Then, knowing that she needed him to lighten the mood, he nipped her knuckle and added, "Of course, it's a good thing I finally got the telepathy stuff under control. Hearing everyone else's thoughts wasn't just confusing; there were times when it was downright embarrassing!"

Miles away, another couple sat and rocked and watched the stars appear, a few at a time. The Big Dipper, Cassiopeia, the Pleiades—or Seven Sisters, as her dad used to call them. Julie felt the sadness creep into her heart as she and Dave sat and watched for shooting stars. Their grandsons would be leaving soon, and the wonderful days of exploration with them were coming to an end—at least for a while. *It's been eye-opening watching Jesse and Mike*, thought Julie. *And Angela. And Joey, who showed up every time he could think up an excuse to pop in. They grow so quickly in so many ways. I'll miss their noise and excitement ... seeing them latch onto a concept, and that light in their eyes when they truly "get it". Gaining independence. Having more confidence in who they are and what they can do. I just hope they've learned some of what they may need for the future when they're old enough to try to find the secret in Crystal Mountain. It's such an unknown to all of us.*

"Hey, Julie," said Dave.

Startled, she turned to him. "Did you say something?"

Dave squeezed her hand. "Where did you go, babe?"

"Oh, I was just thinking how lonely it'll be here soon; how much I'll miss the kids. And yes, I know we're lucky to have had them this long."

"I've thought about that, too. Watching their faces when you're telling stories, hearing them laugh when they're chasing fireflies, hearing Angela get all serious and making the boys back off when she senses the little critters are scared. Seeing the mountains through their eyes, walking the trails, reading the signs. Heck, they've even gotten so they enjoy sharing the chores," Dave chuckled. "We've watched them discover a whole new world and file away all the salient facts for future reference. It takes me back to when Jeannie and Chris were small. It makes me feel young again."

An unexpected gift from their transition to the Fifth Dimension was that Julie, like many others, had physically regressed and rejuvenated. To her delight—and her husband's—her body was again lithe and strong; breasts firm and high; her hair, the warm, soft brown of her teens; and her eyelashes long and curled. Every wrinkle and age spot had faded away, leaving a clear, glowing ivory complexion kissed by pink roses.

"We *are* young, sweetheart. Young enough to make babies again ... if we should choose to ..." Julie stole a glance at her husband out of the corner of her eye.

"Hey, wait a minute! Now don't you go getting any ideas, woman.

We've got kids scattered all over the place already, and I can hardly keep track of the ones we've got!"

Julie grinned at his reaction. "Don't panic, honey. I'm just teasing."

"Whew! I'm glad to hear that!" he smiled. He had fallen in love with this vivacious, nurturing woman with the big smile and sparkling eyes, partly because he never knew what to expect next from her. His life with Julie certainly was never dull, and Dave knew *that* wouldn't change no matter what dimension they ascended to.

"Hey, babe, the boys are tucked in, and so are the girls." He leaned over to drop a kiss on her temple. "So let's stop rocking our youth away. Come inside and I'll rock your world!"

Julie answered with a raised eyebrow, then stood up and pulled Dave to his feet. With a gentle kiss on his lips, she whispered, "I'm at your command, my love." The chairs rocked on as they went inside.

"Grandma! Grandpa! Wake up! It happened again last night!" Jesse was so excited, he couldn't stand still.

Groggy, Julie opened her eyes and raised herself on one elbow. "Jesse? What is it? Are you all right? What time is it?"

"It's morning, and you have to get up! I've gotta tell you about last night. Please get up!"

Dave grunted as he rolled over. "Rise and shine, Jules, m'love. This is what you said you'd miss."

Julie kissed Dave's nose. "You, too, big boy. Up and at 'em. Meet you in the kitchen, Jess."

Coffee brewing and juice in hand, they listened as their excited grandson began his story. "Well, you know how I've been hoping that Dorado would come back and take me on another trip somewhere like he used to. Like when he took me to the big space ship? It's been so long since I've seen him. Well," he paused for effect, "he came last night! He's been busy with other kids he said, getting them ready for whatever they have to accomplish someday. They all have assignments like our family does. There are places all around the world that need to be 'awakened.' That's the word he used. And we all need to be trained. And it won't be easy for us. But now it's *my* turn again! He's the *greatest* E.T. ever! I can say *anything* to him, and he doesn't laugh or say I'm too young."

"That's wonderful, Jesse, that he came back," said Dave. "Where did he take you? What did you do?"

Jesse took a deep breath and another gulp of apple juice. "You'll never guess."

"I couldn't possibly. Don't keep us in suspense. Where?"

"To the Great Pyramid! We went to the Giza Plateau, and I saw the Sphinx and everything, and then, we went inside the pyramid!" Jesse jumped up, hardly able to contain himself. "It was so awesome, Grandma, and just like you described it. We went in the King's Chamber, and the Queen's, and he showed me where the history of the world is all encoded. And it tells the destiny of the universe, Dorado says!"

"The Great Pyramid is one of the Seven Wonders of the World, Jesse, and a really powerful spiritual monument. How did you feel when you were inside it?" Julie asked.

"I thought I'd be scared but I wasn't. I felt tingly all over and a little dizzy. I kept seeing pictures, like movies, in my head. Dorado said it was the energy. We sort of floated through the pyramid ... and ... and then ..."

"Take a breath, Jesse. Go on."

"And the best part is ..." He lowered his voice as his eyes narrowed and became very serious. "We went underneath it. There are rooms there that people don't even *know* about yet, even in the Fifth Dimension. And

Dorado said I was being initiated, and that it would help me with my mission and those pyramids we saw inside Crystal Mountain, Grandma."

Chills ran up and down Julie's spine. *It was such an incredible vision —and the real beginning of the assignments. Initiated. What did that mean? I wonder if Mike, Joey and Angela experienced the same journey with Dorado.*

"No, not yet, Grandma," answering Julie's unvoiced question. Jesse continued, "They will someday, but for now, it's just me because I'm more ready, because of my training in the space ships. That's why I was only a little bit dizzy, even before Dorado helped me remember one of my past lives. That's what he said it was." Jesse had calmed down, and the childlike demeanor changed to one of maturity and awareness. As though acknowledging the weight of his responsibilities, Jesse sat straighter and continued, "Dorado said he'd be back, that I've still got a lot more to learn. But he said I was to be the *leader.* That's what I've been before, when I wore a uniform. It was pretty awesome. Boy, I wish Uncle Jon was here so I could tell him, too. He understands."

Dave gave his grandson a manly handshake. "You'll make a great leader, Jess. We know you've got what it takes."

Pride filled the boy's chest. "Thanks, Grandpa. You know I'll do my best." And giving each grandparent a smile and a hug, Jesse headed to the barn to share his news with Misty.

"Oh, Dave, I wish Jon was here, too. We've had no word or thought or image of any of them since they left. Do you think they're all right?"

"I pray for them every day and night just as you do. Right now we both need to believe in them and trust in Spirit."

"I do, I really do. I just wish I knew for sure."

Chapter Four

"What are we going to do, Jon?" Chris whispered, his eyes filled with fear. "Ellen's really sick, burning up and half out of her mind. The hospitals are next to useless, and they're overcrowded anyway. This could be that super-strain of malaria, or encephalitis, or some tick thing—Lyme or, God forbid, dengue fever. Jon, if it's that, most people don't live to tell about it! I'm scared."

"Let's face it, Chris, we need to get home. We haven't found a trace of Jerry. We've been all over this hell hole for days, eating bad food when we ate at all, not getting any rest, living in squalor. No wonder she's sick. It's time to get out of here. Take her home so she can heal. We can come back and try again for Jerry."

"How, Jon? How are we going to do that? Ellen can't even stand, let alone travel through dimensions. She's stuck here and I can't leave her. But you should go back and let the family know what's going on."

"No way, bro. We're in this together and we stick together. I'll see if I can find some clean water; some food. Stay with her, Chris. Keep her talking and keep doing hands-on energy work. I'm sure it's helping."

"Count on it. But be careful, Jon. The smoke out there is thick enough to cut with a knife, and no one's safe on the streets. Not even you."

"Not to worry. I'll find something." He gave Chris a quick hug and kissed Ellen's hot brow. "See you in a while, crocodile."

"Later, alligator."

The feeble attempt at childhood humor was a small comfort.

* * *

Man, thought Jon, *this must be what hell is like ... or hell on earth.* Fires lit up the night sky, turning the smoke into a rusty haze. Los Angeles was out of water, and the flames spread, unchecked, out of control. Here and there, looters smashed and grabbed, not caring who got hurt in the process. Jon's lungs burned and his eyes stung, filled with ash. *There's got to be food and water somewhere. Come on, Gabriel, you got us into this. How about a hand now?* A burst of flame punctuated an explosion that was way too close for comfort, and Jon ducked onto a side street, back to the walls, keeping to the shadows. *Okay. If I can't find food here, where do I go?*

And the answer came: North.

Sure, the San Joaquin Valley? Farm country—at least it used to be. Yeah, that's north. And I'm still strong enough to get there, and, God willing, make it back.

Jon wiped sweat on a dirty sleeve and tilted his head from side to side to release the tension. He slowed his breathing and cleared his mind as he focused his energy.

The land was flat. Dusty. Not a vestige of green in sight. A broken sign, blasted dull by wind-driven sand, creaked and banged in front of a deserted gas station. Jon walked closer, straining to make out the words. *Bake-something. Yeah, sure looks like it's baked. My God! It's Bakersfield. What happened to this place? Where are the farms? The farmers? This is beyond drought.* He shivered as the wind blew hot. *One thing's for certain, I'm not going to find water in this purgatory. So where to now? Maybe up by San Francisco where I used to surf ... before the world went nuts. That's north. There's moisture off the ocean. Yeah, that could be it.*

It took more time and energy than he would have wished, and he hoped with all his heart that it wasn't more time than Ellen had to spare. But before long, Jon found himself in a fog-enshrouded field. The cool moisture was a blessing in itself. Lying fallow and nearly barren, the area that once fed cities now offered up only a single head of cabbage and a few potato plants. *Can't go wrong with Colcannon,* Jon smiled, knowing that Great-Uncle Clarence and the rest of the Irish forebears had to be smiling, too. *Sure could use that cow of yours about now, Uncle.* Remembering with great fondness his Mom's stories of her favorite uncle squirting milk straight from the cow to a waiting kitten, Jon straightened his shoulders and began to dig with his hands. The soil was soft and moist, and the potatoes still firm. When his pockets were stuffed, he took off his shirt to use as a makeshift knapsack and filled that, too.

"Okay, Gabriel, one more time." Hopeful now, the old Neil Diamond lyrics played in Jon's mind:

This is my time, and I like being free.
I know I can do it, if LA is there for me!

"Okay. I'm on my way to LA again." He closed his eyes and focused on Chris and Ellen, and ... nothing happened. *I can do this. I've got to do this. I will do this.* He took a deep breath and once more brought Chris and Ellen into his third eye. "I am there," he whispered. But he wasn't.

"Dammit, Gabriel, I've got to get back to them!" Panic rose in his throat, tightening his chest. "They need this food. We need each other! Please! Help me!" Unable to stay still, more frightened than he had ever been in his life, Jon began walking. Then running, tripping over the uneven ground and repeating his plea with each step.

"Jon."

Like balm, the distant, yet familiar voice eased through the layers of exhaustion and panic in Jon's mind.

"Jon."

"What ... ? Who ... ? Who's calling me? Who's there?" *Am I hearing things? Have I lost my mind?* He slowed again. Stopped. Concentrated.

"Jon!"

It blew through the fog coming in off the Pacific. Drawn by the invisible cord that was hope, Jon stumbled toward the sound and the surf. When he collapsed on the sand, his strength, like the tide, was at low ebb.

"Jon! Look at me! I'm here. It's Ekor."

Stunned and trembling with relief, yet hesitant to accept that his salvation could actually be at hand, Jon fought to focus. "Ekor! Oh, thank God! How did you find me? Can you help? I'm in really big trouble here."

Ekor was a Mer being, a dolphin whose telepathic communications were highly evolved in many languages and multiple dimensions. Years before, they'd met in San Francisco Bay, bonding over water sports, and Jon had been naïve enough to think that his immediate understanding of Ekor's chirps and squeaks was an uncanny ability that he'd just ... acquired. Jon had come to realize the truth of it, as well as just how much Ekor had taught him during the days following the Shift. It was a friendship precious for both.

"Well, Jon, you really did it this time—pushed yourself *far* too far. This *is* the Third Dimension, remember? Fortunately for you, I sensed your distress and was able to lower my vibrations to match yours, at least for a while. Yes. I will endeavor to assist your return to Los Angeles, but I cannot guarantee its success. Frankly, I can't imagine why you want to go there in the first place!"

"Ellen's there, Ekor, and Chris. And she's really sick. We've got to get strong enough to heal her so we can go home." Noting the dolphin's quizzical expression, he added, "It's a long story."

"Of course it is, and I do understand why you have to go. So ... to begin. First of all, my dear Jon, you've got to come into the surf and put your hands on my back. I'll transfer all the energy I can while you concentrate on your destination; just like a 'boost' for one of those old automobile batteries. Let's see if we can 'turn you over' as it were."

"Where do you come up with these things? It's not like you've ever had your flippers on a steering wheel." Shaking his head in amusement, Jon started into the surf. "Turn me over ... you bet. Here I come." Teeth clenched, he sucked in his breath when an amazingly cold wave washed over his belly. "This is the fun part, right?" And praying that his bundle of produce wouldn't come untied, he advanced into the waves.

The undertow was strong and the currents unpredictable. Jon wondered if he could possibly negotiate the surf and still manage to hold on to his precious cargo. Ekor swam close, and Jon, desperately trying to keep his footing and remain upright, finally laid his hands on the dolphin's smooth back. Feeling a strong and immediate burst of comfort, he closed his eyes, breathing deeply until Chris and Ellen came clearly to his mind.

The acrid smell of smoke assaulted his nostrils and stung like the devil. "Thank you, God! Thank you, Ekor! I'm back!" Jon shouted, as he opened his eyes to disaster. Confused, frantic, he scrambled up off the sidewalk and looked around. *Where am I? This isn't where I left them. Or is it?* His heart sank as he realized that the smoke was coming from the building which had contained their "borrowed" room. Looking up, he saw flames skittering out onto a small balcony on the top floor—as, next door, another structure pancaked, one floor crushing down upon another. *Earthquake? Gas explosion?*

"No! No! No!" Jon dropped the bundle of food where he stood and ripped off a piece of the shirt to tie over his nose and mouth. "I've got to find them!"

Julie woke in a cold sweat which kick-turned into a burning fever. Panic radiated straight from her gut. "Dave—Dave! Wake up!"

"What is it, Julie? What's wrong? Are you sick?"

"Yes … no … something's *wrong!* I'm so hot, and my heart's beating a mile a minute. I feel panicky and I don't know why. This isn't coming from me, Dave!"

He could feel the bed shaking from her shivering. Her eyes were huge, and damp hair clung to her face. "Okay, hang on. I'll get some ice."

"No! Don't leave me. Something's going on. It's the kids. We've got to tune in somehow. Stay here with me! Don't leave me!"

He didn't argue. Taking her in his arms, he held her tight, stroking her back to soothe and comfort. "I'm here, Julie. I'm right here. It's okay, babe, it's okay. Tell me what's happening. You're safe with me."

She closed her eyes, drawing on his love and strength. *Deep breaths. Letting go. Going deep. Deeper.* Her tremors quieted and her body went limp. The movie in Julie's mind became clearer as the city sounds grew louder. She smelled smoke, felt heat, and couldn't quite suppress the scream.

"What is it, Julie? What are you seeing?"

"Jon! Oh God, Dave, it's my baby! The building's on fire and he's in it! Oh no! This can't be!"

"Julie, what else do you see? Tell me! Are Chris and Ellen there?"

"I don't know," Julie sobbed. "Wait. Wait. I think I think I see them. It's so smoky." She coughed, feeling the harsh smoke in her lungs as though she were there. "Yes, yes, I see them. They're still in the building. Chris has Ellen in his arms. He's staggering. Oh God, Dave, she looks …

"What, Julie! What does she 'look'?" Dave was shouting.

"She looks ... dead! Something's horribly wrong!" Julie was shaking violently again. "Jon's trying to find them. He's got something tied over his face, but it doesn't do any good. He's coughing. I can hear him yelling to them. Dave, help me. We've got to hold the energy for all of them! We've got to guide Jon to them!"

"Yeah. Okay." Dave's breath was shallow, his heart pounding. He knew he couldn't level himself enough to see what was going on, but he knew Julie's connection to Jon was the strongest of the family ties. If she could get to Jon ... if he could help her get to Jon. He took her hands, and palm to palm, gathering his strength, pushed his energy to her.

"Chris! Ellen! Where are you?" shouted Jon. "I'm coming! I'll find you! Hang on!" His throat was raw from coughing and yelling. "Chris, if you can hear me, for God's sake, yell!" Painfully, he crawled up endless stairs and bent low to feel his way along smoke-filled hallways. It was incredibly hot, and the smoke was densely toxic. He was lost in the dark, disoriented, and he had no idea what floor he was on.

And then he did! More, he knew it was the right one. Something was pulling him along. "Chris! Ellen! I'm coming!" Eyes streaming, coughing up smoke, choking down fear, Jon dropped to his knees and crawled. "Come on, bro, *we gotta get out of this place—if it's the last thing we ever do!*"

A shadow moved down the hall.

"Chris! You animal! Hang on! I'm coming!"

Intense heat surrounded them, like the air itself was ready to flame. Trusting that he was in touch with a guiding force, Jon shoved his hands under Ellen and locked onto Chris's arms. "Time to play fireman, bro. Come on. Let's skate on outta here."

They found the stairwell and descended, step by careful step, praying for guidance, for survival, until they stumbled through the door, choking and gasping for air. Hair singed and eyes squeezed nearly shut in pain, they staggered across the street and sank down, panting. Speechless, they looked back just in time to see a huge fireball blow through the door they'd just come through. Debris rained down around them.

"Jesus." Chris looked at Jon. "What happened, man? And how in God's name did you find us in there?"

Jon shook his head. "I honestly don't know, Chris. I got back here and the building was on fire. Dropped my stuff, ran inside. Man, it was deadly. I couldn't see a thing, but then I felt like I was being led to you. You must have been sending out signals."

"Not me, Jon. I didn't have the juice. You'd been gone so long, I didn't think you were gonna make it back. And even if you did, I didn't think that you or anyone else could get to us, let alone get us out. I was just praying we'd go quickly. I honestly didn't think we'd make it."

"Ellen ... Chris? Is she ... ?" Jon shifted his attention to her.

"She's alive. But we've got to get her out of here. Now. She's fading."

"Chris, I almost didn't make it back. I wouldn't have if Ekor hadn't come to my rescue. I just don't know where we'll get the strength to translocate back to the Fifth. I don't think either you or I have it right now, and I know Ellen doesn't."

They sat quietly for a time, each lost in their own thoughts until Chris broke the silence. "Jon, Ekor was your teacher, wasn't he? Well, Ellen and I had teachers during the Shift, too. Remember Mary and her daughter, Emma? They were about to be raped, or killed, or both before I brought them back to the apartment in Raleigh. They were angels—literally, I think—and they got us through the whole transition thing. Without them, we wouldn't have made it. They said they'd always be there for us, that they're part of our spiritual family. Do you think if we called them ... ?"

"Hey, it sure wouldn't hurt to try."

Ellen moaned as they cradled her between them. Despite the fact that she was unconscious, Chris asked his wife to concentrate on Mary and Emma, too, knowing that she was still aware at some deep level. Then, he and Jon visualized the two black women in their third eyes, and calling their names, asked for help.

"It's not working, Chris. They didn't come," said Jon.

"Not yet. We're going through dimensions here. Keep your focus!"

A shimmer of light began to dance just at the edge of their senses as a familiar voice rose over the crackling and snapping of the fire, and Mary took form. "Chris, what has happened to you?"

"Mary! God bless you! Am I ever glad to see you! We need help badly. It's a long story and we don't have much time. Ellen's really sick, and we've got to get her back to the Fifth before it's too late. We've all been here too long, and we don't have the energy stores to go home. Can you help? Please, can you at least help Ellen?"

"Hush now, Chris. Let's see what we can do. Jon, how you feeling?"

"Whipped. But I'll give it all I've got. Do you think you can help us, Mary? We really need to go home. We need the folks." The thought of his mother almost broke him. Boy, did he ever need her.

"Emma? Are you here?" asked Mary.

"Yes, ma'am. I made it through." Emma came to her mother's side. "Hi, guys. Hang in. We'll get you home somehow." She sat down on the sidewalk and took Ellen in her arms. Ellen moaned again, curling her body toward Emma. "She's real sick, Mama. We'd better hurry."

Under Mary's direction, the little group gathered close, held hands, and focused on their destination. "We'll have to go all together," said Mary. "Emma, you keep Ellen close to you, and I'll work with these boys." The heat in the women's hands became visible light as they chanted, calling on a Higher Power for help.

A familiar pull through the dimensions—*it's sort of like trying to walk through deep water and fight the undertow*, Jon thought. Time passed, shapes and lights came and went, motion ceased. Exhausted but hopeful, the travelers opened their eyes and found themselves on the deck at Wind Dancer Ranch.

"Mom! Dave!" Jon cried, trying to get to his feet—to get to his mom.

He didn't make it to upright. Couldn't have. Even if he'd found the strength, the family had closed in on them; enveloped them. Drawing them in, hugging, sobbing, and thanking God for yet another miracle.

Safely back in the Fifth, Ellen was still desperately ill. Julie immediately turned to Mary, aware of the special powers this woman and her daughter possessed. Mary smiled and assured the family that with time and nurturing, Ellen would heal completely. Now that she could breathe again, Julie made sure that her guests were comfortable and had everything they needed for their healing work. Then she set to work on Jon and Chris. The two were physically depleted, but with the three-way tag team of Julie, Dave and Jeannie, they had no choice but to rest and enjoy the pampering.

After several days of constant care-giving, Mary announced that she and Emma were going for a walk. Julie was about to object, concerned that although improved, Ellen was still not entirely "out of the woods." Chris put a hand on her arm. "It's okay, Julie. Whatever Mary does, it's for a good reason. Trust her. We learned to, and it paid off."

Mother and daughter walked away slowly, raising their arms and turning in a circle every now and then, until they came to a clearing in the midst of a stand of Lodgepole pines; a mystical circle where Julie had planted flowers and often came to meditate. The women nodded to each other and returned to the house.

"Okay, we found it. Dave, you will carry Ellen and follow us, please."

"Ah ... sure ... okay," he said, glancing back at Julie as he scooped up his sleeping daughter-in-law and prepared to follow her caregivers.

"Lay her down right here." Mary pointed to an exact spot.

"Should we get a blanket or pad or something?" Dave asked.

"No. I want her body to be in direct contact with the earth. Now, bring me four white candles, and if your woman has some white sage, we can use that, too."

Emma patted his arm reassuringly, reading his mind. "It's a vortex. A place that generates intense healing energy and strong vibrations. My mother will call on Ellen's guardian angels to help us hold the energy so she can better use it to heal. You'll have to trust."

"I do. Believe me, I do. I'll get what you need."

The family gathered, sensing that they, too, were needed. White candles burned at the four points—north, south, east and west—as Mary smudged Ellen, Emma and herself with the sage. She asked Angela to do the same for the rest of the family. On either side of Ellen, the family knelt, holding the energy, directing it to her. Mary positioned herself at Ellen's head, Emma at her feet, and swaying slowly from side to side, they passed their hands over her body, radiating heat and healing.

As the trance deepened, their chants and soul songs rang through the forest, floating upward to the heavens, while the energies deep inside the vortex were drawn up like psychic spring water. Her family focused on Ellen's etheric body, seeing it healed in their minds, while cloudy beings—her angels—drifted over and around her; embraced her.

The candles flickered and went out as Ellen's body slowly relaxed.

She was covered in sweat, as were Mary and Emma. Ever so slowly, her eyes opened, and her lips curved into a weak smile when she saw her husband. Chris, tears streaming down his cheeks, gently took her in his arms to rock her like a baby. The family and the healers quietly slipped away, leaving the couple to themselves.

Back in Julie's warm and comfortable kitchen, Mary sipped her green tea and spoke. "She'll be all right now. Ellen is supported by so many high level energies. They came in through the vortex to do the rest of the healing work, and all we had to do was hold the vibration for them. I thank the Lord we could help."

Appreciating the kinship with a fellow healer, Angela crawled up in the big woman's lap and put her arms around Mary's neck. "I love you, Mary," she whispered.

"And I love you, too, little one. Thank you for your help out there."

"I'm so glad you let us help. Can you and Emma stay here forever?"

Mary laughed. "No, my pretty angel. We have more work to do in other places. But if you ever need us, we'll be there for you. You know this."

After warm hugs and profuse thanks, Mary and Emma said their good-byes. As the two women disappeared into the twilight, Julie heard "Hallelujah!" ringing out from the direction of Crystal Mountain and smiled.

PART TWO

Six years after The EarthShift

Realize that you cannot help a soul unless that soul really wants help and is ready to be helped. I tell you to send that soul nothing but love and more love. Be still and wait, but be there when that soul turns for help.

Eileen Caddy (1917-2006) – God Spoke to Me

Chapter Five

Pine needles and fallen aspen leaves redolent with the scent of fall crackled and crunched under the horses' hooves. The creak of saddle leather played counterpoint to bird songs as they moved through the peaceful forest. As they passed through a clearing, Julie and Dave lifted their faces to the light and saw a circuit of brilliant blue which backlit whipped cream clouds drifting lazily around the mountain peaks. They watched a morphing tableau of images—birds, animals, fish, faces—and Julie thought of carefree days when her boys were little and playing "the cloud game."

"Look! Look! It's a big boy lion!"

"No, you dork! That's a monkey for sure."

"Ha! You're both dorks! It's Jeremy Bonneville!"

Poor Jeremy had always tried way too hard to be just like everyone else. His biggest shortcoming wasn't his failure at that pursuit, but that he never did manage the fine art of just being Jeremy. Julie smiled and closed her eyes to send him light. Warm memories, crisp fall air, pine-scented breezes ruffled her hair. "Oh, Dave," she sighed, "it doesn't get much better than this, does it?"

Dave smiled in agreement. He was relishing the feel of barely controlled power beneath him as Orion shifted smoothly, negotiating a trail so overgrown as to be practically non-existent. Here and there, fallen tree trunks and stands of saplings necessitated small, pleasant detours for the horses and riders. "You know, Julie, it's been way too long since we did something like this just for ourselves. Even in the Fifth, it's still too easy to take on everyone else's problems and worries—or at least to feel like we should." He paused. "Bad word, 'should.' There should be no 'shoulds'—Ha-ha—should there?"

Julie giggled, understanding perfectly and recalling the kids' reactions at their announcement that she and Dave were going camping for a few days—maybe even a week! You'd have thought *the kids* were the parents. And overprotective ones, at that.

"Don't get lost." "Take plenty of food." "Do you have a compass?" Then, most revealing of all, "What will we do if we need you?" Even the grandkids were surprised by their "big adventure." Obviously, it was time.

Misty, glossy bay coat glowing rich auburn in the sunlight, tossed her head and snorted in agreement. Squirrels and chipmunks zigzagged across the trail before them, noisily chirping their annoyance at the interruption of winter food gathering. Julie held the reins loosely, rolling easily with Misty's smooth gait and breathed in the good, clean scent of horse and well-soaped leather and, when the breeze shifted, the occasional whiff of her mate.

Dave was enjoying the scenery as much as his wife, but he enjoyed watching her even more. During the last six years, they had become aware of many lifetimes they'd shared as friends and as lovers. Now, here, finally, they were able to experience this lifetime as man and wife. Dave considered Julie to be the most beautiful, sensitive, loving woman he had ever known, and the depth of the love they shared still knocked his spiritual socks off.

Julie reined in, waiting for Dave to come up beside her, and reached for his hand. "I love you, too, sweetheart—to the depths of my being. When I look in your eyes, I still get that same straight-to-the-gut thrill I did so many years ago when we first met."

"And I sometimes forget you can read my mind." He grinned and gave her hand a squeeze before adding, "But if you're reading me now, you're gonna start blushing!"

With a cocky grin, Julie nudged Misty with her heels and charged ahead shouting, "Okay, lover! You come get me and we'll see who blushes!" Her taunting laughter drifted back to him like music.

The smoldering embers of the campfire were slowly dying, but the glow surrounding Dave and Julie, snuggling in their sleeping bag, would last the night. They'd decided that making love under the stars on a soft bed of pine needles was nothing short of heaven on earth. Dave held Julie close and she nestled against him. Breathing deeply, relishing the sweet scent of her hair, he hugged her even closer, turning slightly to cradle her head on his chest. She listened to the rhythm of that beloved heartbeat, felt the reassuring warmth of his body and, saddle sores forgotten, drifted off to sleep and wondrous dreams.

The vast silver ship was gleaming in the night sky. Julie spread her arms, flying up to circle around it, free as a bird—a clever crow, a gentle dove or even a fierce eagle—twisting and turning to her heart's content until curiosity finally got the best of her, and she had to just peek in; to see what was inside the incredible craft.

Her vision changed and her heart skipped a beat. She saw an immense room. White. With chairs, rows on rows of them. White, too. Immaculate. Innocent. Pure. *An empty classroom*, Julie thought. And simply from wondering if she might be able to gain entrance, she found herself floating inside. Soft ethereal music filled the air, delighting her. A stage, just a platform, set off in soft, deep blue, occupied the front of the room, and above that and to the right, was a small, discreet balcony, large enough for one or two people. Drifting easily up to it, Julie settled into a blissfully comfortable chair. The music played on as she relaxed into a thoroughly peaceful trance state.

She was vaguely aware as the room began to change color. Soft blue light reflected off the walls, floor and ceiling until even the air was tinged in blue. And then Julie was no longer alone. Appearing out of nowhere as far as Julie could tell—one or two at first, then a scatter, then large groups of beings flooded in to fill the seats. Not surprising to Julie, appearances were mixed. There were the so-called *Greys*, the aliens depicted in tabloids decades ago with large black almond-shaped eyes and big bald heads. A few, possibly *Reptoids,* had lizard-like features. They were sitting alongside *Pleiadeans* and *Sirians*, as well as various sizes, shapes and colors of *Humanoids*. And there were those who simply defied description. But whether they'd sprung from apes, antelopes or amoebae, everyone seemed to understand each other in some wonderful, universal way.

As one, the beings started to glow, getting brighter and brighter as their bodies morphed into pure energy. Narrowing her eyes against the brilliance, Julie scanned the audience again, trying to discern what it was all about. When her eyes came to rest on the four chairs at the front of the hall, and the four small beings which were taking form in them, her heart nearly stopped. These were familiar. Known and beloved. These were four of her grandchildren. Struggling, gasping, she tried to fly down to them, but she couldn't move. She called to them, shouted, but could make not a sound.

This is just a dream, a lucid dream, she told herself. *Stay calm. It's not real. You can wake up any time you want.* But in her heart of hearts, she knew that wasn't true.

Jesse, Joey, Mike and Angela, bathed in blue light just like the others, were holding hands as they watched the stage in seeming anticipation. It came as no surprise to either Julie or her grandchildren to see Dorado materialize behind the podium. She was aware that he could shape shift at will, but tonight he appeared as a human of medium build, his kind face a cross between gnome and wizard. He was a welcome sight.

"Good evening!" His voice bounced off the walls with enough force to move houses. "Oh, my!" he said, clearing his throat. "Sorry, my friends. It's been awhile since I've spoken to such an ... *energetic* group. Let me conserve my enthusiasm and reroute that energy to better uses!"

She sensed amusement from the assemblage at this small glitch with the technology, but Julie herself was still agitated; fretting about her grandchildren. Although Jesse knew Dorado, she wasn't sure if the other kids did. Julie herself hadn't seen him since right after the EarthShift at the big bonfire in Wind Dancer's meadow. Built at Dorado's request to light the way for transitioning souls coming into the Fifth Dimension, she thought of that time as The Big Reunion. It was then that Dorado had introduced the family to the Archangel Gabriel who had appeared to announce assignments for Jesse and the others. An introduction to an archangel. What an incredible, yes, downright awesome experience for everyone. *The energy in this room is just beautiful!* Julie thought as she relaxed just a bit. *And look at Dorado's smile when he looks at the kids sitting there in the front row!*

"My friends," Dorado began again, "this is one of our more important gatherings. It is time to step up the energy, raise your vibrations. You may wonder whether you, as individuals, can make that much difference in the world. Believe me, you can. When two beings come together, their power is increased sevenfold. Add more beings and those energies can be increased exponentially. The capabilities of those here today have already increased. And you've only just begun! You come from many galaxies, because the future involves everyone; connects everyone; all beings in the universe. The teachings and energies you receive here today will spread across your worlds. You will guide your families—your siblings, your parents, and yes, even your grandparents—to expand the capacities of their Fifth Dimension abilities."

Julie thought she saw Dorado aim a quick smile in her direction.

"And now, my beloveds, as I help you with this meditation to raise your vibrations, your teacher will lower his. We will work together. Please release all your tensions and take three deep, centering breaths."

Julie, with all the others, followed Dorado's instructions, and was immediately aware that power was building, within and without. As the visible light in the room pulsed and intensified, an imposing mass of sparkling energy—*it looks just like the phosphorescence in sea water*—began to take form on the stage.

A being. A force. A soul of astounding energy and major proportion. Julie wasn't sure if she was hearing with her ears or if this new voice simply filled her entire being, but there was no doubt in her mind that she was, once again, in the presence of Archangel Gabriel. She was aware that he prayed, that he spoke of manifestations in other galaxies; other dimensions. Drifting through levels of awareness and unable to fully comprehend the depths of this new material, she still snapped to attention when Gabriel addressed her grandchildren.

"I'm pleased with your progress, dear children. You are being prepared for one of the most important missions in your world. Your assignment, to discover the secret of Crystal Mountain, is a necessary step in the struggle to preserve humankind on earth. It will demand tremendous wisdom and strength, and no less, courage and trust. You appear now as children, but you and I know better. Your souls are, indeed, very old. The energies you've experienced here this day will help to increase your abilities, allow you to magnify your own spiritual levels;

find access to more of those souls. Now is the time to challenge yourselves, test yourselves, and in this way, prepare yourselves to succeed in your mission. It will be ... burdensome ... for your family to understand and accept that you must take these risks. But one will, and she will be your foundation."

This time, Julie was absolutely certain that both Gabriel and Dorado turned to smile directly at her.

"Trust yourselves. And lean on each other. You've already advanced in your maturation by virtue of the Shift and the Photon Energy, but tonight you've moved to a new level. When you leave this gathering of souls, you will have added, in earth parlance and appearance, several more growth years to your bodies and a great deal more wisdom to your minds. This will astonish and befuddle your loved ones, but we can help them to accept the changes with a minimum of awareness."

Julie watched as the blue light surrounding the children deepened, the color vibrating with intensity. Both the physical bodies and auras of Jesse and Joey, Michael and Angela were growing in stature as they took on a more adult physique. *Talk about growing up before your eyes!* Julie thought. *Puberty the easy way! No angst. No acne.* She glanced over to see Gabriel looking directly at her and cocking an eyebrow in amusement, and sheepishly, she looked away.

Suddenly, she felt herself getting lighter, losing substance, and then Julie was floating once more in the vacuum of space outside the ship. Seeing the brilliant blue jewel which was Earth in the distance, she raised her arms to fly back at an astounding speed.

Sunlight bled vibrant pink onto the snowy mountain tops before spilling over and into the valley and filling it with warming yellow light. Birdsong announced the new day as Julie tried to stretch and found herself wrapped tight in her husband's arms. Wiggling a bit in an effort to turn over without disturbing Dave, she took note of the morning sky where the colors of the sunrise were softening. It was then that the memories of her incredible dream flooded back. *Whew! What a bizarre imagination I've developed since the Shift*, she thought.

At the twins' home, Steve and Megan were stunned. They stared at the two gangly teenagers, speechless.

"What's for breakfast?" asked Mike, his voice cracking as he rubbed his eyes and shuffled to the table. "I'm starved."

"Me, too," said Jesse, oblivious to the effect their appearance was having on their parents.

Steve found his voice first. "What in the name of heaven happened to you two?"

"What're you talking about, Dad?" asked Mike.

The boys did their usual unison shrug and eye-roll, and then a shocked double take.

"Well, I'll be! Hey, Jess! What's that on your face?"

"What? What's on my face?"

"Go check it out in the mirror, man. You've got zits!"

"Well, so do you!" Jesse shot back, more than a little peeved to be picked on by his brother before he was hardly awake. He glanced down at his way-too-short pajamas, then inspected Mike's equally poor-fitting outfit.

"Oh boy." He sank into the nearest chair. "Let's all sit down. I think I know what happened."

Megan was shaken to the core by the sudden appearance of two strange young—no other word for it, these were—*men* in her kitchen. But as odd as that was, she was still certain that they were, in fact, her sons. Girding up her mental loins, she sank into a chair beside Jesse, took his hand in hers and, marveling at the change in its size and texture, said, "By all means, Jesse, we'll sit down and you fill us in."

"I thought it was just a dream," Jesse began. "Remember, Mike? How we went to the space ship with Dorado last night? And then Gabriel showed up and did this ... *thing* so we'd be more ready for the big adventure." His deep voice, cracking again as he spoke, was as annoying as it was surprising.

Mike laughed. "I don't remember a thing. But you sure sound funny!"

"Yeah, just like you," Jesse grumbled. And with that, he began to recount the details of the previous night's journey for his twin and their parents.

Oddly, Mike was as shocked as Megan and Steve. "Are you serious, Jess? Why can't I remember? What a blast that must have been!"

"Yeah, it was righteously cool, for sure. There were a lot of strange beings there; E.T.s from everywhere in the universe. And it was the first time I've seen Angela in a class." His eyes grew large as the full significance of that memory hit him. "Uh, oh. She's changed, too. And so has Joey. And I think Dorado said he'd include Erica, too. Man! If they don't remember either ..."

Mike jumped up. "We've gotta get there. Aunt Kathy and Uncle Bill will be freakin' out, and so will Aunt Jeannie!"

"Now wait *just* one minute, you two!" Megan scowled at her sons. "You're in your pajamas, for Pete's sake, and you not only look strange, you look more than a little foolish. At least try to find something that fits before you go translocating again."

Steve, struggling to take it all in, broke his silence. "Um ... I just got a couple new shirts and a couple new pairs of jeans, guys. They're on the top shelf in my closet. Help yourselves to the shoes. But hands off the Rockies tee shirt!" He smiled wanly at his wife, "This is gonna be worse than school shopping, isn't it?"

Laughing, the boys left the kitchen, their deep voices—with an occasional soprano accent—drifting back to where Megan and Steve sat, just looking at each other.

"What next?" said Steve, shaking his head.

Chapter Six

Ruled by an unholy triumvirate of ignorance, brute strength and chaos, the Third Dimension embraced a doctrine of blind fear. Wars escalated and fears of terrorist threats held the world in their grip. Distrust, disrespect, cynicism, and negativity of all forms became chronic, while paranoia, schizophrenia and all manner of phobias and mental disorders flourished acutely. New strains of deadly viruses and mutant bacteria popped up daily until breathing masks—big, ugly, still largely ineffective ones—were being worn in every country, by anyone who could afford or steal one. The more people needed each other, the more it seemed that the forces conspired to drive them apart.

The tortured Earth and her peoples suffered earthquakes, tsunamis, floods and tornadoes while solar flares and the eruptions of sub-marine volcanoes bred more and more extreme weather. Magma rising from the trembling core sent clouds of hot ash, reminiscent of Pompeii, raining down to choke cities, followed by lava flows which seared, then entombed entire regions.

The groundwork had been carefully laid. Tended with love and care, Ellen's healing was now complete, and Chris and Jon were back to full power. And since the memories of their last, nearly disastrous trip were vividly etched in their minds, each of them approached their work in the Third Dimension with even greater caution.

During previous journeys back, Ellen, Chris and Jon had learned firsthand the truth of the old adage, "You can lead a horse to water but you can't make him drink." That it isn't possible to change the beliefs of others unless and until they're ready in their own hearts and souls. The three had been gratified by their successes, but progress was slow, working mostly one-on-one with a few small group operations when conditions allowed. Even so, many families had made their transitions into the Fifth, thanks to their tireless work. Large scale facilitating was dangerous, and just because they were working at Gabriel's behest did not mean they weren't vulnerable.

With Jon's help, Chris and Ellen initiated an underground network, a movement, slowly spreading information about the Photon Energy or whatever the scientists were calling it. They explained the dynamics of the massive energy cloud; its position, spinning around the Pleiades; its intersection with Earth's orbit. Vibrations, Zero Point, and most important, the energies allowing souls who choose unconditional love and positive energies to transition to a higher dimension were presented. Create hope and curiosity, and follow it up with the "Big Pitch" as they called it. They didn't pressure anyone, just asked them to keep an open mind. Once enough people attained a love-not-fear attitude, a gathering would take place.

And today was the day. The first ingathering was scheduled to take place in the hills outside Los Angeles. Jon had found a beautiful valley, miraculously unspoiled by the devastation around it, within reach of those whose motivations were sufficiently strong.

Chris, Ellen and Jon called on all the help available in the spirit world to hold the energy, including a call to a Higher Power, the Universal Energy, and to Gabriel, who had gotten them into this in the first place. Then, covering *all* their bases, they asked for intercession from any other available angels. And finally, Jon called for Ekor to enlist the help of his

Mer friends.

The sun rose, strong and bright, promising a clear day in the valley. Ellen, shivering with excitement and anticipation, held Chris's hand and asked, "Can you think of anything else we need to do?"

"Not a thing. The technology is what it is—or isn't—and the bottom line is that it's simply going to have to suffice. I'm just hoping like hell we'll be guided about what to say. Being a ... well ... the next closest thing to a tent revival preacher is a far stretch from my old career as a cop," he added, shaking his head. "But hey, if people come, if they're open, then we have a shot at awakening their hearts and souls and helping them transition. So I'll preach if I have to."

"Don't forget Jon's here, too, honey, and he's always been comfortable in front of crowds. That amazing comic timing of his really helps sometimes."

Chris frowned. "I'm not sure comedy is what we're about here, El. This is serious stuff."

Jon overheard the last few comments as he strode up to his partners. "Come on, guys. Humor's the very *best* way to teach anyone anything! Chris, you remember those classes people had to take after they got speeding tickets? How they tuned out if the material got too serious? Lectures and preaching don't sell. But make people laugh with you, and they'll stay with you 'cause it makes 'em feel good. *If* you recall, Gabriel has a great sense of humor—sort of a cosmic one, but really good. So lighten it up. Okay?"

A grassy meadow, six or seven acres worth, lay at the floor of the valley, and it was all crowded. So were the hillsides. Families and singles, males and females, young and old, gathered on blankets or sat on the sweet grass. They'd taken a large step toward conquering their fears simply by agreeing to attend such an event. But waiting for something hopeful, yet still unknown ... it was hard. Nervous, a bit subdued, some quietly shared food and feelings with their neighbors. The sound system, hastily installed on the makeshift stage, would be necessary to reach the outer limits of everyone assembled. And judging from its appearance, it might need angels of its own. The trio stood, holding hands, asking for guidance and support. It was time.

They slowly walked onto the stage. Ellen, flanked by her husband and Jon, went to the microphone first.

"Blessings! Thank you all for coming! May I have your attention, please!" Hearing her words over the buzz of the speakers, the chatter of the crowd subsided. "Thank you all for coming. My name is Ellen, and this is my husband, Chris," she said with a nod in his direction, "and this is my brother-in-law, Jon. The size of this turnout tells me that many of you are looking for something more in your lives, a faith to hang onto; to believe in." She raised her voice a notch. "Do you feel the need to let go of your fears and live in a peaceful, loving way?"

An affirmative response echoed across the valley.

"Well, we want to help you achieve that," she continued. "And the first step is to truly understand that what you *believe* is what you'll get! Are you ready to begin?"

The answer was loud and enthusiastic. Yes, they were ready.

Chris stepped to the microphone. "I know you've all read about and heard about the Fifth Dimension and transitioning by now. Well, I want to share with you how it was for my wife and me. I was exposed to the concept of the Shift from my dad and step-mother. But I didn't buy into it. As a matter of fact, I thought they were nuts. I won't go into all the details, but Zero Point and photon clouds sounded way too New Age for us. But if preparing for this so-called 'EarthShift'"—and here, Chris made quotation marks in the air—"if storing food and water would keep them happy, then hey, why not?

"By the time the actual Shift happened, I'd had time to read more, research more, see more. Our faith was strong. The belief that we *are* all One, all connected in this universe, is how we continue to live. Whether you call this *love*, energy, God, Prime Source, Universal Mind, Mabel or Henry, it's all the same. That energy is in and around you. And me. Around all of us." The simplicity of his words and the honesty of his presentation pulled his audience like a magnet. Smiling, he stepped back to make room for Jon at the mic.

"Hi everyone! You know, a speech is very much like having a baby—easy to conceive, but hard to deliver." The audience gave him a little soft laughter. "So here's the deal. My job today, *as I understand it,* is to talk to you. *Yours*, as I understand it, is to listen. If you finish before I do, just hold up your hand." He was rewarded with a solid round of relaxed chuckles along with a few good belly laughs. He had them with him now.

"You may not believe this, but I'm going to tell you anyhow. I've got the greatest guide and friend in the world. He helped me through the change and recently saved my life. Using mental telepathy, he explained the unexplainable to me when I needed it most. His name is Ekor." He paused for effect. "Ekor is a dolphin."

A murmur rippled through the crowd.

"And there's more. My mom and I have a special connection. We've worked on it, through many lifetimes. We can communicate with our minds no matter where we are. Actual conversations! And now, in the Fifth, we—all of us—can translocate to another place by simply filling our minds with the image of a person or place.

"Now," he continued, "before you all try and disappear before our eyes, you have to understand that while it's an easy thing to do in the

Fifth Dimension, it's just about impossible for you here in the Third. But as you grow and your minds open, that's going to change.

"There's so much that's unseen in this world that you *can* come to understand and know about. It's glorious, joyful, peaceful, loving—a heaven on earth. Some of you may ascend today, some next week, some next year. It's all up to you—not you *in your mind*, but you *in your heart*. You *in your soul.* You can't just decide, *'Well, gee, that sounds like a trip. Guess I'll try it.'* Sorry, it doesn't work that way. When you're truly ready to embrace the change, to live the change, it will just happen."

Jon took a drink of water and surveyed the crowd. He looked at Chris and Ellen, who nodded and stepped back to their chairs.

"We're going to do a meditation now. I'll guide you if you choose to join us. If not, that's okay, too. I want you to be as relaxed and receptive as possible. This is the first step toward enlightenment." Jon had no clue what he would say or do next, nor did Chris or Ellen. They simply trusted that they wouldn't have come this far if it wasn't meant to be.

Jon embraced the vibrations intensifying within his body and those flowing out into the surrounding valley. Many in the audience were already in a deep meditative space when, knowing the power of visualization and that a picture speaks a thousand words, he called on the angels for a sign; something that would demonstrate the "other" world and help all these souls to continue along their journey. He added a personal plea, noting to Gabriel that since they were here on his orders, they'd be really grateful if he'd give them a hand this first time out. And then added a postscript to please, please make it a smallish-sized sign since it was not their intention to create a holy-roller atmosphere. A gentle breeze began to blow.

"Please close your eyes and take three deep ..."

A terrified yell pierced the calm. "They're coming up the mountain!"

Other voices joined in. "They're coming for us. There are truckloads of 'em! And there's a tank!"

"They'll kill us all! For God's sake, do something!"

The rumble of the approaching vehicles grew from a low hum to a thunderous roar. Clouds of dust charted the army's progress.

Confused and frightened people began to jump to their feet, grabbing blankets and children, preparing to run for their lives as Jon shouted over the microphone.

"Everyone please stay where you are! Stay calm. You *will* be safe. They cannot harm you! Please, stay calm! All those soldiers out there know is fear. They don't understand love, and they don't want *you* to know or understand it either. They especially don't want you to change; to be able to transition. Stay calm. Don't play into their hands!" The terror in the crowd had lessened fractionally, but sensing that wouldn't be the case for long, Jon turned to Chris and Ellen. "What the hell do we do now?"

"Pray, Jon!" said Chris.

"Pray like you've never prayed before!" Ellen shouted.

The crusaders joined hands, facing the milling throng. Jon's deep voice resonated. "We call on a Higher Power and the angels. We need your help *now*. These people have come to us in good faith. They want to live in love and peace. If we're doing the right thing, please be with us here, and keep everyone safe."

People hesitated, beginning to be aware of ... something. Children, more aware than their parents, pulled on their parents' hands, pointing.

"We ask you to help all of us here today to join together in visualizing the convoy *stopped*." Jon raised his arms speaking directly to the crowd. "Believe that our angels and our guides can help us! Join hands to create a flow of energy too powerful to penetrate. See the soldiers and their trucks stopped. You don't need to know how. There is no right way. Just see it stopped. *Now*!"

A stillness slowly descended as people reached out to their neighbors. Unsure at first, Jon's voice pulled them together. A wave of energy vibrated across the meadow, and a golden glow, something richer, fuller than sunlight, encompassed them. Human chains formed as the sounds of prayers resonated and were lifted, carried upwards on the wind. And still, the militia continued its slow advance.

Jon felt that they were holding the very lives of those people—hundreds of them—in their hands. He became aware of the young man who had screamed the first warning, pounding on the stage at his feet, and realized that his own trust had never been tested to this extent.

"This won't work! This is bullshit! Jesus, man, you got us into this! *Do* something!" His dark unkempt hair and scruffy beard hid most of his face, and in his eyes, there was pure terror.

Squatting down, Jon grabbed his hands. "Hey, buddy, come on. Calm down and look at me. Trust me! It *will* work! We're all helping you. All you've got to do is believe it!" Pausing, focusing on the man's face, the world suddenly tilted as Jon realized just whose eyes he was looking into. Shaken to the core, he cried, "Oh, my God! Is ... is that you, Jerry? Are you Jeannie's Jerry?"

Around them, the vibrations of the group were increasing, raising the energy frequencies. Jon could feel the buzzing, tingling sensation in his body. The man yanked his hands away.

"You're nuts. I don't know who you are, but you're crazy! Dangerous! I thought this group thing might be a good idea; give me some answers, but I was wrong. Dead wrong. I'm gettin' outta here. I'm gonna surrender! Then at least I won't get shot!" He turned and ran toward the approaching vehicles.

"Jerry! Jerry, come back! It's me, Jon!" Jon jumped off the stage and followed Jerry's zigzagging path through the crowd, trying desperately to reach Jerry before it was too late. But as he watched, the darkness enveloped his long lost brother-in-law, and Jon's heart was filled with pain. *He doesn't remember and I can't reach him,* he thought. *But he's alive. And he was willing to come here to try. Oh, Jeannie, I'm so sorry. He's just not ready.*

No one seemed to have noticed the drama unfolding as Jon rejoined the others on the stage and joined the chanting, making the sound of "Ohm" over and over again. The crowd caught on, and soon a continuous hum filled the valley. Their collective thoughts now acutely focused on stopping the invasion. They were blindly unaware of what they were manifesting.

Heavily armed soldiers, trucks and tanks suddenly smashed into the invisible, yet impenetrable barrier which had formed. The oncoming troops were stopped cold. Angry and frustrated, registering no visible impediment to their progress, they rammed it again and again. They fired their weapons at it, but the bullets just bounced off, dropping uselessly to the ground.

Jerry ran headlong toward the troops, shouting, "Hey! I'm with you guys! I made a mistake! I don't know who these people are!" He hit the wall at full speed and knocked himself out cold.

After a time, the captain's voice boomed over the bullhorn, calling for his troops to retreat. He turned to his first lieutenant and growled, "I don't know what's going on. I can't see a damn thing up there. It's whacko, bizarre, weird, and I don't like it. Come on, let's get the hell out of here. We're needed back in the city!" Exhausted and injured soldiers were lifted or thrown into the trucks which turned themselves around and followed the tank back down the road.

Jon slowly brought the crowd out of their meditation; back to the renewed peace of the valley. As the people realized what had happened, they stood in awe. They might not have the words to explain it, but they were well on their way into their enlightenment. The power of their prayers would not be forgotten. Hearts now open to a higher consciousness, they wouldn't, couldn't, go back to their old ways of thinking. The news of their experiences would soon spread to others in the Third Dimension, and other doors would be opened—just a crack.

Enjoying a well-deserved group hug, Jon, Ellen and Chris held onto each other, overcome with relief, bursting with joy to have played a part in another miracle. It appeared that a totaled Jeep was the only remnant of the thwarted invasion. That and the body of the man named Jerry.

"I've got a pulse, but it's really weak!" said Jon dabbing at the blood which flowed from a huge gash on Jerry's forehead. Dirty, smelly, emaciated. *Must have been living a pretty hard life,* Jon thought. There was no doubt in his mind that the guy was Jerry. The beard and long matted hair would hide his identity from most people, but not from his family.

Moving closer, Chris realized just how conflicted his own feelings were. Even *if* this disreputable character was his sister's lost husband—and he wasn't the least bit sure that he was—Chris remained firmly unconvinced that helping him through a transition was the answer, not after all the pain he'd caused his sister. Then again, Jeannie loved him and wanted him back.

"Is he alive, Jon?"

"Yeah, but he's in trouble and I don't know how long he'll last. We can't move him back to the Fifth until—or if—he's ever ready to go. He has no memories of the past. His life with all of us is gone. I wish he'd come around so we could at least get him to someone here who can take care of him."

Ellen sat down by Jerry's head and gently put her hands over his face. "We can't just sit and stare at him. Chris, go to his feet. Let's bring some energy through to him. Visualize the vortex at Julie's where I was healed. Do whatever feels right."

Nothing ventured, nothing gained, thought Jon, as all three began a soft chant. They sat there a long time.

Chapter Seven

Jeannie had taken over all the ranch chores in Julie and Dave's absence. It made for long days and occasionally some aching muscles; but in the usual course of things, she enjoyed the animals and the work and found it all hugely satisfying. So when, at the end of a long but extremely productive day, she found herself feeling nervous and antsy—even snippy with Angela—instead of basking in the glow of her accomplishments, she wondered just what the heck was going on.

What is the matter with me? The ranch is running smoothly. Maybe it's just having to handle everything by myself. And I know my baby girl has changed a lot. Sure, that's a lot to swallow, but it's not like I haven't had to make adjustments before. Lord, I just wish the folks would come home! Something doesn't feel right. She wandered down to the greenhouse to pick some fresh greens for lunch, thinking that if she didn't know better, she'd swear her shadow felt too damn tight.

"Angela! Time to eat!" No response sent the irritated mother on a child hunt. *Strange. Angela's always hungry by now, and she's always so good about coming when I call.* She found Angela in her bedroom, sitting on the floor and staring at a photo of her father, oblivious to everything else. Jeannie walked slowly to her daughter and stood, staring down at the framed picture of Jerry taken before Angela was born. The familiar lump rose in her throat as she focused on the handsome face with its dark eyes, the brown hair curling slightly over his ears, the smile. God, she so missed that smile. Jerry had enjoyed his friends, his work, their life together. He'd been a good provider and a loving husband, despite a few sharp edges.

But he wasn't the least bit interested in joining me on any kind of spiritual learning path—trying though, warming up a little to the concept of angels, spirit guides, gut instinct. It was just that the days of the Shift really spooked him, and the final straw was seeing the hole in Angela's spine after expecting a perfect, healthy baby. I know he was overwhelmed, in shock. It was horrible. But dear God, when Zero Point hit its peak and he just ran out into that storm and the dark and the winds ... and he never even held our daughter. She reached out and softly stroked Angela's curls.

Angela startled a bit and turned to look up at her mother, eyes full of tears. "Mom, you've told me that story before, but where is he now? Why isn't he here with us? Will he ever come home? Doesn't he know we need him? That *I* need him?"

"Sweetheart, the transition changed us all so much, and not everyone changed in the same ways. Your father wasn't ready to ascend, so now he's vibrating at a lower level. With all that's happening in the Third, he can't think right, can't even remember his old life. At least, that's what we've been told. He doesn't know about you, and I'm just lost to him. It's okay to feel sad, to cry, honey. I do once in awhile, too. And it's important to keep sending him love. Don't ever forget how much he wanted to have a child. To have you. He just doesn't know."

"I could go back and look for him there, like Uncle Chris and Uncle Jon and Aunt Ellen."

Jeannie's heart froze. "No, honey, it's way too dangerous. You're too young yet, and besides, I need you here. You know you have some very special things to do when you grow up."

Angela turned to her mother, *that look* written all over her face. She stood, stretched to her full height and summoned her most assertive attitude. "Well, I don't know what *those things* are and I *am* grown up. What could be more important than finding Daddy and making you happy?" She shoved her father's picture at Jeannie, turned on her heel and stormed out.

Jeannie stared at the picture, then hugged it to her breast. The thin veneer of her control cracked, then burst, and tears of despair and loneliness flooded through. Her heart breaking, Jeannie cried for her own pain, and that of her daughter. "Why, why, why, God? Why my Jerry?"

When the torrent subsided to a trickle and the pain eased to almost tolerable, she washed her face and went looking for Angela.

"He has no pulse! Chris, do CPR! Do something! Damn it, we've got to bring him back! God help us, we can't lose him now!" Jon was beside himself. "Jerry! Jerry! Can you hear me? Dammit Jerry, don't you dare leave us now. Come back! You have to come back! Jeannie needs you so much, man ... and Angela needs you. You *cannot* die now!"

Minutes passed. Sweating profusely, Chris had no idea if they could save Jerry, but he wasn't about to stop. Ellen was totally focused on running the energy through his body while Jon yelled and cajoled and, most important, prayed harder than he'd ever prayed in his life.

And then, a flicker. A tiny bump of a heartbeat. Jerry's eyes moved slightly behind the lids and he trembled a little. Consciousness was returning. Suddenly, Jerry gasped for breath before twisting onto to his side and retching miserably. When he was done, exhausted and dazed, he rolled onto his back and squinted at the trio leaning over him.

"Who are you?" he mumbled.

"You don't remember us, but we know you from years ago. We want to help you," Jon ventured.

"Are you real? Are you ... I mean, I don't know. There was a bright light and ... people. Are you ... Were you there? Did you see it?" He didn't really look at Jon. He was still looking inward.

"Jerry, you just had an NDE, a near death experience. You died and then came back. You're going to be okay, buddy. Probably got one hell of a concussion, but that'll heal. Who did you see? Did you see anyone you know in the light?" asked Jon.

The words came slowly, and in a whisper. "Yes. No. I don't know. It was like ... foggy. But it felt good. It felt so good."

"Try to bring it back, Jerry. It's really important for you to remember."

"Why do you keep calling me 'Jerry'?" He paused. "They did, too. My head hurts. I must be going nuts."

"No, you're not. Think. Keep going. What did you see? Who did you see?" Ellen spoke softly, still doing hands-on work.

"It doesn't make sense. It looked like ... an angel. You know, like you see in pictures. He ... she ... whatever it was, made me look at something like a ... a movie screen." Jerry closed his eyes, and they could tell that he was struggling to go deep within himself. When he spoke again, they could barely hear his words. "I saw someone, a woman I think. She was in, like a room, made of glass. I watched her picking stuff, maybe plants or something." He was breathing heavily.

"And there was a kid. I felt so much pain. I don't know why." His voice caught. "She, the woman, was crying. She was crying hard." He paused.

"Go on, Jerry. What happened next?" Chris asked.

"This guy, this ... angel guy. He didn't talk, but I heard him in my head. That's creepy. He said, 'You have to go back, Jerry.' Then I was spinning. It was like being sucked through a tunnel, and I heard someone yelling 'Come back, Jerry.' But I didn't want to." He paused and opened his eyes. "That's it." He took a deep breath and scrubbed his face with his hands, wincing when he encountered the broken skin and huge bump on his forehead. "What the hell happened? Who were those people? And who the devil are you? I don't believe in angels!"

Lunch was on the table. Angela, subdued but largely unrepentant after her outburst, was waiting for her mother.

"I'm sorry I hurt you, Mom, but I'm not sorry for my feelings. I'm not a little girl any more. Things have happened, I've had experiences, and I'm afraid you're going to have to get used to it. Someday, if no one else has found my dad, I'm going to. He may not understand, he may not be ready to ascend, but I need some closure. We both need it. Right now, considering how long we've waited, it's a little hard to believe in angels myself!"

"How on earth can you say that when you know an angel helped deliver you? Gabriel is a huge part of our lives."

"Well, maybe Gabriel. I don't know! I'm just so confused." Angela's eyes were drenched and miserable.

"I know, I know, I know, my baby! I am, too. But no one, no matter what the dimension, can change anyone else. They have to want to change themselves. It's a hard lesson. If your dad is ever ready to make that shift, he'll come back to us. And in the meantime, we have responsibilities here." Jeannie took a deep breath, and turned a bright smile on her daughter. "How about some lunch and a long walk in the woods?"

"Sure, Mom." Smile wobbly and sniffing just a bit, Angela sat down beside her mom. "I'd like that. Guess we could both use a change of scene."

"Thank heaven we found some really good people to watch over him." Ellen's nurturing nature had been obvious during her interrogations of possible caregivers for Jerry. "He sure is one stubborn guy, though," she said, shaking her head. "If he hadn't still been in a daze, I doubt he'd have gone with them. If he'll stay in one place, we can at least keep track of him. So, what's our next step, guys?"

Chris cleared his throat. "Well, we've already met with the coordinators who'll follow up on the people who were here today. They'll make themselves available to answer questions and help guide the ones ready to move on; support the rest until they are. Jon, I know you need to get back to your work with the kids in San Francisco and elsewhere. Ellen and I could use a break, and we want to report in to Dad and Julie and, of course, to Jeannie. So I propose we do what we do, and go t'heck home! Okay with you guys?"

"What are we waiting for?" Jon, Ellen and Chris hugged their farewells, and in an easier, happier state of mind, disappeared from the Third Dimension.

Chapter Eight

San Francisco had never looked better, and it wasn't lost on Jon that a large part of the reason might be his last daunting visit back in the Third Dimension. Inhaling a deep breath of clean ocean air, he decided that the light seemed brighter, the bricks cleaner, the water bluer and the hills more spectacular. He stretched out on the rocks and let the sun warm his bronzed body while cooling breezes laden with Pacific moisture caressed his skin. *Sheer heaven, that's what this is.*

The rhythm of waves crashing just below his feet nearly lulled Jon to sleep, and it might have been the hint of a dream that carried the memories of his first meeting with Ekor at this very spot, years ago. He smiled. *I bet it took me a full minute just to close my mouth,* Jon thought, *communicating with a dolphin! Unbelievable!*

"I sure do miss you, Ekor," he whispered to the wind.

And the wind returned, "Well, why didn't you say so, silly man?"

"Wha ... Hey! Ekor? Is that you?"

"May I ask who else talks to you while doing back flips and double gainers out here in the surf?"

Jon burst out laughing. "You son of a gun! You're something else! Hey, I'm glad you came. I've missed you. You are absolutely amazing, man! How did you know I was here?"

"Now Jon, that's a ridiculous question even for a human! Especially after all we've been through. No, I won't honor it with an answer. But I will ask *you* a question. What are you *doing* lolling about on the rocks when there's so much *work* to be done?" Ekor executed a perfect back flip with a half twist, dove deep, and popped up to "walk" on his tail, smiling his perpetual smile, waiting for Jon's answer.

"Ekor, if you know as much as you seem to, then you know exactly what I've been doing, and that it's for everyone's good that I take a short break and get rejuvenated!"

"Yes Jon, I'm sure you feel that way. And perhaps I'll agree with you. By all means then, rejuvenate! And I do hope you enjoy yourself immensely. Today." Ekor went on, "You did a fine job down there, Jon, and we of the aquatic dimensions acknowledge it. I know you're working with many children who chose to stay with their families in the Third. Trying, as they might, to help their parents see and understand. Not an easy job—yours or theirs, I must say—but a very brave one. God bless those children. For their love and their convictions. And you, for all that and your work besides."

Ekor paused, collecting his thoughts and Jon waited. "As I know you're aware, Jon, there are many groups of *orphaned* children who were brave enough to make the shift to the Fifth alone. They're here in special homes and you've worked with many of them already. Today, however, I'm concerned about one particular group currently on the other side of this bay. When you're ready, you'll need a boat. And before you ask, no, you can't just translocate. It's important for them to see the boat and to know that you're not some sort of ghost or spirit popping in, and then—POOF!—disappearing as though you were never there at all! These little souls need an extra bit of ... what was it your kind called it? Oh yes! T.L.C. The acronym for Tender Loving Care. And who couldn't do with a good dose of that from time to time?"

He's always just one step ahead of me, thought Jon.

"One *leap*, Jon. I don't take steps. Anyway, right now, they're in need of someone to show them some loving attention, like a daddy or big brother or favorite uncle for a day—play ball, tag, games, swing, read, tell silly jokes and laugh, Jon. These poor dears so need to laugh. And the highlight of the day—and I'm not saying this just because I'll be the star of it—will be when you bring them all to the water's edge, and then I shall take them for rides. Contact with a dolphin is amazingly healing as all the most learned scientists have often said, not only physically but emotionally as well. This is what I will offer them. You will go, won't you?"

"Okay, okay. You win. Of course I'll go. In fact, this sounds like a blast—no, not an explosion, just 'a really fun assignment'. I'll get a boat early tomorrow and buzz across. You'll come when I call you?"

"Harrumph. Really Jon, you wound me! What do you think? And now, I must be off! I, unlike you, am working today." The dolphin dove deep, exploded up out of the water, twisted into a magnificent triple spin, and dropped flat on his side with a huge splash which covered Jon with sea water. Jon coughed and spluttered, and Ekor disappeared as quickly as he'd come.

What a day! San Francisco Bay was choppy, but the salt spray and breezes were exhilarating. Jon had almost forgotten what it was like to use an old world method of transportation, *really old world!* His muscles strained under the plain cotton tee shirt as he pulled the oars, shooting the little boat through water. *It's a long way across but I've got plenty of time. At least the tide's going with me.* He sang sailor songs; "Michael Row the Boat Ashore" and "A Pirate's Life for Me". Even his own version of "Row, Row, Row Your Boat" before dredging up the words to a few older, saltier sea chanteys that made him laugh, but were obviously not intended for young audiences!

After a substantial chunk of work and more time than Jon had expected, the bow ran aground on a sandy beach on the bay's west side, and Jon leapt out to haul the little craft up above the tide line. Looking up, he sighted a likely looking building and, grabbing his supplies, headed off across the warm sand, stretching out his overworked muscles as he went. *I bet they'll think I look just like Santa Claus—ha! Make that Sandy Claws—carrying this big bag of toys.* And glancing down at his shadow, added, *OK, so Sandy minus 200 pounds!*

Mounting stone steps flanked by fragrant beach roses, Jon knocked on the door, and when it opened, he felt the impact so strongly, it was almost a physical blow. Jon found himself staring into the smiling eyes of the most beautiful woman he'd ever seen. Classic even features, long satiny blond hair, clear golden skin. The brilliant blue of her eyes reflected the blue of both the sky and the Pacific—or perhaps *they* reflected the blue of her eyes. When she gave him a radiant smile, Jon's only cogent thought was that if she glowed any more, she'd be sporting wings and a halo.

"Hi ... um, I ... ah ... I'm ..." *Dear God, what's my name?* "Jon! I'm Jon. And, ah, I'm uh ... I'm here to ..." *Good grief! I'm stuttering!*

"Yes, I know, Jon. I'm Sara. Please come in. We're all so excited. The boys and girls are waiting for you in the courtyard. It's this way." And turning, she strode off down the hall, without waiting to see if he followed and seemingly unaware of his massive attack of nerves.

Struggling to simply *get a grip, for Pete's sake!* Jon shouldered his pack, thinking, *Okay, so did Ekor tell her I'd be coming, or was she reading my mind. And if she was reading my mind, then please would somebody just put me out of my misery now because the most gorgeous woman I've ever seen in my life just saw my best interpretation of a complete fool! Please let it be Ekor! Please, oh please, let it be Ekor!* "Hey! Wait up!"

To say that the waiting band of little boys and girls gave Jon an enthusiastic welcome is the highest degree of understatement. But once he'd caught his breath and peeled a small child or two off each leg so he could maneuver, Jon quickly went about the business of giving the kids his full and undivided attention. Small gifts from a big, jolly guy—even without the jelly-belly—work wonders to break the ice, and since Jon was using his intuition to match his gifts to the interests of the youngsters, he was cracking ice like a Coast Guard cutter in Baffin Bay. There were no skates or sleds, but special books, games, hats, shirts, and stuffies made the day nearly as good as Christmas.

Later, mingling with the kids and staff, chatting and hugging and playing, he was also working to discover little bits and pieces about the woman whose mere presence was still clouding his mind. From some of the other nurses and aides, Jon learned that Sara was in her early thirties, a single parent, and a widow. He didn't need anyone to explain her obvious devotion to her four-year-old son, Scott. Jon knew that Julie would describe Scott as "cute as a bug's ear." He took particular note that the boy hung back from the crowd, and that he never moved far from the security of his mother.

"Hey, Scott, how about I give you a piggyback ride?" said Jon, approaching the boy who looked at him through eyes as striking as his mother's.

Scott backed up a little further behind Sara.

"Come on, buddy. It'll be fun." Scott wasn't buying it.

"Sorry, Jon. Scott's just a little insecure. But we're working on it, aren't we, buddy?" She crouched and took Scott's hands in hers. A minute later, she turned back to Jon, gently stroking Scott's head. "Let's go sit on the porch for a minute while the kids enjoy their toys."

As Scott settled down to turn the pages of his new book, Sara said quietly, "He hasn't said anything verbally for a year. When his father passed, he just stopped speaking, like a part of him turned off. Neither

Scott nor I had any idea Kevin was going to cross over. We still don't know exactly how or where or why, just that he has. He left a message saying that it was something he had to do, that we should get on with our lives, and for me to explain it to Scott when he was old enough to understand. As though I'd know the answers he hadn't shared with me.

"But you know, since we transitioned, I think I do understand, and I think it's all right. At least I've come to terms with it, living here in the Fifth, with Scott, and mostly *in the moment*. It might sound callous or hard, but I can deal with it. I have dealt with it. Scott though, he's very tender, and still extremely upset. We communicate very well using our minds, Scott and I, but not everyone can read his thoughts, and when they can't, it's difficult for him. He'll open up—if you're patient."

"I'm so sorry, Sara, for your loss. For Scott's. I'll go slower with him. We have the whole day, and there's a special treat at the end." Noting her grin, he added, "Which of course, you already knew."

"Yes, I know about Ekor. He's very special, and he certainly thinks the world of you, Jon." She flashed her dazzling smile and rose to herd her playful charges together for their next game.

As the shadows began to lengthen, Ekor appeared, sharing stories and jokes and accenting them with chirps and clicks. Mental communication with "a great big fish" was something the kids just took for granted—what a wonderful dimension—and they took turns holding onto his dorsal fin as he towed them around in the blue waters of the cove. Sun sparkled on the water and laughter sparkled in the air. A perfect close to a very special day.

Jon had managed to draw Scott out of his shell a time or two, but suspected that leaving his mom to ride a dolphin like some kind of aquatic cowboy might be just a bit more than Scott could handle, right up until he felt a tug on the right leg of his shorts.

"Hey, Scott, what's up? What can we do for you, big guy?" Jon knelt down to Scott's eye level and found that he could easily share his thoughts.

"You want to ride Ekor, too? Is that really what I'm hearing?"

A faint nod and an expectant glance in the direction of the dolphin said it all. Jon looked at Sara who shrugged and smiled. It was obviously fine with her, even though she was as surprised as Jon.

"Okay, buddy, let's go find the big fish." Jon was actually nervous at the thought of letting such a small, delicate child loose in the ocean—heck, the kid wasn't much bigger than Ekor's nose!—but in they waded, as far as Scott could go. There was a pause. Then, as Sara watched, Scott looked up to Jon, gave a nod and a small smile, and was scooped up in Jon's strong arms to continue his journey to dolphin-friendly depths.

What happened next was beautiful to see. Ekor approached slowly, nosing up to Jon and Scott. Then, Scott reached out and put his hand on the dolphin's snout. Instantly, the connection they made resonated with such deep trust that Jon and Sara could feel it, too. Scott leaned forward and Jon settled him on Ekor's back, making sure that his small hands had a good grip on Ekor's fin. Then, without any hesitation at all, Ekor swam away from the shore. His small passenger sent a big smile back over his shoulder to his mom who waited on the beach, then pressed his face to the dolphin's back, thrilled by Ekor's strength and the depth of their connection.

It was a long ride; much longer than any of the others. When Ekor finally brought Scott back to shore, the boy wore a smile that stretched from ear to ear. He slipped off Ekor's side, trusting Jon to hold him up, and his tiny hand stroked Ekor's snout as he listened intently, nodding. Then, man and boy walked back to the beach where Sara was anxiously waiting.

"Mommy, Mommy!" Scott shouted, and hearing him, everyone

turned to stare. "I *talked* to him! He talked to *me!* He told me things. He's my friend! Oh, Mommy, I love him!"

Relieved, stunned, utterly undone, Sara dropped to her knees and hugged her son as tears streamed down her cheeks. "Oh, my sweetheart, I love him, too. And I love you so very much."

Scott put his hands on her cheeks and looked deeply into her eyes with wisdom beyond his years. "I love you, too, Mommy."

Jon's eyes glistened. He had so much to thank Ekor for already, but at the top of today's list, was the introduction to the woman he already knew he would ask, one day very soon, to be his wife, and for the precious boy he wanted to be his son.

PART THREE

Eight years after The EarthShift

For the animal shall not be measured by man. In a world older and more complete than ours, they move finished and complete, gifted with extensions of the senses we have lost or never attained, living by voices we shall never hear. They are not brethren, they are not underlings; they are other nations, caught with ourselves in the net of life and time, fellow prisoners of the splendour and travail of the earth.

Henry Beston (1888-1968) – The Outermost House

Chapter Nine

"I still can't believe I let her take off with her cousins *just like that,* Julie! She's only eight, for Pete's sake!"

"Jeannie, honey, I understand what you're feeling, but you know that the *number* of years just isn't as important here in the Fifth. She's really so much older in so many ways. Things are different here, not like they were in the Third. The kids need to explore, stretch their abilities, try their wings and all those other euphemisms that are supposed to make moms feel better about it when their kids strike off on their own. Try to think of it as two weeks of summer camp, OK? It's good practice for the kids and for us. You know that they'll be taking many more journeys before this is done, and that they have lots of help on lots of levels. Try not to worry."

She knew instinctively that Jeannie needed reassurance; because, dammit, she needed a good shot of it herself! So Julie set aside her own fears and anxiety and wrapped her mind and heart around the tenet which would give her the greatest degree of peace—living in the moment. It was strange that fear hadn't been totally eliminated from their lives. Not yet. They were treading the tenuous middle ground, letting go of the Third and fully embracing the Fifth. *Obviously,* thought Julie, *we still have some work to do, some explorations to make, and miles to go before we sleep.*

Everyone who had transitioned in the EarthShift had gained so much spiritual ground, but before the final ascension, there was still a lot left to do. Gabriel's "assignments," given when he appeared at their first big bonfire at Wind Dancer, had laid that out in no uncertain terms. Julie, like everyone else, wanted the best for her loved ones. *But the fact is,* she thought, *everyone has to continue to learn their own lessons in order to grow. The ultimate challenge for parents, as hard as it is, as hard as it's always been, is to give kids the time and freedom to learn for themselves. Some things never change.*

Julie blew out a big breath to release residual tensions and swung her arm around Jeannie's shoulders. "Come on, kiddo. Let's go see if we can find some choke cherries for jam. Then when the kids get home, we'll make a big batch of Nanny's hot biscuits to put it on. We'll be their heroes."

"How many miles have we gone, Jesse? Is it time to make camp yet?" Angela slid her backpack to the ground and stood, hipshot, panting just a little and working hard not to show it. She wanted to prove that she could keep up with the boys, but her gear was getting heavier with each step. Sensitive to his younger cousin's unspoken needs, Jesse walked over to stand beside her, looking down the steep ridge which overlooked a beautiful lush valley. A pair of mountain goats made short work of climbing the hillside, and Angela was more than a little envious of their agility.

"I'd guess we've gone about eight miles," said Jesse, "but it's been pretty tough terrain. I say we go down into the valley and camp by the river. We can get a fire going, maybe take a quick swim and chow down. It's getting late anyway. Okay with you guys?"

"I'm more than ready. Come on, let's go." Joey was starving as usual. "Maybe we can catch some fish for dinner, too, and keep an eye out for berries. We'll need to supplement our food supply if it's gonna last for two whole weeks."

They began their descent at a much slower pace than the goats. The trail, such as it was, dropped nearly vertical in places, and stones moved under their feet when the weight of their packs threw them off balance. But it was the bellow of an elk that did it. Mike whipped his head around looking for the elk, and as he did, his foot slipped on a loose stone. He pitched forward, out of control, and began a long, rolling tumble. The cousins heard him yell in pain as he slipped and skidded down the embankment, breaking bushes, loosening rocks and grazing trees as he went.

"Mike! Oh my God, help him!" Angela screamed in horror.

Slightly below, leading the descent, Jesse and Joey tried to make a grab but weren't quite quick enough. Mike plunged past them, followed by a small rock slide that pelted down like super-sized hail. They watched Mike's arms flailing as he tried to grab something, anything, to slow the fall. Then, throwing his arms up to protect his head, he disappeared from sight, and his panicked shouts faded away.

Jesse's heart was in his mouth. He'd just watched his brother fall a long, long way while getting hit by big rocks—possibly on the head. He might be badly hurt ... or dead. Jesse forced the breath in and out of his lungs. Mike wasn't supposed to be vulnerable like that. Mike was strong. He was their protector, their warrior. How could this happen? Tamping down the rising panic, Jesse launched himself down the incline calling for his brother.

"Jesse, be careful!" called Angela. "You're kicking up rocks and they'll hit Mike. Move more to the right—and watch where you're stepping!"

Sensing that Angela was "tuned in," Jesse moved right. "Mike! Where are you? We're coming! Hang on!" Joey and Angela followed, taking great care not to dislodge more rocks. They all kept shouting encouragement to Mike, but were answered by silence.

Back at the twins' home, Megan and Steve were strangely unsettled.

"It's been four days, Steve. Where do you think the boys are?" As with Jeannie, it had been quite a struggle for Megan to let her boys go off on their own for a two week stretch. *How could they have grown up so quickly and so much?* She knew they were responsible and intelligent, certainly highly intuitive. Sure they were, and that was good. Still, it didn't change the fact that she'd prefer to keep them tucked safely under her wing for a few more years.

"They are where they are, Meg." Steve was trying his best to be Mr. Cool when he felt really anything but. "Look, there's absolutely nothing we can do about it except trust in them, and *try* to trust that E.T. guide of Jesse's. As much as it's out of character for me to say it, I really do hope Dorado is keeping an eye on them. I'm sure we'll hear from them any time now, babe."

Megan was doing her best to trust, just as Steve had said, but at the same time, there was no denying a bone-deep unease fluttering around the edges of her consciousness. And if that wasn't bad enough, she was unbelievably frustrated that she was currently unable to tune in to any kind of psychic contact with her own kids. Completely out of touch.

It took just minutes and felt like hours. Angela was the first to spot the red backpack and to realize that the young man under it wasn't moving. "Oh no. Please let him be all right, please!"

Mike was out cold. His arms and legs were scratched and bleeding, and blood oozed thickly from his head and face. Joey checked for a pulse. "He's alive but don't move him. We might make it worse. Let's see if we can get that pack off him." Jesse carefully undid the straps and Joey lifted it up and away. Angela wet a towel from her water bottle and began to carefully wipe blood away so they could better assess the injuries.

"Joey, you've had more experience at healing than we have," said

Jesse. "He needs help, and we'll back you up. Can you scan his body? See if we can move him? We should get down this pitch and into the valley before dark if there's any way possible."

This was the biggest challenge Joey had ever faced. As a kid, he'd healed his own bumps and bruises, even a badly twisted knee, but compared to this, anything he'd done before was like comparing Band-aids to brain surgery. Centering himself, Joey placed his hands on Mike's head and brought in the Higher Power energy, visualizing it running throughout the body. He looked for bleeding, tears, broken bones, anything internal that wasn't right; all the while, willing the energy to heal wherever it was needed.

He began to whisper a running commentary. "Okay, I don't see any breaks. There's a bad concussion, a sprained wrist. There's something in the knee. Maybe a pulled ligament or torn cartilage, lots of cuts and bruises. He's hurting, but nothing looks life-threatening. We all need to work on him. Concussion first ..."

The attentions and emotions of his cousins were raising Mike's vibrational rate. After only a couple minutes, his eyelids flickered as he struggled to regain consciousness.

The others could have danced when Mike opened his mouth and a logical, reasonable question popped out. "What happened?"

Jesse leaned close. "Hey, bro, you slipped and took one hell of a fall. But you're going to be okay. We'll get you down off this perch when you're up for it."

"Ohhhh. Sure. I'll try to ... Oh! Oh man. Everything hurts. How ... ?"

"Don't talk, Mike. We'll tell you all about it later. Right now, you need to save your strength. You're gonna need it." Angela, still wiping blood and tending small wounds, asked if he could sit up.

Mike nodded and allowed himself to be helped up a bit before he was forced to admit that he felt really sick to his stomach. For a warrior, he wasn't doing a very good job. Struggling to get his legs under him so he could try to stand, he discovered that his knee wouldn't bend and hurt so badly he doubted it would hold weight. His head was dizzy and the nausea increased with even the smallest effort. Desperately afraid he was going to cry, or hurl, or both, he lay back down and closed his eyes, concentrating on his breathing.

The cousins knew that a change of course was in order. Using every ounce of ingenuity they could muster and the materials close at hand, they fashioned a crude sledge. Two saplings, snapped off during Mike's fall, were laid parallel, about eighteen inches apart, then stabilized with fir boughs crossed and woven back on each other. These were fastened at the edges with vine and bits of string. Three sleeping bags were placed on top for padding and Mike was carefully lifted into place. The fourth bag was wrapped around everything and everyone's belts were used to secure him. As afternoon turned toward evening, they began the trip down.

Makeshift as it was, their stretcher worked like a charm. The route was bumpy and tedious, and when their speed outstripped their caution, Mike's groans served as a reminder. Dark shadows had crept up to swallow most of the hillside when they reached the valley floor to settle into a grassy clearing beside clear running water. A fire was soon blazing, and Joey was busily catching fish for dinner while Angela finished tending Mike's wounds. Jesse made splints for Mike's wrist and knee, and by the light of the campfire, they covered any remaining open wounds with bandages until he began to look a little like a mummy. Some hot, sweet tea helped settle his stomach, and even though Mike would have preferred to be left alone to sleep, the cousins peppered him with questions until they were convinced he was coherent, albeit grumpy. Lastly, they gathered for another session of hands-on healing before falling into their own sleeping bags, utterly exhausted. If any animals came to inspect the visitors during the night, none of the four knew about it.

Aching muscles for everyone arrived with the morning sun, and for Mike, there was an extra scoop of ache. Their warrior wasn't in any shape to protect anyone or anything at the moment, so Jesse, Joey and Angela gathered their wits for one more healing session. They recognized their abilities to heal as one of their best gifts and an important part of their training, but now especially; it was vital that they succeed at it.

Mike knew he had to get better quickly, for his own sake, as well as to prove to their parents that they were capable of facing and solving whatever challenges the mountains, and Gabriel's assignments, might bring. So he relaxed himself, body and mind, when Joey sat on the ground and gently lifted his dully aching head into his lap. Angela sat on his right side, Jesse on his left, and as one, they breathed and centered before beginning their visualizations of Mike's injuries.

By unspoken agreement, they laid up to rest, explore and meditate. They caught fish and gathered berries in cups, pots and hats to supplement the supplies brought from home. It was telling of the cousins' close bonds that Joey, who could and did eat anything, anywhere, anytime, made sure that Mike got first dibs and as much nourishment as his body required. By the end of the third day, Mike was limping only slightly, his dizziness was completely gone, if not the tender lump on his head, and the cuts and bruises had all but disappeared. They had things to do and places to go, and they knew it; but this experience had shown them that trusting their own instincts and making sure they looked after each other came first and foremost. They were working on trusting their unseen guides to help with whatever came next.

"I think I'm ready to move on, guys. If we take it slow—you know, just not climb any fourteeners," he said with a grin, "I just might make it." And with that, their respite ended. They packed their gear and hit the trail to the beat of, "we can, we can, we know we can" which became their mantra as they tackled the hills and valleys of Colorado's forests.

Chapter Ten

"I miss Joey, Mom." Even though Erica had been little more than a baby when the Shift occurred, she remembered bits and pieces of it with photographic clarity. When she was worried, she remembered it often. *Darkness. Wind. The scramble to find candles because Aunt Jeannie was in labor. Pressure. Darkness. Joey putting his hands on Aunt Jeannie's head, and no one minding or telling him that he was in the way. The strange man coming in out of the darkness to deliver the baby, to deliver Angela. The strange man had known Joey, and Joey had known the man. The man was nice, comfortable. The man was light, even in the darkness.*

But especially when she was worried, the memory which played in Erica's head was Uncle Jerry running out the door and disappearing into the wind and darkness. It always made her sad. Especially since she knew that the cause of his panic was Angela's spina bifida which had been completely healed during the Shift. For Erica, the possibility existed that someone loved could be someone lost. And now her brother was off in the mountains, and she wasn't. He wasn't lost. Just out-of-sync. But she still didn't like it. Not one bit.

Recognizing that the cause of Erica's moodiness was her big brother's absence, Kathy tried for an outlook modification. "For goodness sake, Erica, Joey's strong and capable. And the twins and Angela are watching out for him. He'll be back soon, baby. Come help me bake some chocolate chip cookies for when they get home. Those are Joey's favorite."

"Food is Joey's favorite, Mom." Tossing her blond curls, Erica scowled at her mother before reluctantly stomping her way to the kitchen. Kathy smiled and thought, *Oh yes, our little girl isn't going to stand for being left at home much longer.*

At Wind Dancer, Jeannie was fretting, too. "Dad, couldn't you and Julie just do your thing and tune in to the kids? Make sure they're okay and safe and ... ?"

"I've got a better idea. How about a game of checkers or something? You know we can't interfere with their learning. They're in good hands, Jeannie, much more experienced hands than ours."

"I know, I know, I *know*, Dad! It's just that Angela's the youngest and a girl, and ... and after losing Jerry, I just couldn't face losing her, too."

Dave put his arm around her and led her out to the deck. "Honey, you know that what they're doing is bigger than we can possibly imagine. And we can imagine pretty darned good. But this is stuff they need to learn in preparation for the real deal. Knowing who they are and what Gabriel expects of them—well, I'm just so proud of my granddaughter and grandsons. And I have faith in their abilities. You need to, too."

Jeannie put her head on his shoulder and heaved a deep sigh. "You're right, Dad. I know you're right. It's just that sometimes I feel so alone. Believe me, I'm grateful to have you and Julie. I just still miss my husband. I guess that's probably silly after all these years, but maybe someday ... " Her voice drifted off into the twilight as they stood watching the pink of the setting sun reflect off the peak of Crystal Mountain.

With the others' help, and the regenerative powers contained within his own improved DNA, Mike's recovery was fast. He might still have a tiny limp when his knee grew tired, and just a twinge in his head when he moved too fast, but he couldn't complain. He was just grateful that he hadn't totally screwed up their assignment and well aware that he might have been killed.

The cousins continued their journey following the river. Mike continued to fish for their dinners; not his favorite pastime, but something he could easily do to contribute and not risk re-injuring his knee. It had been *amazing,* he thought, to feel the others' healing energies working through his body. Even though he'd seen it and done it before, it still blew him away to witness the full power of that energy, especially when they were combined. Comforted by those thoughts, he turned his mind to Jesse. His brother was getting more and more serious by the hour; not joking around—just intense and distracted. He'd have to poke Jesse a little and see what he could find out. Knowing his brother as he did, Mike figured it would take him a while to get past, "Everything's fine."

Jesse was having dreams again. Dorado-instigated, high-resolution, several steps beyond Technicolor dreams. As reassuring as it was to know that their special guide was around and keeping an eye on them, *I just never know when he's going to appear and scoop me up for another space journey. Not that that's bad, but this just isn't the right time,* Jesse thought. He'd always shouldered a certain amount of responsibility for his cousins, but at times like this, the weight of that responsibility could be overwhelming—even for a 14-going-on-40-year-old.

Thanks to increased exercise and a somewhat sparse diet, all four kids had dropped a pound or two during their time on the trail and were all feeling great about their toned young muscles. The plans for the journey hadn't included any particular destination, just the experience of facing the unknown on their own, and they'd handled their explorations, meditations, and even Mike's accident well enough. Now, Jesse felt that it was time to head back home, and if they were going to make it before the supplies ran out, they needed to make tracks.

Dammit, thought Jesse, *why do I have this weird feeling something is missing. Or maybe that we're just not seeing something that's right here under our noses. So far, everything's been ... normal. We haven't seen any strange behavior in the animals or signals in the sky. I've listened for sounds, music, words, messages of any sort and gotten nothing. I wish Dorado could just give me a clue.*

"Ow! Jeez, that hurt!" Jesse yelped.

"Hey, your nose is bleeding, buddy! What happened?" Joey grinned. "Aw, did that mean old branch reach out and bite you in the face?"

"Knock it off, Joey. I didn't see it."

"Hey, sorry Jess. Didn't mean to get your shorts in a knot."

"Forget it. I'm fine. I was just thinking about something else." He glanced at the tree. "What kind of tree is that anyway? Anybody seen one like this before?"

Angela walked around the tree, placing her hands on the rough trunk. "Hmm. It feels weird, guys. It really feels alive. Vibrating. Very strange."

Mike came over and inspected the tree, too, looking at it closely, sniffing it, running his hands over the bark. Then, he stepped back and gave it a whack with the sapling he was using for a walking stick.

"Ouch!"

"Whoa, did you guys hear that? I swear that tree said 'ouch!'"

"That's because I did say it, Michael. And now that you've ruined my cover, I might as well join you for a while." Slowly, and with great flare, the tree melted and morphed into a smiling Dorado.

"I've been nagging Jesse in his dreams, but he's been very adamant about not letting me in. I figured a little knock on the head might wake him up. Obviously, I picked the wrong kind of tree. Silly me! So now I'm out in the open with no protection at all." He scowled at Mike. "And please don't go around hitting trees with that thing."

"Sorry, Dorado. Never again."

"Good. Now my dear children, we all know why you're on this grand adventure, don't we? What I mean to say is *this* adventure ... here, now, lately, the past week. Not the big one coming."

Jesse found his voice, adolescent croak and all. "Dorado, I'm sorry about the dream thing. I really am glad to see you. We've had a few challenges, but I think we've about got this trip whipped. And yeah, we're *so* on our training for the Big One in a few years, right guys?"

"That's certainly the main focus, Jesse. It's also to help your parents adjust to the idea of letting you *do your own thing* as they used to say in the Third. That's more difficult than you can imagine, even with the added wisdom of your own years and those given you. But there's a bit more to do before you return home.

"You each have a certain role to play and special strengths needed for the success of your mission. Being able to blend your talents, to get along with each other, treat each other with respect and support. These are major requirements. So far, I'm very impressed. Good training, if I do say so myself."

"You're so modest, Dorado," Joey quipped and received a sardonic look from Dorado in response.

"Yes, well, as I was saying: There's one thing which you haven't, to date, experienced. This you must do. Crystal Mountain emits an enormous amount of energy. If—no, *when* you decide to take this challenge, you'll understand the full ramifications of my words."

Dorado continued, "To that end, I would suggest that you immediately embrace the task of *sensing* the mountain. This is an exercise which will help you, even *guide* you, when it's time. Tasting this energy at this time, and in this fashion, will allow your bodies to make the proper adjustments. And there will come a time, dear ones, when the demands upon you will be so great that any system out of balance may overstress other systems. The cost for that could be very great. Just a thought, my dear friends."

"You know, Dorado," said Angela, "It's good to have a new exercise to work on. We've been working on being independent and surviving on our own, but pretty much, it's just been a big camping trip. It's good to be reminded of the bigger picture."

"Very insightful, my dear. You all might consider attempting to connect with the mountain before you get any closer to home." He turned and arched a brow at Jesse. "No space trips for now, Jesse. Relax and enjoy the scenery ... and watch out for low branches. Perhaps you need to raise your focus, so to speak. You never know what you might see. So I'll be off now." And he was.

"Wow, that guy is awesome," marveled Mike.

"He's the best guide in the universe, if you ask me. He has a good sense of humor, but he can be serious, too. I think we should get started on this mountain energy stuff. What do you guys think?" asked Jesse.

"Sure. What do we do and how do we do it?" asked Joey.

Jesse looked around. "You see that hill ahead of us? It's not far and not too steep, so Mike's knee should be OK. Let's climb to the top and tune in. We'll never know what we're missing until we try it. Angela, you lead this time."

With a happy, confident smile, proud that Jesse had tapped her to break trail, Angela strode off, careful not to hit any trees with her walking stick.

They reached the hilltop in short order and sat down, cross-legged, to enjoy a gorgeous view of Crystal Mountain. Jesse led the meditation, guiding them into a deep trance, asking the angels to keep them safe and allow them to experience the energy of Crystal Mountain. Surroundings diffused into fog as they went deeper. Into an emptiness, a silence. They were floating. Attached to nothing. Stretching out toward whatever lay on the other side of the stillness.

Suddenly, there was a great pull on them from inside the darkness. Their ears heard a growing hum, their skin felt a tingling, a heat. Time was rushing, or dragging, and it didn't matter because they were feeling a power unlike anything they had ever felt before. Their stomachs grew nauseous. Fear took root. They were alone.

The hum grew to a buzz, and the buzz grew louder until it was a whine or whistle which filled them from the inside out. Their bodies began to vibrate and feel prickly, the way a foot does when it's been asleep and the circulation returns.

Mike spoke, and the sound came from a far distant place. "Where are we? What's happening to us?"

"Wherever it is, I'd like to go back to where we were," whispered Angela. "I don't feel so good." She and Mike hadn't had as much experience with out-of-body journeys as the others, and fear was increasing her physical symptoms to an alarming degree.

With that conscious wish, the spell was broken. Angela felt the vibrations slow. The tingling stopped and her queasiness eased. She was aware of the earth beneath her body, the smell of the forest in her nostrils, the songs of birds in her ears. They were back!

"Wow! What a trip!" said Joey. "That is some powerful energy. Was that coming out of the mountain, like from the inside, you think?"

"I imagine so," said Jesse. "It felt like a vacuum pulling on me. And loud, too. I don't think I'm ready to completely give in to it, though. I didn't know whether we were together or if I was alone until I heard Mike. You sounded like you were in an echo chamber, Mike."

"Yeah, well guess what ... I *felt* like I was in one! I still feel weird. I'm not ready to mess with that stuff yet."

"Personally, I think it's a darn good thing we did. Now we've got an idea of what we'll be dealing with someday. I'm thinking we'll have to learn to control just how much and how far we let it take over. Dorado was right. This isn't just a fun-and-games mission, but we've got a couple of years to learn everything we'll need. For right now, though, let's hit the trail. There's a good chunk of miles between us and a big home-cooked meal with seconds at Grandma and Grandpa's." Jesse shouldered his pack and headed down the hill. Still a little dazed, the others followed.

The vortex experience, drawing on the mountain's power, had been sobering. More even than holding a lightning bolt. Julie's grandchildren had touched the power of the universe. Dorado, watching his young charges from a distance, was satisfied with their response to the Crystal energy. Still, there was so much more for them to learn. They'd soon be ready for another lesson on the great silver space ship, and he would ponder awhile before deciding whether the next should be as a dream, or if the four would be ready to open their minds while fully conscious.

Chapter Eleven

The day after Ekor first put them together, Jon went back across the Bay to see Sara and to talk and play with Scott. For days after that, more than a week's worth, he continued to visit. Then came the time when he needed to return to the Third. Jon told them that he wouldn't be long and that he'd see them again when he got back.

In that absence, Sara and Scott spoke of Jon often. Phrases like, "Jon told me ..." or "Remember when Jon ..." seasoned their conversations. Sara told Scott that she enjoyed the way Jon could join in any conversation. How he would add bits and pieces of trivia, or ask challenging questions, filing the answers away for later use. Scott told his mom that Jon made him feel safe. And special. And loved. And that Jon smelled good and gave good hugs, even when his beard was scratchy. And Sara agreed.

Two days later, it was late in the evening, and Sara and Scott were sitting on the sand, watching the sunset paint the sky over the Pacific when Jon shimmered onto the beach and walked toward them. They scrambled up, shouting his name and ran to him, leaping into his arms, kissing his face. Welcoming him home. And they were a family.

Sara and Jon would marry in San Francisco so Ekor could take part. Without him, they might have met—eventually. But considering the circumstances, they weren't about to deny the absolute perfection of his sense of timing. Sara and Jon were in total agreement that theirs would be a small, simple ceremony with family and a few close friends, and the preparations for it were nearly complete. The time for vows was fast approaching, and Scott was so excited he could barely contain himself.

"Mom, are *all* the kids coming? Our new family? I had so much fun with Angela and Erica when we were all together. Are they in the wedding, too? And what about the twins ... ? And Joey ... ?"

"Hey, buddy! Slow down! How can I answer so many questions when they're coming at me so fast? I can barely remember what you asked!" Sara laughed. What a joy it was to hear his voice after the long year of silence. Scott had definitely conquered his emotional block, thanks to Ekor and Jon.

"OK. Yes, *all* the kids are coming." Scott danced in place, grinning from ear to ear as his mother continued. "All the family is coming, and in one way or another, they'll all be part of our ceremony. But, since you've been wound up tight all day, and I don't want to have a sleepy helper tomorrow, you need to get yourself off to bed." She leaned down to give him a big hug and a kiss on both cheeks before touching her lips to his. "Scoot! Rest up! We have *so* much to do tomorrow!"

At Wind Dancer Ranch, Jeannie knocked on Angela's door for the third time. "Come on, sleepy head. Time to get up. We need to make sure your dress for Jon and Sara's wedding fits." Again, no answer. "Okay, young lady, you've had your warnings. I'm coming in and I'm armed with kisses!" Jeannie knew her daughter was in the throes of another big growth spurt. There were many changes after the training hike with the boys. The most difficult for Jeannie was that Angela had become very sure of herself, rebelling if there was even a hint that someone might be treating her like a child. *Which she still is,* thought Jeannie. *It must be early puberty causing the mood swings.*

Another change was that, like Jesse, Angela had developed the ability to block her thoughts, closing off her mind so it couldn't be read.

Jeannie's pain of losing her husband and Angela's pain of losing her dad had always been a burden they'd shared. Now, she worried that her daughter was struggling to manage a load that was just too heavy for her young heart to bear. *After all this time, it's still just not knowing that's most difficult.* She opened the door and walked across the room to sit carefully on the bed.

"Angela. Sweetie ... " She carefully pulled the blanket down, revealing neatly rolled towels and blankets.

"Angela! Oh, no! *Angela!*" She blindly stumbled into the hall, her shouts echoing through the house, and bringing Julie and Dave on the run.

"What is it? What's happened?" Jeannie was white as a sheet and her heart was beating like a jackhammer. Seeing the bloodless face and the shocky eyes, Dave grabbed Jeannie in his arms and held her tight. "It's okay, it's okay. Take a breath and tell us what's happened, babe. Tell us what's wrong."

"She's gone," Jeannie whispered. "She faked her body in the bed. She's gone and I don't know where!"

"She's probably in the barn, or on an early walk. Or something." Julie grabbed at answers, not believing them as she said them. "Come on. Let's go see if she left a note." Julie strode off toward Angela's room. "We know she can take care of herself and wouldn't want you to be upset, Jeannie." She did a quick survey of the room, her eyes fastening on the envelope labeled "MOM," propped against a lamp on the dresser.

"Look. Just as I thought. Here's a note." Julie handed the envelope to Jeannie and said, "Let's hear what escapade she's cooked up this time."

Jeannie began to read.

> *"Dear Mom, I'm sorry if you're freaked out when you read this. Please don't worry about me though. I know I'll be all right and I'll be back very soon. I know I can do this. By the*

time you're reading this note, I'm hoping that I'll have found Dad. I'm going to bring him home to you, Mom. I love you. Angela"

"Oh God! No! She can't do that!" Completely undone, knowing all too well the extent of danger her daughter was facing in the Third Dimension, Jeannie began to sob quietly in her father's arms.

Dave was powerless to do anything except hold her and whisper inadequate reassurances. Stroking Jeannie's back, he met his wife's eyes and read the deep concern in them. At that moment, Dave felt strongly that he'd failed his daughter on so many levels. He hadn't helped her get over Jerry's loss, or to recover Jerry from the Third. And now, he hadn't prevented his granddaughter from taking off on her own, into that war-torn, disease-ridden chaos. Helplessness rose as bile in his throat as he stroked Jeannie's hair and muttered soothing sounds.

Julie gave them both a hug and whispered, "I'm going to get in touch with the others."

Julie put off telling the grandchildren about Angela, opting instead to direct her thoughts first to Chris, then Jon, and finally to Bill and Steve. She worried that, as headstrong as especially Mike and Joey were, they might end up teleporting back to the Third to help, and having one child back there was one too many. Support for Jeannie was at the top of the Must-Have List, followed closely by a decision on who would go back to find Angela.

As Julie started to bring Jon into her mind, she couldn't help thinking that with a wedding coming up within the week, Angela's timing could hardly be worse. And then an image of Angela, standing proudly beside Jeannie and Jerry, floated up. Julie shook her head, realizing that all her granddaughter wanted was to bring her dad back for the family gathering.

Oh sweetie, if it hasn't happened in eight years, how on earth do you think you can pull it off in less than a week? As she embraced the overwhelming poignancy of Angela's pain, Julie closed herself inside her meditation room to briefly set aside her armor of control, and weep.

Chapter Twelve

Angela's first thought was, *Wow, I made it!* It was quickly followed by a wave of fear and a sea of questions. *Where am I? What should I do now? Where should I go? I should've brought the guys. Where's my dad? No, the guys wouldn't have let me come. How can I find my dad?*

She looked around and saw small, dull cement buildings and a few houses, drab and neglected, all with broken windows. A swirl of dust spun across the street, rattling the tin cans rusting in the gutter. The area appeared deserted, but when a hint of movement caught her eye she realized that someone had appeared on the street corner a block away. She dropped to her knees behind the rotting carcass of an abandoned car.

Angela needed to talk to her angels and a Higher Power. She needed to make sure they had crossed over into this other dimension with her. She called on their energy, apologized for hurting her mother, thanked them for getting her this far, and asked for their guidance. All her life, she had believed with every bit of her heart that she was never alone no matter how lonely she felt. And even now, that held true.

Feeling a little better, she rose cautiously, squinting in the sunlight, and peered through the cracked and grimy car windows to focus on a tough-looking man dressed in camouflage and carrying a huge rifle. He turned in her direction, and Angela's breath caught in her throat. She froze, waiting. After a minute, he lost interest and disappeared down an alley, leaving the street deserted once more.

Weak and trembling, Angela slumped to the sidewalk and leaned against a rusting fender as the enormity of her actions—or inactions—hit home. *That man was real. His gun was real. No one here is playing games,* Angela thought, realizing just how precarious her situation was, and she didn't even know if she could return home.

She tried to reassure herself. *The others have done it, but they're older and more experienced.* She searched her mind for bits of Julie's wisdom. *What's that saying? Sure, that's it: Pull yourself up by your boot straps and get on with it.* She breathed deeply, trying to gather her courage. *Yes, that's what I've got to do. Right now, before I think about it too much! I've chosen this mission, and I'd better get to it.*

She moved quickly to the shadows, keeping low and staying watchful. *This certainly doesn't look like a place I'd find Dad. Or a store with food in it. Or a safe place to stay. I need to find someone to talk to. Someone besides that huge guy with the gun.* Her skin crawled just thinking of him. *He was probably just trying to protect himself.* Whether it came from the man's real intentions or she was beginning to feel the Third Dimension influences, she really didn't believe it.

Angela continued a short distance up the street, then slipped into a garbage-strewn driveway behind a rundown house. Yes, it was nasty, but she didn't think traveling on the streets was safe. She congratulated herself on remembering to bring a container of water and some snacks for emergencies. Then, she complimented herself on her choice of black pants, black shirt and black jacket. *What all the best-dressed spies wear!* Then a trash can lid crashed beside her, and something ran right over her feet chased by a mean, skinny cat. She squealed a little as she realized that the something being chased was the biggest rat she'd ever seen, and scared all over again, she waited for her pulse to settle.

Moving on, she finally located a sturdy house with a bit of grass in the yard and knocked quietly at the back door. Getting no response, she tried the door knob which turned easily. She swung the door open cautiously and called out a "hello," but only a cold, hollow echo bounced back.

She stood in the kitchen and studied the room. On the table, a dust-covered coffee cup was anchored to the table with cobwebs. Beside it lay a yellowed newspaper. The date on the front page was the date of her birth eight years ago—the date of the EarthShift. The full impact of what that meant crumpled Angela into a chair. *One of three things happened here*, she thought. *Whoever was here either transitioned to the Fifth, or got captured, or died.*

Her emotions were up and down like a roller-coaster. *Okay Angela, let's think. Did the whole town disappear? Is there anyone left behind, and if they're here, will they talk to me? Will they be helpful or hateful? Fearful or brave? Is it even possible that my father is still living in this miserable place?*

She glanced down and noticed that the newspaper was called The Los Angeles Journal. *So maybe this town's near LA. That's where Uncle Chris, Aunt Ellen and Uncle Jon held their big gathering. That story was really frightening, but at least they saw Dad. So why haven't they been able to find him on return visits? Maybe he's okay and still living with that family that took him a couple years ago. It's someplace to start.* And so, Angela decided, was the blood relationship with her father. *Our connection still has to be inside you somewhere, Dad. It just has to be. The sooner I reach you, the better.*

Angela had no idea of the turmoil she'd created back home. Wedding plans on hold, Jon, Sara and Scott journeyed to Wind Dancer and gathered with the family. The kids, Scott included, were asked to take care of ranch chores and assured that they'd be brought up to speed shortly. They didn't much like being left out of the loop, but enjoyed visiting the horses and playing with the other animals.

Supporting Jeannie, while convincing her that she'd be foolish to attempt the trip back to the Third to search for Angela, was the adults' primary goal. Not an easy task. Constantly reminding her that she didn't have the training or experience, they brainstormed about what steps to take and who should take them. They reminded her how easy it was to get lost in the Third, geographically and spiritually, and this, she was told over and over again, would not help her child.

Logically, Chris, Ellen and Jon should go. They were aware of the dangers and already committed to helping others in the Third. They had experience, and would have the best chance at locating Angela. They were also doing their best to ignore their doubts about finding one young girl all alone in LA, if she'd managed to make it there; let alone all the other places she might be in that vast wild world. They knew they would be looking for the proverbial needle in a haystack.

Adding to their difficulties, they had to assume that Angela might not want to be found. If her goal was to find Jerry—and they knew it was—and if it was within her power, Angela would likely block her location until she had reached her goal.

It was time to fill in the kids and ask for their help since Jesse and his cousins already had an inside track to Dorado, and through Dorado to Gabriel. If they were going to find Angela and bring her home safely, they'd need all the help they could get.

"Why the hell did she *do* that?" Jesse was furious. "She's too young and she doesn't know what she's doing. You guys would never let us go there, not even *together!* Never mind just one of us alone."

"You're right, Jess, but she didn't give us a choice," Dave spoke quietly. "I think she's been getting herself ready for this for a long time, but couldn't tell us, figuring we'd freak out. She was right. But it doesn't do us any good to get angry. The situation is what it is. What we could use now is any guidance we can get from your friend Dorado. It might help us decide what to do to help Angela. God only knows where she is ... literally. What do you think? Could you try to communicate with your friend?"

"You bet we will, Grandpa. We'll all try. But I have to warn you, that he—they—are really stubborn about having us learn our own lessons. They put obstacles and choices in our way to help us grow, but they don't give us hints or demonstrations or maps to show us the way. It's for us to choose, so we'll learn. They might feel the same about Angela."

"Yeah," added Joey. "We've found that out the hard way, especially the last two years. If we start to get too cocky about our abilities, we usually get thumped on the head or something, just to keep us humble. But we'll do what we can, right now. Mike, are you with us?"

"Absolutely. Let's do it."

But before the boys could begin, Erica spoke up. "I just need to say this: Angie may be young, but she's determined. Single-minded. Even stubborn. You all know that. Women—and I put her in that category now—are strong to begin with, and I'm sure you've felt her strength right from the moment she was born. She's proved that she has unique gifts on every expedition you guys have made; your so-called camping trips into the wilderness. I'm feeling really strongly that you—we—shouldn't interfere if at all possible. Don't get me wrong. I want her back safe and sound and now. But, being a girl with a dad I love right here, I think I'm tuning in a little more on Angela's needs and desires, and what kind of help she really needs." Erica's eyes filled with emotion as she looked at her dad, and Bill moved over, put his arm around her shoulders and squeezed as he bent to drop a kiss on her head.

Julie was still processing. She remembered the relationship she'd enjoyed with her own dad during his long and energetic life, and even more, the one they'd grown into after his passing. His guidance from the other side had been invaluable throughout the time of the Shift. Even now, he was always there when she needed him.

She cleared her throat. "I know that what Jesse and Erica have shared with us is wisdom beyond their years. We need to listen to them. Let's not rush into anything right now. I suggest we get quiet and see if we can tune into anything or anyone. That's the first step."

"I agree."

"Let's do it."

Soon, energy was vibrating around the room at an intense level, but with a certain degree of caution. If they focused too strongly on the Third, there was the possibility of falling back into it, and no one wanted that to happen now. The information they received was sparse. Chris relayed that Mary was sending, "Let her be. Don't interfere." Dorado was pleased with Erica's analysis and emphasized that the lessons to be learned weren't just for Angela, but for all of them. Ekor, usually wordy, sent only, "Trust."

Then Julie felt Gabriel's energy, and softly spoke his words:

"I watch over all of you, something I trust you know. Not every happy ending is the right ending. Not everything sad is wrong. Things might turn out the way you'd like, or they might not. How they turn out will surely be for the good of all. What you believe is what you will see. What will become. Have you forgotten that? You must believe it for yourselves. Angela must believe for herself. She must do her own manifesting. This is not easy in the Third Dimension, but that is the dimension of her choosing. I caution you against interference. Go on with your lives. Keep Angela in your prayers. Bless you all. I leave you in love."

Chapter Thirteen

Angela summoned her resolve and reminded herself of all the lessons she'd already learned. Especially the ones about belief and trust. She had asked for guidance, and now she would have to trust that it would be given. And, she had to trust that she would find her father. How, was out of her hands.

Of immediate concern was finding food because her snacks hadn't lasted long. She searched the cupboards of the long-abandoned kitchen looking for anything that might still be edible. A jar of peanut butter with the seal still intact, two cans of creamed corn, one of white beans, another of beets ... *yuck* ... and a small can of sauerkraut. *Not exactly home cooking, but this'll keep me going for a while.* She found a dusty but functional backpack in the hall closet and packed in the cans. Then, realizing that some utensils would come in handy, she rummaged through the kitchen drawers and located a knife, two forks and four spoons of various sizes. Luckily, she remembered that she'd need a can opener and found a slightly rusty, manual one in a box labeled "Emergency Supplies." It also contained a waterproof canister of matches, a small bottle of tablets for water purification, and an odd silver "emergency blanket" folded up in a little bag no bigger than her fist. She put it all in the pack along with some band-aids and a long-expired tube of antibacterial ointment.

Angela was quickly coming to grips with her lack of experience and realizing that she'd been painfully naïve about the multitude of differences between the Third and the Fifth Dimensions; conditions here, just in general. She concluded that what she desperately needed was a whole new set of problem solving skills. *OK Angela! You're smart and capable and imaginative. Let's figure this out.*

A big plastic bag would work as a poncho if it rained, and a baseball cap with *Lakers* printed on the front was certainly worth having, and would keep the sun off her face. She searched for something to carry water in when and if she found any, and hoped that whatever germs had been on the three pint-sized empties in the recycling bin would be long gone. She dropped the bottles in the pack and zipped it closed, as prepared as she could be under the circumstances. Angela blessed the unknown owners and thanked them for her supplies, then closed the door behind her, checked for big men with guns, and moved quickly away from the main street.

"Keep walking. Trust that I'll go where I need to," became her mantra. Every now and then she would stop, look, listen ... and then swallow the hard lump of fear that kept rising in her throat. Every shadow, every sound, amplified small fears until they seemed monstrous and huge. She maintained her control through sheer willpower and fierce determination.

At the edge of the town, the lot sizes grew larger and the houses were fewer, farther in between. The air was improving a little, but cover was growing sparse. Head down, she ran flat out across an open lot, then sank down against a tree and reached into her pack. Memories of fish and berries with the guys didn't make the peanut butter any more appealing, but her belly was very empty and beginning to protest. Angela sampled a finger-full, then nearly choked when she heard a motor coming her way. The tree and some low bushes provided all the protection she was going to get, so she scrunched herself as small as possible behind them and peered carefully through the leaves.

The scene was right out of Uncle Jon's stories. A dull, dirty khaki-colored truck. Lots of men in the back. With guns. Really big guns. In that moment, Angela realized just how grave the danger really was, and by the time the truck went out of sight around the corner, and the men's deep voices faded away, her heart was nearly leaping out of her chest.

I've got to find a safe place so I can sleep, but jeez, these houses give me the creeps. The light was fading and she was completely exhausted, but she plodded on, watching and listening for danger. A mile—or an eternity—later, she spotted an old barn. It had lost most of its paint in the weather and the denuded boards had been silvered by the rain and sun. A few boards were missing, but remembering the comfort of Orion and Misty's barn, Angela ran stumbling through the rutted field toward it and discovered that the door was stuck tight.

She worked her fingers in beside the jamb and wrenched it open, praying for the safety of a loft and the comfort of soft hay. She found both at the top of the rickety ladder which butted up against a second-story half-floor where bales of hay rimmed the walls, and loose hay was scattered about the center. The old roof was thankfully intact so there was no wet or mold, just dust. *Lots and lots of dust,* she thought as she stomped and sneezed her way around, hoping to scare off all the creeping little critters. *I am a brave and grownup woman,* Angela reminded herself, *or at least I am until I touch a mouse.* And with that thought, she settled into a nest of hay, wrapped up in her strange shiny blanket.

The loft door was unlatched and swinging back and forth as the wind blew, its old hinges creaking mournfully. Angela found it comforting. She was bone-weary and feeling as safe as she had since she'd arrived, so sleep came quickly. But in her dreams, she ran and ran, pursuing the unknown, pursued by the unknown.

Bright sunlight burned between the barn boards, warming the loft and its inhabitants. Angela stirred, pushing the blanket down and throwing her arms over her face. When a gust of wind slammed the loft door shut with a bang, she sat bolt upright, looking around wildly. She found herself alone except for two small mice skittering across the floor, and as she'd seen them first, she was thankful. Rising quickly, she folded her blanket and stored it in its little bag, then reviewed her choices for breakfast. Without water, she was simply too dry to face more peanut butter. The beans might have more liquid, but they were chalky on a good day; at least they were without some tomatoes, onions, olives and maybe a little feta. *Sauerkraut for breakfast. As Charlie Brown would say, 'BLEAH!' Ditto, beets.* Trying to convince herself that it was somehow related to cornflakes, she opted for the creamed corn which turned out to be ... *pretty tasty. OK, so it's one step up from kindergarten paste, but hey, it's filling!*

Her need for water was acute, but there was neither hose nor spigot in the barn. *Water. First order of business.* Slipping the pack onto her shoulders, she paused to utter a prayer for guidance, then carefully made her way back down the ladder and out into the world. The sun warmed her face and lifted her spirits, so she decided to follow its light, at least until the morning chill was gone.

A couple of hours later, Angela noticed a line of dust rising in the distance and made a beeline for a dry ditch in a nearby field. Lying as flat as she possibly could, the grass and weeds provided some camouflage—and made her sneeze. As the big trucks passed by, she was grateful for the throaty roar of diesel engines that drowned out everything else. Turning her head to the side and raising it only slightly, she saw one truck with canvas panels tied up along the back. An assortment of people leaned stiffly against the sides, all looking scared. As the trucks drove on, she wondered where the people were being taken; why they'd been taken. Angela shivered, even though the sun was now hot and high, and acknowledged that her legs ached and her feet burned, that the sun was doing a real number on her skin, and that she was scared. And then, she moved on.

She came to another neighborhood with more houses, also empty and as desolate as the rest. Definitely not welcoming. It was lunchtime and she dug around in the remnants of an old garden, thrilled to find a volunteer cherry tomato sporting a dozen small red fruits. Hungry enough to not be picky, she ate them all, then picked any others which showed even the smallest hint of redness to take with her. She moved on, pulled by her determination, wondering how her family was dealing with her absence. The ache in her heart lingered as the miles fell slowly behind.

The next small town fascinated and delighted her. Angela imagined it was very pretty, once upon a time, with its back streets laid out, not in squares, but curves. Angela walked the empty sidewalks like a wandering ghost, or maybe someone from that old TV show that her grandmother had talked about—Twilight Zone. At any rate, she admitted that as near to normal as things looked, they just felt ... strange.

A torn curtain in the window of a small stucco house moved, at least she thought it did, and her heart skipped a beat. Had someone peeked out at her? She ran to the door and knocked, praying that someone would answer and that they would be ... *Nice. Helpful. Dad*.

But there was no answer. She pounded until paint chipped off on her hand. Still, no one answered. No one came. *Just my imagination,* she thought, heaving a sigh.

She trudged on, always listening for vehicles, always on the lookout for soldiers, always feeling jumpy and horribly, horribly thirsty. "I've got to find water," she mumbled, a bit startled to hear how raspy her voice had become. A half mile later, she came upon a small pond. "Wow! Ask and you shall receive. This is a miracle! Thank you, angels!" She waded in, clothes and all, relishing the feel of the water on her skin. She filled the bottles, dropped a purifying pill into each one—*no sense in getting sick in this no-man's land*—and screwed on the tops. Her shoes made squishing noises as she headed out, sipping water that tasted heavenly.

The town was larger, or she was more tired, than she'd first thought; roads curved and wound in all directions. Angela lost track of time, plodding on, head down, and trying to avoid the cracked sidewalks, trailing vines, and overgrown weeds that threatened to trip her. The lump in her throat was back, growing bigger and bigger, as she finally admitted to being dreadfully lost as well as alone, and not knowing where to turn or what to do next. The tears began to spill as she collapsed onto the front steps of the next house, seeking shade and a place to think.

Angela, sniffed, sipped more water and leaned back against a post. Then gasped in utter disbelief. There, across the street, was the small stucco house with the torn curtain. How could this be? She'd walked in a huge circle and wasted all that time and energy! For nothing! She wiped the back of her hand under her runny nose and made dirty wet streaks across her face. It was just too much.

Julie and the family were at a standstill on both wedding and rescue plans. Jon and Sara insisted that everyone's focus should be on Angela, and all agreed, knowing that Jon and Sara's marriage deserved more focus than they currently had to give. Time after time, they gathered to try and tune in to Angela's energy. And time after time, their vibrations bounced back like a tennis ball off a brick wall. Frantic, frustrated, Jeannie was feeling more helpless with each passing day. Erica was making a habit of wandering the house, stomping from room to room; one moment scared that something had happened to her cousin, the next, bursting with pride and certain that Angela would be back any day with Jerry at her side. Julie kept reminding everyone, including herself, to breathe, relax and be open.

But most of the time, it didn't help much.

Dave, Chris and Jon were deep in discussions, considering every conceivable course of action for finding one little girl in such a staggeringly large area. It was in their favor that they knew where and with whom Jerry had been left. If any of the players were still alive in the Third, there was a chance that their energy might draw the rescuers to their general vicinity. It was a long shot, true, but it was quite possibly their only shot.

The sun had set and night was falling in Colorado. Julie and the rest of the family were painfully aware that wherever she'd landed, night was falling on Angela, too.

Chapter Fourteen

Angela stared at the small stucco bungalow and slowly got up off the step, more determined than ever to get inside. *There's a good reason for me to be back here,* she thought. *A direction. Food. Water. A miracle.* Again, she knocked on the door and when no one answered, she banged and beat on it. She tried the knob, rattling and turning it, then shoved and slammed it with her shoulder. But the door was either locked or stuck tight. Carefully making her way around to the back, she tried that door with much the same results.

To the right of the back porch, she noticed a half-opened window; ground level, but pretty high up. The wooden hose box from the neighboring yard would give her a good boost, but it was bulky and heavy, and it took her some minutes to drag it through two yards worth of neglected shrubs and center it under her goal. Even standing on the box, she could barely reach the frame. Frustration made her all the more determined. Taking off her backpack, she carefully piled the cans of vegetables into a graduated stack, largest on the bottom, the little can of sauerkraut on top. Carefully placing her toe on the cans and bouncing a little to check for stability, Angela launched herself upward, hitting the bottom of the window and forcing it up another inch. It took balance, concentration, time, and it hurt like the dickens, but eventually, she increased the opening to well over a foot. Enough of an opening to launch herself through without concussion. She hoped. *Toe on the cans, push with the back leg, bounce, launch, grab!* And then, her head and chest were inside, her belly resting on the sill. She hauled herself forward, kicking and wriggling, until her hands reached the floor and she pulled herself through.

Her entrance had left her a little bloody, a lot tired, and she wondered if she'd be able to walk by tomorrow, but she had persevered. She was inside, and that felt very good. She found an old dish towel there in the kitchen, and after dampening it with a little spit, she began to try to clean her collection of scrapes and cuts. The wounds were mostly superficial, but bloody and dirty, and they stung like the devil. She held her hands over them and visualized healing energy, but soon realized that she'd left most of her healing abilities in the Fifth.

"Put your hands over your head!"

Angela screamed, dropped the towel and nearly fell as she jumped up to comply.

"My God, you're just a kid! Who are you? Where'd you come from?" The voice sounded harsh and no-nonsense, but what really worried Angela was seeing the sun glint off the long barrel of his gun as the man walked toward her down the darkened hallway.

"Oh, please don't shoot me. I can explain everything—or at least I'll try. I'm looking for my father. I came from ... ah ... Colorado. Um, it'll take a little explaining, but I promise I don't mean any harm. No one answered so I thought the house was deserted. You see, I was looking for water. And food. And shelter. All the houses seem to be empty." She tried to smile a little. "I'm just so glad to see a living person! Please, mister, if you could just tell me where I am so I can figure out where to go ... please." And with that, Angela's eyes overflowed, her tears etching pale tracks through the dirt on her sunburned cheeks.

The gun barrel lowered until it pointed at the floor, and the man holding it stepped fully into the light. His clothes were ragged; his beard and hair were long, gray and unkempt. Angela took a step back, thinking that this might be just another bad guy with a gun, but then, feeling the presence of her angels, she raised her chin and looked him straight in the eye. "Well? Will you help me or not?"

He'd been ready to send her on her way, but just couldn't seem to. The emphatic "No" he was planning came out as, "Yes. Yes, I will."

She blew out a relieved breath and leapt forward to throw her arms around his waist and nearly took him down in the process.

"Hey! Okay. Careful there! Take it easy, little one. How about you sit down and tell me what's going on. And please, keep your voice down. You never know who's gonna be sneaking around. I'm sorry I scared you, but it pays to be careful. No one knows we're here, my wife and I. We've been safe for—well, I don't know how long. Feels like forever, living on whatever we can scrounge. But we decided right from the time the troubles commenced, that we *wouldn't* be taken by those gun-toting yahoos! For the record, I don't have any bullets for this gun. It just looks loaded. Now, young lady, tell me your name and what the heck you're doing here all on your own."

Angela introduced herself and explained her predicament as well and as quickly as she could. She kept waiting for the man to roll his eyes and kick her out of the house, or at least tell her she was nuts. But he listened quietly, even fetching the dish towel for her as tears stopped and started, coursing down in rivulets when she explained how her father had been lost and how much she needed to find him.

"Thank you for telling me your story, Angela. I do hope you'll find your dad. You've taken on quite a challenge for a young'un. Tough to do. Maybe impossible." He hesitated, shaking his head. "Sorry, you don't need to hear that sort of thing right now. Let me go get my wife. She's a whiz at first aid." He got up and walked back down the hall.

"Wait! I don't know your name!"

With a smile, he stepped back and stuck out his hand. "It's Walter, Angela. You just call me Walter. The wife is Emily. Now you hang on right here. I'll be back in two shakes."

Walter. Emily. They could be Dopey and Grumpy for all she cared. They were alive ... real people ... and she wasn't alone any more. Maybe they'd let her stay the night. She'd share her peanut butter with them. Maybe they liked beets! Maybe they could tell her.

The sound of shuffling feet brought Angela out of her reverie.

"Well, my word. Walter, this is just a young girl, for heaven's sake. Dear, dear child, how did you get here?" Not waiting for an answer, Emily scuffed off to the sink, gray curls bouncing, and reaching underneath, brought up an old fashioned dish pan, a bar of soap and a large bottle of Clorox. "You sit right down there and we'll get you all fixed up."

Seeing Angela's horrified look as she filled the basin, Emily chuckled, "It's OK, child, this is really just water in here. Those military hyenas would grab a bottle of water quicker'n'a lick, but they aren't much interested in bleach."

As Emily got down to her nursing, Walter shut and locked the window, then unlocked the back door and went outside. He put Angela's things back into her pack and returned the hose box to the neighboring yard, making sure to fluff the shrubs and scuff out all signs of tracks. He took the time to do it right, but noted that the sun was sinking toward the horizon. And went back inside to prod Emily along. They needed to get their new charge tended and settled in quickly before they lost the light.

The sun was Angela's alarm clock once again. Sitting up in a small bedroom—in an actual bed no less!—Angela stretched, rubbed her eyes and wondered if she'd overslept. *But in this reality, the actual time doesn't really mean much.* Sun and dark. Warmth and cold. Thirst and hunger.

These were the driving forces. And since hunger was currently making her belly rumble, she shoved her feet into her sneakers, grabbed her jacket and headed downstairs. And if, on her way, she poked around just a bit, trying to find where Walter and Emily had gotten themselves off to, she thought it could be excused as part of "getting her bearings."

Like all the other houses she'd seen—well, as much as one could see by snooping through the occasional window—this one appeared abandoned and dirty. All the bedroom doors were left open. All of them were nearly empty except for the one she'd used. She still couldn't figure out where her benefactors were, and only refrained from snooping in the closets because that was just rude. Walter's cheery greeting, which came as she was standing in the kitchen debating whether to open her last can of corn, nearly scared her to death.

"Did you sleep all right, young lady?"

"Oh! Jeez! Wow! You startled me. Yes, I slept just great, Walter. Thank you so much for the blanket and pillow. They were so cozy and soft. I hope I didn't wake you."

"No, Angela. We're running on the same time clock as you. Sun up to sun down. Can I get you something to eat?"

"Oh yes! Please! I mean, if you have anything. I didn't see anything in the cupboards," she added, blushing a bit because she'd already looked.

"No, you wouldn't see anything there. We have to keep up the appearance of no one being here. Sure don't want to be caught by the so-called police force, so we're real careful. It's sure not the life we dreamt of so many years ago, but at least we're together, still free—sort of—and nobody's ordering us around and telling us we can't pray how we want to."

Angela thought about her mother, grandmother, grandfather and the rest of the family back in the Fifth. All the work Uncle Jon and Uncle Chris and Aunt Ellen had done, helping enlightened souls cross over. "But

I don't understand. If you feel that way, why are you still here? Why haven't you made the Shift?"

"That, my dear, is a long story and one we'll get into in a bit. But right now, what would you like to eat? Or maybe I should ask if you'd be willing to try what we can come up with."

"That's a silly question," Angela laughed. "I can and will eat pretty much anything you're willing to give me. And I have some peanut butter and other stuff to share."

Walter smiled and smacked his lips as though tasting something wonderful, and actually felt saliva forming in his mouth. "Peanut butter ... what a treat! You'd best hang onto that peanut butter and savor it, little lady. That's a rare indulgence these days. A rare indulgence, indeed. If you'll just wait right here in the kitchen, we'll bring you something."

Where on earth are they getting their stuff, Angela wondered. *They're very secretive. But I guess I would be, too, given the circumstances. I need to find out what they know and be on my way. Who knows how long I've got before the family comes looking for me, and I've just got to find my father first!*

Breakfast looked a lot like sticks and weeds with some berries thrown in for color, but it was fairly tasty, and it wasn't beets. When they heard a truck rumbling in the distance, they hit the floor as one and lay there, barely breathing, until the sound faded away.

"I've got to be going. I don't really want to 'cause you've been really kind, but I've got to keep going. I'm not sure where to exactly, but I need to keep looking for my dad. Thank you so much for your hospitality. My family will be so grateful when I get back and tell them ..." Angela trailed off. "And I will get back. Soon." She didn't feel nearly as strong as she was trying to sound. "So, I just need to get my backpack."

"Well now, you know you're welcome to stay just as long as you want. We'll do our best to take care of you. But if you have to go, we'll help you with that, too." Walter paused and exchanged a look with Emily. "But before you leave, little one, let me ask you a couple questions."

"Sure, Walter. What do you want to know?"

"You've told us the circumstances of your father's disappearance, and that your aunt and uncles finally located him somewheres 'round here and put him in good hands. Just what do you intend to do when you find him?"

"Take him home."

Emily leaned over and put her hand on Angela's. "What if he doesn't know you, hon? What if he doesn't want to go home with you?"

Walter and Emily were surprised to see the fierce determination in Angela's young eyes. With maturity beyond her years, she replied, "I'm ready for that. He probably *won't* know me. How could he? But I truly believe that there are bonds between my father and me that will overcome every obstacle. He'll come to know me ... eventually. And he'll remember my mother, and he'll want to be with us. I just know he will. He just *has* to!" She took a deep breath. "And I'll stay here until he does. I'm not going home without him."

Walter and Emily exchanged looks which spoke volumes about their respect for Angela's resolve and her love for the father she'd never met. Without a word, Walter took Angela's hand, patted it gently and led her back through the house. Emily quickly removed all evidence of the meal and followed them.

The corner of the deck overlooking Crystal Mountain was Julie's special place. Here, she felt physical and spiritual serenity, and a great inner peace which facilitated the deep meditations she found essential to her life. She wanted desperately to connect with her granddaughter; to know Angela was all right. But she just couldn't get through.

The dogs snuggled up against her, sensing her struggle, offering their special comfort. If she could only see Angela with clarity for one instant, but her only impression was a short statement in muddy colors through dirty glass: "Call off the guys." Julie knew her abilities well enough to know that the message was real, and it was all she was going to get for now. *Call off the guys. Give her time. Lord! Jeannie's not going to like that one little bit.*

Walter opened a door in what had likely been a small office. Inside, it appeared to be a simple closet, empty except for a few musty clothes and some old hangers along a center pole. Willing her eyes to adjust quickly, Angela watched as he ducked beneath the clothes and carefully propped up a section of flooring. Beneath it, she could see the outline and hinges of a trap door. Walter lifted the trap and turned, stepping onto the ladder. He started down, beckoning her to follow. She stepped closer. The space below was dark and smelled slightly of mold.

"It's OK, honey. Just watch your step and go slow." Emily arrived behind her, waiting to go last so she could reset the panels.

Angela climbed down and paused at the bottom, still holding the ladder, watching as Emily started down, closed the trap door and listened to be sure the flooring had dropped back into place over it. *Feels like a major case of claustrophobia*, she thought, but managed to get it under control when Emily stepped off the ladder beside her, put an arm around her shoulders and squeezed. A candle, carefully set in a small plate of water, threw a soft light on what was obviously their living space.

"I want you to meet a friend of ours, Angela. He might be able to help you." Walter led her into another small room.

Angela's senses were under attack. An unpleasant smell stung her nose. She was disoriented in the darkness and stood, squinting, trying to see more; straining to hear. Then, as her pupils adjusted, she realized that there was a man sitting in a corner on the floor, his head bowed. His hair was long and dark and stringy. *Disabled?* she wondered, glancing at Walter. Clearing her throat, she whispered, "Hello. I'm Angela. What's your name?" There was no response. No movement. Louder, she repeated, "Hello. I'm Angela. What's your name?"

The man twitched as though annoyed at the intrusion.

Walter squeezed her hand, encouraging her to go on. "Talk to him, honey. Go ahead. Sit there beside him. He can help you."

It took some effort, but she steeled herself to sit beside the man on the corner of his old comforter. She reached out, took his hand and asked a third time, "Who are you? I'm Angela."

As he turned his head and looked into her eyes, she completely lost her breath. Shock didn't begin to cover what she felt, and she was afraid she might pass out. *No,* she thought, *I can't pass out now!* Surprise, joy, love—all these and more flooded through her. "Oh my God! You're my father!" she whispered hoarsely.

Jerry just stared. No sign of recognition showed on his face. Discomfort, puzzlement, even embarrassment. But it was clear that he had no idea who this person was, or why she was making such a bizarre claim.

With love, intuition and restraint, Angela delighted in the knowledge that while imperfect, her dream was coming true. It grew more possible by the minute. Her father was found. This man who had loved her mother, who her mother loved still. He had no idea what had been left behind during the torments of the EarthShift. He simply couldn't access those memories. But he would. She would make sure of it. She would succeed. Her goal was sitting right here by her side.

Chapter Fifteen

Eight years of living as a lost soul had taken a toll on Jerry. He had no real memory of his life prior to the last eight years, only a dark void with an occasional flicker which he worked hard to ignore. All he remembered was his struggle to survive—against earthquakes, floods, drought—everything nature could find to throw at him. And as hard as that was, the man-made terrors were even worse, more reprehensible.

In the days after the world went mad, terrorism in all forms ran rampant, exploding with wanton disregard for kindness, morality, for life—for anything but chaos, and the blood-lust required to maintain the harsh rule of the Gestapo-like military. The military which Jerry had run from, then joined with, then run from again when he'd witnessed things, been ordered to do things so abhorrent that his very soul bore the scars.

He remembered making his way to that weird meeting in the hills, hoping he might find answers. But it was too freaky. Strange. But he'd tried so hard to get his mind around it. Then the soldiers had come and things had gone crazy. He had gone crazy, and he'd gotten knocked out. He had a vague memory of being rescued ... saved ... tended. Those people had told him strange things about knowing him and wanting him to go back with them. But back where? He had no idea. And they'd scared him almost as much as the soldiers. And he'd blacked out again. Then, all he remembered was waking up in a car, being told to stay down, stay out of sight, and a bumpy road that went on and on.

That was two years ago, and his life since then had been wrapped up in this little hellhole. He hated it. Living in the dark, living in fear—of just about everything. But it was okay. He helped Walter and Emily find food at night, and they were kind to him. They talked, once in awhile, about that day in the hills. What they remembered of the speeches, and something about getting to a different world if you could just change your thoughts.

He thought Walter and Emily already seemed to think in that new way. They sure acted it—love, trust, just plain goodness—but when he asked them why they didn't go to that other place, they said they couldn't leave quite yet. And that's all they'd say. Sometimes, when his spirits were at low ebb, Jerry wondered if it wouldn't be easier just to kill himself. Escape this miserable excuse for a life once and for all. But he'd grown fond of Walter and Emily and he knew they needed him. So he'd stay. And they'd survive.

But now, there was a new piece to the puzzle. This girl. Such a pretty little thing with such intense eyes. Eyes so intense they made him want to turn away. She'd called him her father. *Where the devil did that come from? I've never been married. I don't have a kid. And I sure as hell wouldn't want to raise one in this godforsaken place. Still, she's so pretty and she seems like a sweetheart. Better to keep her here with us than for her to be out someplace on her own. Bad, bad things happen to kids on their own these days. I can teach her how to stay safe. Maybe she knows how to play cribbage, and if not, I'll bet she could learn.*

As Angela studied Jerry, her emotions ran the gamut. Excitement that she'd found him, fear that she might never be able to access the part of his mind which held his memories of her mom. And yes, memories of herself. She couldn't help but feel sad she'd lost so many years with him, and since the Third had a way of turning up the negative volume, she couldn't deny her own tiny bit of residual anger that he'd left them in the first place.

She'd need to process *all* her feelings for her father. Bottom line: He'd deserted them just when they'd needed him most. That was one bitter little pill. Angela also knew that the anger and sadness she felt could, if she wasn't careful, lead to feelings of shame, even inadequacy on her part. She heard that little voice in her head whisper, *if I hadn't been so messed up, so imperfect*—and she squashed it like the nasty bug it was. Sure she'd had problems. And she'd healed them. Yes, her dad had had issues. And she was here to help him get past them. She would heal her heart, and in so doing, heal her dad as well.

Recommitting herself to the challenge, she began to study Jerry's face like a science project. His black, curly hair and beard emphasized the pale, sun-starved skin. His clothes, worn and not terribly fresh, hung loosely on his tall, nearly skeletal frame. The brown eyes, sparkling and warm in the photo she'd studied at home, were now veiled and distant. Their sparkle, gone. *The eyes are the windows to the soul,* she thought, vowing to reach that soul if it was the last thing she did.

Quietly watching as father and daughter discovered the first threads of their bond, Walter and Emily backed slowly out of the room. They embraced in the dim candlelight, and stood close together, wiping the tears from each other's cheeks.

Days passed as Angela learned and quickly became proficient at cribbage. She and Jerry played literally hundreds of games. As they played, she was able to coax out the broad strokes and some of the smaller details of how he'd spent the last several years. And when she felt he was open to them, she shared a few stories of her childhood, carefully avoiding too much talk about her mother. For now, she also stayed away from the actual event of the Shift, and especially her own birth. She sensed she had to move slowly, gain his trust—and, she hoped, his affection—before advancing to more difficult subjects which could scare him or close him off entirely.

From the start, Angela gravitated toward Emily for comfort; a cozy grandmother figure. Walter quickly became a surrogate grandpa. Seeing her ease with them made it simpler for Jerry to model himself into a role as her mentor and guide; something a bit more than big brother, but for now, a bit less than her father.

He and Angela explored the surrounding area, always at night, always on guard for sounds or movement, anything which could expose them and betray their friends and the hideout. Angela had never appreciated the sun and its warmth as she did now when the best she could hope for was to steal a few golden minutes here and there, continually on guard. She always insisted that Jerry had to join her, not because she was fearful, but because his pallor worried her. Sure enough, a faint hint of color soon returned to his cheeks.

They grew closer. With some miraculously sharp scissors found in a neighboring house, she made short work of his long hair and all but a soft fuzzy fringe of beard. Walter and Emily could barely contain their amusement when Jerry, insisting that turnabout was fair play, held out his hand for the shears. There was trepidation on both sides as he carefully trimmed Angela's golden curls. There was no denying the affection and pride when he held up a small mirror for her to check his work.

He began calling her "Angie." But as she still didn't feel he was ready to face fatherhood head on, she continued to call him "Jerry."

During her alone times, Angela was painfully aware of how much she missed her family, and the knowledge of what her absence would be doing to them weighed heavily. Though her determination never faltered, she began to consider the possibility of attempting to contact someone ... else.

Someone outside the family. Someone who could pass on a message. She had no idea if such a thing could be done, but the feeling of rightness that the idea gave her convinced her that it was worth a try. She adopted a new mantra: "I can, I will, I am. I am doing this, I have done it." *Yes, make it a done deal in your heart and the universe will find a way to manifest it. How many times have I heard Grandma Julie give that lecture?* Repeating it again and again, she wondered how long it would be before she would *feel* it and know something had happened.

Chapter Sixteen

Back home at Wind Dancer Ranch, Julie was severely frustrated. Her attempts to contact or at least get a read on her granddaughter continued to hit the proverbial brick wall. Jeannie was more frustrated still, and the two women commiserated frequently. Gabriel's message had been loud and clear—simply put, "Don't try to find her. She must follow her own path." But Julie didn't believe for an instant that Gabriel had any idea how difficult it was to keep the family, and sexist as it might sound, the men especially, from just mounting up and translocating back to the Third, figurative guns blazing.

Chris and Ellen were still making forays back to teach and help people to transition, but for now, they were being sent to locations far away from LA. Clearly, the word was out that any and all interference with their missing niece was *verboten*.

So when Julie called a family gathering, and that now included Sara and Scott, there wasn't much doubt in anyone's mind that Angela would be the main concern and primary topic of discussion. Once they were all gathered, they found out differently.

"We've been doing a lot of thinking about this, so don't think that it's just a spur-of-the-moment thing," Julie began, "but we think that the wedding plans have been put off long enough."

"Here's the deal," Dave picked up the ball after mouths had dropped open, eyes had popped, and more than one gasp was heard. "We all know how much Jon and Sara love each other—something about those sparks popping off 'em every time they get within ten feet of each other—and how much they want to begin their life as a family. So we thought it made a lot of sense to make the most of the happy diversion of wedding plans to keep everyone's minds off what we can't do anything about anyway. Not only are we honoring Jon and Sara, and of course Scott, we're also honoring Angela's choice. This is what we feel she'd want. And yes, it won't be the same without her, but ..." he paused. "What does everyone think?"

They all started talking at once and the room's energy ramped up several notches. No persuasion was necessary, because everyone was so grateful to have something positive to work on and think about. Julie laughed and gave Dave a knowing look as she reclaimed the floor.

"Okay, okay! Let's get some input from the future bride and groom here. I know they want to do this in the San Francisco area, but that's about all the specifics I know. How about filling us in so we can get this show on the road?"

And with that, the planning began again.

After a couple short but very busy weeks, the happy couple was in shock at the family's hard work. "Oh Jon, I can't believe our big day is tomorrow. I've waited for this for so long. Lifetimes." They were wrapped in each other's arms as silver moonlight shimmered its way toward them across San Francisco Bay. As Sara smiled, as her eyes glistened in the moonlight, Jon cupped her face in his hands and kissed her with aching tenderness.

"I've never seen anyone so beautiful in my life. I love you, Sara, with everything I am and everything I've got. Tomorrow's just the beginning." As the reality struck, a grin split his face. "Hey! I'm going to officially be a dad! I'm gonna have a son. We're gonna be a family!" He grew serious, "And I'm going to be there for both of you for the rest of our lives."

"And I'm going to be there for you, darling. We're so incredibly blessed to have found each other. And Scott and I are so lucky to have stumbled into your big, loving family! And we all have Ekor to thank for it."

"Big time. Sara. Ever since I met him, he's helped me, taught me, saved my life ... and now, he's given me my life." Jon turned his head and leaned down to sniff her neck, then ran his lips along the soft length of it. As Sara shivered, he looked out on the water. "He said he'd be here for the ceremony. Sure hope he doesn't get called away on something else."

"I have a feeling Ekor will move heaven and earth to be here for you ... and me. But especially for Scott," Sara said, smiling. "Everything's going to be so beautiful. Wait till you see the flowers Erica's done. And the boys have written a song they're going to sing for us. Don't worry. I got a preview, and there's not one mention of underwear or a single bad pun. Your family has done everything possible to make our wedding perfect." She paused. "I just wish Angela ... "

"Oh baby. Me too. We've got to keep on trusting that she's all right. If she just wasn't so darn young to be out there on her own. I dream about her all the time, but I just can't get through to her. Any more than anyone else is able to." Straightening up and walking off a few steps to release some of his tension, he continued, "I know what it's like in the Third, damn it. I sure hope she's not right in LA proper."

Jon stared up at the night sky, feeling the exasperation and sadness he always did when he thought of Angela, on her own, back in the Third. But being the bright young man he was, he shook off the negative thoughts, strode back to Sara, did a quick pivot in front of her presenting his back and gestured for her to climb aboard.

"Lady Sara, your steed awaits! Mount up, gorgeous, it's time to tuck our young prince into bed so he won't fall asleep walking you down the aisle tomorrow!"

With the grace of a gymnast, Sara leapt lightly onto Jon's back, and he galloped back up the path making silly horsy noises to make her laugh.

Miles out to sea, Ekor, who had been eavesdropping only a little, smiled his dolphin smile, well pleased with the results of his match-making.

The family was up bright and early greeting a warm, sunny, picture-perfect day. Puffy clouds drifted across a brilliant blue sky as white gulls soared and swooped gracefully over blue water. In the kitchen, Julie was knee-deep in very hungry people, especially the growing teenagers. Since their last Gabriel-induced growth spurt, it seemed they'd acquired the ability to simply inhale their food—no mastication necessary. But once fed, they quickly excused themselves to go practice their song for the wedding.

On the lawn, Jeannie, Megan and Ellen set up tables and decorated them for the buffet lunch while Scott ran from place to place, group to group, absolutely beside himself with excitement. All his mom's students were coming and they'd get to see him be the *main man*—Jon's term—and give his mom away. He thought back to when she'd first asked him to do that; how he'd told her "No!" that he didn't want to give her away, that she was his mom and he didn't *ever* want to give her away. And he'd even cried a little until she'd explained that it wasn't *really* giving her away. It was more like *he* was telling Jon that it was okay for Jon to come and be part of their family. And, she told him, he'd get all the cousins, and aunts and uncles and even Grammy Julie and Grandpa Dave. He'd decided a while ago that that was a really good deal. And when Ekor showed up, maybe he'd give rides again. How awesome would that be?

Sara was enjoying Erica's company as she indulged in the female rituals of wedding preparation. As Erica chattered about the challenges of growing up as a girl cousin outnumbered by her boy cousins, Sara slipped her dress over her head.

She'd felt it was hers the minute she'd seen it. So simple, a long sleeveless dress in two layers of pearly silk, the sheer overskirt worked with the tiniest hint of pattern. It flowed in an unbroken line from the curve of her breasts to the floor, taking its shape from the exceptional body it covered.

Her veil—headdress really—a simple gather of the same sheer silk as her dress, had been carefully hand-sewn to a wreath of white flowers gathered by her students in the meadow behind the school. She would carry a bouquet of those same flowers, accented with blue and yellow blooms which the children hadn't been able to resist picking. Erica had used every ounce of her artistic talent to arrange them all and tie them with pretty ribbons that would take on a life of their own in the breeze. Sara needed little in the way of makeup; a tiny smudge of color at the edge of her lids and the lightest of lip glosses. Her glow came from love and anticipation. It wouldn't be long now.

The haunting sound of Steve's flute drifted through the window with the gentle breeze off the ocean. A knock on the door brought Sara out of her reverie as Julie stepped inside, then stopped dead in her tracks. "Oh, Sara! You look like an angel! Absolutely ethereal. I'm so happy you're going to be part of our family. I love you, honey. We all love you."

"I love you, too, all of you. Oh Julie, I'm going to cry."

Quickly taking both Sara's hands in hers, Julie looked her straight in the eye and, in her no-nonsense way, said, "No, you're not! You don't have time for it! We can all have a good cry *after* the wedding." She leaned back, surveying from top to toe. "My baby is one lucky guy! Now, we're ready for you. Come on, Erica. Time to join the others."

Jon was in place, looking incredibly handsome in white slacks and a soft, white shirt, open at the neck which set off his healthy tan. His longish, sun-streaked hair, paired with bright blue eyes, would make any girl with eyes weak in the knees. Julie knew she was a bit prejudiced but didn't care in the least. Her baby was a catch!

Mr. Martin, a sweet older gentleman—a judge in another life who volunteered at the orphanage—had been thrilled when they'd asked him to officiate. He waited, smiling at everyone, dapper in the conservative suit which, for him, was a requirement of his role.

Jon thought that over the weeks he'd known and loved her, he must have built up some small degree of immunity, where Sara was concerned. It wasn't reasonable to think that the woman, as striking as she was, could keep on stealing his breath and fogging his mind. The instant she stepped out on the porch, he knew he'd never be immune. And more, that he'd thank his lucky stars for it! He was dazzled. And she was breathtaking.

Scott, posted on the top step, looked up at his radiant mom and reached for her hand. Everyone there simultaneously smiled and misted when they heard his breathy, "WOW!" He led her slowly across the beach to where Jon waited, and as they'd practiced, Scott took Jon's hand and put it together with Sara's. It was his job, and he was taking it very, very seriously ... until the moment his eyes went wide and he forgot his instructions and everything else, shouting, "Look!"

Ekor broke the surface launching into a mile high flip followed with a series of rolls and somersaults, and ending with a tail walk. Everyone applauded as he glided toward shore, smiling his huge smile, squeaking and whistling approvingly. The wedding party was now complete, or as complete as it could be. The judge stepped forward to ask a blessing.

The service was as untraditional as it was meaningful. The boys' song was original, heartfelt, and maybe just a tad off key in places; but the love they projected more than made up for a handful of sour notes. Julie read poems from Anne Porter, Elizabeth Barrett Browning, and Khalil Gibran. Everyone watched as Jon made his vows to Sara, then turned and dropped to his knees to make vows to Scott. Incredibly moved, Sara dropped down so that they were all on the same level. Then, holding hands with "both my guys" promised her love, friendship, respect and support, and noted that "This is just the beginning."

Dave, his voice smooth and mellow, sang "In My Life" looking straight at Julie. A gift for the happy new family ... and his wife. When Mr. Martin finally introduced "Mr. and Mrs. Jon Cramer," Scott let out a yelp and jumped squarely into Jon's arms.

"Now I can call you Dad, right?"

"You better believe it! I'm gonna love being your dad." There wasn't a dry eye on the beach. Then there were congratulations, hugs and huge smiles all 'round, followed by a hefty spray from a dolphin's tail.

"Ahem," Ekor began. "If I might have your attention for just a moment. I have a message for all of you. Angela has asked me to tell you that she is well, that she misses you, and she'll come home when it's time."

Jeannie started to sag onto the sand until Dave caught her in an iron grip, and everyone asked the same questions.

"What else did she say?"

"When will it be time?"

"Where is she?"

"Has she found her father?"

Ekor's big head moved slowly from side to side. "I'm sorry, but that's all I know. It was difficult for her to send any message—but that much was clear. She doesn't want you to worry, she's all right at the moment, and as she misses you, I'd say that her love is implied."

Jon waded into the water to give Ekor a hug. "Thank you. Thank you so much. You've just made this day more special than we could have dreamed. How about some special wedding cake to celebrate? We have either fish or crab?"

"Lovely. And thoughtful. I'll take both. I imagine I'll need to fuel up if I'm to take all these children on rides, eh?"

"You know it, man. You've got your work cut out for you with this crew, and Scott's just itching to be your first passenger."

It had been the best possible day, and as the sun began to set, firing the clouds into a rainbow of colors, the family said their goodbyes and took a very tired Scott back with them to Wind Dancer for a short vacation with lots of Grandma Julie's cookies.

Alone in their cottage on the shore, Jon and Sara found they had no need for more wine as they relaxed on cool cotton sheets, bathed in moonbeams and candlelight, exploring the wonders of each other's bodies. Textures, scents, skin cooled by the breeze, the warm silk of Sara's hair. Contented sighs and lingering kisses became soft moans and luxurious stretches. The night birds called to each other as the two lovers became one.

Chapter Seventeen

Life was far from easy. In fact, parts of it were downright unpleasant in the dim little cellar that was their home and sanctuary. There were only so many games to play, so many books to read, stories to share—not to mention the sparse and tasteless diet they subsisted on. Privacy? Well that was nearly non-existent. But still, the bonds of friendship grew, and Angela's determination to gain Jerry's trust never faltered.

It was hard for Angela to accept that her exposure to the Third had stripped away the lion's share of her Fifth Dimensional gifts. She especially missed her ability to intuit and share other people's thoughts, because as a result, she sometimes found herself second-guessing what Jerry's answers meant. They talked survival, shared trivia, told jokes. They talked philosophy—up to a point. But she still didn't dare bring up their personal connection—not yet.

Time and time again, she nudged him into talking about the LA event and his accident. How empty his life had felt, like big pieces were missing, and the way he'd felt drawn there. He admitted he'd felt really hopeful for a while. He'd been surprised by that. Little things puzzled him—especially the three strangers who'd called him by name. Angela knew that her intro to that topic would need to circumnavigate any mention of trucks and soldiers if she wanted Jerry to be open to it, because whenever he talked about them, he invariably grew agitated and withdrawn.

He admitted to Angela that he'd been afraid of being captured and of what he knew they'd do to him afterward, and that turning away from the ideals which were so hopeful, well, it made him feel like not much of a man. She seemed to understand his fears. To forgive them. Sometimes, she seemed so old for one so young.

"So Angie, what's on our schedule for today?" He watched her busily writing in her little notebook—her "personal diary"—she called it. "I don't know about you, but I could sure use a few minutes of sunshine."

She closed her pad and tucked it into her backpack. "If Walter will let us, maybe we could just sit in the backyard and soak up some vitamin D. We haven't seen any trucks out there for a while. Maybe they've given up on what's left of this poor town. We certainly haven't left them any signs that would make them think anyone's still here. How about it, Jerry?"

"Sure. I'm definitely up for that. And you're right about it being really quiet lately. I'm still not taking any chances, especially with you, kiddo. You're tough, but I don't want you fighting off any Mongol hordes today! I might be good for a Samurai or two, but those Mongols just wear me out!"

"Jerry! You made a joke! Excellent! Let's get going. I've got the world's worse case of 'cabin fever.' When Mom and I had it, we'd go for long walks in the woods at home. But right now, a little sun in the back yard sounds absolutely perfect!"

Jerry fought to deny the appeal—and increasing clarity—of the images that came to mind when Angie talked about her mom and things they'd do. *Pipe dreams. Fantasies. Nothing to do with me.* Dismissing it, he grinned broadly as his petite chum turned up her charm and batted those big blue eyes at Walter, who obviously didn't stand a chance.

Cautions, precautions, warnings, rules, regulations and edicts. They wondered if Walter was going to demand a blood-oath before he allowed them outside. Leaning against the foundation, her curls pulled back in a ponytail to allow more rays to be absorbed, Angela and Jerry spoke in low voices "just in case." As usual, the subject of food—or lack of it—came up.

"I bet we could find a new house to break into. Close by. One with full cupboards ... peanut butter, honey, raisins. Even salt would help. We'd be really careful, Jerry. Just think of how excited Walter would be!"

"Sorry, kid. We promised Walter. Think of how upset Walter would be if we got caught! We just can't take the chance."

Whether it was the Third Dimension's influence or the foolishness of youth, a glint fired in Angela's eyes. "Well, I'm a lot smaller than you and I can move really fast. I'm going to scout around and see what I can find!" And she was off and running.

He tried to grab her, but she'd caught him unawares—and she was just too fast. "Damn it, Angela, come back here!"

She tossed him a little smile. A "catch me if you can" look over her shoulder, and disappeared through a gate.

"Great," he mumbled and took off running after her. *If anything happens to her, I'll never forgive myself.* He caught a glimpse of her, two houses down, crouched by the front steps and looking like a midget spy; an eight-year-old playing cops and robbers, and she managed to elude him every time he got close. Jerry was getting more and more frantic, swearing under his breath, because she knew all too well that he couldn't yell or make a scene for fear someone—the wrong someone—would hear.

Two more houses and she struck pay dirt when a door creaked open enough for her to slip inside. She found a small pantry off the kitchen, and in a small corner cupboard, pushed far in out of sight, was a glass jar of fruit, a can of something called Spam, and yes, even a small jar of peanut butter. The crunchy kind. Praying for courage and hoping to goodness that she wasn't reaching into a mouse nest, she leaned in further and hauled out a true prize, a 4-pack of toilet paper. Emily would be ecstatic.

She scooped her stash into an old paper bag and tiptoed back through the living room. She grabbed three old paperback books—it didn't matter what they were—from a broken bookshelf, then headed for the door.

Over the years, the floorboards by the front door had been soaked by rain and baked by the sun, resulting in some very severe warping. Angela hadn't noticed under layers of dirt and dust, but when it caught her toe, she went down hard, spilling her treasures in all directions.

No one heard. No one heard. Everything's OK. Frantically, she scooped books and cans and toilet paper back into her bag.

"What the hell do you think you're doing?" The unfamiliar voice was cold, no-nonsense and menacing to the max.

Angela's heart simply stopped. Looking up slowly, her eyes passed over black military boots, camouflage pants, and before she got to the shirt, she found herself, for the second time in her life, staring into the business end of a gun. Three military types on full alert stood just outside the front door, and the one with the voice, an enormous man—six-four minimum, heavyset, unshaven, unsmiling, his eyes hidden by mirrored sunglasses—was now moving toward her.

Angela's mind was in overdrive. *Who are these guys? How did they find me? Where's Jerry?* Fear and panic hit her stomach like sour milk. *How could I have been so stupid! What if they find Emily and Walter? What are they going to do with me? I hope my dad doesn't try to save me! He could get killed!*

"Come on, kid, let's hear it. We ain't got all day. Ain't nobody around this town. Ain't nobody supposed to be. So what the hell are you doin' here? Answer me, you little bitch!"

A furious flush rose up under Angela's skin as pure, sheer outrage warred with fear. If these animals thought they could treat her this way, if they thought she was going to tell them *anything*, if they thought they were going to ruin her plan and keep her from taking her dad home ...

well they damn well had another think coming. She just had to remember who she was, and hope she could stay strong enough.

Jerry had seen it all. The front door, slightly ajar, the three military creeps striding up the street had him scurrying for cover. He flattened himself against a wall, pleading, "Please God, let them walk on by. Don't let them find her ... please. Please!" But the open door had caught the soldiers' attention too, and as Jerry watched helplessly, they crept up onto the porch. Then, there was a crash and he saw them smash the door back, weapons raised, and for one absolutely mind-numbing second, he'd been sure they were going to shoot first and ask questions later. He'd nearly jumped up to take them on, but logic prevailed. Three big men with rifles would make short work of him, and he wouldn't be much help to Angie lying in a pool of blood. Better to wait for the right moment. For an opening.

He was still looking around the corner when he heard glass breaking. That was followed by yelling and swearing, and suddenly, there were cans and books flying in all directions accompanied by Angela's high-pitched screams and an occasional threat or curse from the men. As scared as he was, the sight of a line-backer-sized military hard-ass hopping around on one foot, holding his knee and yelling "You little bitch!" almost made him laugh. But when he heard "Goddamn she-cat!" followed by a slap, and then nothing from Angela, fear rose in his throat, as bitter as bile.

Seconds later, they brought her out, hands tied behind her back and a gag in her mouth. They went back the way they'd come; the two with Angela dragging between them, her feet kicking, seldom touching the pavement while the third man walked behind, gun at the ready, still cursing Angela furiously. When he declared to the others, "We ought to just torch this whole damn town!" Jerry's heart sank to his toes.

It was a dusty, bumpy, uncomfortable ride. Angela passed the time trying to memorize each right and left turn, and the speed and time in between, because she'd need to know the route when she escaped. As scared as she was—about a 12 on a scale of 10 at the moment—she told herself that she *would* escape. At least they hadn't gotten her dad. She prayed he was safe. And Walter and Emily. Then she remembered talk of burning the town, and panic knotted her gut. They were in very real danger, and she was responsible. Plus, they'd be so worried about her. She vowed that no matter what these jerks did, she'd *never* give them any information.

The truck bounced up the narrow dirt road and finally stopped beside a dozen or so more, parked in a small clearing. A line of tents had been pitched against a windbreak of trees, and more soldiers moved around the compound. Angela blocked out all thoughts of her mom and home and sniffed back her tears as she was yanked from the truck.

Chapter Eighteen

Scott's visit had been a true joy. Getting to know their newest grandchild put Julie and Dave in the best of moods, and Scott explored and learned and peppered them with questions from sun up to sun down. But now, he was back home in San Francisco with his mom and new dad; loving school, loving his playmates, and especially loving the visits from Ekor.

Without Scott to distract them, there was simply too much time to miss Angela. Her light-hearted laughter and silliness had been such an intimate part of life at Wind Dancer. Now, they walked a tightrope trying to balance their own emotions while making sure Jeannie had enough support to stay strong, too.

Jeannie shuffled out of her room and headed toward the coffee pot, half awake, definitely distracted. Intercepting, Dave folded her into a hug and kissed her forehead, then held her at arm's length.

"Hey, what's up, pretty girl? You look like someone pulled the plug and your stuffing fell out."

"I don't know, Dad. My heart's been flipping and flopping all morning. Feels like something crawled inside me just to interfere with the circuitry. I guess that sounds pretty overblown and ridiculous."

"More like worrisome. Should we call someone? Check in with the experts; run a few tests just to make sure you're OK? I'll call Julie and—"

Jeannie interrupted, "No Dad, it's nothing like that. Nothing physical. I'm just ... off."

"Well, if something's off, let's sit down and talk about it."

They filled their cups and carried them to the table where they could look out at Crystal Mountain towering above the meadow. It didn't take long for Dave to figure out that what was off was Angela. Undoubtedly, Jeannie was missing her. Dave knew, because Jeannie's pain was his pain. For the last eight years, Jeannie had experienced the deepest pain of her life, because Jerry wasn't with her to share her greatest joy—Angela. With Angela gone, Jeannie's balance leaned tenuously toward a darkness that was growing, night by night, dream by dream. Hoping that by sharing, some of the darkness and weight would be lightened, Jeannie, her eyes drenched and overflowing, shared the previous night's horrors with her dad.

"Honey, we have to remember that her angels are with her. They won't interfere with her learning whatever it is that she needs to learn, but they'll be there to support her and make sure she's okay." He wasn't able, one hundred percent, to convince himself that was true, but he'd still do his level best to convince his daughter.

"It's okay, Dad." Jeannie smiled wanly, patting Dave's hand. "We'll both do our best to believe that and—"

"Well of course we'll believe it!" Dave interrupted, but Jeannie cut him off with a knowing look.

"Forget it, Dad. I can read your thoughts." They both sighed. "I just wish I could read Angela's."

Jon was having substantial success with his kids; those Third Dimension children who had stayed behind to be their parents' teachers, helping them break through barriers of old fears and belief systems, expediting their transitions to the Fifth. His work in the Third, nearly all one-on-one operations, was both fulfillment and challenge. At times, it felt like the numbers would always be overwhelming, but he was assured by Ekor and other guides that he wasn't working alone. People in other countries, even from other planets and dimensions, were volunteering in similar ways.

As a rule, Jon connected only briefly with families after their transitions, to touch base and assure that all was well. But anyone who'd ever heard Jon talk about his kids knew he felt something very special about the one he called his little angel. Whenever he needed a lift, checking in on little Colleen and her family, now happily acclimating in the Fifth, was a surefire way to get it.

His life with Sara and Scott was his own personal miracle. They'd come together in the way of old souls, a shared knowledge which filled the heart and nourished the entire being—mental, physical and spiritual. They fit together like peas in a pod.

Sara loved her work, loved her orphans, and they loved her right back. Scott was so happy with his new family, and so proud of his mom, that he never showed any jealousy about the other kids. Instead, he seemed to accept them as part of a really big blended family.

Yet as blessed and happy as they were, as full and rewarding as their lives were, they all carried with them a nasty, nagging little itch lurking in the backs of their minds. Worry and concern which never quite disappeared, and which was continually exacerbated by frustration. And there it would remain until Angela returned to them.

Chris and Ellen worked in the Third Dimension as often as they were allowed, creating undercover operations with large groups formed to spread the word. On their early expeditions, they'd learned many lessons the hard way. Now, they were effective, seasoned practitioners who found great satisfaction in the job they did.

But this day, Ellen felt neither effective nor seasoned. She sighed as she watched her husband pace from room to room in their small apartment like a caged animal. It was driving her nuts.

"Okay, Chris, what's wrong? What is it, honey? What's crawled under your skin? Time to spill it or take it for a walk 'cause watching you is giving me indigestion."

"Yeah, well, I wish I could help you out, but I don't know what the heck is going on. Something's wrong. And no, I don't know what. I've checked in and the family seems to be all right. Our plans are all set for our next trip through the dimensions. But something's ... off. I tried to reach Mary last night to ask her if she had any input, but that didn't work either."

"Maybe we need to take a little vacation, Chris. We could go up into the mountains for a few days. Or to the shore. Or we could visit your folks, see the nephews and nieces. Well, the boys at least, and Erica." Immediately, Ellen's hopeful, happy mood went south.

"Dammit! Dammit! Dammit! Yeah, that's it. It's Angela. I worry about her all the time, El! It's like this *undercurrent* of fear that never goes away. My sister is hurting, and I can't find a way to make it better. It's driving me nuts!" He banged his fist on the table and sent the coffee cups jumping. "Damn it, Ellen, praying for her safety is fine, but after so long, it's just not very satisfying." He dropped into a chair, deflated. "Sorry. Flashback to the Third. Really, I'm sorry."

"It's okay, baby. I understand how you feel. What I don't understand is how a girl so young can be so darned determined! We just have to believe that she's following her path, and that her path will lead her home. Come on, get your jacket and let's go for a walk. You need a change of scenery before you wear holes in the carpet. And we both could use some fresh air."

Chapter Nineteen

When Jerry got back to the bungalow and had to tell Walter and Emily what had happened, he just didn't know how. He struggled to stop shaking and get the words out. He struggled to hold onto his anger, knowing if he didn't, that his fear and hopelessness might eat him alive.

"And now, I don't know what I should do. I don't know where they took her, or what they'll do to her. She's so young. Just a little girl. Those bastards could really hurt her!" Overcome, Jerry closed his eyes and crumpled, sliding down the wall until he came to rest with his knees drawn up and his face in his hands. "I love that kid. Didn't want to, but she just sort of ... marched right on in, you know? And now I've managed to lose her and put you guys in danger at the same time. It's my fault, damn it! Sun or not, careful or not, it's just too damn dangerous to be outside. Ever! It's my fault."

A tearful Emily dropped to her knees and wrapped her arms around him. She was crying for Angela; feeling that loss. Fearing what might befall the child. But more that that, she cried for the child's father, this tortured man who had finally admitted his love. And Angela wasn't around to hear it.

Walter was a whole different kettle of fish. "For God's sake, Jerry, pull yourself together! I had the final say on you two going outside. Should've known that Angie would push the envelope. That's what comes of being young and impulsive, in case you haven't noticed. Bottom line, this was not your fault. So here's the deal. What's done is done. But right now, we need a plan. Fast. And that doesn't mean running off willy-nilly either. I know you love her. We love her, too. And I know she loves you. So it's time you knew, my friend, just exactly who you're dealing with, 'cause right now, you don't."

"What the hell are you talking about, Walter? I know wh—"

"Just shut up, Jerry. I've got the floor." Walter had spent far too much time holed up, nursing and caring for Jerry, to let him wallow in self-pity for long. "Before you take off on some wild goose chase, Jerry, there are things you need to know. Emily, get him something to drink. This is going to take awhile."

Walter pulled out Angela's backpack, unzipped the inside pocket, and brought out her diary. "You're going to read this. Yes, you are, so don't shake your head at me. It'll explain a lot. You probably won't believe it, and that's okay for now. Just be aware there's a connection between you and Angie that goes much deeper than simple friendship. When you're done, if you want to go looking for her, we'll stock you up with supplies, and we'll pray for you and see you on your way. And we'll be right here waiting when you come back ... or at least send some good news, Lord willing."

"Walter, this is her private journal. I don't have any right to read it. And even if I did, I don't have time!"

"Yes, you do. On both counts. Sit. Read. Now!"

Reluctantly, Jerry opened the small, dog-eared book and began.

The first part of Angela's diary repeated things she'd been told about the shift—the EarthShift. She told of earthquakes, solar flares, storms and tsunamis. How her birth had happened in the midst of that. How she'd entered that world of darkness, wind, pressure; born with spina bifida. How her father—not a believer—had been distraught, undone by the sensations they were all experiencing, then unable to accept the imperfection of his child. How he had run away into the wind and darkness, never to return. How, later that night, her young cousin Joey had somehow known that she was healed. How, when the adults had checked, they'd discovered it was so.

A miracle had happened, one her father hadn't shared, because he was never found. His faith had simply not been strong enough to allow him to ascend to the next dimension. Angela wrote of the pain the whole family had experienced because of his loss; most poignantly, her mother's grief at losing the man she loved so dearly. How her mother continued to believe that he would, one day, return.

Jerry read on, through the story of Jon, Chris and Ellen's traumatic experience in the Third when they'd seen ... *Jerry? "He's been unable to break through and open his mind."* This was spelled out in her childish handwriting.

Angela's journal told of a daughter's determination to find her father and bring him home, and tears stained the page that talked of holding his photograph, looking into his eyes. *"I know we'll connect if I can just look him in the eyes. I know what I have to do. I know I can find the strength to do it. I have to find my father or die trying."*

A picture of Angela's life was coming together, but the connection between Jerry and the Jerry in the journal was not. It was a sad story, no doubt about it, but he just didn't get why he had to read this thing when all he wanted to do was get started on his rescue mission. Except that Walter was guarding the door like a sentry, and no one was going anywhere until he said so.

"Well, I did it this morning. Mom is going to be awfully upset with me, and now I'm in a strange place. It's sure not like home. It's dirty and lonely, and the men I saw scared me. I'm glad they didn't see me. I will, I

know I will, find my dad. I'll know. But will he know me? That's the big question. I'll just stay with him until he does, even if it takes me forever!"

The entry was dated six months ago, Jerry noted. But he still didn't understand where she had come from. It sure sounded like one heck of a trip the kid had been on, and he marveled at her stamina and courage. He read about her fears, even panic at times, of sleeping in barns, ducking the military types, scrounging for food and water, missing her family back home, and then ...

"I can hardly believe it! Today I found my father! It just all came together through the most amazing set of circumstances. Thanks to Walter and Emily (who seem like really nice folks), I found him. He has no idea who I am. He looks awful, all scruffy and pale and skinny, but I could tell from his eyes. I'll have to be patient. I am NOT going to let him get away again."

Jerry looked up at his friends; doubt, disbelief, and a torment of contradiction on his face. Walter simply nodded yes. Jerry went back to the diary, frowning and sometimes shaking his head as the last months of his life rolled by in the little book. Their adventures. Finding food together, playing games, talking, just surviving. Her continued loneliness, missing her family—especially her mother. Through it all ran Angela's stubborn determination to retrieve her father, to reach his soul and awaken it, and her repeated assertion that her father was, indeed, Jerry. He read about her trying to send a message to the family that she was all right and praying that they would forgive her someday.

The last entry was dated two days ago.

"Sometimes it's really hard staying here in this cellar. Emily and Walter are like grandparents to me and I love them dearly. They've given up so much to take care of my father. God will surely bless them. I hope they'll make the transition with us when the time comes. But sometimes I

get really discouraged and wonder if it ever will. Whenever I try to bring up something of Dad's past life, he cuts me off—doesn't want to hear it. If I could just break through on one small thing, I think the flood gates would open. Maybe he's scared of that. Maybe he'll never remember how much he loved Mom, and how much he was looking forward to having a child like Mom told me. I've got to get us both out into the sun soon, or we're going to get really sick. Maybe tomorrow. I just love him so much even if he doesn't know who I am."

"She's making this up. She's young. She has a vivid imagination. What do you guys know? Is there any truth to what she's saying? Have you read this, too?"

Walter answered, "We don't need to read it, Jerry. We've known the story ever since your family entrusted us with your care. 'Course we had no idea that this little sprite of a girl would find her way back to this hellish mess to look for you. I've never known anyone with as much courage and determination as Angela.

"So what I know is this—you've got to find her. Maybe in the process you'll come to accept what she's written. Emily and I are too old to go out crawling around looking for her, but you can. You call on your angels. No, don't shake your head at me! You have them ... and they'll help guide you if you just open your heart and listen. You're one lucky man to have a daughter like her, and I pray to God you don't lose her, and equally important, that she doesn't lose you. If you're ever able to move on and accept what we know to be true, to make the transition, we wish you well. You'll carry our love and blessings right along with you. Now, get what you need, and get out of here."

"But what about you? Will you be here when we come back?"

"I don't know. We'll wait for you, but I'm hoping you both go where we won't find you ... into the next dimension. Don't worry about us.

We'll move on when it's time."

"Walter. Emily. I don't know how to say this, but I ... I just love you both. I thank you for saving me, and for giving me a home. I want to see you again." Jerry choked up and felt self-conscious about it.

Emily gave him a big hug and a kiss on the cheek. "We love you, too, honey. You're a good man. You'll be okay. Godspeed."

Walter and Jerry shared a man's hug, trying to stay strong and gruff, but feeling squishy inside. "Here's some food and water. You'd better take her backpack, too. We don't have anything else to offer you except our prayers, but we've got lots of those. Be very careful. Open your heart and listen. Now go on and find our girl!"

Chapter Twenty

Jesse had been receiving nudges from Dorado; dreams mostly, urging him to gather his cousins and continue training for their mission. Today, he got straight-out conversation. He'd taken a long solo bike ride and stopped by the lake to sit quietly and enjoy the peace and beauty.

"Well, Jesse, it's nice to see you again! Oh, sorry, my boy. I made you jump."

"Jeez, you should give me a little warning, ya know? Why are you here, Dorado?" he asked, knowing the answer already.

"Because, Jesse, I feel that you and the boys are slacking a bit on your commitment. And yes, I understand why. It's not the same without your young cousin. She's part of the agreement. But, she's not here, Jesse, and who knows when she'll return ... even *if*." Dorado raised his index finger. "No, no, don't say a word. Angela's got her own agenda, and I've been given strict instructions not to interfere with it. And you boys are not to interfere either. You have work to do, and Angela would be the first one to jump on your case. If she were here."

Jesse looked pained. "You just don't understand. We need to find her, help her, protect her. She shouldn't be *there*. And it was dumb to leave!"

"My goodness, aren't *we* being judgmental? Since you're not in her skin, how could you possibly know where she should and should not be? I know it's frustrating that you can't get into her head. But you're a master at keeping people out of yours, so why shouldn't she have the same right and ability? She's set up a block that makes it a challenge even for me, let alone her poor guardian angel. And that's all I'm going to say about it."

"Thanks, Dorado! I'm really glad to hear that," Jesse smiled and meant it, knowing that his special E.T. guide had just shared his knowledge that *someone* was watching out for Angela, even in the Third. "So what else is on your mind?"

"I want you and the boys to go off on another so-called camping trip. It's still not time to tackle the mountain, but it *is* time to feel its energy again, and to become aware of some other energies that are growing stronger near there. Not particularly good ones. No, in fact, not good at all. You'll need to protect yourselves well—and be prepared for anything."

"When do we have to go, and how do we prepare?"

"Leave within a day or two. Preparation? That's what this adventure is about, dear boy. You have things to learn ... all of you. And now I must leave. Good luck. And be careful."

"Wait a minute! I have some questions. Dorado? Where are you? Doggone it! Why do you *do* that to me?"

He headed home knowing there would be lots of questions and no small amount of concern from his parents. The guys would jump on a chance to take off on an adventure, but for Jesse, his role as leader was currently a very heavy burden. This trip would be without Angela, without her healing abilities, and yes, without her feminine intuition. He had to admit that he'd miss the whole package.

"I think we're all set," Mike announced after checking the packs for the third time. "We've got food, sleeping bags, and warm clothes, just in case. Everything we'll need."

"Are you sure there's enough food, Mike? You know how hungry I get. Last time I got really sick of berries." Mike and Jesse knew that Joey's life revolved, to a great degree, around his stomach. "How far are we going? Are we going to be doing a lot of climbing? Where's my hat? I need a hat."

"For crying out loud, get a grip, Joey. This is a working trip, not some fancy recreational camp-out." Jesse was struggling a bit to stay positive. "Come on, Mike. Let's say goodbye to Mom and Dad."

Ten miles the first day seemed like a reasonable goal, and after achieving it, they were all glad to stop and make camp. It might take a few days to work up to their full potential, but now that they were "on the road" so to speak, they felt better about being there. They began to look forward to whatever challenges might be coming their way. Jesse had repeated Dorado's instructions, and they'd all agreed that at the first sign of any weird vibrations, they would speak up, and speak up fast.

"So tomorrow we'll head north toward Crystal Mountain. We know there's an energy that wants to keep us from ever reaching it; to keep us from finding and revealing the secret. That's where we need more experience," Jesse explained, "so maybe it's a good thing Angie isn't with us. She *is* just a girl, you know."

"Wow! Don't ever let Erica hear you say something like that. Talk about tough people. She'd kick your butt." Joey knew his sister well.

They all laughed and crawled into their sleeping bags, settling down for a good night's sleep.

Jesse sat bolt upright, drenched in sweat, heart beating a mile a minute. The fire was out and it was pitch black; not even a moon. "Hey, wake up guys," he whispered. "Something's wrong!"

"What, what is it? Jesse? Is that you? It's the middle of the night, for cryin' out loud. Go back to sleep. I'm supposed to be the protector, and you need to let me be that, not scare me half to death." Mike sounded tired and peeved.

"Yeah, okay, but do you feel anything strange? Something got to me. I don't know what. But it wasn't a dream. I can remember those."

Joey was awake now, too. "Do you want me to start up the fire again, Jess? I can make a torch or something."

"No, I'll be okay. That was really bizarre, though. Maybe I'm just worried about whatever's out there trying to keep us away. Go back to sleep. It'll be daylight in a couple of hours."

"Sure, bro." But Mike was now more awake and taking Jesse's concern a little more seriously. He knew his brother wouldn't joke around. "Just wake me if anything else happens."

It took Jesse a while to quiet himself, and a while longer to stop jumping at every small sound coming from the surrounding darkness, but eventually, he, too, joined the others in sleep.

As darkness gave way to the cold light of dawn, Jesse wondered if he *had* dreamed the whole episode. Something—or maybe someone—had penetrated his sleep in a negative way, and he couldn't quite bring it back. So he pushed the uneasiness away, frustrated but resigned.

The boys ate, packed up, and headed out. They wanted to end the day camped near the base of Crystal Mountain, which would make for a very long hike, but the weather looked perfect.

The miles ticked by and the hills grew higher—or felt that way as the boys' energy began to wane. Joey finally called a halt, claiming he was nearly starving. They found a shady area and dug around for their next meal. Megan had actually made peanut butter sandwiches and tucked them into the last few inches of space in Mike's bag. Her sons had kidded her at the time, but now that tune was changed as they sent waves of gratitude her way.

"Good grub. Full as a tick!" Joey quoted an old cow poke line as he patted his belly. “Thoughtful mom, you guys. We probably shouldn’t have eaten them all at once.” Actually he wasn’t feeling too great, experiencing a little dizziness that he hoped was due to the altitude. “I guess we should hit the road.”

They shouldered their packs and struck off, each boy desperate to not be the weak link, and all discussion of speaking up at the first sign of “weird energy” was conveniently forgotten.

Chapter Twenty-one

Angela was petrified but not about to admit it, even to herself. With her hands and feet still bound, she was stuck inside a very hot, very smelly tent. Hungry to the point of pain, desperate to pee, the minutes dragged by. Had she been claustrophobic, there was no doubt she'd have been screaming. Even though she wasn't, the idea held some appeal. Suddenly the tent flap flew open and in strode another large, gruff, grungy man clad in the ubiquitous camo fatigues.

He rolled her over roughly with his booted foot and said, "I hear you've been a pain in the ass for my men. That stops *right now!* 'Cause *right now*, you're gonna tell me what you were doin' in that town, who you were doin' it with, where you were holed up, and where in hell you came from."

Angela lay there, not moving, not speaking.

She was rewarded with a not so gentle nudge with the boot. "Hey you! You might be just a kid, but that don't mean shit to me. You're gonna talk or you're gonna suffer, you little bitch. Now what's your name?"

Angela closed her eyes, but they flew open when she was grabbed roughly by her shirt and hauled vertical as though she were nothing more than a rag doll. A quick shake snapped her head back, torturing her stiff spine, and she was slammed into a chair before she could even yelp.

"You don't seem to understand how this works." Her tormentor paused, pulling a nasty looking knife from the scabbard on his belt and leaning down to pinch her chin with his free hand. He laid the flat of the blade on her cheek and exhaled amazingly foul breath right into her face. "You see, *sweetheart* ... " He smiled without humor and twisted the knife until the point of the blade pricked the tender skin by her eye. "I run things around here. And what I say goes. Now unless you want a little eye surgery, or maybe a few scars on that pretty white cheek, I suggest you get with the program and give me some goddamn answers! You tell me your name! Right frikken' now!"

Angela had never been easily intimidated but had to admit that on a fear-factor scale of 1 to 10, this guy was a solid 12. Despite the temperature, she was shivering and simply couldn't comprehend not answering. "My name is Angela." It came out as a croak.

"That's better. Now what's your last name?"

A quick evaluation and she concluded that telling him wouldn't make any difference anyway. But hoping for a little give and take, she tried to look as pathetic as possible and pleaded, "Please sir, could you just let me go to the bathroom? I'm really afraid I'm going to make a mess. And then I can tell you more. Please?" Maybe she could get more bees with honey, as Grandma Julie would say.

"Hmmm. Okay. Our facilities aren't great, but I guess it beats crapping with the rats in deserted houses. No funny business, though, or you'll be sorry."

She was uncuffed and led outside where she discovered that he hadn't been kidding about the facilities. To say that the makeshift outhouses weren't "great" was an understatement, but in her desperate state, she held her breath and took care of business.

On the way back to the tent, her captor allowed her a cup of water which helped clear a little of the dust out of her mouth. He told her that as long as she kept cooperating, they could do without the shackles. If she was going to make a run for it, she had to avoid shackles at all costs, so she drew on every ounce of maturity and common sense she possessed to keep her jailer happy, and herself safe. As long as she was guarded by the big man himself, any thoughts of escaping would have to wait.

She answered his questions honestly when the answers didn't matter, and lied through her teeth when they did. She was certain God would understand.

When there was a lull in the inquisition, she gathered her courage and asked, "Sir, just who are you, and where are we? I'm so lost. It would help me a lot to know a little about this place."

"Ha! Like I'm gonna to tell *you* anything. You just keep calling me *Sir* and we'll get along just fine. I'll tell you this much—we're just outside what's left of LA" He burst out laughing, feeling powerful and in charge. They didn't get many prisoners any more, and this one was cute, a real spit-fire. She'd be a challenge, one he might get to enjoy in a more personal way sometime real soon, just as long as he kept her close by. Wouldn't want some other brainless idiot to take her away from him.

"Okay. I'm gonna get you settled in my tent for now. You'll be guarded 24/7, so don't even think about doing anything funny. Try to run and you won't live to tell about it. Got it?"

"Yes ... Sir." Tonight she'd start working out a plan.

Jerry had no idea how to go about finding Angie. He knew the general direction, and was painfully aware that he needed to be on the lookout for more trucks and unexpected sentries. He reached the edge of town and lost the protection of houses. Staying away from the main road, he made sure he was always in range of a place to take cover quickly. His progress was slow, but every hour brought him that much closer to finding the kid. He hoped. Sleeping in the brush with night sounds and animals skittering around reminded him of his first years in LA when he'd suddenly found himself sitting on a sidewalk, battling the rats for territory. He'd had no idea who he was then, and still didn't, not really. His life was a blank slate up to that point.

Since he didn't want to spend the time scavenging for more, Jerry rationed out his meager supplies. Less sleep, more hunger and thirst made staying positive more and more difficult. The third night, things really got to him, and his imagination overflowed with thoughts of what might be happening to Angie. His emotions, repressed for so long, simply boiled over; from rage to fear to bitter, bitter sorrow. He hadn't known he could still cry.

"God," he whispered, "I don't know how to talk to you, but Angie did and she said it felt good. If you're out there and you can hear me; if your angels are around and haven't got anything better to do, I could sure use some help. I don't know how to do this. Never believed in this stuff. But this kid needs some help. She says I'm her father, and I can't buy that, but I do know I love her and want her safe. Show me where to go, where she is. I promise I'll do my part. Um ... I guess that's it. Please ... and thank you."

He could handle feeling a little self-conscious. Hell, he felt downright ridiculous, but maybe just a little more hopeful. And if anything heartfelt had *ever* come out of his mouth, this prayer was it. Emotionally drained, he dropped off into an exhausted sleep.

Chapter Twenty-two

Nobody ever said the Rocky Mountains were an easy climb, but some days—and this was one of them—they were darn near impossible. Joey finally called a halt, saying simply that he needed a rest—which was true. What he didn't say was that his head was aching, his skin felt a size too small, and his stomach, three sizes too big. He was scared that he might be coming down with the flu or something. But that didn't make sense, because physical sickness really didn't happen in the Fifth Dimension. Knowing that scared him even more. What the devil was happening?

"Hey, guys, we need to talk, but first I've just got to sit down. I've got some stuff going on ... head hurts, stomach hurts. I just feel strange all over. Not normal, y'know? Are you guys feelin' okay?"

Jesse dropped his pack and sat down beside Joey. "Well, to tell the truth, I don't feel too hot either. Figured it was the heat and the climb, but yeah, I pretty much feel like crap. What about you, Mike?"

"Same. Like Uncle Jon when he had the measles or mumps or whatever it was. Without the rash. I didn't want you to think I was just pooping out on you. So what do you think is going on, Jess? Think it's that other energy Dorado was talking about?"

"Yeah, that's what I think," said Jesse. "Especially since we're all feeling it. This isn't good, but Dorado warned us it might happen. Let's hang here a while and see if we can adjust. Or maybe we should try and tune in to it. You know, try to figure out what it is and how to deal with it?" Back in leader mode, he was looking for answers and taking responsibility. "Guess

I should have said something sooner."

"I thought it might be the peanut butter sandwiches," said Joey with a sickly little smile. "I'm really glad it's not."

Jesse was a bit apprehensive, knowing this was only the beginning of their trials and something Dorado expected them to handle on their own. "Let's dial it in, guys. It's energy, and it doesn't feel good to me, so be careful. Pay attention to what you get and we'll share when we come out of it." They stretched out on the soft pine needles, and breathed themselves into the silence.

Swirling down, deeper and deeper still, Jesse reached the point of losing touch with his body. Usually in this level, he was a true light being, slipping smoothly away from his physical self and traveling wherever he wished with a mere thought.

This was different. This was ... wrong. He found himself in a dull, brown, stagnant energy, choking instead of flowing. He felt cold. Sluggish. Bogged down. He tried to hang back, tried to withdraw a bit to watch. He waited for something more to happen. For anything to happen. Nothing did. But when he would have raised his vibrations and returned—to his body, to warmth, to his cousins—he discovered that he was held fast, bound by that cold, stagnant brown which was bonding to him more with each passing moment. He was losing touch with himself—every level of himself—and drowning in the choking, malevolent energy.

"Jesse, come with me. Let go and come with me." The voice was smooth, female, and comforting.

"Who's that? Who are you? Show yourself to me."

"You can see ... that is, if you think you can handle it." The response came in the same appealing tones, but now, with just the slightest edge.

"I don't see anything."

"Don't worry, dearest. Just follow my voice. Come with me. Just let yourself sink down into my arms. I'm waiting right here for you."

It was such a soft and soothing voice, so tempting, so seductive. Jesse knew he was meditating. Part of him still knew that Mike and Joey were close by, but he'd never experienced anything like this, and thinking of Mike and Joey was so much work. He wasn't used to feeling so dizzy, especially when he was meditating. And he was tired. So, so tired. He struggled to remember to breathe. The brown energy made it so hard. Why couldn't he get free? He *should* get free. He really *needed* to be free. He felt that need to the depths of his soul.

"No, I won't! I don't know who you are or what you are. Leave me alone! And *let ... me ... go!*" His control was off and his thoughts fuzzy, but his agitation was growing.

"I only want to help you, Jesse." Now the voice had more bite. *"I know how tired you are."* But it quickly dropped down into a syrupy sing-song. *"Come on now, dearest, just let yourself go and come with me. You'll be fine. Your friends won't even miss you."*

"My friends? My cousins! Of course, they'd miss me. That's nuts! Who the heck are you anyway?"

"Jesse, all you need to do is just let go of your reality. I can offer you a better one with no cares, no missions. Just fun! Come. Come with me, Jesse."

"No! Let me go! Leave me alone! Mike! Joey! Dorado, help me!" Jesse's body lay still as death, but his spirit was putting up one heck of a fight.

"Jesse! Jesse! For the love of God, wake up!" Mike yelled as he shook his brother's limp body.

Jesse's eyes flew open for just a second, then rolled back in his head.

"Jesse, come back! It's Mike, your brother! Joey, yell to him! He's fading again!"

Joey leaned forward and slapped Jesse sharply across the face. Mike was shocked, but Joey said quietly, "We've got nothing to lose, Mike."

Slowly, like moving through knee-deep mud, Jesse slogged forward until he felt the brown energy begin to lighten, both in density and color. Faint voices called his name. They sounded much more urgent than the lady's voice in the brown mist. Yet part of him had wanted to do as she'd said. Had wanted to just let go.

"Jesse! Come on, bud! You can do it! He's coming out of it! Come on, man, we need you. Come back. We love you. Come on, Jesse!"

The voices were getting louder and clearer. He wanted to open his eyes, but someone had glued the lids together. He tried to speak but his mouth wouldn't work. He tried again, but couldn't even moan. Still struggling to free himself of the last clinging bits of the energy, he was internally pleading, "I'm trying, Mike. Keep calling. Please don't let me go."

Suddenly Jesse's body stiffened and his eyes flew open. They fixed briefly on the boys leaning over him, before he rolled away to retch up great quantities of stuff too foul and brown to be peanut butter alone. When the spasms ended, Mike wiped his brother's face with cool water, and with Joey's help, they propped Jesse in a sitting position against a tree.

"Jeez, Jess, are you okay? Can you talk to us? What happened? You scared the crap out of us!" said Mike.

Jesse cleared his throat and whispered, "Yeah, me too."

"Well? What the heck happened?"

Jesse swallowed, cleared his throat and opened his mouth to speak. But all he could manage was to whisper, "You first."

"Okay, I'll start." Joey jumped in, sensing Jesse's persisting weakness. "Well, I guess it's a safe bet that we had nothing close to your experience,

Jess ... thank goodness. We both went into a meditation state pretty easy. Right, Mike? But then, I started feeling real dizzy, and then came this nasty, dark cloud sort of out in front of me. When it started moving closer, it scared me so much I just bailed out. Landed back in my body right here about the same time as Mike. We talked a while. Seemed like we'd had the same experience. And then we got this vibe that something was really wrong with you. I'm thinking it was that cloud thing that got to you. Uh ... maybe *into* you." He glanced quickly in the direction of the vomit.

"Yeah," rasped Jesse, and took a sip of water from his canteen. "I started out OK, but when the sludge came, I was helpless. Powerless. That stuff was just so ... *brown*, you know? Dorado warned me, but, man, I really didn't have any idea. We're gonna have to be really careful 'cause I can tell you guys, this is no game any more. Whatever is trying to stop us is not fooling around! We really need to get better prepared, but I don't know how we're gonna do that. I'll tell you one thing—I'm sure glad you called me back. My head's still pounding. I was almost gone."

Mike shook his head. "That was too close. It wasn't like any of the energies we experienced before." He squeezed his brother's shoulder. "How about we pack up and head back to the ranch? You OK to travel, bro?"

Jesse thought about home and smiled. "Yeah, I'm good with that."

Mike swung his pack onto his shoulders. "I don't know about you guys, but I've had enough excitement for one trip. Let's go home, find Dorado and get him to answer some questions. Find us some spiritual weights to lift. Something! Anything! Just so we're better prepared next time."

"You've got my vote!" Joey jumped up, shouldered his own pack, and started down the trail.

Feeling more grounded every minute, his headache eased by the good spirits of his cousins, Jesse followed. He couldn't have agreed more about their need for preparedness. It was humbling to realize that even in the Fifth Dimension, he'd just come up hard against something that felt very much like what would've been called "evil" back in the Third. He had lots to think about. And he needed home.

Chapter Twenty-three

Angie was calling for him; crying and calling for him. "Dad, help me! Please!" He ran toward her voice, stumbling, falling, struggling to get up. Struggling to keep running. But as hard as he ran, he made no progress. The mud was too deep, too slippery. His lungs were burning. His heart was pounding. Sweat was pouring into his eyes, nearly blinding him. Where was she? Why couldn't he find her? He yelled, but he couldn't make her hear. He saw her face, tear-streaked and pleading, calling to ... yes, to him. And someone else was there, too, just at the edge of his consciousness. A woman. Was she talking to him? Crying for him? *Angie! Hold on, Angie, I'm coming!* He stumbled on.

Something was pulling at him, jerking him, yanking at his clothes. He fought to free himself because he had to get to Angie. *What the hell is grabbing at me?* And then, he heard a low growl. His breath caught as he fell again and struggled to rise. Then something was on him, biting his face. He tasted fear. And mud.

He woke up fighting, coughing and struggling. His first feeling was relief that it was just a dream. But when he realized what he was seeing, he gasped, kicked and scrambled back, trying to get away. A huge ugly dog, his huge ugly mouth filled with huge ugly teeth, was still lunging straight for his face. Jerry yelped, jumped to his feet, tripped over a root and fell on his butt.

"Easy, boy, easy. Good dog. Nice dog. Nice unbelievably big ugly dog." As Jerry held out his hands in an effort to fend off the beast, it pounced, landing both forefeet square on his solar plexus. Jerry's breath whistled out as he folded up like a lawn chair. Thankfully he did have presence of mind enough to cover the vulnerable back of his neck with his clasped hands.

He waited for the attack, but it didn't come. What came was a tentative sniffing at his hands, his hair, his ears. And then a cold nose poked through to nudge his face. *What the hell?*

Jerry slowly lowered his hands to look at his attacker and quickly realized that it really wasn't as huge as he'd first thought, but that it was quite likely the source of all the mud in his dream. *Filthy, medium-sized, 50 pounds at most, pricked ears, brown coat.*

"Jesus H. Christ! It's a goddamned coyote!" And he quickly reached down to shove at the beast's paws which had slid down from his chest and were making their way toward more ... tender parts. The coyote backed up a step and waited.

Jerry got to his feet, one eye on the coyote, and brushed at his clothes, struggling to remember anything he knew about coyotes and coyote behavior. *OK. Pack animals, shy critters.* "So what are you doing here, pal?" *Adaptable. They'll eat most anything.* "Well, I suppose you'd do OK with all the rodents, but you still don't look like you're that much better off than the rest of us." *Lots of Native American legends about them. Clown? Trickster? Shape-shifter?* He looked hard right into the animal's eyes. "No, that's just too damn weird. You're just a coyote."

Seeming to accept the pronouncement as fact, the coyote walked around Jerry, grabbed his pants leg and yanked.

"What the ... ?" Turning, it walked a few steps in the general direction of Jerry's travels, stopped, and looked back as if to say, "Well, come on. We haven't got all day." Shaking his head, Jerry gathered his things and struck off, but the coyote quickly caught up and began crowding him, nearly walking under his feet; forcing Jerry toward the new path.

"Cut it out!" Jerry tried to maneuver around it, but the coyote blocked his every turn. *Now I know what sheep feel like!* He thrust, the coyote parried. He zigged, it zagged. It went on and on until it became like a dance. *And damned if you don't think this is funny,* Jerry thought as he feinted left, still not quick enough to get by his new playmate. They stopped. A face-off. Both panting a bit, Jerry bent over, resting his hands on his thighs; the coyote waiting for his next move.

Suddenly, Jerry burst out laughing, "Okay, buddy, I've got nothing to lose, and damned if you're not the most determined critter I ever met in my life. Well, except Angela." The coyote cocked his head and yipped once.

So they walked together, always on alert, and Jerry had time to consider his dream. He hadn't remembered one in years, but this was playing back in his head like a movie. Real. Some parts as clear as crystal, sharper than a knife. And as painful. He could still hear Angie calling to him. She thought he was her father; she thought of him like that. As much as it scared him, part of him wanted nothing more than to be that "Dad" she'd cried out for. *Poor kid. She's in big trouble. I've just got to find her. Wait. Was there someone else there? An angel? No ... someone was just saying "Angela." Sure. That must be it. But no. There were two people crying, someone besides Angie. Someone ...* That part of the image wasn't as clear as Angela. The other woman was *different. Beautiful, like a reflection in an old mirror. What was she saying? She was pleading. Yes, she was pleading with me about something. Such a pretty woman ...*

Jerry stumbled over a rock and nearly went down. *That's what I get for daydreaming.* He stopped to collect himself and had to smile as the coyote seized the opportunity to mark his territory on a low bush, then scuffed the scent with his hind feet before trotting on. *Following a coyote, for Pete's sake! Well, Angie said I needed to lighten up and trust. I'm trying, Angie. I hope it pays off.*

Suddenly the coyote growled softly and crouched; ears up, nose twitching.

"What's up, buddy? See something?" Jerry started to turn and look, but at that moment, realized that it wasn't a sight, but a sound which had alerted his new friend. He hit the ground, working his body back into the scrub as the engine noise grew louder. *This isn't good. Or maybe it is. If there are trucks around, it might mean that she's around here, too.* But *damn,* that truck was getting close. Cold sweat trickled down his spine as he waited, barely breathing, praying to ... well, he supposed it was God. The "Big Power" that Angie had talked about. He almost smiled when he realized he was doing it.

The sound faded and Jerry's companion got cautiously to its feet, alert and watchful. It gave a great shake, from nose to tail, a coyote version of, "Whew! That was close!" and trotted off, cutting a trail through the brush. One ear was constantly cocked back, making sure that Jerry was still on track, while the other twitched here and there; a second line of defense to its keen nose. They continued on for hours, finally reaching a stand of trees which offered both shade and cover.

As Jerry prepared to get some much-needed rest, he pondered the what and why of his companion. He decided that the bottom line was just simple gratitude for the company. The close call with the truck led him to believe that they were coming closer to the bastards who'd grabbed Angie. So he'd play *Follow The Coyote* for a while longer and see where it led. Right now, he'd rest. He pulled a pack of very stale crackers out of his pack and ate them, drank a little water, and watched the coyote forage for pine nuts under the Pinyons. He hoped they'd find water soon.

Dozing in a thicket while the coyote stood watch, Jerry felt the dream return and welcomed it. He wasn't scared this time. Still, his heart wrenched at the vision of the beautiful woman—clearer now—pleading, crying, holding a photograph in her hands. He wanted to see that picture; see who she was crying for; asked to see it and jolted awake when he saw his own image in the frame. *That's me! Why does she have a picture of me? I don't know her. What the hell is going on? Maybe the stress is just driving me nuts.* His muscles were still tired and sore, and he ached right down to his bones. It would be so easy to give up. He'd hardly thought it when the coyote was at his side, head laid quietly in Jerry's lap and looking up with sympathetic eyes that said, "Come on, pal. Angie's waiting. Let's keep moving."

Jerry struggled to his feet, rubbed his hands over his face and raked them through his hair. His clothes were sweaty and tattered. He was skin and bones, had no weapon, and his best friend was currently a coyote. Compared to him, Don Quixote was an Iron Man. But he was all Angie had, and somehow, he had to be enough.

"Okay, buddy. You lead the way, 'cause I sure don't know where we are or where we're going, and damned if I don't think you do. Go for it. I'm right behind you. But if you're going to lead me into battle, you need a name. I'm thinking 'Sam.' Sentinel Sam." The coyote, seeming to understand, wagged his tail. "If we find our girl, Sentinel Sam, I promise you, I'll find a way to get you the biggest steak you ever ate." Cheered by both thoughts, they moved on with renewed purpose.

Chapter Twenty-four

Jeannie was feeling terribly alone, and increasingly sick. Earlier, she'd quietly excused herself and retreated to her room before it had become obvious. Now she sat, Indian style, a soft wool blanket wrapped around her, shaking and shivering in front of the roaring fire she'd built up in the little corner fireplace. Even though she still wasn't able to connect with Angela in the Third, her mother's intuition was sounding alarms that *something* had happened to Angela. She brought the pictures of Jerry and Angela down from the mantel and laid one on each knee, stroking them tenderly with a finger now and then, as chills wracked her body. Staring at her daughter's happy face, the first tear escaped and trailed down her cheek.

She turned to Jerry's photo; the warm dark eyes, the shy smile. Regardless of his faults—maybe even because of them—she'd fallen for him, tumbling quickly and deeply into love. Even now, that love was alive and well in her heart. She'd long since forgiven him for leaving them. She knew that the events of the Shift, coupled with Angela's birth defect, had simply overwhelmed him. That didn't make him a bad man; just a man who hadn't been ready to handle everything the universe had thrown at him.

But now their daughter was back in the Third Dimension searching for him, trying to bring him home, and, Jeannie felt, in big trouble. And here she was, powerless to help either one of them, except with prayers. Tears still falling, she got up and crawled into her bed, standing both pictures on the low bureau where she could see them. She pulled the covers up to her nose and took one deep and trembling breath, then another, and a third. Closing her eyes, Jeannie held her daughter and husband in her heart, surrounding them with her light.

Sam the coyote prowled cautiously ahead, ears pricked and constantly twitching, eyes scanning, tail low. Jerry followed in full stealth mode, also low, also alert. They'd crossed two dirt roads before melting back into the trees; a fairly dense area offering some semblance of safety. Sometimes, Sam would drop to the ground, ears flicking, every muscle tensed, a position which never failed to make Jerry's heart beat so fast he thought it might just fly right out of his chest. Then Sam would move on, swiftly at times, cautiously at others, and at every twig that snapped under Jerry's feet, he would send disapproving looks back over his shoulder.

They both hit the ground fast and hard as voices drifted back to them through the trees. The words were indistinguishable, but the tone was clearly angry. Men. More than two, and rough, if judged by the voices. Jerry had no reason to believe otherwise.

Sam bellied forward as Jerry ducked from tree to tree, cold sweat dripping, popping out on his forehead and trickling down his back. Close enough to hear each word, they stopped. *Okay,* Jerry thought. *Now to find out if Angie's here. This has got to be the place. Gotta stay out of sight. Gotta be smart. Gotta get closer.* As though he'd heard Jerry's thoughts, Sam crept slowly forward, inch by agonizing inch, until there was movement through the trees.

Angela forced herself to *make nice*, swallow her distaste, and answer politely whenever the self-proclaimed "man in charge" spoke to her. She'd heard her Mom and Grandma Julie talking about bullies and male chauvinists one day, but had never run into one—until now.

Currently disgusted, and more than a little nauseous, she let the spoon clatter back onto the tin plate filled with today's portion of mystery-meat stew. It looked more like something for zoo animals than people. *Like vultures maybe,* she thought. *I might be able to swallow my pride, but there's no way I'm going to be able to swallow this mess, no matter how much my stomach hurts.* She drank her water, thankful that it was at least palatable, and hoped no one would notice she hadn't eaten.

Yesterday, her muscle-bound "guardian" had brought her a stale granola bar—a treat for behaving herself, he'd said—and she'd eaten it, for no other reason than to keep up her strength. She knew it was only a matter of time before payment would be demanded. *At least he's keeping the other creeps away from me for now,* she thought. *But the day will come, and I've got to be ready to fight.* She curled up into a protective ball and closed her eyes to escape her surroundings, at least visually. Planning her escape was her top priority, and she needed to think of a creative, fail-proof way to do it. So far, she had nothing. At least the chains were off—another reward for being "such" a good girl. *Think, Angela! Let's show Mr. I'm-In-Charge about good girls!*

But her mind wandered, and she couldn't focus the way she needed to. Instead, she mentally replayed all her experiences since she'd translocated here to the Third, especially the time with Emily and Walter, the time she'd finally had to get to know her dad. She'd been so happy. Now, she was just so tired; so weary of it all; so worried about her family back home as well as here. *Where are they all? I hope Mom's all right. Oh God, I've found my dad, but will I ever get to see him again? I can't cry. I can't.* Her tears were ruthlessly sniffed back.

"What's the matter, sweetcakes? Cold? Want me to warm you up?"

"I'm fine! Or I will be after I go to the bathroom again. That nasty stuff you call stew is running right through me! Please! I need to go! Right now or I'm gonna make a mess!"

"Okay, okay, just go around back, and for Christ's sake, stay out of the way of the other guys. And stay close. No funny stuff or you'll be sorry. And you come right back here fast when you're done."

Angela fled a little way into the bushes behind the tent and made some groaning and gagging sounds. She felt fine—at least as well as could be expected—and the fresh air helped steady her. Crouching behind some bushes, she was gauging her chances of a successful escape if she just started running when something streaked past her, howling like a mad thing. Some sort of dog, snarling, fierce, knocking over men, spooking the poor skinny horses staked out among the trees. The stray dogs that hung around the camp looking for scraps joined in the ruckus, upsetting untended cook pots and fighting among themselves over the spillage. Tents emptied as men came running out to see what was going on, and that included Angela's jailer, who ran into the middle of the fray, red-faced and screaming for order.

When somebody grabbed her arm and slapped a hand over her mouth, she spun around, ready to fight with everything she had ... and looked straight into the warm dark eyes of her father.

She'd never run so fast in her life, nor had Jerry. The yelling and howling faded, but the two rifle shots were too close for comfort. And Jerry was terribly afraid that Sam had been on the receiving end of them. He couldn't regret anything that had happened. The coyote's crazy performance had allowed him to spirit Angela away. But he felt horrible to think that it might have cost Sam's life. If that was the case, he would always be grateful, and he would show it by keeping Angela safe from here on in.

More than two miles later, when they finally stopped to catch their breath, Angela wrapped her arms around Jerry's waist and was clutched close in return. Words weren't needed and they couldn't spare the breath for them anyway.

They ran on again, knowing only that they had to put distance between themselves and the compound. Three miles, four. Then the woods came to an abrupt halt and so did they. Before them stretched open fields, too dangerous to cross until night. On their knees, working hard to catch their breath, their heads jerked up at the sound of rustling and crackling, nearly on top of their hiding place. Angela stifled a scream as Sam burst out of the trees and skidded to a stop beside Jerry.

"Oh, my God! Sam! Sam!" Jerry threw his arms around the animal and pressed his face into the dirty fur. "Hey, you're bleeding! Buddy, you shouldn't have raced in there like that. But you made a heck of a distraction. Angie, this incredible guy led me right to you. And then he created a diversion so we could escape. I don't know how or why, but he's tame as a dog and smart, too. I owe him, big time!"

He turned back to Sam. "But you're hurt, buddy. You're hurt bad. Look. There's a hole in his thigh. Damn it!"

Jerry wrapped his arms around Sam again and smoothed the fur on his head. Sam licked his face, his tears, and thumped his blood-spattered tail. For a moment, Angela could only stare and struggle to take it all in.

"Dad, we'll take care of him. I know he'll be okay. I know he's connected to our angels. But right now we've got to get someplace where we'll be safe and there's water so we can get that leg cleaned up. We're gonna need something to bandage it, too."

"Not just connected to angels. He *is* an angel, Angie. I asked—no, I *prayed* for help. I thought I was going to die out in the fields. I came so close to being caught—but if I got caught I couldn't help you. He knew, Angie. Sam knew. He helped me find my daughter."

Angela stared at Jerry. "Dad? Did you just say 'daughter?'"

"Wow ... Yes. Yes, I did." Jerry looked as stunned and overwhelmed as she did. "Angie, it's happened. I *know*. For the first time, right now, I *know* it's true! Somehow, you found me. And you believed in me. And Emily and Walter. They believed in me, too. How? Why? There's so much I need to know, things I don't remember."

"After all this time, all the prayers, all the hope. And now we owe your big breakthrough to a coyote. Perfect!" Tears thickening her voice, she shook her head in baffled amusement. There was so much to talk about, but this wasn't the time or place to do it. They had to hide, and quickly. Sam dragged himself to his feet, gave her a soulful look, and started walking along the edge of the meadow, keeping to the trees. Father and daughter, their arms around each other, followed behind without words or hesitation.

It took a long time, and it hurt to watch Sam's limping gait. Twice they had to dive for the bushes when hunting parties had thrashed by, swearing and yelling. Angela couldn't imagine any place Sam could take them that the men with guns wouldn't know about or find, so she was delighted as she followed him through a wall of alders hung with wild grape vines, and found the mouth of an enormous culvert with a trickle of water running along its bottom. Water and shelter. Just what the angels had ordered.

Inside, Sam rolled over on his side and licked at the water while Jerry backtracked to scuff out their footprints and shake the vines back into place. By the time he finished and came inside, Angela was tearing the sleeves of her blouse into bandage strips and carefully tending Sam's wound. They weren't out of the woods yet, but they were together. And, they were family.

Chapter Twenty-five

"Mom! Dad! Where are you? Something's happened with Angela! I know it! I feel it!" Jeannie burst through the barn doors, sending chickens flapping and goats hopping.

Dave came running, dogs close on his heels, sending the goats and chickens back the other way. Breathless, Dave grabbed Jeannie's shoulders and bombarded her with questions. "What about Angela, Jeannie? What did you feel? Did you get through to her? What did she say? What's happened? Wha ..."

"I don't know, I don't know." Jeannie tried to explain, "I just had this *overwhelming* feeling. I'm all goose bumps, my heart is pounding. The hair is standing up on my neck, but ... God! I just don't know!"

"So it's positive, right? Not negative? If it were negative you'd feel bad. *You're* all right. You *are* all right, aren't you? Did you see anything? Get any impressi—"

Julie came to Dave's side, placed one hand on his shoulder and the other over his mouth. At her touch, he closed his eyes and took a deep breath. "Dave. Jeannie. Let's go up to the house. Jeannie, you can slow down and tell us everything. We'll have some tea and decide what we need to do." Putting her arm around Jeannie's shoulders and locking onto Dave's arm with her other, she urged them out into the sunshine.

By the time they reached the kitchen, Jeannie had managed to get a handle on her calm. She and her father sat at the table, holding hands while Julie brewed the tea. While she couldn't define what she'd felt from Angela in any sort of exact terms, she was sure that her daughter had reached a turning point. Since the malaise and chills were gone, she had only to believe that it was a positive one.

Jeannie felt, too, that time was of the essence, so Julie immediately sent out the call for the family to come together. Until now, even the family's combined energies hadn't been enough to reach Angela in the Third, and except for the brief update via Ekor after Jon and Sara's wedding, there'd been no word of any kind. But if the connection had opened enough for Jeannie to receive impressions with this much wallop, it was time to pool their energy and try again.

Jeannie waited on the deck in the sunshine, turning the pages of an album filled with pictures of Angela and Jerry. She looked a little frail, a little shaky, working hard to stay positive. Feelings kept ruthlessly in check for months, even years, were bubbling up. At times, bubbling over, especially as the family began arriving.

In the soft air and slanting sunshine of late afternoon, everyone congregated on the deck with Jeannie for an update. Immediately afterward, each person explored their own connection with Angela to see what impressions they might get. The good news was that they hadn't hit a brick wall like last time, which meant that Angela's "jammer" was definitely turned off. But the results weren't all positive either.

Jon, Chris and Ellen read more fear than they wanted to admit to Jeannie. Jeannie herself was getting deep satisfaction and wonderful, *fuzzy* warmth ... but yes, with some fear as well. She wondered if her daughter was trying to shield her. Julie and Dave received impressions of deep love, dark foreboding, but most of all, a desperate plea to come home.

But for Jesse's crew, Angela's energies amounted to a quick punch to the gut. They all started talking at once and the others quickly jumped in.

"She's there!"

"She let me through."

"She's in trouble!"

"She needs us."

"She's not alone."

"We've got to get to her, bring her back! Now!"

"Hold it!" Dave's raised hand and slightly raised voice brought an immediate halt to the vocal bedlam. "What we've got to do is figure out the best way to help her. She needs our energy, and she needs help. So help me out here, guys. Who goes? What's everybody's gut say?"

Julie was grateful Dave had spoken up because she was busy just then, leveling her own energies to stay tuned in for Angela while staying calm and strong for Jeannie. She knew, too, that they were about to be treated to a large dose of old-fashioned knee-jerk responses which would need to be sorted out immediately if they were going to be able to help Angela.

"I'll go!" Jeannie jumped in quickly.

"Not on your life, little sister. I'm going," Jon countered as Sara squeezed his hand.

Chris and Ellen chimed in. "We're coming with you."

"I'll tell you what needs to happen, and I'll tell you why." Jesse stood up from his spot on the railing, Joey and Mike at his side. They pulled the group's focus like a cat at a dog show. "You know my cousins and I have a bond, ordered by Gabriel, and that we're watched over by Dorado. We're young, but we've handled some intense experiences, dealt with some bad energies. We want Angela back with us like she's meant to be. She needs us as much as we need her. So we three will go back. She'll draw us to her, and we can use our energies and strength to bring her back. You'll all do your part from here. I get that she's ready to split from there now. This is the time. You know we'll do our best."

Mike and Joey stood up, ready to roll, but Steve and Megan stood, too. Still hesitant, still hoping for an alternative that would keep their boys out of harm's way. Julie stepped between them. "Everything Jesse said is true. This feels right to me," she said simply, turning to the boys. "I don't know how you guys got so grown up so fast, but I trust in you, and in your connections to Dorado and Gabriel. You'll need our energy to get you there and back, and you'll have it. When do you want to go?"

"Now." The boys answered, a single voice.

Megan was struggling to be calm but her nerves were jumping, "Wait a sec, guys. What if you land in the wrong place? What if you can't find her? We can't lose you, too!"

Steve put his arm around his wife and leaned his head against hers, "Shhh. We've trusted them in everything they've done, for everything they've been asked to do. We're going to trust them on this."

"I'll get food and water," said Julie, dashing off into the house.

Jeannie stepped in front of Jesse and held out two pictures, one of Angela, the other of Jerry. "Please carry these close to your heart, Jess. Maybe they'll strengthen the connection. And yes," she said, seeing him hesitate, "I think it's important that you take them." Her eyes were shining with tears as Jesse solemnly tucked them inside his shirt.

Julie returned with three small packs which she distributed with kisses to each grandson. Then, the family formed a tight circle holding the three young travelers in its center. It was only a second and they were gone. The family stood a few more minutes, holding the boys in their hearts.

Sam was losing blood. Angela held him, mud and all, on her lap as she compressed the wound and struggled to center herself enough to focus whatever healing energies she could manage. He was trembling a little now, opening his eyes less, occasionally licking his nose as Angela's tears landed on it. Jerry sat beside them, one hand on the coyote's shoulder, the other supporting his daughter's back as she softly encouraged Sam to "just hang on, boy."

"Tell me what to do, Angie. I want to help you with whatever it is you're doing. I want to go back with you, home to your family—*our* family. I can see your mother's face now, and I'm remembering. I know I can change. I know I *have changed*. Grown. I can see now how much pain I caused you all. I've *got* to make it up to you. Tell me what to do so I can help you."

"I love you, Dad. Let go of the bad stuff. Guilt won't help anyone. Do what you were doing at that big meeting in the hills before the soldiers came. Picture Mom. Picture the family. I'm picturing the family and asking them and the angels for help. Hold onto me and we'll do it together."

He felt awkward, but that passed quickly. He could feel his connection with Jeannie; could remember the power it generated, right from the moment they met. He pushed aside guilt and fear, drawing on the warmth of that love and friendship, and for the first time in so very long, felt the possibilities. Felt an intense desire to get home and to see his wife again.

They jolted when Sam lifted his head and growled softly. Struggling to his feet in a wobbly effort to protect and defend, he opened his mouth to bark, but it was stifled when Mike grabbed the coyote's muzzle. Angela squeaked, wide-eyed and jumped up, straight into Jesse's arms. It was a struggle to contain the joy and noise of their greetings, but after many hugs and handshakes, they sat down together and the boys shared their supplies.

Sam was briefly revived by peanut butter crackers and a drink of clean water, but settled quickly back into Angela's lap as first one hand, then another leaned in to rub and scratch. His tail would give a thump, but he was fading. They could all feel it.

They could also feel the trucks rumbling in the distance and hear the pop of gunshots echoing through the woods. They didn't have a lot of time.

Jesse scratched Sam's ears. "Is this furry guy—what the heck is he? A coyote?—is he coming with us? He's hurt, Angie. We can't heal him here, and I don't know if he can make it back to the Fifth."

"He has to, Jess. He led Dad to me and then helped him rescue me. He's so brave and good and loyal. He's going to make it. I'm sure he will."

Seeing her determination, Jesse had to agree. "Okay. Let's see what we can do. Get tight and keep him in the middle. Jerry, you sit in the middle, too. Help Angie hold Sam. We'll ease you both right along with us."

"Ready? OK. Everyone breathe. Center. Block out all sounds, focus on Grandma and Grandpa and the family."

A deep voice came from close range. "Hey, I think there's something behind these vines and trees. I'm gonna check it out!"

"It's time," said Jesse. "See the ranch. Everyone's waiting for us on the deck. Stay focused. Stay open. Be at peace. I am there. We are there."

"We are there!"

"It's a big old culvert. Hey, look! Here's some blood. Looks like they were here. Let's see if we can find their tracks. Should be easy. All this blood, they won't be able to move very fast."

PART FOUR

Ten years after The EarthShift

Our deepest fear is not that we are inadequate. Our deepest fear is that we are powerful beyond measure. It is our light, not our darkness that most frightens us. We ask ourselves, Who am I to be brilliant, gorgeous, talented, fabulous? Actually, who are you not to be? You are a child of God. Your playing small does not serve the world. There is nothing enlightened about shrinking so that other people won't feel insecure around you. We are all meant to shine, as children do. We were born to make manifest the glory of God that is within us. It's not just in some of us; it's in everyone. And as we let our own light shine, we unconsciously give other people permission to do the same. As we are liberated from our own fear, our presence automatically liberates others.

Marianne Williamson (1952-) — A Return to Love

Chapter Twenty-six

"Wow! Baby Gracie is really kicking up a storm today. Honey, feel! Put your hand right here. Yes, there. Now ... wait for it ..."

Jerry was amused by the name. "Baby Gracie" would be "Grace" if she was a girl and "Grayson" if he was a boy because, Jeannie insisted, they were living in a state of Grace. Grace or Colorado, he still turned pale when their child gave a solid kick under his hand, as if to say, "Hey! I'm tired of being stuck in here!" Watching Jeannie with concerned eyes, he asked, "Baby, is this okay? Normal? I mean ... doesn't it hurt you?"

"No, my love, it doesn't hurt. Annoys, maybe. Especially when he or she kicks my book off my lap and I lose my place." She smiled and kissed Jerry's cheek. Her hand had gravitated back to her belly, and she rubbed in slow circles, calming herself and the unborn child. "Sure is anxious to get out of there. Sometimes I can almost see the outline of a little foot." She poked at a moving lump and giggled as it quickly withdrew. "Hmmm, ticklish." Stretching back, she rested her head on Jerry's shoulder and sighed. "Can you believe everything that's happened since you came back to us? I still get goose bumps just thinking about that day."

"It was too close for comfort, that's for sure. I was so worried about Angie. She was so worried about me. And we were both worried about Sam. Amazing how he fits right in here. I love watching him play with Scott. Treats him like a younger, two-legged brother! That coyote would do anything in his power to protect this family. I imagine he's on duty right now, protecting the kids. Angie sure hated leaving with the baby coming so soon."

"She knows we're in good hands, Jerry, and she ... well, she just has to do what she has to do. With you and Julie and Dad right here, I'm not going to worry." And thought, *not about that, anyway*.

Out on the trail, deep in a Colorado forest, Angela's feet were, quite simply, killing her. Not that she'd ever admit it. These adventures into the wilderness were getting harder and harder; more and more of a physical challenge. She massaged and rubbed as her thoughts drifted back over the last two years. Her journey through dimensions. Her search for her father. Finding him. And Emily. And Walter. And Sam. Dear, dear Sam. Being captured. Being rescued. Nearly being captured again. Her prayers that no one be left behind.

Their homecoming celebration had been amazing. Just being able to hug her mom again. And the look on her mom's face when she saw her dad, and when he'd taken her hand and asked if he could come home. Everyone immediately fell in love with Sam, and with the whole family together, he was healed and good to go in about two minutes flat. Little Scott took to him like a long lost pal, laughing like a loon when Sam gave him coyote kisses with that big, eager tongue. Many tears, many hugs, lots of laughter, wonderful food. She had no idea how Grandma Julie found the time to get an old-fashioned Thanksgiving dinner together with everything that was going on.

It took just a little while, especially with the grown-ups, for the strangeness to wear off with her dad, and for everyone—especially her dad—to trust that his enlightenment was for real; to move past the old hurts and distrust. Seeing—*feeling*—the unconditional acceptance and love from her mom for Jerry, not to mention his obvious devotion to both Angela and her mom, took care of everyone's fears pretty quickly.

The only sad note was that, so far, no one had been able to find Emily and Walter, either in the Fifth or back in the Third. And it wasn't for lack of trying. Jon, Chris and Ellen had all "put out the word," so the network of searchers had widened geometrically. Angela consistently prayed that their friends were okay. The thought of them living in conditions even more unstable than when she was there ... well, it just hurt to think about it.

She wanted to at least get a message to them; to let them know she was okay. To tell them her mom and dad were expecting another baby! It would happen. Some day soon, it *would* happen.

She always felt a little pang that she'd missed Jon and Sara's wedding. But then, she'd been able to spend time visiting with them in San Francisco and had gotten to know—

"Hey, Angie, what the heck are you doing? Move it, for Pete's sake! You've got to keep up!" Joey's voice had passed "encouraging" and moved well into the "stock prod" range. Under his breath, but loud enough for her to hear, he mumbled, "Girls. Jeez!" before stomping off down the trail.

He really wasn't that angry with Angela, but the pressure was getting to him. He knew he'd overreacted, but was unable to pull it back. He hiked on, trying to find his calm. *So okay, she's been really helpful sometimes. But females spend way too much time thinking and analyzing and cleaning and talking. I know we're getting close to one of those high-energy, strong-vibration areas, so closing ranks is ... is ... imperative! Yeah, imperative. And what's she doing? Giving herself a damn foot massage! Well, at least she brought us Sam. He'll give us a heads-up when we get close. It'll be soon now. He's acting pretty weird. Agitated, running back and forth, sniffing, growling.*

"Yeah, I feel it, too, buddy. Getting a little dizzy, head's hurting."

Sam's hackles were raised, the hair standing straight up along his spine, and he was whining or growling almost constantly. Just then, Sam decided that no one was going any farther. He spun around, planted his feet in the middle of the trail and bared his teeth at them.

Jesse shouted to the others. "Hey, you all feel it?" Heads nodded. "Okay, so let's move sideways. Try to stay right on the edge of this force wall. We'll see if we can figure out how big the block is. And whether it's protecting something, or just trying to force us back. Let's go." *I sure wouldn't mind if Dorado showed up about now*, Jesse thought. Twigs snapped, leaves crunched, and the heavy scent of pine grew stronger as they wound their way deeper into the woods.

Their feet moved automatically as the miles ticked by. Now that they'd named their goal, their challenge, no one wanted to stop. It was breathlessly hot, even in the shade, and the wall—the force field—was still there; invisible, yet impenetrable. When even Sam looked like he could use a break, Jesse knew it was time to call one.

"We'll just get up this knoll and then stop for a while. We need to take stock, and talk things over before we go any further," he said. In the way of small hills, as Jesse's band got more and more tired, the knoll seemed to grow and grow.

It was a full fifteen minutes before Joey crested the top and shouted back, "Hey, wow! Look, guys! There's a lake!"

"What's with all the mist?" asked Angela, reaching Joey's side. "It's really thick. Can't even see the other side."

"Yeah," Mike chimed in. "Reminds me of that heavy mist during the Shift when we were in the cave. Kinda spooky, but I bet the water's gonna feel just great! Come on, guys!"

Mike took off down the hill at a gallop, Joey at his heels. They reached the shoreline, kicked shoes off and threw socks every which way, and waded in beside Sam, who was already muzzle-deep and slurping busily.

"Hey, this feels great!" Mike called.

"Come on down!" Joey had scooped cool water, splashed his face, and was rubbing off layers of sweaty grime. Mist or not, this was the best thing since sliced bread as far as he was concerned.

Angela and Jesse had descended more slowly, more cautiously, looking around for anything ... off. For both of them, there was just something strange about that mist. Still, Sam wasn't leery about the water. In fact, he'd finished drinking and was currently swimming circles around Mike and Joey, his skinny tail swishing back and forth like a rudder.

"Come on, Angie. Let's pick out a good camp site. We'll need some wood for the fire and some rocks to line the pit. The lake still gives me the heebie-jeebies a little, but the guys don't seem to feel anything weird." His smile was still a little tentative.

"I'm with you, Jess. But a swim would sure feel good. Let's just look around and get the fire laid first."

Sam came out to join them, sneaking up as close as possible before shaking enthusiastically, covering them with spray. Angela swore he grinned when he did it. *Males!* she thought. *They're all the same. Jokers, every one of 'em.*

Sam stayed close, sniffing and marking turf and giving a deep-throated growl now and then. But he didn't stop them or try to move them along. They gathered firewood, picked some berries, and returned to a spot on the shore which offered not only more driftwood, but a scatter of rocks as well. Jesse wondered if there were fish in the lake. If so, and if they were biting, they could stretch their supplies a bit further. He and Angela scooped out a pit, lined it with stones, and soon had a fire ready to light.

Jesse gave a yell. "Okay guys! Time to come out and talk about what we do next."

Refreshed, and feeling only a little guilty about missing the camp prep, Mike dried off and surveyed their little piece of the world. "It's not a bad place. Has some water—even if it does look weird—and you found some berries. I don't know about you guys, but I don't feel any strange energy here at all."

"Agreed," said Joey. "I say we spend the night, swim in the morning and decide what to do then."

"Sounds like a plan," seconded Mike. "I'll make the poles, and Joey and I will see if we can work some fishing magic."

Jesse held up his hand. "Hold on a minute. That's all good, but before you take off to fish, Angela and I think we need to make a raft so we can do a little investigating. We just have to get creative. Think like engineers. Gather some stuff, figure out how to hold things together. Maybe use our belts to start with. That sort of thing."

"Great! We'll see what we can find in the way of logs 'n' stuff while we're fishing!" To Joey, most everything was an adventure. It was one of his best features. He and Mike walked off down the shore toward an outcropping of ledge which would give them access to deeper water.

Angela had concerns about the raft project and voiced them. "I'm worried about this mist, Jess. It would be real easy to get lost in it. And I think it's going to have to be a small raft or else we'll never be able to launch it. So at least one of us would need to stay back here with Sam."

"It's got to be a two-man rig, I think," said Jesse. "Joey and I need to do the exploring. You and Mike should stay here and keep the home fires burning. We can keep yelling so we won't get lost. Sound carries on the water, so we'll hear each other. And we can whistle if the yelling isn't enough." He still sensed her reluctance. "And you'll have Sam."

They talked, walked, dragged back wood for the fire and even a couple logs they thought might work for the raft. The fish had been biting, so Mike and Joey returned like conquering heroes. Later, with full stomachs, everyone crawled into their sleeping bags to settle in for the night.

When they slept, Sam slept too, but lightly, raising his head now and then, whining just a little. But it was enough to wake Angela, who roused herself and reached over to stroke his head. Lying there, under the star-strewn canopy of the western sky, she thought she heard the sound of a woman's quiet laughter. But since no one else seemed to hear it, she chalked it up to her imagination, and she *had* been thinking about her mom.

Chapter Twenty-seven

Morning came quickly. Before long, a large, sturdy raft took shape, fashioned from lengths of quaking aspen the cousins found only a short walk from the lakeside. Mike figured the wood had been abandoned by some pre-Shift logging operation, and was pleased that it was not only still solid, but completely dry. A combination of wild grapevines and bittersweet served to lash the pieces together.

The biggest problem was figuring out how to flip the finished project so that the two last pieces of larger, bigtooth aspen, laid cross-wise to support the "deck" and provide additional buoyancy, would be on the bottom. The cousins tried lifting; then they tried levering. Angela suggested they drag the raft the rest of the way into the water to try a weight/counter-weight arrangement. There was much grumbling from the manly men, but after they had tried and failed several more times, she insisted that they give her plan a try. Vindication was sweet when the craft teetered up on its side before toppling over with an impressive splash. Even the boys had to cheer.

Paddles were fashioned by tying pieces of canvas ground-cloth around two forked branches, and as quickly as that, Jesse and Joey climbed aboard, ready to set sail.

Even though the mist didn't appear to be as thick as it had the previous day, Mike was still nervous. "Look, I don't think the folks would approve of any of this, especially us splitting up. So don't go out so far you can't see land, and make sure you can hear us. And don't be gone long. Okay?"

"You're just jealous 'cause we're going and you have to wait on shore for your turn," Joey laughed.

"Yeah," Mike mumbled. "I wish that's all it was."

The splash of the paddles reassured him for a while, but that was before the mist rolled back in—boiled in, actually—like the heavy smoke from spring bonfires, just before the flames burst through. "Jesse! Joey! Talk to me! Can you hear me?"

"We're doing fine, Mike! No problem except this mist. We'll come back closer to shore! Hang on!" Jesse was in need of a little reassurance himself. Things seemed fine, but he still felt that something was off.

On the shore, beside Mike and Angela, Sam was pacing rapidly. Ears twitching and eyes alert, he was definitely *not* comfortable with the goings-on. He barked his concerns with his coat bristling up so much he looked ten pounds heavier. And then, Angela heard it again; the distant sound of female laughter. *It's just the breeze blowing through the trees*, she tried to tell herself. But she really didn't think so.

"Mike, did you hear that?"

"Hear what?"

"Someone laughing?"

"Nah. You're just spooked by this mist, Angie. And I bet you're worrying about your mom, aren't you? Hey, it's too early for the baby to come, right? Relax. The guys'll be back with us on dry land before you know it."

She nodded, desperately wanting to believe him. "That's probably it. But let's keep yelling anyway. It seems like forever since we heard them."

"Jesse! Joey! We want to hear you. Give a yell!" He paused. "Come on, guys, how about a whistle!" Again he waited. "You hear anything?"

"No. Yell again." Her uneasiness built, blossoming into full-blown apprehension when Sam started barking. There was still only silence from the lake. "Wait. There it is, Mike. Can't you hear that?"

He stood, tilting his head, listening intently. "That's sure not the guys. Is it? Sounds like a ... bird? Or maybe the wind, or ... yeah, you're right. Maybe a little like someone laughing."

Without warning, Angela screamed, loud and ear-splitting as a fire siren, before she called again. "Jesse! Joey! You answer us! Right now!"

But her orders were drowned in the mists.

Aboard the raft, the sailors' concerns were also growing by leaps and bounds. "Hey, Jess, I can't hear them any more, and I can't see a thing except this cloudy foggy crap. Can you hear anything? I can't even hear Sam barking."

Paddling steadily with a worried look on his face, Jesse replied, "Uh-uh. Nothing. Man, we are *lost*. This is like some weird Never Never Land or something. Can you tell which way we came? Should we turn around? *Did* we turn around? It's like a white-out on a ski slope. I can't see a thing, and man, I really do *not* like it!"

"Neither do I. Keep listening. I don't think we've gone that far. But if we can't hear them, they can't hear us, so let's keep yelling."

"I'm getting hoarse. Let's yell together. On the count of three. One. Two. Three! Mike! Angela!"

But the only sound was the quiet slap of water against the logs of the raft, and the drip of water off their paddles. "Come on, Joey, paddle. We've got to get to shore somewhere. Then, we'll just walk back to Mike and Angie."

"I am paddling, for cryin' out loud! Sam! Bark for me, buddy!"

The day wore on. They waited.

"It's getting really cold, Mike. Let's start the fire. I'm not all that hungry, but we should eat something so we stay strong enough to keep yelling. Poor Sam. He just keeps pacing and whining and looking out there into that damn mist. He's making me nervous!" Angie was ready to jump out of her skin.

"Yeah, we'll start the fire. And maybe Sam will feel better once he's eaten. I don't know what this deal is, but it must be something we're supposed to figure out. The wind's shifting a little now, so they'll probably just drift back in. When they do, we'll hear 'em. Or Sam will, for sure."

"You're pretty calm about this, Mike."

"I'm not, really, but I don't know of anything else we can do at this point. I *have* to trust they'll be watched over, Angie. You do, too." He smiled, trying to reassure his cousin and by so doing, convince himself that all would be well. For a time, it almost worked.

"I've got this awful feeling we're going in circles, Jess. My arms are about to come off." Despite the cool dampness, beads of sweat dotted Joey's brow, and his shirt showed dark patches under his arms. "Maybe we could just listen and drift for a while?" Joey asked hopefully.

"Okay, but just 'til we've rested." Sweating too, Jesse sent a weak smile, and added, "At least we shouldn't get a sunburn with this fog."

"Yeah. Something to be thankful for."

As though on cue, the light grew brighter and the fog lifted to reveal ...

"Land!" they shouted in unison, paddling hard until the raft ran aground on a sandy, but unfamiliar, shore. Beyond the sand, there was no living forest; rather, an odd grassy verge littered with the upturned and weathered root systems of older, much larger trees than those in the aspen grove by their campsite. Standing close by Jesse's side, Joey surveyed the odd landscape and shivered. Jesse turned to meet his eyes and nodded.

"Weird and then some."

They wedged the raft between two rocks on the water's edge, and after stretching a bit to work out the kinks in their arms and backs, walked along the dusty, narrow path which wound back between the massive roots, gleaming silver in the sunlight, their dark shadows reaching out like giant tentacles.

When buildings came into view—plain, small sandstone structures, built beside the path—Jesse's eyes grew wide. "Wow! This looks like something I read about in my history class. Hey! Look over there! People! In weird long robes. Let's go see if they can tell us where we are."

And feeling more alien than they ever had aboard Dorado's space ship, Jesse and Joey walked toward two men who were walking toward them.

"Hi, I'm Jesse and this is Joey. We're sort of lost. Could you tell us where we are?" But rather than answer, the men simply moved by; their gait, an odd, slow shuffle; their faces without expression; their mouths moving to form words the cousins could barely hear and not comprehend at all.

Joey turned and hurried after them, shouting, "Hey! I'm Joey, and this is my cousin. Can you help us? Hello?" He looked at Jesse. "Jeez, Jess, they didn't even look at us!"

"Maybe they're deaf or something? Let's try someone else." But no matter how loudly they spoke or how frantically they waved their arms—or even when, in utter frustration, they pulled on the robes—there was no response. Each and every one of these strange people just continued on their way, non-responsive, emotionless, as though they moved in a waking trance.

"Come on, let's follow them. See what they're up to. Wow ... this is *str-raaange.*" Joey drew out the word and made it two syllables. "Watch this. I can jump right in front of this guy, and he doesn't even flinch. I tap him on the shoulder and he doesn't feel it. This is crazy, Jess."

"Listen to their words. It's a different language. I've never heard anything like it before, and I'm getting nothing from them telepathically except images that look like surreal paintings or hieroglyphics. Where *are* we, and who the heck are these people, Joey?" Panic was rising up in Jesse's gut. "It's like we've landed in some ancient civilization. Where did they come from? Maybe it's some kind of time warp thing, or even another dimension, but it's giving me the freaking creeps."

They followed the oddly vacuous people and eventually reached the mouth of a large cave cut into a wide rock wall from which shot a powerful beam of bright blue light. Without hesitating, the beings shuffled inside, their bland faces reflecting the blue which made them look even more corpse-like than before. Jesse and Joey stood to one side and studied the pulsations of the beam. It was a pure blue, a shade reminiscent of the lights on Dorado's huge space ship, and it was accompanied by the faint sound of laughter—a woman's laughter.

"Hey, we heard that same sound out on the lake," whispered Jesse. "This is beyond bizarre. But we're here, and we need to check it out." When Joey started to object, he added, "We'll be careful. And quiet. The guys in robes can't hear us, but, just in case they're not alone in there."

Starting inside, they quickly flattened themselves against the wall when three more of the strange people came slowly walking out. As before, there was no reaction whatsoever to their presence, so they continued on. The tunnel wasn't wide, but tall enough for all but the tallest of people to walk upright. The blue glow illuminated the curving pathways, and no other lights or candles were visible. Everything was blue. So very blue.

"This place gives me the creeps, Jess. And I'm worried about Mike and Angela. Let's head back and take our chances on the lake."

"This light's getting brighter, Joey. We've come this far, we need to finish it. Mike and Angie will be okay. Just be careful and stay close."

Inching their way around the next corner, they discovered that the cave opened up into an enormous archway through which blue light poured in a nearly material stream. Motioning for Joey to stay behind him, Jesse pushed his backpack into the beam, checking if, being so powerful, it would do physical harm. When nothing happened, he tested with his hand. *Maybe this is the same as the blue light on Dorado's ship.* Encouraged by that possibility, he motioned for Joey to follow and edged inside the arch where he stopped dead in his tracks.

In the center of the chamber stood a crystal, thirty feet tall, the color of a Colorado sky in midsummer, clear as water and incredibly beautiful. So wide at the base, it nearly filled the room, its facets tapered to a point at the top. The sight left them speechless.

"Hello. Please, come right in." They thought the disembodied voice emanated from inside the crystal, until a stunning woman appeared from behind it, gliding toward them. Her luxurious brown hair framed a classically beautiful face, then flowed down around ivory shoulders before curling over lush breasts. A dark blue crystal pendant matched the shimmering gown which clung to her amazing body, and as she contemplated their faces, her soft laugher rippled around them. Her effect on the teens was potent. They were both dumbstruck.

"Welcome to our crystal chamber. I'm so glad to see you here."

Jesse found his voice first. "Who are you? What is the place? How come you can see us but nobody else can? And we can understand you—you speak English—but the others don't. Who are they? Do you know Dorado?"

At the mention of Dorado's name, the beautiful face hardened for just an instant before fixing itself once more in soft, appealing lines. "My, my, my. You *are* full of questions, aren't you? I'm Beryl, Mistress of the Crystal. But there's a simple way for you to know the answer to the rest of your questions and more. And it will make you feel *so* good."

Joey was already feeling *so* good, just looking at her, hearing her laugh, watching her smile. His hormones had kicked into overdrive the minute he'd seen her, and he just couldn't tear his eyes away. Jesse, caught completely off-guard by the woman's overt sexuality, stared at the floor trying to regain his composure.

"Well ... okay. But what is it?"

She flashed him a sugared smile. "All you have to do is touch the crystal. It's magical, you see. Once you've put your hands on it, you'll understand what's truly important. Past, pain, problems? Pffft! A waste of time! Once you understand, you'll join our family and meet more beautiful women. You'll stay here with us and never grow old! Just put both your hands on it. Go ahead. Feel its warmth and energy. You'll know all the answers when you do. Touch the crystal. Touch it now." Joey, clearly under her spell, began moving toward the pulsating stone.

"Don't Joey! Don't go near it! We already have a family, and *they're* what's really important! Back up, Joey. That thing will make you forget *everything;* our family, our mission, everything. That's what happened to those zombies we've been following around. Joey, no!"

But Joey's eyes were already focused on the smooth blue surface and his blood was pulsing from listening to the lady's dulcet tones. "Just a touch with my finger, Jess," he whispered. "It's just a pretty crystal. It can't hurt me." Its influence, and that of Beryl's, was inexorable. If it was magic, it was very strong—and very dark.

Even as he lunged, Jesse sensed it was too late. Before Joey's finger even made contact, a blue arc of energy leapt out to complete the circuit.

Joey's whole body jolted with the shock, shaking from head to foot before he froze, still as death, in place, staring at the blue prisms within the stone.

Jesse spun his cousin around, looking deep into the dulling eyes; watching as the last glimmer of recognition faded. For Joey, there was a brief awareness of a stranger's face. Then that faded, too, as the neurons in his cerebral cortex, parietal lobe, occipital and temporal lobes powered down, leaving nerve impulses working for only the most primitive of body functions.

Jesse held his cousin's non-responsive body as the blue light pulsed, and soft female laughter echoed cruelly.

"We've got to get help, Mike. We can't leave them out there drifting around in the fog. They'll starve. God knows, they may already have. Or drowned! It's been a week and we haven't heard a thing. Sam just sits there by the water, whining. We've searched all we can reach of the shoreline and found nothing. And we need food. I don't know what we can do that we haven't already done, and ... and I'm just scared." Angela's shoulders slumped as she wound down.

"I have one more idea, Angie. I don't think we have a choice at this point."

"What is it? Tell me."

"Sam goes swimming."

"What? No! He'll get lost too, or drown!"

"Listen, Angie. The guys are still out there somewhere. Sam has a sense about how to find people. Look at how he found you and your dad. He wants to go. The only reason he hasn't is because we've been keeping him here. If he can't get to them, he'll find a way back. Bottom line, if we don't find the guys so we can do whatever it is Gabriel needs us to do, well, I just don't think it's going to matter much what happens next."

Head down, Angela walked across the sand to where her coyote friend sat waiting and watching. She knelt in the sand, put her arms around him and lay her head on his, talking softly as she stroked his fur. When she stopped speaking, he pulled back to lick the tears off her cheeks. Then, they both stood up.

"Go on, Sam! It's okay. Find Jesse! Find Joey!" Sam never hesitated. He splashed in, and his powerful muscles propelled him through the water to where he was swallowed up by the mist. Mike and Angela watched, arms around each others' waists, trying to visualize all three of their friends happy, smiling—and coming back home.

Chapter Twenty-eight

"It's too soon! It's *got* to be false labor. The pains aren't consistent. They come and they go. And Angela's not back, so this simply *cannot* happen now!" Jeannie stretched back on the couch, a slight sheen of sweat on her forehead, her mouth set in a stubborn line.

"I know, babe. Here, just let me rub your feet." Jerry was doing his best to calm his increasingly disturbed wife, and a foot rub was the best he could come up with at the moment. "Have you thought any more about the name?" he asked, hoping to keep her busy mind from latching fully onto Angela and her cousins, who'd already been gone long past their expected return date. "I know we'd settled on the Grace/Grayson gambit, but then you remembered that cheerleader from high school ... and you know, now that I think about it, I seem to remember one of those corporate CEO's from all the dot.com scandals back in the Third named Grayson. And somebody would always be calling him Gracie anyway. So maybe we should rethink."

Jeannie turned back from gazing out the window and seized on Jerry's distraction. She was already working hard to avoid dwelling on Angela and the boys and all the possible reasons they weren't yet home.

"Well, if it's a girl, it would be nice to honor Emily," her eyes grew a little teary as she thought of the kind woman who'd tended her husband so well and so long. *Long enough to let him come back to us*, she thought. "And if we do that, her middle name could be Rose, after my nana. Emily Rose. Has a nice ring to it, don't you think?"

"I like it. And if it's a boy, we could call him Walter, and maybe use

Julie's dad's name, Kent, in the middle." Grinning, he went on, "Or my dad's name, Clark. And then there's Jimmy and Olsen. Lane! And Perry White! Yeah, he could be Perry, except if he became a lawyer, he wouldn't have any murderers to represent in these here parts. Or—"

Jeannie was giggling by now, and struggling not to. "Stop! No more! I beg you or I'm gonna have to go pee again. You are so sweet, honey, trying to distract me. Sweet and wonderful and silly. And I love you more each day. I'm okay now, really. *We're* OK. The foot rub is perfect. And it's working. The contractions have stopped," she noted with pleasant surprise, "and now, I'm sleepy." So saying, she yawned and snuggled, drawing the soft tartan throw around her. She closed her eyes and promptly fell asleep.

Jesse was beyond panic. "Come on, Joey!" he yelled, grabbing a limp arm. "We've got to get out of here. We've got to get back. Remember Mike and Angela? It's been a whole day and it'll be dark soon. Please, please, *please* hear me! Look at me, damn it!"

"Calm yourself, Jesse. He's fine. He's content. You just need to relax and touch the crystal." Beryl spoke in dismissive tones. "He can't hear you, you know. Until you touch the crystal, too, you simply won't exist for him. Life is simple here, and sweet. Easy. Always easy. Why don't you touch the crystal now, Jesse? Then you and Joey can be together forever. It's so easy, dear, dear Jesse." Her soft, silky voice was mesmerizing, hypnotizing, but when Jesse swung his gaze to meet them, the perfect blue eyes were icy cold.

Like a siren, the crystal's mistress trilled sensuously on. "You know, your friend should really put his whole hand on the stone. He'd be even more comfortable then. Here ... I'll just help him." And cobra-quick, her hand shot out to grab for Joey's.

Spinning quickly to put himself between Joey and the crystal, and at the same time jerking back away from the woman, Jesse nearly tumbled them onto the ground. Everything in him was screaming to get away from both her and her crystal, as he was more and more sure that both were evil, right down to their cold blue hearts. He regained his balance, planted his body in front of his cousin and screamed, "You stay the hell away from him! Don't you *dare* come near us! He'll fight this! He'll never be one of your slaves. He'll come out of this, I know he will. He has to. He has a family and we have work to do for Gabriel."

"Ah, yes. *Gabriel.*" She hissed it. "Yes, I know all about Gabriel." She tossed her head and purred, "Well, there's no hurry. We who serve the crystal have time. We have all the time in the world." She made no move to come closer, and in fact turned away to gaze lovingly into the stone.

Jesse allowed himself a deep breath, but when he turned to check, he realized that behind him, Joey had wandered off and was now moving back through the archway, turning back down the tunnel toward the outside.

Jesse bolted after Joey, quickly reaching the arch and skidding around the corner as Beryl watched, laughing softly. Joey's usual long-legged stride had turned into more of a shuffle, so Jesse caught up just past the first turn and walked along, close beside him, constantly checking over his shoulder for more aggressive slaves, or their mistress.

He noted Joey's eyes were half-closed, his expression dazed, as though slightly puzzled. He chattered constantly, reminding Joey about Mike and Angie, about home, about Grandma Julie and Grandpa Dave, about horses and fishing and whatever else came to mind, hoping desperately that one of those subjects would be the key that would reach and awaken the sleeping parts of his cousin's mind.

Behind them, the blue light pulsed, and Jesse could hear Beryl still calling.

"You'll never get back to your friends, you know. It's impossible to find your way through the mists! I'd hate for you to drown, Jesse! It would be such a waste! Come back! Come back and join us! Touch the crystal and live happily ... *ever after!*" and at that, her laughter trilled gaily, as though she'd made a terribly funny joke. But it was such cold laughter it sent shivers down his spine. He felt the chill even as they passed through the entrance and stepped out into sunshine.

Moving with the same shuffling stride as the other crystal slaves, like a zombie, Jesse thought, Joey scuffed along the dusty path behind the others. Still, no one tried to stop them or talk to them or paid any attention to either of them. Jesse, more terrified by the moment, alternately whispered, shouted and whistled in his cousin's ear. He grabbed Joey's shoulders and shook him, overjoyed to see the slight hesitation, just a stutter in the blank eyes, but his heart fell each time the spark died, and Joey stepped around him to continue unerringly down the road, following some internal map toward an unknown goal. Jesse walked after him. Thinking. Praying.

Chapter Twenty-nine

It had already been a long, exhausting swim when Sam caught the faint scent and turned toward it. He was weakening by the time the mists thinned revealing a shoreline, then rocks, and then—to Sam's delight—the raft. His paws contacted the sandy bottom, and he waded through the water toward it, sniffing busily. Yes, his guys had been here. The scent was still fresh. He walked out onto the sand, shook himself thoroughly and flopped down for a short rest.

Almost immediately, several of Beryl's slaves arrived, and with great interest, quickly circled around Sam, shaking their heads and speaking to each other in their strange tongue. Unlike their *laissez-faire* response to Joey and Jesse, they were hyper-aware of Sam.

Whether alerted by their scent, their words or just bad vibes, Sam quickly raised his head, aware and wary. And that was the sight that greeted Jesse, still holding onto Joey's arm, as he came around the last ancient root system and turned down onto the beach.

The coyote's sharp eyes locked on. He jumped to his feet, baring his teeth, scattering his onlookers in every direction. As though he hadn't been swimming forever and was utterly exhausted, Sam ran joyfully across the sand, howling and whining in an ecstasy of joy.

"Sam! It's really you! Hi buddy! Oh, it's so great to see you!" Tears were welling up in Jesse's eyes, as he buried his face in the sandy fur. "How did you get here, fella? Man! I am *so* glad to see you!" So deliriously happy were they to have found each other, neither noticed Joey shuffling away with his crystal brethren; like them, showing what could only be described as agitation and fear at Sam's presence.

With their greetings complete, Jesse and Sam looked around for Joey, who was disappearing back up the path. Quickly realizing that they could use this to their benefit, Jesse spoke to the coyote. "Help me, Sam. Joey can't even see me, but he sure sees you! We've got to get him back to the raft and away from these people. Bring him back, boy! Bring him to the raft!"

Doing his best border collie impression, Sam quickly separated Joey from the others and herded him back toward the beach. By circling and nudging, even giving a snap or a growl if Joey tried to evade, Sam managed to move his impaired friend close to the raft which Jesse had waiting, ready to shove off the minute they were all aboard.

It was going fairly well until Beryl and all her slaves surged onto the sand. "No, no, no! You fool! Don't you realize that he'll never be able to see you again?" She stopped suddenly, her eyes locking on Sam, and her voice became less strident, more cajoling. "He can't exist without access to the crystal now, Jesse. If you take him away, he'll die. Now please ... stop this nonsense and come back with me now." She smiled and reached out. "All will be forgiven."

Behind her, the slaves waited; those at their mistress's side swaying in place as others joined their ranks at the rear. Their numbers were growing by the minute, and Jesse had no doubt that they would soon reach critical mass and simply attack. Sam stood watching, his feet planted, a glint in his eye. But when the crystal's cold mistress raised her hand to signal for an advance, he leapt straight at her, blasting a series of barks and howls that made the hair on the back of Jesse's neck stand straight up. Instantly, the slave ranks disintegrated into a milling mass as the slaves' service to the crystal ran hard against their instincts of self-preservation.

"Idiots! Keep that thing away from me! He can't be here!" In a rage

Beryl turned on her slaves, screaming, "You imbeciles, kill the beast! Hurry!"

Joey was physically cut off from the other slaves, but still moved by Beryl's orders which resounded through the slaves' collective consciousness. Obviously afraid of Sam, but feeling the need to carry out Beryl's order, he lunged toward the raft to grab one of the paddles, the nearest thing to a weapon he could find.

"Sam!" Jesse yelled. "Get Joey! Push him onto the raft!"

Sam spun away from Beryl and her army and ran full tilt at Joey, struck him sharply between the shoulders in a powerful leap, and knocked him forward. His head thumped hard, knocking him unconscious, and his body landed, half on, half off the logs. Again, Beryl motioned for her slaves to advance. Wheeling about and leaping back to the shore, Sam recommenced his snarling and barking, ready to fight if necessary, to give Jesse time to escape, but Jesse was already pushing hard, and the raft quickly moved into deeper water.

Jesse didn't even look back until after he'd given one final push as his feet left the bottom. He bellied onto the raft beside Joey, kicking madly. As he turned his head, he saw Sam, still holding the masses at bay. At his whistle, Sam spun once more, splashing into the water, then paddling hard for the raft.

By the time Sam had clawed his way on board, the mist had closed around them, dense and cold. Sam relaxed his guard long enough to sniff at Joey's face, licking and whining, but there was no response. He grabbed the back of his shirt with his teeth, trying to pull Joey's lower half up onto the raft, but didn't have the weight or strength to manage it.

Seeing Sam's struggles, Jesse slid over to help. He rolled Joey to his side, then lifted first one leg, then the other out of the water, before heaving himself up and on.

They lay there, flanking Joey's unconscious body, just breathing. After a while, the cold began seeping in, and Jesse knew it was time to get under way, even if they weren't sure of their direction. He hoped that if Sam had found his way to them, he would also find his way back.

"Okay, Sam. We've got to get back to Angela and Mike. Can you show me the way?" He didn't know what to expect, and hoped that Sam wouldn't just jump off and paddle away into the mist, leaving them behind. Instead, Sam, with a final lick on Joey's cheek, walked to the side of the raft and looking intently into the mist, barked once.

"That way?" Jesse picked up a paddle and began moving the raft forward in the direction Sam was standing. A few minutes later, Sam moved to the left and barked again, looking intently at Jesse, who smiled and asked, "Course correction?" Sam's happy bark was confirmation that they had a system. Now, it was a matter of paddle and pray.

It might have been minutes. It felt like hours, days, even weeks, but then Jesse allowed himself to believe that it wasn't his imagination; the mist was really thinner, and he was beginning to feel the sun's warmth once more. He was near exhaustion and so was Sam. They paddled on, the raft moving slowly through the water. Suddenly, Joey groaned and started to roll over.

"Don't move, Joey! Hang on, and I hope to hell you can hear me!" *Dear God, please help him wake up. And please let his brain function like it's supposed to.* Sam adjusted his direction once more and barked once, then, sniffing the air, began barking non-stop. Jesse, having felt so alone, suddenly was aware that he could feel his cousins with him. "Mike! Angie! Where are you?"

At their campsite, Angela froze for a second before calling to Mike. "Did you hear something? I could swear I heard Sam. Listen."

"Yeah ... Oh yeah! And I hear Jess, too! Hey guys, we're here! Look!

I think I can see them. We're here, Jess! Welcome home!" And they ran toward the water.

Sam leapt off and paddled quickly to shore, not even bothering to shake before jumping all over Angela, who wrapped her arms around him, happy tears in her eyes. Mike jumped into the water and dragged the raft onto shore. He was elated to see them, but worried to see that Joey was non-responsive.

Before he could ask, Jesse spoke. "Man, it's so great to see you. We've got to pool our energies quick and see if we can get through to Joey. Long story. I'll tell you later."

Before they had a chance to move Joey, Angela ran over with Sam at her heels. "What's the matter with Joey? Is he all right?" And hopping onto the raft, she sat and lifted his head into her lap, immediately beginning to stroke and send healing energy to the large bruise on it.

"I'm hoping he will be. Some stuff happened ... " Not wanting to get into the serious matter of the crystal and Joey's contact with it, Jesse tried to lighten the mood. "And it probably doesn't help that we haven't eaten since we left, and you know how Joey gets when he misses a meal—let alone two!"

Angela stared at him. "Two? Misses two meals? Jess, you've been gone nearly two weeks. We've been terrified. We wondered if we'd ever see you again. We thought about going home, getting the family to come and help us look for you, but well, we just couldn't seem to leave without you. We didn't know what else to do, so we finally sent Sam to find you." Her tears, held inside for so long, spilled over and dripped onto Joey's face.

"Two weeks! That's impossible. But ... " He broke off, noticing Joey's eyes blinking open. "Joey? Joey! Hey Joey!"

As his cousins crowded in, Joey cautiously sat up. He hissed as his fingers found the source of his pain to be the huge lump on his head.

Then, looking around at his cousins and Sam, he smiled weakly.

"Hey Jess, did you finally go for a swim?" He paused. "Wow! You guys would not *believe* the weird dream I had."

Chapter Thirty

"Mom! Dad! I'm home! Grandma! Grandpa! Where are you all?" Angela and Sam stood in the sunny kitchen of Wind Dancer Ranch, breathing in the familiar smells, then listening as feet thundered down the stairs.

Julie got there first, grabbing Angela up in a big hug and spinning her around before setting her down, clutching her even closer to rock her back and forth. That's when Dave arrived, wrapped his arms around them both and rocked on with them. Sam sat at a safe distance and observed the goings-on with a look of coyote inscrutability.

Suddenly breaking out of their contented reverie, both grandparents took a step back and began peppering their prodigal granddaughter with exclamations and questions.

"Angela!"

"Where have you been?

"Thank God!"

"We've been so worried! None of us could get a reading on any of you."

"Is everyone all right?"

"Where are the boys?"

"What happened?"

Angela laughed. "Slow down, you two! We're all okay. The guys went home to check in. It was—wow! Well, let's just say it was an interesting and challenging journey. I'll tell you everything when we're all together, but it's a long story."

Julie sighed, resigned to waiting for the details. "Okay, honey. We're just so glad you're home safe and sound. So go let your folks know! They're in their bedroom doing some timing. We think she's in—"

"Labor! Oh m'God, she's in labor! Thank you, thank you, thank you! I got back in time!" She raced down the hall, skidding to a stop, then tapped quietly on her parents' door before turning the knob and disappearing inside.

Julie and Dave heard Jeannie's scream and concluded that this one was not the result of labor pain. "Angie! It's about freaking time you got back here!"

Angela sat carefully on the bed with her parents, sharing hugs and kisses and patting Jeannie's huge, taut belly. Relief from all parties was palpable. Sam came to sit beside the bed, his head on Jerry's knee in a show of male support, his eyes on Jeannie and Angela.

Julie and Dave watched the happy reunion from the door and listened, smiling, as Angela's parents continued where they'd left off, bombarding Angela with questions.

"So tell us all about it, sweetie. Why were you gone so long?"

"I was afraid this baby wouldn't wait for you."

"Are you okay? Is everyone?"

And just then, Jeannie's whole demeanor changed. "Oh ... oh ... wait a minute ... here comes another one." Like a well-oiled machine, Jeannie's team swung into action. Jerry started the stop watch with one hand, held Jeannie's with the other. Angie moved behind her mother to support her back, while Sam crept forward to gently nudge Jeannie's arm until she looked down at him. She smiled as he began panting rhythmically. And obediently, she followed suit. Everyone watched as her abdomen tightened in concert with the hand locked onto Jerry's, which squeezed until his bones all but rubbed together. The seconds ticked by. By the time the contraction wound down, they were all panting together.

"Breathe, baby, breathe. It'll be over in a minute. They're getting closer and stronger. It's okay, baby, we're all here. Visualize turning down the pain dial ... that's it. Good. Good girl. You're doing fine."

"Ohhh, I hate the word 'fine!' 'Fine' is an over-used and meaningless term, and believe me, 'fine' has very little to do with this stage of birthing!" But she slowly relaxed and smiled back at her daughter. "Okay. It's almost gone. Whew! That was a good one. Now, young lady, talk, and talk fast."

And between her mother's contractions, Angela did. She gave a shortened version of what had happened at the lake, left out a lot of details entirely—especially the part about how scared she'd been—but managed to hit all the highlights before Jeannie turned the corner from full transition and headed down the homestretch to pushing contractions.

"And so, everything turned out just great, and here I am. I'm so proud of the boys, and of Sam. And of me, too," she smiled, wrapping it up.

Jerry rose slightly to lean forward and place a gentle kiss on his daughter's forehead. "And we're proud of you, too, Angie. You're amazing. You and the cousins are all amazing, but especially you! And your timing is impeccable."

He looked back at Julie with a question and just a touch of panic in his eyes. Seeing both, Julie moved closer to lay a hand on Jeannie's belly. "I don't think it'll be too long now, boys and girls. Angie, you go quickly and get *really* cleaned up. Dave, how about boiling that water? And Jerry, just keep her breathing the way I taught you. Sam's not cleared for pant-blow!" Smiling, she moved to lift the covers and said, "Let's check under the hood—so to speak."

Moments later, she looked up, beaming. "You know, I bet we'll have another baby in the house within an hour!"

* * *

"OK, sweetie, big breath in, hold it and push to ten, then let it out slowly. Big breath! One, two, three, four, five, six, seven, eight, nine, ten. And let it out slowly! A couple more like that and this baby will be here. Cleansing breath ... good. That's good." Julie looked around the room, assuring herself that everything was in place for her newest grandchild. The room was warm, the light, not dim but lowered a bit to be gentle on new eyes. Music played softly. Jeannie's breaths sped up as another contraction began. "One more time, love! Big breath in and one, two ..."

Dave moved in to wipe his daughter's face with a cool cloth. Angela sat behind her mother, propping her up in the bed; a better position for pushing. Jerry held Jeannie's hand, whispering encouragement, clamps and scissors at the ready on a small table beside him.

When they all joined Jeannie in her cleansing breath—even Sam—Angela started giggling and it quickly spread. The laughter was just what they needed to relax, minds and muscles alike.

Julie knew the next push could be "for all the marbles," so she rubbed her hands briskly on Jeannie's knees and looked her in the eye. "Okay, Momma, when you push this time, you listen to me. Once we have the head, I may need to turn the baby a bit in order to get the shoulders out without tearing you, so I'll say, "Blow!" if I need you to stop pushing. It'll just be for a second, all right?"

"Yeah. Let's do it." Jeannie's voice was hoarse, but strong.

Julie's voice was quiet, but forceful. "Here it comes, honey. Big breath. Hold it and count. One, two ... and here it comes—don't push now, Jeannie. Just blow for one second ... " Julie quickly turned the tiny shoulders and the baby slid into her hands. She gently rotated the child up and over Jeannie's pubic bone to lay it on her abdomen, making sure the mouth was clear and the head turned to allow the mucus to drain.

Gently massaging its small and perfect back, she noted that the umbilical cord was still pulsing.

After a minute of silence, Angela spoke. "Grandma, I was so intent on Mom, I didn't notice. What do we have?" And with that, the spell was broken. With a laugh, Julie's activity began again. She smiled at Angela. "Sweetie, you have a new brother." She carefully cleaned his tiny nose as he pulled in his first breath, then registered his objection to the change from embryonic fluid to air with a lusty wail.

Julie clamped the cord and Jerry stepped in to cut it, looking brave and only a little green. Jeannie had taken over on the baby's massage and, covering her son with the soft blanket, soon moved him up to lay on her breast, gently rubbing his cheek with her nipple. Without hesitation, his mouth opened and he latched on, eagerly exploring this new connection to the comfort of his mother.

As she nursed, the afterbirth was quickly delivered, and Julie wrapped it in another cloth. It would be used to nourish a new tree they would plant in honor of the baby. "Everything looks perfect," she said with a sigh of relief which Dave echoed. "We're going to clean up a bit and make some tea and something light to eat. You guys take the time to get acquainted."

Jerry helped Angela extract herself from behind her mom, and they laid Jeannie back, after adding an extra pillow and fluffing them. Tenderly wiping the damp hair off Jeannie's face, Jerry kissed his wife, saying, "Thank you, sweetheart. What can we get for you?" And suddenly, as if it had just occurred to him, he exclaimed, "I can't believe this is happening after all these years. We have a son!" Straightening, he put his arm around Angela and pulled her close. "And you have a brother!"

"And I have a baby brother! Oh, Mom, you did so great!" she added with a little sob as she jumped up and down.

"I did, didn't I?" Jeannie basked in the glow as her new and perfect son suckled, and as her daughter and husband smiled down at her. Sam looked over the foot of the bed, assuring that all was well.

The new family slept, all together; Angela and Sam sharing the daybed, Jerry and Jeannie with their son safe between them.

Julie sipped a glass of wine as she and Dave watched the new moon rise in a sky peppered with stars. Occasional shooting stars swept across, sparkling tails quickly fading. The Milky Way cut its broad, smoky path through the constellations, and the Pleiades shone, vivid against the black.

"Joshua. Not Grayson or Walter or Kent or Clark or Jimmy or Perry or even Superman! I have to admit, I didn't see that one coming." Julie was thoroughly amused that once the baby had arrived, he simply didn't fit any of the previously discussed name choices and had sort of ... picked his own.

"Remember last night, Dave, when I shook you awake to tell you about my dream?"

"How could I forget? It took me awhile to settle you down, and by the time I did, *I* was wide awake," he smiled as he remembered.

"Sorry about that. But honey, I'm sure it wasn't a dream. It was a vision—an incredible vision! There was a huge star against a sky like this one. Normal stars in the background. But this one star was just enormous with these spikes of light shooting out of it. I know it was a sign. I didn't understand last night, but now, I know it was a sign."

"So are you going to share your wisdom and insight with me, babe, or just drive me crazy with the possibilities?" He affectionately brought her hand to his lips, biting gently at her knuckle.

Julie smiled, but spoke with reverence. "Spirit was telling me—us—that Baby Joshua is a star child! One of those delightful psychic children who arrives without any karma. No past lives, no baggage. A clean slate. They live in joy. It's hard to explain, but I feel this—deep in my soul. He's going to bring so much happiness to all of us, Dave ... and to the world."

A tear glistened on her cheek and Dave kissed it away, drawing her closer. She snuggled in, resting her head on his shoulder.

"We're some lucky family, aren't we?" he whispered.

Chapter Thirty-one

News of Joshua's birth spread quickly, and family members arrived to meet the new baby and congratulate his happy parents and ecstatic big sister.

In San Francisco, Sara debated whether she and Scott should make the trip to Wind Dancer or wait for Jon, who was on assignment back in the Third and out of touch—and had been for a very long time.

The number of children at Sara's boarding school—she preferred to think of it simply as "home"—was dwindling in the best of ways; parents making their transitions from the Third to the Fifth, and joyfully appearing to reclaim their children. Sara was proud to know that a large percentage of these happy reunions had been facilitated by Jon, Chris and Ellen. And while that knowledge made it easier to accept her husband's absence, there were still times when she struggled with her own growing need to have him close. Jon's capacity for love, and his willingness to share it, was what attracted her in the first place, so Sara's logical side fully supported his devotion to his work. But logic, understanding and pride aside, her emotional side ached for his return.

Her life was full—with Scott and all "her" kids at school, it could hardly be otherwise—but this trip had kept her husband away far too long. Despite her positive outlook and her trust that all would be well, a niggling seed of fear was threatening to sprout. She was putting the kitchen to rights after lunch when the screen door slammed, and Scott came barreling around the corner and ran headlong into her.

"Easy does it, you! What's the big hurry?" she laughed.

"Mom, I just had a really weird thing happen in my head!"

Well aware of her son's amazing psychic abilities, Sara's heart bumped. "Can you tell me about it, Scott?"

"It was about Dad! And a girl! She had curly red hair and a funny dress on, and she was laughing, like she was really happy. And he was hugging her! She was really pretty."

Sara swallowed hard. She trusted her husband. Of course she did. But he *had* been gone a long time. With an effort, she brought her attention back on her son as he continued, "She looked about my age, maybe a little smaller." Relief washed over Sara like a cool rain as she thought to herself, *Idiot! You know better!*

"There were other kids around him, too, but I couldn't see them as well as the little red-headed girl."

Sara sank down on a kitchen chair and pulled Scott onto her lap. Still inwardly reprimanding herself for *almost* jumping to a ridiculous conclusion, she said, "You know Dad visits hospitals on the other side, sweetie. I bet that's where he was in your vision."

"Yeah, 'cause I saw the beds 'n' stuff. And, you know, the scary stuff—machines and tubes and trays. And needles! And he had a hairy face, Mom, and he looked pretty tired," said Scott, remembering.

"But then all of a sudden, it was like Dad was ... I dunno ... like he was really *talking* to me. And ... and—let me think—he said something like 'I hope it'll be okay with you, and I really hope Mom will understand.' What do you think that means, Mom?"

Before Sara could answer, Scott's eyes grew wide and filled with tears. His voice trembled as he whispered, "You don't think he's gonna stay there, do you?" And once that ugly snowball started rolling downhill, it quickly gathered both mass and speed. Scott's tears overflowed, spilled down his cheeks as his voice rose. "Maybe he can't get back here! Maybe he needs help! Maybe—"

"No, Scott." Sara put a finger on the small, quivering mouth to staunch the flow of maybes, and wrapped him in her arms to stem the tears. The closeness reassured them both.

"Jon will be back, Scott, and soon. I feel it in my bones. In my heart. Now, more than ever."

"You're right, Mom. I guess I was being silly." Sniffing a bit and wiping at his tears, Scott gave her a wobbly smile. "I feel it in my heart, too!" Then, with the utter seriousness only an 8-year-old on a quest for knowledge can manage, he asked, "But how can your bones feel anything except if they break?"

"Oh, sweet, sweet boy o'mine! You are *so* serious ... and *so* literal! It's just a saying. Now, let's find something good and productive to do on this very nice day. How about you pick up a big bunch of kindling so when Dad gets back we can have a fire in the fireplace and toast marshmallows?"

"Sure thing, Mom! Hey, I think my bones feel like he's coming back, too! I'll bring back *lots* of sticks and we'll have a big, *big* fire!" And he galloped off, screen door banging behind him.

Sara sat for a minute, smiling at the warmth she felt. She wasn't as telepathically adept as Scott, but through him, Jon had been brought so close she could all but feel his arms around her. Yes, he was coming home. Soon.

A perfect fall day at Wind Dancer meant aspens shimmering in varied shades of gold, and Julie reveling in the sweet, rich smell of the greenhouse. *Amazing, the amount of food this little plot produces for us, year 'round!* And what they didn't eat was shared with neighbors and friends.

Dave was feeding the barn animals, enjoying all the scents—horses, goats, chickens, hay, grain, bedding. Orion greeted him as always, gentle lips snapping up the proffered carrot followed by the look that asked. "Now can we go for a good, long run?"

"Not right now, partner. How about tomorrow? Maybe we can get Misty out, too. Give her a little time off from the baby." He looked over into the big box stall beside Orion's to see Misty's foal enjoying a snack from mom, and chuckled when Orion blew, then shook his head, as if to say, "Well, Dave, if that's the best we can do."

Angela came looking for the nanny goat, bucket and milking stool in hand. "Hi Grandpa. Okay if I do this now?"

"More than okay, kiddo. It sure is nice to have the help around here."

"And I sure am glad to *be* here to help!" she laughed.

Dave watched her stride off, so relieved to have her back, so proud of who she was and who she was becoming. But in the back of his mind lay just a twinge of grandparental worry. The time was soon coming when the lessons the grandkids had learned would be put to the test.

Julie's psychic antennae were tingling. She was sure that Chris and Ellen would return soon with another transition group. She was "seeing" a crowd of people holding hands, singing, with a lovely glow surrounding them. Yes, this group was ready to transition, either accompanied by loved ones, or ready to reconnect in this dimension.

Some of the orphanages, temporary homes and schools would soon be out of business—maybe even Sara's. Julie wondered what her lovely daughter-in-law would do next, and hoped that the possibilities included making more grandchildren.

She went into the kitchen to check on her simmering vegetable stew and the sweet, whole-grain bread baking in the oven, before putting together a fresh green salad. Yes, all was right with the world.

As Dave was coming up the steps onto the deck, he heard his son's voice in his head—faint, but unmistakable.

"Dad, we're on our way. See you soon."

He burst through the kitchen door with a grin that stretched from ear to ear. "Better put another jar of tomatoes in that stew, babe! We've got company coming!"

Chris and Ellen's stories from the Third were uplifting, even if they were scary. Their gatherings were much larger now, and spreading to more locations. Ellen described the thrill of seeing whole families in the Third disappear before their eyes, and of the amazing light which could be seen shimmering before, during and even after transitions.

"We just had to come share with you before we even thought of going home," said Ellen.

"And you knew you'd have to answer to me if you didn't!" Dave joked. "We're so proud of you both. Just think of the joy you guys have brought to so many people!"

Chris received his dad's praise in his usual self-effacing manner. "Thanks, Dad. It really does keep getting better and better. Did I mention that this time, we literally ran into Jon? He was flying low! Stopped long enough to say he was on a mission and would explain when he saw us again, and zoom! Gone! He's been in the Third so long, he's actually got quite a beard going. Sara and Scott are our next stop. We'll swing by. Let them know he's okay, just very busy doing something he obviously considers to be terribly important."

Ellen, her arms full of Baby Joshua, rocked happily and added, "But we *had* to come meet this big guy before we did anything else! Oh, and catch up with you guys, of course!" Josh gurgled happily and she leaned down to sniff in his neck. "Makes me want a baby, too."

"Uh-oh..."

"Relax, Chris." She patted his hand reassuringly, then spoke to the others. "We've agreed that it's not the right time. And when it *is,* we've decided to adopt. There are so many kids who need homes. But enough about us! Angela, I want to hear all about your latest adventures with the cousins."

Fire crackled on the hearth, candles burned on the mantle, and love glowed in their hearts as the family talked and laughed together. From her favorite spot on the couch between her mother and grandmother, Angela shared her adventures from the Fifth Dimension with two of the family's adventurers to the Third.

There were, it seemed, always chances to take, choices to make, and love to guide and protect.

Chapter Thirty-two

It was a long-shot. Jon knew it and it made no difference. He still had to try. First, he'd made sure his kids at the hospital were in Nurse Amy's capable hands. His peace of mind required that little Mandy, with her red curls and dimpled grin, be cared for, no matter what happened.

He'd wondered at first, if his close bond with this particular child, out of the thousands he'd helped over the years, stemmed from her resemblance to sweet little red-headed Colleen. It had taken only one short conversation with Mandy for Jon to realize that she was an angel in her own right, and that looks had little to do with the bright light beaming out of her.

The plan, every minute detail of it, was worked out and stored in his head, and thanks to Angela and Jerry, he even had an adequate map to take him where he needed to go. He'd run a fair distance already, but his energy level was still high, nearly as high as it was in the Fifth. He wondered if his stamina might be getting an extra little boost from Gabriel or Ekor—communications with Ekor always gave Jon a lift—or if the wings on his feet were a result of the urgency he felt in each and every fiber of his being. Whatever it came from, he'd take it.

There had been times during his previous visits to the Third Dimension, when Jon had faced an adversary feeling nearly ... invisible. Yes, *invisible*, like a moving shadow; capable of magic and miracles. He prayed for that invisibility now as the miles rolled by, and the rhythm of his feet striking the pavement became his meditation.

In that higher state, he thought of home; his family at Wind Dancer,

Sara and Scott at their house by the shore, walking in the sun, playing on the beach, watching Ekor flip and fly and dive. *God, I miss them! I know Sara and Scott are all right. Probably lonely. God knows, I am, too. No, no. Nothing negative. Just run. I can do this. Yes, I can, I know I can.* The corners of Jon's mouth twitched up as he remembered Julie reading to him when he was a small boy. *What was that book? Oh yeah, "The Little Engine That Could." I think I can, I think I can, I know I can! You can do anything if you have the intention and the belief, the belief that you can. Yes! This is going to work. This is working. I will find them. No, Jon! Get with the program! Believe it like it's already happened! I am finding them. I have found them! OK, so that's a stretch. Go with it anyway! Yes! Walter and Emily, here I am!*

Emily and Walter had lived through tough times, both before and after the EarthShift. First Jerry, then Jerry and Angela, had kept them going, given them something to fight for and cause to stay put. Now, freed of those responsibilities and obligations, but sadly lacking in any kind of positive support, their living conditions had deteriorated so much that the couple was simply overpowered by their fears. They'd tried, again and again, to transition on their own, but their energies were just too low.

Their plan, if Jerry and Angela didn't return, had been to escape; to go far away from their dark, depressing basement. They weren't foolish enough to think they could simply "move to the country" after all that had happened, but they hoped to at least distance themselves from the dangerous military presence and reconnect with real people once more. But after Jerry and Angela had been gone for only a week, Walter had ventured out to find their little town surrounded; totally cut off from the rest of the world.

So their hopes were dashed. They had nowhere to go, no one to turn to. Even finding food was next to impossible, and as Emily said, more and more often, they weren't getting any younger either. No wonder it was so hard to frame the future in any kind of positive light!

Subsisting on the dwindling supplies Jerry and Angela had scrounged from abandoned homes and gardens, Walter and Emily still gave thanks every day. They'd come to think of the troubled, dark-eyed man and his spitfire of a daughter as family, and continued to reassure each other that Jerry and his Angie were still alive ... somewhere, and that they were together. Reassurances about other things weren't as easy.

"Em, I'm feeling really shaky today, like my insides are vibrating or something. It's a little scary. Do you feel okay?"

"Well, I wasn't going to say anything. Didn't want to frighten you. I think the energy's changed. It feels different, but I have no idea why. Do you think we're not eating enough? Maybe we just need more sunshine."

"Probably both. I don't know." Walter gave a tired sigh and held out his hand. "For now, why don't you just sit here next to me and hold my hand. It's about all we've got, and it still beats the alternative."

"Don't ever forget how much I love you, Walter."

"Me too, Em."

Jon rounded the corner and stopped short. *Oh, boy. Way too many trucks. Way too many hard-ass military types. And look at those guns. Crap! I've had it. This is it. It's over. Ekor! Help me, buddy!* Sinking down behind some bushes, he put his head in his hands, breathing hard.

But his head snapped up and his breath caught in his throat when he heard the familiar voice.

"Jon, my dear boy. Do you doubt my long-distance abilities? A little faith, please!"

"Holy cow! Ekor? Is that you, man? How'd you bust through all the

Third Dimension static?"

"When it comes to you, my friend, the connection is easily made. Even when you're high and dry in a miserable desert with crumbling houses, flirting with thoroughly nasty folks who would love to add you to their body count. I shouldn't mention what a lovely day it is here, or that I'm catching herring and enjoying the waves, eh?"

"No. Feel free to leave that part out. Listen, Ekor, I'm in trouble here. I think those 'thoroughly nasty folks' just saw me, and even if they haven't yet, they're searching this area so they will soon enough."

"Fear not, Jon, through the grace of God and the help of your angels, you are, as you've sometimes felt before, invisible. For the moment. It won't last forever, and that's likely a good thing as it could be disconcerting to folks along the way, especially considering how you, in your lighter moods, might be inclined to use such a power. But my suggestion is to make the most of it. Run along now. Run like the wind! Run like you've got a school of great whites on your tail! And Jon, you *are* getting close." And with that, Ekor was gone.

"Ekor, wait! Where do I go? Damn it. Why does he do that? Okay, Jon. Deep breath. I'm going ... right between the big trucks, right by the big mean guys with their big mean guns. Right through the freakin' line!" And Jon was off and running once more. He breezed between a pair of heavily armed soldiers, close enough to know they'd done without showers for more than a day or two. He had to smile when one turned to the other and said, "Whoa! What wazzat?" Jon hit his stride at the next corner and turned north. Ekor was right. He *was* getting closer. He could feel it.

He reassured himself as he ran on. *And we're clear! Wow! All right! Way to go, Ekor! But where the heck do I go now? Keep running. Just keep running and I'll wind up in the right place.*

* * *

Like the rest of the family at Wind Dancer had been, Sara and Scott were happy and excited to see Chris and Ellen. News of the baby, news of the cousins, news of Sam was shared with relish. But news of Jon—any news of Jon—was especially precious in the wake of Scott's visions. They all compared notes, concluding that if something was keeping Jon, it likely concerned a little red-haired girl. Still, Sara remembered Ekor's words and wondered if Jon's current lesson might not include a whole lot more.

Thanks to Chris and Ellen's work in the Third, Sara's school had experienced a sudden mass exodus of children the day before. As fulfilling and heart-warming as it had been to watch all those anxious parents arrive and reunite with their enlightened children, losing so many of "her" kids all at once left Sara a little shaken. And as delighted as she was for those families, the lighter work load was going to make waiting for Jon's return just that much harder. She was riding an emotional rollercoaster.

Sensing Sara's need for company and distraction, Chris and Ellen accepted the invitation to stay for dinner, then helped her prepare a light meal which they shared in the comfortable kitchen. When the dishes were done and the sun began to paint the sky with color, they all took a long walk on the beach. Ellen slipped her arm around Sara's waist as they turned for home, and Chris scooped up Scott and plopped him on his shoulders as the boy began to show the effects of the hour and the letdown after all the excitement. Back at Sara's porch, they shared hugs and kisses all around, and then Chris and Ellen were off for home.

Sara kept Scott company while he brushed his teeth and settled him into bed with his favorite stuffie, an oddly tufted dog which bore a startling resemblance to the coyote, Sam. "Sleep well, darling boy. I love you a bushel and a peck and a hug around the neck."

"You, too, Mom, tons and tons and a cinnamon bun! Do you think Dad will keep his beard when he gets home? If he does, maybe he'll feel like Sam." He was dreamily rubbing the toy's fur against his cheek as he spoke.

"He just might, but I hope he doesn't shed like Sam, or we'll have to brush his face every day." The idea had Scott giggling which was Sara's intent, and after a final kiss, she returned to the porch to ponder and settle.

Dropping down onto the porch swing, breathing in the moist evening air, she watched the sliver of a new moon rising, and thought of other evenings, just sitting here, sharing the quiet with Jon. She remembered his strong arms around her, the warmth of his body against hers, the heat and passion of his kisses. Drawing in a shaky breath, she held it, then blew it out trying to release some of her tension and nerves.

She'd been alone before, but being alone wasn't the same now that it meant being separated from Jon. Lord! This *alone* was a whole different animal.

She pulled up her feet and wrapped her arms around her legs, thinking that if Jon were here, she wouldn't be feeling the evening chill. There were times when he would simply melt her with a look, and times when their closeness ignited stronger needs; to mate, to join. As much as she'd loved Scott's father, the physicality of that relationship had never approached the heat she shared with Jon. Not that a relationship could or should be judged on sex alone—but it certainly didn't hurt. Now if she could only get him home for a while to enjoy it!

She knew Scott was missing him, too. She thought of Jon snuggled up with her precious son—their precious son—on the big, comfy couch in front of the fire; reading books, telling stories, listening as Scott shared his latest adventures with Ekor, or asked for an opinion on what a dream or vision might mean.

Bringing Jon's image clearly to mind, she surrounded him with light. "Come home soon, Jon. I'm missing you. We're missing you." With another deep breath, Sara rose and went in to finish her evening chores, keeping Jon close in spirit.

Jon had run a marathon—maybe two—when he recognized a street name from Angela's map. A right at the next corner, then a left, and it didn't take long to find the little house. *Man! This place has seen better days. I can't imagine anyone living in something so run down, and in the basement to boot. Maybe they're not there anymore. Maybe they've headed farther inland. Maybe they're in the Fifth somewhere. Okay ... so go on in and find out.*

There was no need to break the door because the lock was broken. The squeak, as it opened, was straight out of a horror show, and inside the kitchen a thick blanket of dust covered the table and counters. But the floor showed footprints. Jon headed toward the closet in the back room, aging floorboards creaking under his feet.

Below, Emily and Walter heard him and went cold with fear. Huddled in the darkest corner of the basement, Walter whispered reassurances to Emily. "It'll be okay. We're old. Why would anyone hurt us? And I won't let them hurt you, Emily. I love you with all my heart."

"I know. Hold me, Walter. Just hold me tight."

The trap door was exactly as Angela had described it, *except maybe heavier,* Jon thought as he propped it against the wall and leaned his head over the opening, calling softly. "Emily? Walter? Are you there? Please answer. I want to help you get out of here. I'm Jon, Angela's uncle. She's safe and so is Jerry. Please trust me."

He heard a faint sound but could see nothing in the unrelieved darkness. "I'm here because Angela and Jerry told me where to look. Angela even drew me a map. Please ... are you there? They told me to tell you that they love you and they need you. And I can tell you that my whole family would really like you to come home with me now so you'll be safe."

Jon heard the scratch of a match and saw a small flare of light that grew brighter as a candle moved across the room. As his eyes adjusted more, he saw them, looking so sick and pale and terrified, he wanted nothing more than to scoop them up and get them out. "It's okay. You're going to be okay. Can you see me?"

Emily found her voice first. "Are you really Jon? Angela's Jon?"

"Yes, ma'am. And I can assure you that Angela and Jerry are both safe and doing well at home. And that's what we all want you to be. May I come down?"

"Yes, yes, of course. Oh, I can't believe this is happening. Watch the ladder. Be careful. Oh, Jon, you are a sight for sore eyes." Emily's tears, held back for so long, flowed freely, as did Walter's and Jon's as they all shared hugs and handshakes.

Walter and Emily were so happy and relieved, they felt ten years younger. Jon, having reached his destination and found these dear people who had done so much for his family, was so encouraged he felt he could move mountains.

"I don't have time to explain much right now because this whole place is crawling with paramilitary goons. I know you're weak, but we've got to get out of here. I had a little invisibility thing working on the way in, but since you guys can see me, I don't know if that's still the case. We're going to need a small miracle and I'm hoping I have the strength for it. I'm sure going to try. Jerry and Angela told us that you're spiritually ready, but the trip out of here will be for 'all the marbles.' Are you up for it?"

Walter flipped his thumb toward the ladder and grinned. "Like we used to say in the '60s, son, let's rock and roll!"

Chapter Thirty-three

"Mom! It happened again! I just heard Dad's voice in my head. But it was sort of ... jumbled. He still has a hairy face, only now, it's dirty, too, I think!" Scott was nearly bouncing out of his sneakers.

"What did he say, Scott? Can you remember?"

"It's just words, Mom. I heard him say 'Help' and 'Ekor' and ..." His face fell as Scott realized the words he'd just put together. "Mom! We need to do something! I think Dad needs help!"

Trying to hang onto whatever calm she could muster, Sara struggled to find a positive outlook and not give in to abject fear about what might be happening to Jon. "We should go to Wind Dancer and talk to the family. See if they've tuned in to anything."

Scott considered for only a moment before shaking his head. "No, Mom. We need to call Ekor. Right now. Let's go out on the beach. He always comes when I call him, you know."

"Okay, sweetie. You're right. Come on! Let's move!" And taking Scott's hand, she bolted out the door and headed for the beach where, like magic, they found Ekor waiting, jumping and flipping, sending showers of spray skyward.

Sara didn't know where to start. She struggled to hold back her tears and keep her fears in check. Ekor would understand, but she really didn't want to scare Scott. The minute Ekor spoke, the matter was out of her hands.

"Sara, my dear, honest emotions don't have to be denied. Your feelings are absolutely valid and entirely understandable, even by someone as young as your son. He requires honesty, not protection."

Eyes glistening, Sara nodded and squeezed Scott's hand.

Ekor continued, "That's better. Now Scott, tell me what is happening with our Jon. You're missing your daddy, aren't you?"

"An awful lot. But we called you because I heard him in my head, you know? And I think he needs help because that's what he said. And then, he said your name." He trailed off, "We're just kinda scared because we don't know where he is or why he said 'help.' You can help him, can't you, Ekor?"

Ekor flipped himself upright to "walk" on his tail a bit and appeared to be thinking. "I expect you're intuitive enough, Scott, to know that I'm tuned in to Jon pretty much all the time." Scott nodded rapidly. "Yes? I thought so. And you know that there are also many, many angels around him. Of course, they're around you—all of you—as well. No matter where you are, all the time."

Scott still clutched his mother's hand and she, his. But watching Ekor, listening to Ekor's thoughts, and being reassured that their angels were hard at work, gave them a great deal of comfort.

Ekor continued, "And you're well aware, thanks to your mom and dad, that it's everyone's responsibility to learn their own lessons. Or sometimes, to manifest what might be necessary to achieve certain results which they desire. To 'get the job done' so to speak. Your dad has taken on such a responsibility, and is, right now, facing a personal challenge for a very good reason."

"But ... " Scott was struggling. Responsibility and lessons were fine, and he understood their importance. But if Jon needed help, Scott was ready to argue for more.

Smartly cutting off any debate, Ekor interrupted. "I have such faith in Jon and such faith in both of you; his abilities to help all those people in the Third Dimension. And such faith in both of you, your abilities to cope without having him here. Trusting. Keeping the faith."

Scott leaned into his Mom. "Okay, Ekor. It's just so hard sometimes. Sorry we bothered you."

"Me too, Ekor," said Sara, rubbing Scott's shoulder. "But I'm so grateful for the pep talk. Please watch over Jon."

"Jon is in good hands, Sara. Good spirits, too. And never feel sorry to be in touch. You always brighten my day. Speaking of that, it's such a beautiful one, it would be a shame to waste it. How about a little ride before I have to get back? Come on in, you two! The water, as they say, is fine!"

"Can we, Mom?"

"Absolutely!" With no regard for clothes, they splashed in and rode off over the waves. Three beings, connected by fate, faith and their love for Jon.

As brave as they were acting, Emily and Walter were terrified to *just let go* and trust in their ability to escape safely. It was a lot to ask, and Jon sensed the block they were setting up. He probably had a small one of his own, especially since his instincts told him that his shield—his invisibility—was gone. He didn't feel the presence of any other outside help either. *This might take a little longer than originally anticipated*, he thought, and he wrapped each arm around a thin pair of shoulders.

"Okay folks. Here's the deal ... " Jon paused as a clap of thunder shook the house and rattled the windows.

Walter jumped. "I think it's going to rain. That doesn't happen very often here. I'm afraid we don't have raincoats any more."

Jon laughed, grateful for the simple distraction. "You know, Walter, I don't think I'll melt and I bet you won't either. I wish we could just teleport out of here, but I'm thinking that we're going to have to do this the old-fashioned way and hoof it."

"Jon, it's been so long since we've had any exercise at all. I'm afraid we're just going to slow you down. You should go back. Tell Jerry and Angela we send our love and that we'll be along ... sometime." Emily's face reflected both disappointment and resignation.

Jon leaned over to kiss her forehead. "Emily, if you think for one minute I'm going to leave you guys here, then I'm going to have to lodge a serious complaint with Angela 'cause she obviously left out some of my best points. Now let's think about this. We're going to work with what we have. Do you two remember any place around here that's more sheltered? Less guarded? Some place where we have the best chance to avoid being seen?"

Silence.

"Take some deep breaths, and don't try to think about it. In fact, try *not* to think. Let things come into your mind on their own. If you get anything—image, sound, smell, whatever—just let it come." Jon suggested.

They stood, breathing deeply, eyes closed. Several minutes passed before Emily spoke.

"Walter, do you remember that place we found? Oh, it was so long ago. There was that big rock at the bottom of the hill where we used to sit and have picnics. It has a little view, not much, but there weren't any houses. It was just a wild area with big trees, not quite an official park, and there was a road that ran right through it and out into the country."

Walter blinked and smiled at her, a faraway look in his eyes. "You made the best fried chicken, Emily. And potato salad ... with dill. Sure I remember. I don't know, though. It's a ways away. Could be pretty dangerous just getting there."

"Walter, if Jon wants to try something, we can darn well take some chances and try it ... unless you really *like* being stuck here!" Emily's challenge was punctuated by a flash of lightning and sharp clap of thunder which made them all jump.

"No, Em. I don't want to stay here." He glanced at Jon. "If that's what you think we should do, we'll try it." They all looked up as the sound of rain grew from a hiss to a dull roar.

Jon cleared his throat. "We've got to pick the path and just go. This sounds like a good choice, and the rain may keep some of the patrols off the streets and out of our hair. It'll be wet and the lightning is dangerous, but I say we give it a shot. Are there things you need to take with you?"

"It's all just *things*. As long as we have each other, we'll be fine," Walter said, winking at his wife. She dropped her eyes, demure as a schoolgirl, and Jon had to laugh.

"Then let's all ask our angels to be with us and go find ourselves a nice picnic spot in the rain." He moved toward the ladder.

Jon led the way up and checked for intruders before helping Emily, then Walter, up and out. They replaced the trap door and moved carefully through the kitchen and out into the downpour. Through the backyard and into the next, Jon scouted ahead, moving slowly and cautiously. Block by block, they made their way through the neighborhoods, hair dripping, clothes clinging, cold seeping into flesh and bone. Only once did they see any sign of military presence. The glint of lightning off a gun barrel which protruded from a carport brought them to an abrupt halt. As they skirted the far side of the property, they could hear a number of male voices and determined that it was likely a small patrol taking shelter, waiting for the rain to let up.

But the storm showed no sign of letting up and, in fact, it intensified. Jon walked to the beat of his inner litany—*we are guided, we are safe*—and

Emily and Walter did an admiral job of maintaining their pace. The three reached a more rural area and trudged on; unfazed, unerringly determined.

At last, they reached the hill. Below sat the big rock; huge, wet, silhouetted like a primordial beast against the electrified sky.

"You weren't kidding about the 'big' part, were you? Good job," Jon told them. "You guys are troopers."

But the next flash of lightning had Walter grabbing Jon's arm and pointing. "Look, Jon. You see that big tree over there to the right? I think that's a tent behind it."

"What? Oh ... yeah, I see it now. Nobody around, though, from the look of it. How do you feel about this hillside? All this rain, it's going to be slippery as the dickens, and we won't have much cover."

"You know I'm worried about Em. But don't underestimate our spirit or gumption. You tell us what to do and we'll do it, both of us. Wherever you go, we're with you. But Jon, we haven't got much to lose, and you have so much. If it comes to leaving us behind, son, you just do it, okay? Just take good care of Angela and Jerry for us."

"Jeez Walter, I can sure understand why my family loves you guys so much. We're going to do this. Together." The lightning forked through the sky once more, and Jon squinted into the darkness. "Hey! Look over there. Is that a Jeep or a truck? To the left of the tent and a little behind it."

"I think it is. Emily, can you see it?" Years of living in the dark basement had proved to Walter that Emily really *could* see in the dark.

"It's a Jeep, one of those open ones. It's backed in there. Must be full of water now." Emily fought to keep her teeth from chattering.

"I say we appropriate it and hope we can get far away before the goon squad realizes it's gone." Jon knew that even as game as they were, neither Walter nor Emily would make it much farther by foot.

Feeling Emily starting to shiver beside him, Walter was ready for anything. "You bet! Em, take my hand. Jon, lead the way!"

Jon thought that current conditions warranted the term "Wrath of God," and as they began their slide down that final hill, thunder boomed, lightning cracked, and the rain simply liquefied the ground under their feet. They slipped, slid, fell, and finally reached the bottom where Jon gathered them close as they plotted their final move to the Jeep.

"Okay. This is it. We're going to run over to the left, then head back along the woods. Even with all the rain and thunder, we're going to have to be really quiet. You can see how close the Jeep is to that tent. Walter, if we can pull this off, do you know the way out of here? Is there a road, or should we go cross country? What's the best way to stay out of trouble?"

"If we can see it in this rain, the road should be about a hundred feet in front of the Jeep. If we turn left, it gets us away from this tent and takes us out into the country. There used to be a cow path that crossed it a ways up, but that might've grown over by now."

"We'll take our chances and hope. Okay. Once we start, no talking, no noise. When we get to the Jeep, I'll drive." *Please God, let there be a key in it,* Jon thought. "Walter, you help Emily up into the back, then get in beside me. It won't be a comfortable ride, but like my Great Aunt Rita used to say, 'It beats riding Shank's mare.'"

They stood, catching their breath another minute while the rain pelted down, feeling more like pebbles than raindrops.

"If the wind keeps blowing in this direction, the people in that tent won't even hear the sound of the engine. This storm is great cover." Walter grinned and added, "Gotta be nuts to come out in this weather."

Jon nodded in agreement. "Let's pray the roads are still holding together. You guys ready? Are you with me?"

All three clasped hands. Emily spoke the words they were all thinking. “God be with us.”

Jon gave his crew his biggest, most encouraging smile. “Head ’em up, Move ’em out!”

They moved carefully, slapped by wind-driven rain, blinking water out of their eyes, staying alert in case one of the residents of the tent should venture out. Leaving the shelter of the tree line, they closed in. The tent, aglow with lantern light, revealed the shadows of two men playing cards at a small table. As the would-be car thieves began their transit, one of the men stood, grabbed his rifle and headed out. Jon put out his arms, and Walter and Emily quickly dropped back into the shadows. Jon had no choice but to crouch where he stood, hardly daring to breath.

The tent flap almost hit Jon as two hundred and fifty pounds of military might strode forward. But when a fierce gust slapped him with rain, pine cones and a few not-so-small branches, the soldier executed a quick about-face and dove back inside, pulling the flap behind him. Jon struggled not to laugh as he heard, “The hell with that! Deal the god-damned cards. I’ll wait ’til it lets up or piss in a bottle, but no way I’m going out in this!”

After a deep breath, Jon motioned for Walter and Emily, and the three crept safely by the tent and rounded the Jeep. Emily struggled up into the back. Jon gave thanks that the key was in the ignition and signaled a thumbs up to Walter as the older man climbed in beside him. But when he turned the key, nothing happened. He tried again. Nothing.

He was beginning to panic when he glanced back at Emily, quietly sitting in the back seat, her hands clasped, her head bowed. *Trust*. The voice resounded in his head. Smiling, Jon turned the key a third time, and the resulting roar was music to his ears. Quickly shifting into first, he drove forward, looking for the turn, found it, and gunned the motor. Mud flew as the Jeep swiveled on the slick muddy road. He could barely see beyond the hood, but somehow, Walter kept pointing—first one way, then the other. There were potholes, huge axle-busting ones, but they bounced through them for a half mile without serious incident before Jon slammed on the brakes, skidding sideways.

"What the ... ? Walter, this looks like a dead end. Do you know where we are?" he shouted above the storm.

"Hang on. Let me take a look ahead! If anyone comes, you get Emily out of here." And with that, Walter swung out of the vehicle and jogged off into the low brush between two large trees. Jon reached back for Emily's hand and gave it a reassuring squeeze which she returned.

Before they could really start to worry, Walter sloshed back into view. "I think this is the cow path—or I should say it once was. The road continues up ahead, but it goes back toward town. I couldn't find a fence to stop us if we turn here, but God only knows if we can make it over that old trail. It would be hard to see on a good day, let alone in this."

Emily, struggled out of the back seat, gesturing for Walter to take her place as she moved into the front. "We can do this, Jon. We can do this right now. This rain will hide our tracks and keep the bad guys indoors. You keep praying and I'll keep pointing!"

"Atta girl, Emily! Show us the way to go home!"

Chapter Thirty-four

Even back in the Third, swimming with dolphins had been recognized as a healing, spiritual experience—often with a hefty price tag, but money was, after all, the root of so many problems in that dimension. In the Fifth, without the influences of commercialism and capitalism, cooperation between species had grown geometrically. Ekor's attachment to Jon and his family was living proof that things were, in fact, going *swimmingly*.

The ride with Ekor had been a godsend for Scott, now in a high state of glee at the prospect of regaling his friends with their adventures. In the way of small boys, once his anxieties were relieved, his appetite had been stimulated. Now, fed and bathed, he slept peacefully between clean, white sheets with an angelic smile on his handsome little face.

Not so his mother. Like Scott, Sara found her mood lifting and her cares floating away as they'd sailed the bay with Ekor. Back at home, she'd enjoyed making dinner—Scott's favorite pizza with fresh basil, mozzarella and tomatoes on homemade crust with just a grating of fresh parmesan on top—and the subsequent bathing, reading and sharing time. Like Scott, she'd dropped off to sleep the minute her head hit the pillow. But now, she was wide awake and seriously considering the possibility that she was losing her grip on reality, if not her mind.

Over an hour ago, she'd gasped awake with the uncomfortable sensation of being *overpowered* by water. Not drowned exactly, but close. She'd told herself that it was just a dream. She'd tried to go back to sleep, but managed only to dose, fitfully, waking again and again with the same sensation—water, extreme wetness, extreme discomfort; the feeling she'd never be warm and dry again. Finally, she tossed the covers aside, put on her robe, and after checking on Scott, walked the short distance to the beach.

Sitting, burrowing her feet into sand still warm from yesterday's sun, Sara wrapped her arms around her knees and breathed in the stillness. Listening to the gentle lapping of waves took her back to her wedding day; the beauty of it, her connection—physical, emotional and spiritual—with Jon, sharing his joy that his family was with them, and, of course, everyone's joy with Ekor's appearance and the message from Angela.

All those connections. Those messages sent and received over space and time and dimensions. Sara realized with a jolt, that all her feelings added up to something going on with her husband. She was sure of it. And hadn't Ekor said as much? Lessons? Responsibilities? Choices? Ekor hadn't actually said "Danger," but Sara was nobody's fool. Jon was in the Third. No one had to say it. Danger was a given.

Feeling the tension, she stretched, raising her arms toward the silver crescent rising over the trees. A few clouds were drifting, stars twinkled as they always had, and as she watched, the steady light of a space ship orbited slowly over the bay. Ah, the miraculous things one grew accustomed to in this new dimension.

She was still debating a visit to the rest of the family. They'd understand her concerns and share them. Why was she hesitating? Was it that Jon wasn't at her side? For so long, her life had been Scott and "her kids." And then, Jon had slipped into their lives, fitting like the last piece of a complex puzzle. To complete the picture, to complete her family.

By her marriage, Sara had linked up with another family—a number of other families—other puzzles, other pieces. And they'd accepted her, welcomed her and Scott with a warmth and openness she could hardly believe. Yes, the rest of the family was a pretty smooth fit, too.

So why was she hesitating? She really didn't know. What could she tell them? If these strange perceptions made no sense to her, how could she possibly explain them to anyone else? No. For now, she would wait, and pray, and keep her own council.

She closed her eyes, picturing Jon's handsome face; strong jaw, straight nose, those wonderful creases by his mouth when he smiled, his eyes—especially his eyes. Those clear, intensely blue, obsidian-sprinkled, twinkling eyes. How she missed that twinkle.

Her thoughts became a prayer, *Please keep him safe. Please bring him home to us. We love him so much. I love him so much.* She widened her scope, as she always did, asking blessings for "her" kids—the ones who were missing their parents and trying to cope in a new dimension—and for all those parents of *her* kids who were still stuck in the Third. *My kids ... Jon's kids. Strong bonds.*

For a few troubled minutes while the dark of night turned toward the light of dawn, she considered calling for Ekor again. He might not share details or give as firm a confirmation as she'd like, but he was always a comfort. In the end, she opted just to trust that all would be well, that her prayers would be answered.

She rose, brushing off the sand and turned toward home, smiling when she caught the flash of a dolphin's tail as it fractured the silver track of moonlight dividing the dark waters of the bay.

In the spirit of "misery loving company," Sara might have found it reassuring that the night's plague of sleeplessness was not limited to San Francisco.

At Wind Dancer, in the deepest part of night, Julie had been wide awake for some time. Beginning to be frustrated, she snuggled close to

Dave and whispered, "Honey? Are you awake?"

"Oh yeah. Sorry if I bothered you, babe."

"You didn't. I just can't sleep."

"And the problem is?"

"All I can say is *water.*"

"Interesting. Me, too."

"What do you think that means?"

"Not a clue. I'm not getting anything really earthshattering. Just sort of like ... an update? Does that make sense?"

"Exactly!" Julie was relieved that they were on the same page, and showed her relief by snuggling even closer.

Dave pulled her closer still, pressing warmth to warmth and stroking down her back as his lips found hers and nibbled, seduced. "And since we're both awake ..." His hands continued on their way, cupping her buttocks and adjusting her position so more of her body quickly awakened, and in awakening, expected ... needed ... craved.

Bright moonlight shone through the windows of the Children's Hospital in Los Angeles, the glow illuminating Mandy's angelic face as she knelt, resting her chin on her hands. She'd crept out of bed the minute Nurse Amy had finished the last check. Mandy's acute hearing picked up the other kids' soft breathing, an occasional cough or snore, beeps, calls for help, and the quiet footsteps of nurses as they answered those calls, traversing the corridors, doling out meds and warm blankets, taking temperatures, and sometimes—the times Mandy liked best—sharing a hug and a bit of time.

She sighed and whispered, "*La misma luna*. Nurse Amy says that means 'the same moon.' I'm calling you that 'cause I know you must be shining on my friend, Jon, too. He's a wonderful man. Please watch over him and make sure he's okay. I really want to see him again, even if ... " She smiled at the memory, "even if his beard does tickle. Please send him my love. And thank you for keeping me company tonight." She turned and quietly pulled her blanket and pillow off her bed, then curled up in the pool of moonlight on the floor.

Angela, awakened by her own disquieting dreams, had passed Joshua's room just as he finished his middle-of-the-night feeding. Arming herself with a burp cloth, she scooped him out of Jeannie's arms, and sent her sleepy mother back to bed. "Come with me, big guy. Let's have a little sib time." Now, she sat, pensively rocking, studying her brother's perfect features as the moonlight turned them to ivory.

She thought of Walter and Emily, as she often did. It seemed like forever since she'd come back from the Third, and no one had brought any word of them since. She wondered if they were still alive and feared that they might not be. *Why can't anyone find them?* Or if they might have transitioned and landed in some far off place. But she'd tried, time and again, to contact them telepathically, to no avail. *Will I ever find them again? Will I ever know for sure what's happened to them?*

Neither Angela nor anyone else in the family found it strange that the love she felt for Walter and Emily was comparable to what she felt for Julie and Dave. One set of grandparents connected by blood, the other, by heart. And though she didn't talk about it—didn't dare to think about it, really—part of her wanted desperately to go right back to the Third and seek them out. If only she didn't have so much to do here. So much to learn.

"And an adorable little brother to help take care of. Yes, I do." She bent to kiss the velvety head and breathe in the sweet smells of baby lotion and breast milk. Joshua cooed and nestled closer as the squeak of the rocker soothed them both.

Suddenly, feeling that click of connection and smelling just a hint of the peppermint gum Jon always carried, Angela knew that her uncle, still on assignment in the Third, was checking in. "Please, Uncle Jon," she whispered, "Wherever you are, come home soon and meet this little guy. He'll love you as much as I do. And if you happen to hear anything about Walter and Emily, I know you'll do what you can."

Angela might have been surprised that what Jon could do included barely avoiding some substantial trees, plowing through low bushes and slamming over an unexpected washout that dropped the Jeep with a bone-jarring thump as they careened along Walter's "cow path." As Emily peered into the rain and darkness, pointing the way, he sailed along, trying not to think about who or what was following them. Emily groaned now and then as her arthritis protested the rough ride, but she, like Walter, was "game."

They drove on until their bodies ached from the bumps and the cold, and their eyes ached from straining to see. But their hearts grew lighter with every mile. Jon slowly became aware that the light was changing. The storm was lifting. They were approaching dawn.

As the light increased and the rain dwindled, Jon swiped a hand through his hair and managed to slick off the worst of the wet that continued to run into his eyes. Beside him, Emily unpinned her long braid and wrung it out onto the floor before pinning it back in place. And then, bright sunlight broke through the clouds. Jon, shivering in its warmth, thought he could feel the steam rising off their bodies.

Walter glanced over his shoulder at the ominous black cloud behind them, still flashing with forks of lightning, and said, "Well, I'm not sorry to leave that behind us!" He earned an indulgent look from his wife and a belly laugh from his driver.

Minutes later, they all cheered as the Jeep burst through a last stand of trees, and they found themselves on an actual asphalt road. *Deteriorating, yes, but still, such an improvement. And,* Jon thought, *it's leading us away from the military and back toward the hospital and friends.*

For Emily, just being out in the fresh air and sunshine was enough to make her laugh with joy. When Walter grinned at her from the back seat, she knew she felt twenty years younger. In that heartbeat, they both felt sure that everything was going to be okay. They had no idea where Jon was taking them, nor did they need to. They'd taken a new hold on their faith with both hands and were ready to move whatever mountains needed moving.

The morning sun was warm on her face and she was having such nice dreams. Mandy tried to roll over and go back to sleep, but someone was shaking her arm, telling her to get up.

"How did you come to be here, young lady? Haven't we spoken before about the proper place for little girls to sleep? Never mind. It's time for breakfast now, so go get yourself cleaned up, then get back in your bed and wait for it."

Mandy yawned and rubbed her eyes, "Yes, Nurse Amy. The moon was just so beautiful last night. I was thinking that the same moon was watching over me as watches over ... well, all sorts of nice people, huh? Guess I fell asleep before I could get back in bed. I'm sorry."

The nurse's kind eyes crinkled. "If that's the worst you do, my love, we'll count ourselves lucky, eh? I think I know a little bit of what you're feel—" She broke off as the sound of sirens pierced the morning stillness and Mandy's eyes grew wide with fright.

"Those are sirens! That means the mean men with guns are coming, doesn't it? Are they going to take us away?" Her face paled even more and tears welled in the big frightened eyes.

Nurse Amy scooped her young charge up and plunked her in bed. "No, Mandy. I won't let them. And besides, the hospital is an off-limits place. We've been promised."

"But Nurse Amy, that's what my Dad said, that our town was safe, and the bad men had promised to not come there. But then they did. They came more and more, and they hurt people. They hurt my Mom and my Dad. Why did they do that?" Tears overflowed as the memories came flooding back.

How many more children will I see suffering from PTSD along with everything else they've suffered? Nurse Amy wondered. "Hush now, lovey. We want to get you well, isn't that right?" Mandy solemnly shook her head. "Well, in order to do that, we all need to think good positive thoughts, right? So for now, you just lay back in your nice safe bed, and I'm just going to quickly check and make sure everything is okay. That's my girl."

With a little sob, Mandy nodded. "Yes, ma'am. But will you come back and tell me if I should go hide from the men again? They scare me."

Jon could hear the sirens as though they were inside his head. Somehow, word had gotten back to the local militia that had obviously been watching for the Jeep. Praying he could outrun them, Jon wove through the city streets, low on gas and high on adrenaline. He hoped his passengers wouldn't get whiplash, and that the sputtering Jeep would make it. The familiar outline of the hospital loomed ahead. Not far now. "Come on, baby, you can do it!"

Then, a military truck pulled out of a side road, right into their path.

"Damn it! Hang on!" Jon yelled as he jerked the wheel hard right, sending the Jeep up over the curb, squeaking through the impossibly narrow slot between a mail box and an awning before he jerked it left and bounced back into the street on the far side of the truck.

As the Jeep sped the last two hundred yards toward the hospital, Jon heard tires squealing and sirens dying as several of their pursuers slammed squarely into the truck, leaving the bulk of the soldiers effectively cut off by their own moving barrier.

Sliding into the hospital turn-around, Jon slammed on the brakes, depositing the last of the Jeep's tire tread on the asphalt. Wasting no time, he jumped out and ran around to help Walter with Emily, "Come on, you guys, run! Into the building. Fast!"

With heavy boots pounding close on their heels, Jon fairly carried the aging couple forward and up the steps. He flung open the heavy glass doors, shoved Emily and Walter through, slipped in himself, then shoved back hard to close them. From the front desk, he heard a familiar voice say, "Welcome back, Jon" as the heavy locks engaged.

Thump! Thump! Two burly soldiers hit the glass and were repelled back. "Open this damned door! You can't do this! They stole our Jeep! Let us in! *Now!*" Now, there were soldiers pounding on the doors, first with fists, then with gun butts.

Jon, Emily and Walter watched in amusement as a lilting voice addressed the soldiers from the little box over their heads. "Hello. Welcome to Children's Hospital. May we help you?"

"Open this goddamned door, you idiot!"

"I beg your pardon. I can't seem to understand what you're saying. Could you repeat, please?"

"We want those assholes that just ran in there! Open the fuckin' door!"

"I'm so sorry, sir. You know we can't allow you inside. It's in the agreement. If that's all, then have a good day."

"Bitch! Come on, men. We'll find another way. The side's sealed tighter than a damn drum. Spread out. Set guards at all the doors. If we can't find an opening, one of us can pretend we got a kid there or something. We'll get 'em. I said, *spread out!*"

Jon watched the soldiers leave. The young woman behind the front desk was holding together, smiling, but shaking like a leaf. "I was really afraid they'd crash in the door." Wasting no time, she picked up a microphone, pushed a button, and sent out an alarm for all the doors and windows to be secured before she alerted the staff with the details of what was happening.

Damp, exhausted and out of breath, Jon and his merry band collapsed like shipwreck survivors into the large chairs in the lobby and concentrated on just breathing. Jon was praying hard that the hospital's security would hold, and that his actions wouldn't put the young patients in harm's way.

Nurse Amy walked through her locked-down ward, hugging and reassuring ten frightened children. Outwardly calm, she managed to quell their fears a bit, but she knew if she was honest about it, she herself was scared to death. The banging on the door nearly did her in.

"Amy! It's me, Jon, and I've got a couple friends with me. Please let us in. The soldiers aren't here." *For a while, I hope.*

Mandy scooted to the foot of her bed and leaned out to peer through the tiny window in the door. With a squeal, she jumped down and flew across the room.

"Mandy, wait! It might be a trick!"

But the nurse's warnings were too late. Mandy flipped the lock and turned the knob. As the door swung open, she leapt into Jon's arms, wrapping her little legs around his waist and her arms around his neck.

"You came back! I was so scared. I tried not to be, but ..." And then she simply dissolved, burying her face in his neck as sobs wracked her small body.

Jon stood, rocking, crooning. He held her tightly, cupping her head with his hand, and whispered, "I promised I'd be back, Sweet Mandy. Remember? I told you I'd come back for you."

When her tears subsided, he accepted the tissue offered by Nurse Amy—whose own eyes were none too dry—and wiped Mandy's face. Then, settling her on her pillows, he sat and made a big show of wringing out his shirt where her tears had added to the leftover dampness from the night's travel through the storm. All the other children, well used to Jon's clowning, laughed uproariously.

When the laughter quieted, Jon began. "Nurse Amy, boys and girls, I'd like to introduce you to two very special people. Their names are Emily and Walter, and they want to get to know all of you."

Emily and Walter were closely scrutinized for several seconds. The children observed the damp, ragged clothes, the windblown hair, the soggy shoes; then zeroed in on Walter and Emily's kind eyes and open smiles. Already wired from the excitement of sirens and possible break-ins, the kids spilled off their beds and ran forward to attach themselves to hands and knees, jockeying for position to get close to these grandparent-like folks.

Nurse Amy relocked the door, then turned, shook her finger at Jon and scowled. "And do you think, young man, that you can run off, scare us half to death, then come bursting back in with the military hot on your tail? And just because you bring us a couple nice visitors, all is forgiven?"

Jon, for all his beard and scruff and exhaustion, managed to look like a recalcitrant 8-year old as he cuddled Mandy, held her hand, and nuzzled her hair. As he'd known she would, Nurse Amy simply melted. Stepping close, she ruffled his hair before leaning down to drop a kiss on his brow.

"Well, you're right, you rogue." And she turned to beam at Walter and Emily who had now moved into some chairs and sat with children on each knee, surrounded by more, obviously wasting no time in getting acquainted.

Jon gathered his thoughts and prepared to lay out the facts of their next, even bigger challenge.

Chapter Thirty-five

Sara turned from the kitchen counter to put the eggs back in the fridge and nearly broke her neck when she tripped over Scott, who'd snuck up behind her. "Whoa! Scott! You scared me to death! What's up with you, kiddo? You've been in and out and 'round about, and mostly under my feet all day long. Feeling okay? What's going on?"

He shrugged, hitching a small shoulder in a perfect imitation of a Jon move which made her smile. "I dunno, Mom. I'm just kinda missing everybody. I always miss Dad, but I keep thinking about Grandma and Grandpa and all the rest of the family. 'Specially Angela. She makes me laugh, and she plays games with me and takes me on adventures." He heaved a big sigh.

"So I heard. I wonder ..."

"What, Mom? What do you wonder?" Sara was sure that Scott was already tuned in on her thoughts, so she dragged out the words as she turned back to her cookie dough.

"I wonder ..." Scott was fairly dancing out of his shoes as Sara turned back and scooped him up, smudging his nose with a floured finger. "I wonder if we could drag Angela away from little Joshua for a day or two. I'd enjoy her company, too!"

"Yeah! Mom, you're the best!" The thought of having another female around would be fun, and obviously would do the trick to perk up her son. "Tell you what. Let's finish baking these cookies off. Then we'll pack some up, find something to drink, and head down to the beach. We'll see if we can connect with Angela at Wind Dancer. What do you say?"

"Yes! Yes! I say yes! Can I help with the cookies? How long will they take? Can we turn up the oven to make 'em bake faster?"

Angela was sharing some quiet time with Julie on the deck. She'd practically memorized the book she was reading, but wasn't inspired to find another. She hadn't felt like riding or gardening. Swimming or fishing wasn't as much fun by yourself so she'd dismissed that, too. She was missing her cousins and wished that Jesse would plan another trip. *Somewhere by the water,* she thought, *just not a strange lake with mist and nasty blue ladies and crystals.*

"Angela!"

She jumped.

"I was beginning to think you were asleep with your eyes open!" Laughing, Julie reached over and patted her granddaughter's leg. "Sorry to startle you, Angie, but I have an idea. You've been doing a stellar job of tending to your mom and Joshua, but I was wondering if you might not enjoy a little break for a day or two. Babies do tend to sleep a lot of the time, and there are three more of us here to give your mom a hand when she needs it."

"Were you reading my mind again, Grandma? 'Cause I was just-thinking about the same thing."

"You were thinking pretty loudly, honey. It wasn't hard to catch the drift. Where do you want to go?"

"Well, I hadn't really decided on a place. But somewhere with water. I was even thinking about getting in touch with the guys and seeing if they wanted to hike by a lake." She noted her grandmother's raised eyebrow and look of disbelief. "Well, a different lake. But now that I think about it, I think maybe it would be a great time to go see Sara and Scott and all the kids."

Julie relaxed, "That beach is gorgeous, and it would be a wonderful change of scene for you."

"Maybe I could help Sara with a project or something. She's talked about wanting to get a greenhouse going. And Scott and I had a great time when he was here before. He's a neat kid. So smart." She closed her book with a snap. "And The Boxcar Children, Harry Potter and The Hardy Boys have got to be more interesting than this! Think they'd want company?"

Julie smiled. "If the company is you, I'm absolutely sure of it. See if you can tune in. If you need a boost, I'll give you a spiritual hand. Somehow, I don't think you will."

Angela relaxed, leaned back on the porch swing and closed her eyes. Breathing deeply, she centered herself, smiling when she caught the scent of chocolate chip cookies. As quickly as that, she was gone.

Mother and son sat cross-legged on the beach, eyes closed, breathing deeply. Beside them was a pretty basket packed with hot cookies, a cold bottle of fizzy water, and three cups with slices of lemon.

"Hey, Scott! Hi, Sara! One of those fizzy waters for me?"

"Angela!" Scott scrambled off the blanket, sand flying in all directions. "Did you hear me wishing you'd come and see us? Wow! Mom, we did it!" He grabbed Angela's hands and swung her around in a quick ring-around-the-rosy move as she laughed.

Sara felt her own spirits lift as she watched. "I expect Angela had something to do with it, too, Scott. Angie, I'm so glad you dropped in, so to speak. We both needed to see you. And here you are! I'll never understand how it works, but it does!" A tiny frisson of concern passed between Sara and Angela as they felt a ripple of other forces gathering. "We'll talk later, but maybe you two have things to do first?"

Scott was tuned in on Angela and only Angela. "Oh, yes! Yes, we do! Come on, Angie! What do you want to do first? Build castles? Have a race? Go for a swim?"

"Scotty-boy, castles can wait. I'll race you to the water 'cause I could sure use a swim."

"I'll beat you. I can run really fast!" And he sprinted off.

"You didn't wait for the count, you monkey! One, two, three, go!" And Angela sprinted off behind him.

Sara smiled as the two splashed into the blue water, and registered equal parts of relief and foreboding as the silver bullet of a dolphin broke the surface half a mile out. Yes, something was definitely in the wind.

It was difficult to think when alarms were sounding all over the hospital. Then the public address system crackled to life, "There has been a breach of security on Level One, East Entrance. Interior lock-down is in effect. Do not—I repeat—do *not* open any doors until the intruders have been removed."

"Damn," Jon muttered under his breath. "I'd hoped we'd have a little more time." All eyes were on him as he looked around the circle.

"Okay gang, we've talked about all this before." The children were holding hands and pressing in to get as close to each other as possible. Their eyes darted between Jon's face and the door. There were a few tears. The adults were doing their best to reassure them, but it was a struggle.

Emily and Walter had kids in their laps and at their sides, as did Jon whose lap was shared by Mandy and a small boy named Henry. "So, we're all going to stick together and think our very best, most positive thoughts. Good things. Like how much we love each other, and how much God loves us, and how many angels are watching us and helping us *all* the time. Nurse Amy, you sit right over there beside Walter."

"Jon, I hope you'll understand—you, too, kids—but I'm staying here. We have so many children in the hospital, and I'm needed here. I'll be okay, so you don't need to worry about me. I'll miss all of you, and I'll pray for your safe journey and great adventure!" She smiled, even as her eyes filled. "I know it'll be a wondrous thing."

Jon had to try one more time. "Are you sure, Amy? There's a lot you could do in the Fifth, too."

"I'm very sure, Jon. You might say, an angel whispered in my ear. Hey now, my darlings, no tears." And swallowing her own, she quickly made her way around the circle, hugging and kissing everyone—even Walter and Emily. "I'm going to sit on that chair over in the corner 'til you're gone, and I want each of you to concentrate really hard and do exactly as Jon says. Will you promise me?"

There was a chorus of "yeses" as Amy leaned down to press a final kiss to Jon's cheek. She whispered, "Please take care of them, my friend. I'll see you again someday. Now hurry. The lights in the hall are flashing."

Fighting down the panic in his gut and struggling to replace it with calm, Jon issued his instructions. "Squeeze in as close as you can, kids. Close your eyes and just breathe with me." He was reassured and moved to see each small, serious face now reflecting the serenity of deep meditation, in spite of the ruckus going on around them. "That's great. Perfect. Now comes the good part, we're going to picture in our minds ..."

"Hi, Ekor! Look! Angela came for a visit and we've been swimming!" Scott was jumping up and down and splashing. "Can we go for a ride?"

"Not right now, Scott. Right now, we all have something incredibly important to do."

Sara had watched Ekor's approach and waded into the water to stand with Scott and Angela. "Tell us what to do, Ekor."

"Good, we're going to jump-start some energies. Please come close to me and hold hands. Focus on Jon. Breathe deeply and concentrate. Keep all your thoughts positive. Bring him into your thoughts with love. See his smile. Feel his hugs."

And drawing in a deep breath of his own, Ekor submerged between them. His energies were always stronger under water.

Chapter Thirty-six

Nurse Amy had heard about transitioning. She'd studied it, believed in it, took comfort in the promise of it, and prayed one day to participate in it. But what she had just witnessed ... well, that was just a miracle!

Now that she was alone, she rose from her chair in the corner, shaking her head and smiling until the door crashed open and three big men in camouflage burst in.

"Where are they? Where are those miserable, thieving sons'a'bitches? You tell us right now and don't bother to lie! That little girl out in the hall told us they were in here!" Bad-tempered and smelly, the incensed soldier had invaded Nurse Amy's personal space and was screaming directly into her face.

Calmly, wiping the spittle off her nose, she gestured around the room. "As you can see ... *Sir*, I'm the only one here. And since I'm getting the room ready for sick children, you ... *gentlemen* will have to leave."

"Bullshit! Just bullshit, lady!" The man's color deepened to a disturbing shade of burgundy as he turned to bark out orders. "Wallace! Check that door over there. Jackson, look under the beds. Those car-stealing bastards are in here somewhere."

"Hell, Sarge, it's just a bathroom. Ain't nobody in there." Wallace was more willing than his commanding office to believe the pretty nurse and his own eyes. "The only person here's the nurse, just like she said."

Amy knew her knees were going to buckle if they didn't leave soon, so she added another verbal jab. "That's right, Mr. Wallace. Just me. And since I've work to do, I'll thank you to be on your way so I can do it."

Defeated, the Sergeant growled and turned to leave. "Come on, men. We'll just check *all* the rooms. We've had guards on all the exits, so we know the scum didn't get away. Let's go! I want every damn room searched!"

"Stand down and lower your weapons!" Amy heard the commotion in the corridor as the soldiers were greeted by another group of big men carrying weapons of their own. The heated argument over jurisdiction between the soldiers and city police was the icing on Amy's cake. As the voices rose, she went about stripping off the bed linens, whistling a very happy tune indeed.

Up to her chest in the Pacific, holding hands with Sara and Scott, and feeling Ekor against her thighs, Angela knew she'd seen this kind of light before. Even through closed lids, the flash was brilliant. Her eyes flew open and she began to splash toward the beach squealing, "Emily! Walter!"

Sara and Scott weren't sure what had happened, but knew they'd had a hand in it. The circle of people now sitting on the sand was obvious, but until Jon, seated on the far side, stood up, they thought it was strangers. For Scott, it was the grin.

"Dad!" he screamed as he pounded out of the water and up the beach.

For Sara, it was the eyes, brilliant blue and twinkling, locked on hers, even as he bent to scoop up their son.

Sara walked slowly up the beach, listening to the enthusiastic reunion between Walter, Emily and Angela. She stored the image of her son peppering Jon's cheek with kisses, and felt her heart swell when she saw the small face with bright blue eyes and a halo of bright red curls peering at her from behind his leg. Putting aside her own needs for the moment, she faced her husband and gently laid her fingertips on his cheek.

"Hello, Jon. Welcome home." Then, she dropped down onto her knees to touch the child's cheek and welcome her, too. She was rewarded with a shy smile.

"Hello, sweetie. We've been waiting for you."

Jon's relief was huge and instantaneous. He dropped back down to sit cross-legged on the sand, shifting Scott to one knee, and pulling Mandy around to plop her on the other.

"Hi, I'm Scott. I saw you in a vision. What's your name?"

"I'm Mandy. Do you live here?"

"Yup, with Mom and Dad ... um ... this guy ... Jon. We work at the school and swim in the ocean and sometimes we visit Grandma and Grandpa at Wind Dancer Ranch in Colorado. Would you like a cookie?"

Ever a mom, Sara picked up on that immediately. "Scott, how about if you take Mandy and the others over to school and get them some cereal or a sandwich *before* we start on the cookies? And then, show them the clothes cupboards and let them find something to wear, could you?" She turned to the rest of the children, still sitting in their circle, taking in their surroundings and watching the adults for clues about what to do next. "How about that, kids? Stick your feet in the ocean, then go get something to eat? Find some clothes that don't smell like a hospital? Sound good?"

Scott scrambled off Jon's lap and held out a hand for Mandy as the others got to their feet, brushing sand and trying to look everywhere at once.

Ekor burst up into the air to twist and somersault before landing with a resounding smack. A few smiles wavered a bit as the kids considered the wisdom of sticking their feet in an ocean which contained such an enormous, if handsome, beastie. For Scott, it was a chance to be a hero.

The prospect of introducing all these new friends to Ekor was thrilling. "Come on, Mandy! Come and meet our friend, Ekor!" And without a trace of hesitation, she ran with him toward the water followed by the nine other newcomers.

Angela, with Walter and Emily in tow, moved to follow. "We'll just go along and make sure they find everything. And don't eat all the chocolate chip cookies! We'll eventually be on the playground." And they left Jon and Sara by themselves.

Leaning together, their feet warmed by the sand, their faces warmed by the sun, they needed—and took—a minute just to settle; to actually grasp everything that had happened. Then, Jon turned to lay his face on Sara's hair before lifting her into his lap where he wrapped himself around her and held on for long minutes.

"My God, how I missed you, Sara. I love you so much."

"I was trying not to be scared, Jon, but I was. We couldn't reach you. Then Scott saw you in a vision, heard you talking, calling for help, and Ekor came, and told us you were on a mission and—"

"Shhh. There's so much to talk about, and we will. But right now ..." He rose with ease, still holding her in his arms. Sara thought that if they'd lived in the Antebellum South, the easy show of strength would certainly have given her "the vapors."

"Right now, what?" And opening her eyes, she instantly recognized the quick change of mood in his.

"Right now, I'm absolutely filthy. So ..." He bolted toward the water.

"Jon, no!" But she was laughing as he took them both under, and smiling when they surfaced to find Ekor walking on his tail and whistling.

The moonlight glistened on the water as Jon and Sara returned to the beach and sank down onto their blanket with a mutual sigh. Flat on her back, Sara's words were soft and slow. "Whew! This has been quite the day! Thank goodness everyone's settled in for the night."

"Amen to that!" agreed Jon.

"Emily and Walter are delightful. I'm so glad they've decided to stay on with the kids. They have so much to give."

"To all of us."

She rose on one elbow. "Can you imagine anything more different? To go from just the two of them all the time, to being around all these kids? And here with all this sun after that dark basement."

Jon turned to her and spoke with emotion. "It was *such* a horrible place, Sara, but they'd tried to make it a home." He paused. "They're anxious to see Jerry again and meet the rest of the family."

"And there'll be plenty of time for that once they catch their breath." Sara chuckled, "I should say 'if' they catch their breath. There are a couple live wires in this new bunch of kids."

Jon grinned, "You think? Thanks for finding clothes for them. Did you see the look on Emily's face when you found her the ribbons and barrettes for her hair? I'll bet it's been years since she had anything but rubber bands, and even those were in short supply. Can you imagine how it'll be for them to be warm and clean? To have a full belly? And I bet that soft, clean bed is going to feel *so* good to them!"

"Soft, clean and *dry*. I bet it'll feel like heaven." She rolled over on top of him, supporting herself on her elbows and studying his face; savoring the warmth of his body as she began to kiss his cheeks, his nose, his eyes. "Talk about feeling like heaven."

Jon quickly reversed positions and found her mouth with a groan. Oh, how he'd missed that mouth. When he raised his head, Sara reached up to pull him back, but shaking his head, he said, "I'm going to feel dishonest if I don't ask you this before any more time passes ... and I'll understand if you say 'no.' Okay?"

Now, Sara was worried. "Okay. But hurry up and ask. You're scaring me."

"The little red-headed girl ... Mandy?"

Sara smiled, "That would be the one who posed for Raphael's angels in a prior life? The one with the adoring blue eyes that find you the minute you come into a room?"

Jon nodded, toying with his wife's hair. "That's the one. Sara, she's had such an awful time. The militia killed both her parents while she was hiding upstairs in the attic. When she finally came down, she found their bodies. Her scars are so deep, but she's so ..." He searched for the proper word, but Sara found it first.

"Precious. She's precious."

"Yes. Exactly. The minute I met her, I felt like I'd known her, well, forever. And from what I can tell, it's a mutual thing."

"I'd have to be deaf, dumb and blind—and not have a clue about who you are—to have missed that, my love. So what's your question?"

Jon's body had tensed. Sara could feel his agitation growing and thought it was really very dear. Like a school boy asking for his first date—or Jon, during their own first tongue-tied meeting. He struggled to get the words out. "Well, um, I ... I thought ... I was wondering if we ..."

Sara took his face in her hands, holding him still so she could look directly into his eyes. "Jon, I think it would be a great idea for us to adopt Mandy. Would that be all right with you?"

He lowered his forehead to hers. "You knew all along."

"Yes. Scott was picking up on some very strong vibrations the last few days."

"And you're sure it's okay?"

"It's absolutely okay. In fact, it's absolutely wonderful! I thought I'd have to wait to have a daughter, and now, she's here! And such a sweetheart. Scott will be thrilled to death. Did you see how they latched onto each other this afternoon? Of course, we'll have to talk to him and make sure he has a say in how things play out. Does Mandy have any idea?"

"Not yet." He paused. "Hey! Maybe, if Scott is okay with everything, he could ask her. Think he'd like that?"

"I think he'd love that. It's perfect."

Jon grinned and his eyes sparkled. "Sara, are you absolutely sure?"

"Darling," she whispered. "If I were any more sure, there'd have to be three of me. Oh, Jon, I love you so darn much!" And this time when she pulled him down to her, she didn't let him go for a long, long time.

Scott's forkful of syrup-drenched griddle cakes hovered just short of his wide-open mouth. "What? You mean Mandy will be my for-really-real sister for ever and ever? We'll be a family?" His sticky lips curved into a delighted grin as he pushed back from the table to jump up and yell, "Oh boy!"

Sara and Jon exchanged smiles before Sara answered. "Yes, Scott, we'd all be family. We'd still be *almost like* family even if Mandy lived at the school, so if you're uncomfortable about any of this, it's okay to—"

Scott's hearing had turned off at "Yes." In his mind, it was a done deal, and he had a new little sister named Mandy. Uncharacteristically interrupting his mother, he shouted, "Hurray! Can we go tell her right now? Where's she gonna sleep? She should probably have a room of her own, right? Or she could stay in mine in case she's afraid of the dark. Wow! Can we take her to Wind Dancer and tell the guys? I can show her the horses and we can play with Sam and—"

"Wait! Slow down just a little!" Sara grabbed a napkin, dunked it in a water glass and went to work on the sticky mouth and hands. "Let's take a minute and make some plans. Just the three of us, for now."

"I think the room is a great place to start, Scott." Jon agreed. "Mandy's had a very rough time of it, and I'm sure that having a real home and a room all her own will mean a lot to her. Did you have some ideas?"

Managing to twist away from his mother's cleaning efforts, Scott bounced around the table. "I've got some sea shells I bet she'd like, and she can have all my stuffed animals except for Sam. And I've got lots of books and toys and art stuff we can share. Mom, you made me special curtains. I'll bet Mandy would like ones with ... waves, maybe. Yeah, blues and greens, 'cause she really liked playing in the ocean and playing with Ekor yesterday. I'm gonna go look in the cedar chest, okay?" And he bounced off down the hall. "Oh! And we can take the little table out of the play room so she'll have a place to draw, and I have an extra chair that's the right size and ..."

Jon reached over, took Sara's hand and pulled it to his mouth. "Mmmm. Maple syrup. You were right. I didn't need to worry." He nibbled her knuckles. "Honey, this means so much to me. Like one more thing that I've been waiting for. Like finding the last piece of a really complex puzzle and having it slip right in, you know?"

To his surprise, Sara burst out laughing, "Oh Jon, I couldn't have said it better myself! Come on. Let's go make sure Scott doesn't drag out every piece of material I own in the quest for curtain perfection. And you, Mr. Handyman, can think about putting up a few shelf brackets so our daughter will have a place for books and toys."

Jon's eyes twinkled as he pulled Sara up and into his arms. "Our daughter. Oh Sara, I really like the sound of that!"

If anyone had any doubts about joining the family, it certainly wasn't Mandy. Pink-cheeked and bubbling with health after her transition, she and Scott had whooped like banshees and run around like dervishes after he'd asked her to be "my sister, for real."

The evening's celebration had included a special send-off supper at the school, with fruit salad and pizza and a huge chocolate cake delivered by Walter and Emily, who led a rousing chorus of "You are good. You are great. You deserve chocolate cake!" before cutting slices for everyone. Then came a barrage of "milk toasts" wishing Mandy well in her new family—and in her new room, too.

A week later, Mandy got her introductions to the rest of the clan as they arrived, group by group. Jon watched in amusement as Mandy chattered away with Erica and Angela in a female bonding session, and Sara's heart swelled when she saw the beginnings of a first crush—or several—when Mandy met Jesse and the boys for the first time.

One night, after an enforced afternoon nap, Julie and Dave took Mandy for a late-night walk on the beach to introduce her to special stars and constellations, telling her that before long, it was likely that she, too, would be exploring those distant worlds; having grand adventures and meeting all sorts of interesting new beings.

Emily and Walter shared a happy, and only slightly tearful, reunion with Jerry—Emily said that she missed his beard—and connected with Jeannie and little Joshua in the way of true grandparents. Julie and Dave welcomed them warmly into the family, saying that another set of grands was just what everyone needed, and that when they needed a break from all the kids, they should come and visit at Wind Dancer.

Later, when all was quiet on the Western front, Jon and Sara, each holding a small hand, sat on either side of Mandy's bed.

"Mom? Dad? Are you sure I didn't die and go to heaven?"

"Oh no, dear Mandy. You brought a piece of heaven to us!"

PART FIVE

Twelve years after The EarthShift

Somewhere, something incredible is waiting to be known.

We are star stuff which has taken its destiny into its own hands.

The loom of time and space works the most astonishing transformation of matter.

Carl Sagan (1934-1996),
Ann Druyan (1949-) and Steven Soter (1943-)
– COSMOS: A Personal Voyage

Chapter Thirty-seven

In the Third, during the lifetimes of Grandma Julie, her parents and grandparents, the world shrank at an alarming rate. Intercontinental travel, which took weeks or months by ship—and some of her forbears had, in fact, sailed on and even captained those ships—had been reduced to a matter of hours aboard supersonic transports or SSTs as they were called. In 1865, when Grandma Julie's grandfather was still toddling, Jules Verne wrote of men traveling to the moon. 104 years later, that fiction became fact.

Transcontinental communications matured from transcribed dots and dashes which were delivered as yellow, expressionless telegrams, to full-color, real-time audio and video images of vocal and facial expressions.

Cities grew, flowering out from ports and manufacturing centers, ebbing and flowing over the years as transportation improved, allowing for people to benefit from careers in the city while enjoying home-life in the country.

From the Journal of Angela Mathews

At Julie's knee, Angela had learned the art of journal-keeping. And, like her grandmother, she had a natural affinity for the written word. Her cousins were alternately amused and frustrated that she put so much effort into recording mankind's history, her own history, her family's history, and especially the history of Jesse and his cousins. Amused that she was truly compulsive about it—especially since one of the main tenets of life in the Fifth was *living in the now*. Frustrated when there were things to be done and Angela's response was, "I just need to finish this paragraph."

But over the years, her cousins, the boys—now, young men—had come to understand that the old-fashioned practice kept Angela grounded; helped her to put things in perspective; and often, helped her see "the big picture" when it might otherwise have been lost in the tumult of their trials and discoveries. And of course, they were all glad that someone was keeping track of Grandma Julie's cookie recipes!

Angela had never voiced it, but another important element of her journals was that they were ... well, her legacy. It was important to her that no matter what happened, her baby brother especially would know who Jesse's band had been in this life, as well as what they had been charged to do, and how hard they'd worked to do it.

The seasons had turned once more toward spring. The days warmed as the sun climbed higher in the sky, softening the soil as Earth gathered herself for new growth. Young shoots were waking, reaching toward the light, and new leaves were building at the tips of branches, ready to unfurl and begin the alchemy which would change golden sunlight to vital, rich green foliage.

For some weeks now, everyone in the family, especially the four cousins, had sensed an increase in the vibrations emanating from Crystal Mountain.

No one talked about it much, and everyone did their best not to dwell on it, but they all knew that the final test was at hand, and that the stakes were incredibly high. After so many years of preparation, the mountain was calling Jesse to complete the journey; to play out the final chapter of the story begun long ago by the archangel Gabriel after the EarthShift, when the family had gathered around the first great bonfire at Wind

Dancer Ranch.

Wind Dancer was stirring now in the early morning chill. Delicious smells of coffee and baking wafted up from the kitchen. Joshua's pattering footsteps ran down the hall, and a shriek of laughter followed when his mother scooped him into her arms to blow raspberries in his neck. The backdoor slammed and Dave was heard announcing that today was a very "good egg day, indeed."

And at the antique desk in her room, Angela was busy tying up literary loose ends.

My mom tells that I was named Angela for good reason. I have grown in the Fifth, but my roots began in the Third. I come from sturdy stock. I have been tended with care and nurtured with love. I continue to grow in the Light.

Every day is such an adventure in this dimension. So many souls have made the transition from the Third, and Chris and Ellen deserve a lot of credit—even if they don't want anything said about their work. Really, for anyone to make the trip back and face the hardships and evil that goes on back in the Third every day. Their dedication and courage is just amazing.

Jon has continued to work in pediatric wards of hospitals in the Third, and he's helped lots and lots of kids to transition. That's a double benefit because, in the process of transitioning, they're healed!

Mandy, Emily and Walter are proof positive of the strength of Jon's love and what he can accomplish with it. Mandy still calls him her angel now and then, but Emily still reminds him about how gray her hair turned after their wild ride in the Jeep when they were fleeing from the militiamen!

Sara and Scott have been hard at work at the school, tending and encouraging kids who transitioned before their parents. The good news there is how many of their parents have finally seen the light, so lots of those families have been reunited. And the very best news is that Sara's expecting again. It'll be a gorgeous and very lucky child, to come from those parents and be welcomed into such a loving family.

Erica is such fun. So artistic, so feminine, and yet so aware of how strong she is. It might be because she's spent so much time waiting for Joey to come home from our adventures, and that she's never been allowed to come along. But if Erica was still in the Third, she'd definitely be rabblerousing for equal rights. As Grandma Julie once told me, "She'd probably have Carrie Nation tattooed on her breast!"

Our parents—all our parents—are so supportive, even if they're not always comfortable with what we have to do. I know that part of the whole parental deal, especially for parents who grew up in the Third, is to protect. Because we've all grown up so fast, I can only imagine how hard it's been for them to let us do what we've been called to do and to control their fears when we're cut off from them. Just to let go and trust that we'll be back. As brave as we've had to be, they've been equally brave, because they've been the ones left waiting. Not easy, as I learned at the lake.

Some of my trips with the guys have been a lot scarier than our folks ever knew. We've always been instructed to block them from contact while we're out, and let's just say that we might have forgotten to tell them more than a few of the details. I think it must be a lot like what Grandma Julie says about raising children. "You love them so much that all you can think of is protecting them. When they hurt, you find yourself praying that you can take the pain in their place."

God bless Dorado for his help and guidance. He's been one big source of strength and support for us through the years, much like Ekor has been for Jon. I wish he could be with us at Crystal Mountain, but we all know that it doesn't work that way. Everyone made it clear in our last workshop that we're ready. So now, it's all up to us. Wow ... so we just have to be sure that nothing comes between us and our true selves.

Whatever waits for us on Crystal Mountain is calling. It's very important that we live in the now and take things one day at a time—probably one moment at a time. I've spent some time with everyone, even Misty and Orion and our old goat, Mert. Not to say goodbye, necessarily, but so I can carry them all with me. They're my touchstones, the relationships that make all the difference.

Jesse has been reading more lately and shared this quote with me. He thought, and I do, too, that it's a lot like what we're feeling now. It was written by Martin Luther King, Jr., a man who fought for his people back in the Third, right before he was assassinated.

> *"Well, I don't know what will happen now. We've got some difficult days ahead. But it doesn't matter with me now. Because I've been to the mountaintop. And I don't mind. Like anybody, I would like to live a long life. Longevity has its place. But I'm not concerned about that now. I just want to do God's will. And He's allowed me to go up to the mountain. And I've looked over. And I've seen the Promised Land. I may not get there with you. But I want you to know tonight, that we, as a people, will get to the Promised Land. So I'm happy, tonight. I'm not worried about anything. I'm not fearing any man. Mine eyes have seen the glory of the coming of the Lord."*
>
> *Martin Luther King, Jr., April 3, 1968*

In many ways, I think that the Fifth Dimension might actually be the Promised Land, so I'm not expecting to be assassinated. In fact, I've told Gabriel that we're expecting a huge bonfire here at Wind Dancer, like the one we had after the EarthShift. I don't really remember that one since I was barely born, but I've sure heard a lot about it.

PS: Even though I don't expect to be assassinated, with so much riding on this mission, we have to accept that anything could happen. I don't want to move on just yet, but just in case, I want everyone to know that I'm concentrating on being happy tonight, and not worrying about anything, and not fearing any man. We four have certainly seen a lot of glory and expect to see a whole lot more.

"Angela! The boys are here." Angela could hear the nerves in her mother's voice. "Come get some food—you need fuel—and tell me what else you need in your backpack."

"Coming, Mom. Just a sec."

Okay. The boys are here. Gotta go. I'll take a new journal with me and leave this one here. If you guys are reading it, know that I love you all so very much. I'll always be with you ... one way or another!

Love, Angela

Chapter Thirty-eight

Jesse smiled as he watched Sam weaving back and forth in front of them and behind them, marking his territory and checking their perimeters. They had no idea how old the coyote had been when he transitioned to the Fifth with Jerry and Angela, but they knew there was a powerhouse of energy wrapped in that wiry little body. Sam put in twice the miles, probably got half the sleep, scavenged his own food—not that he didn't appreciate a treat or two—and was a source of both security and comfort. And they couldn't have made him stay behind if they'd wanted to.

The cousins were walking quietly, each communicating with a Higher Power in their own way. Each requesting strength or guidance or protection or wisdom. Each seeking their own peace. Each knowing that even though they walked together, every step was a statement of individual courage.

They'd walked this path many times over the last few years, so it was familiar. And then, like the throwing down of some metaphysical gauntlet, it wasn't familiar at all. *Part of the challenge*, Jesse decided as he smoothly made the shift from relying on his eyes to relying on his intuition. He glanced back at the others, still moving smoothly without even the tiniest of missteps, and shared a grin with Angela as Sam skinned back his teeth and growled low in his throat. After the events at the lake, Sam had little tolerance for the unnatural, especially when it concerned his adopted "pack."

The cousins still carried shadows of their dealings with Beryl and the frightening power of her crystal. For Angela and Mike, the two weeks of helplessness while they waited for Jesse and Joey's return still haunted their dreams.

Joey saw his inability to resist the evil beauty of the woman and the crystal as a nearly unforgivable weakness. His actions had put Jesse in immediate danger, and ultimately could have doomed them all. No matter what the others told him, he had carried a heavy burden of guilt.

Jesse, always strong, centered and psychically skilled, felt his failure to protect Joey and the team should certainly mean the appointment of a new leader for their final mission.

They had returned home to rest and heal. They'd had communion with beings of both substance and light. And after a few days of pampering by parents, grandparents and siblings, they'd come together. Together, they'd meditated, and meditating, they had all reached a level which allowed them to recognize the importance of the lessons learned from their "mistakes." The truth of the saying, *things happen for a reason,* was now written upon their hearts.

Subsequent training journeys with Dorado to various spaceships and other worlds had built upon previous lessons, and had exposed the cousins to myriad attendees of myriad species. Telepathic lessons, understood by each individual in his/her own language, were the norm. *If only they'd had this in the Third,* thought Jesse. *I'll bet things would have been so different if people could just talk.*

"Hey, Jess! I've gotta take a break for a few minutes, okay?" Mike shouted from the rear.

"We all do," seconded Angela. "This looks good. Shade trees."

"And I'd like a little snack," Joey chimed in, living up to his nickname of "The Bottomless Pit."

Jesse put his pack down. "Good idea. Good timing. The trail's gone strange anyway. We'll regroup and see if we can get a read which direction we need to travel. Um, Joe? You *are* going to share those, right?"

Joey grinned, then looked pained as Jesse held out his hand for the cookie tin. There were packets of all their favorites, lovingly baked and packed by Grandma Julie. Nanny Rita's Filled Cookies, Manga's Chocolate Chip, Ruthie P's Snickerdoodles, Elsie's Valentines, Sammy's Sugar Cookies, and Mrs. Young's Brownies—with and without nuts. How many times had they felt this love and reveled in their connections to these long-gone women who'd nourished their own families with love and baked goods?

The air was sizzling at Wind Dancer Ranch, and not necessarily in a good way. The entire family was anxious about Jesse and his gang leaving on what would hopefully be their final mission. And Julie, especially, had recently become aware of an increasingly large buildup of magnetic energy. She was sure the effect was being felt in all of Mother Earth's dimensions.

Such effects rippled out, reflecting in human beings and animal species alike, and it wasn't helping Julie's nerves one bit that she recognized the same jumpiness and confusion she'd felt years ago when things were building up to Zero Point.

Where did the time go? Julie wondered. The intervening years between the family's transition and now had sped by—sometimes frustrating, sometimes a bit frightening, always exciting—with everyone concentrating on *living in the moment*. So it was with a certain degree of surprise, when she realized that they were coming up on the next big transition. And just like the last time, no one really knew just what to expect, except in broad strokes—

That it would be incredibly important.

That it would be another huge step in the predicted Shift of the Ages.

That it would be the cut-off point for souls still in the Third, still unable to open their minds and hearts in order to transition to the Fifth.

Well, Julie admitted as she went about finishing up in the kitchen, *I learned a long time ago that living in fear was a waste of energy. Things will be whatever they will. I'm pretty good about 'living in the now.'* She paused to lovingly run her fingers down the two frames which hung by the door, placed so that everyone could read them. Inside were old-fashioned samplers, colorful cotton threads stitched onto a linen background. The first said, *"If You Believe It, You Will See It."* The second, *"Live in Love, not Fear."* The grandchildren kept them decorated with meadow flowers, and Julie recognized them as a source of personal power. Taking a deep breath, she read them again, grabbed a jacket, and stepped out into the spring sunshine.

Believe it, see it. Love, not fear. Drawn to the barn, the company of the horses, the richness of scents—animals, hay, grain, leather—and the possibility of a fast, head-clearing ride, Julie strode down the well-worn path. *Believe it, see it. Love, not fear. Believe it, see it. Love, not fear.*

In his family's portion of the ranch house, Josh toddled from room to room, searching for his sister, his voice achingly sad. "Mama, where my Annie?" He couldn't quite get his mouth around Angie yet, and no one seemed to mind the dropped "g," least of all, his sister.

"It's time for her to go on another camping trip with the guys, sweetie. She'll be back soon." *I pray to God she'll be back soon*, Jeannie thought.

"Why, Mama? Why Annie go?"

"It might be hard for you to understand just yet, sweetie."

"Why?"

"The angels asked them to. Angie and the guys have a job to do, so they had to go away for a while. But the angels will watch over them just like they watch over you and me and daddy and all of us."

"Angels. I like angels. They're my friends."

"That's right, Josh. And we have to ask them to take special care of Angie and the guys, and remember to thank them for helping to keep us safe, right?"

"Yup. But I miss Annie ... and she misses us," he sighed, and his mother did a little double-take as she realized how strongly Josh was tuned in to his big sister. "Will you read me a story, Mama?"

"I think that sounds like just the thing. You go get a book and we'll go out on the deck and sit in the sun."

Beaming a smile that would put the sun to shame, he ran off on sturdy little legs to find his old friend, Mike Mulligan.

Chris and Ellen dropped in on Jon and Sara. The plan was to spend some time with them and check in on the kids at Sara's school who were still without parents. Neither Chris nor Ellen had spoken of it aloud, but they both knew that when the time was right, when their trips back to the Third ended and transitions had ceased, they would open their home to one or more of these unclaimed children. They had already opened their hearts.

Ellen was helping the kids put the finishing touches on a huge sandcastle, smiling to herself, tasting how wonderful it would be—a home, a family, building that wonderfully simple day-to-day life.

Watching her as he and Jon and another group of youngsters dug a series of canals and bridges at the water's edge, Chris knew exactly what she was thinking and he smiled, too. He thought they were ready for the next Shift, whatever it might bring, but now, relaxing here with family and kids, he wished he had a little more insight about it. All he had was the strange vibrations which had plagued him for months. Only now, they were stronger.

"Hey, Jon, have you been feeling the—"

"Yeah, I have and I am. So has Sara. The children don't talk about it, but they're so active, I'm not sure they'd even notice. Wonder what it means?"

"Somehow, I think we're going to find out in the not-too-distant future. Kinda makes me want to be with family."

"You know you can stay here as long as you like, bro."

"Thanks, Jon. We appreciate it."

Megan and Steve missed their boys, though at 18, Jesse and Mike hadn't really been boys for a long time. *It's a lot like being a parent of a secret agent*, Megan thought, not in a kindly way. Still, even with the stresses and tension of the training missions, their sons' growing years—the love, the challenges, the laughs—had been wonderful.

Megan was pretending to read a book on the porch and having little success with it. She knew from experience that the hardest part of parenting was letting go. Heaving a deep sigh, she told herself, *At least they're with Joey and Angela, although that often means more trouble, planned and unplanned.* That made her smile, but she still wished she wasn't feeling quite so uneasy.

Steve joined her on the porch swing and offered a shiny red apple. "You've been a good mom, Meg; a good teacher. They'll take care of themselves."

"Thanks, honey," she said, taking a bite. "But this time is different. Something big's coming this time, and it's unsettling."

"You know, I bet Bill and Kathy are feeling just as uptight as we are. Joey's gone and I'm sure Erica's feeling a little left out. She's been doing terrific work for a 13-year-old. Talk about a full and challenging agenda!

How about we pay them a visit? Strength in numbers. I think we could all use a little support right now."

"Oh, yeah! Let's go!"

Jerry and Dave grumbled when it was their turn to take care of the greenhouse. *Just a male thing,* Julie decided. At least Dave had someone to share the chores with now. Belly laughs echoed from the glass dome, and she smiled as she lifted the lid on her stew. She breathed in the pleasing aroma of herbs and vegetables. *Angela's favorite. No, no. Don't go there, girl,* she scolded herself and turned to find Josh watching her intently from his little chair by the window, a slight frown on his handsome little face. If it was difficult in the Third for parents to keep their own counsel, it was darn near impossible for a grandparent in the Fifth to keep hers!

"Come on, little man. Let's go see what Grampy and Daddy are doing. Maybe we can help."

He jumped up, put his tiny hand in hers, and led the way to the door.

Chapter Thirty-nine

"Man, my feet are sore. I hope we camp near a stream or river so I can soak them tonight." Angela had given her boots a good workout and was pleased that she was having no trouble keeping up with the guys. "How are your paws, Sam? I bet you'd like a dip in the water, too." She stopped a minute while Sam leaned against her knee, his eyes closing in pleasure when she scratched his ears.

Jesse was hoping to find water, too. It was their fifth day out, and they'd gone through most of the food in their packs. If they found water, Mike was a demon with a fishing pole. They could sure use the protein.

The weather hadn't been bad. They'd been spared any late spring blizzards, but the vibrations were growing so strong they were all having headaches and even a little nausea from time to time. Jesse knew they could survive by scavenging nuts, berries and wild greens, but he also knew that so much roughage sometimes played havoc on their digestive systems.

"Okay, guys. We'll stop. Take a little time. See if we can adjust to what's going on with the vibrations. Then we need to keep an eye out for signs of water." Nearly as one, they dropped to the ground and reached for canteens.

After a short rest, and the unspoken realization that they'd done about all the adjusting they were going to do and didn't feel much better, they stoically shouldered their packs and resumed their march.

They were in their fourth mile of rough terrain when Sam, who'd run ahead, let loose a piercing howl.

"Jeez, Sam. How about not telling the world where we are, buddy?" exclaimed Joey, looking around for the cause of Sam's excitement.

"Hey, look over there, through the trees. Listen! It's a river! Come on, gang! Last one in is a rotten egg!" And he was off and running, the others close on his heels.

The water, coming straight off the melting snow pack, was absolutely freezing. Whooping and screaming, the cousins sluiced off the day's dirt, drank their fill, and emerged clean and refreshed. With an eye on the late afternoon sun, Mike used his knife to cut a long sapling which he fitted out as a fishing pole while the others gathered wood and kindling for a fire.

There were grumbles about their meager fare for supper. Angela had picked a full pot of young dandelion leaves and scavenged some wild onions and even a few pine nuts which the squirrels had missed last fall. She dressed the "found" salad sparingly with her personal bottle of oil and vinegar to cut the dandelion bitterness, and thought it looked pretty appetizing. But when Mike appeared with two trout, she was quick to join Jesse and Joey in giving him a rousing cheer, even if the fish were a bit on the small side.

Loaves and fishes ... well, leaves and fishes, Joey thought, wishing he'd saved at least one of Julie's cookies. He told himself that if only he had one, he wouldn't even mind splitting it four ways. But when his mouth watered at the mere thought, he was honest enough to admit that maybe that was stretching the truth just a bit.

The sun was setting, and as the cool evening air settled in, Jesse lit the fire and gathered them around it. He sensed a flagging spirit in his team, and knew it was essential that they talk about it. Joey had already voiced the possibility of returning to Wind Dancer in the morning "for a good meal." Jesse was pleased when Angela squashed the notion like a used paper cup.

They were bathed and fed, but before they slept, they had to be fired up and refocused. Jesse knew they all had to renew their commitment.

The embers glowed. Light reflected off clean, healthy faces. Sam settled at Angela's side and laid his head in her lap. The sounds of the river and the night surrounded and soothed them.

"We're five days out and we all know that we're getting closer, right? The vibrations are increasing, but we're handling it. This is what we've trained for all our lives, and Gabriel and Dorado believe we're ready to do whatever it takes. *I* believe we're ready to do whatever it takes."

The cousins all nodded their agreement.

Sam sat up, stretched, and trotted off on another patrol.

"Sure wish you'd have a dream about all this stuff, Jess. Maybe get Dorado to drop in or something. I know that's a long shot, but it would be great to know for sure that we're on the right track."

"I know, Joey. But that's just not how it works. You know it. I know it. So let's concentrate on what we have—great training and great backup. Nobody's got better backup than we do, right? We can do this, right?"

Smiles and fist pumps all around.

Jesse smiled, "So let's get some sleep and we can get an early start in the morning."

Resigned to the task ahead, the cousins fed the fire, crawled into their sleeping bags, and bid each other goodnight. Sam split his time between patrolling the woods around them and catching quick naps curled in the bend of Angela's knees. As a guard against the night creatures, there were none better.

But that night, even the night creatures fled as evil stalked the woods.

Morning arrived all too soon. Blinking against the bright sunlight,

Joey reached out and slapped Jesse's sleeping bag. When there was no response, he gave the lumpy pile another annoyed whack.

"Come on, slug-a-bed. Shake a leg. You're usually the first one up."

The bag didn't move and Joey prodded further, finding only lumps of bag and pillow—nothing of his cousin. Instantly awake, Joey's heart shot into his throat as he yelled, "Hey! It's empty! He's not here! Jesse's not here!"

Mike and Angela went immediately to high alert. Sam ran over to check out the bag, growling softly, and continued his search of the area, moving out from the fire, nose to the ground. No one had seen Jesse leave. No one had heard Jesse leave.

They began to shout.

"Jesse! You could've waited for us, you know!"

"Where the heck are you? Jesse!"

"Come on, man! This isn't funny!"

"Come out now! We need to get going!"

Annoyance turned to fear when the only answer to their cries was an echo bouncing back at them from the barren cliff across the river.

"Jeessee ... Jeessee ... Jeessee ...."

Silence settled, as heavy as the morning mist.

"Oh, boy. We've got a problem," said Mike. "He's done this before—wandered off to explore—but this feels different. I really don't think he's exploring."

"Same here," nodded Angela. "I know about disappearing, and he wouldn't do this of his own free will, not now. He knows we're a team. If it were another space trip, he'd be back by now. Or we'd have gone with him. I'm definitely worried."

"All right! All right! Don't panic," said Joey. "Let's just stay calm and think and ... Damn, we need him! Right here! Right now!"

"Face it, Joe. He's not here. And whatever happened to him could happen to any of us at any time," said Mike. "We've got to stick together. So let's huddle up and see what we get. I'm vibrating like a banjo string. It's got to be the mountain ... or whatever's in it. Or whatever *wants* to be in it." Mike bore down hard. He wanted to be strong. He *would* be strong for his twin. "Come on. Get in the middle, Sam. Okay, guys. Hold hands and try to tune in to Jesse so we can figure out what to do next."

Jesse was looking at a barren landscape. *Moonscape might be closer to it,* he thought. *No premonition, no warning, and here I am. Where the hell am I? Not a tree in sight, nothing. Just ... emptiness.* He turned to look behind him and the movement brought on a wave of dizziness and nausea so strong he had to put his head between his knees and pray that last night's fish didn't swim upstream.

This is not good. This is NOT Dorado. Evil stuff. And whatever it is, it doesn't want us to reach our goal. Where are the others? Are they okay? Were they zapped away, too? What the hell do I do now? Okay, Jesse, get a grip. Don't panic. That's what they want. To disorient me, get me off track, scare the crap out of me. Well ... mission accomplished. But I can't just sit here. There's more to this.

Random thoughts were flying through Jesse's head when a gust of cold air swirled up around him. He shivered and was watching his breath turn to smoke when a familiar voice broke the silence.

"Hello, Jesse. How lovely to see you again."

"Where are you, Beryl? What do you want?" he shouted, jumping up and looking in all directions.

"Why, Jesse," she purred. "You're such a smart boy. I'm sure you know the answer to that question."

"I don't know anything about you except that you're a damned evil thing. Go away and leave me alone!"

"Hah! You make me laugh ... *boy*. I've come to get you, and I will. In fact, I already have, haven't I?" Jesse could hear the smile in her voice and it infuriated him.

"Over my dead body!"

The air went absolutely still and the temperature dropped sharply as Beryl's whispered response reached Jesse's ears, now burning with cold. "Be very careful of your words, Jesse. I prefer you alive, but don't aggravate me too much. You're in a bit of a ... *pickle?* Isn't that what you're kind says? Yes, well, it's just a mess, isn't it?" Her voice hardened, "The bottom line is this: You're in no position to call the shots here, sweetie. I call them." She paused. "Think about your friends," she purred. "I wonder where they can be ..."

"You can't get to my cousins. Sam's with them."

"Yes," the voice went slow, slick, wicked. "But he was with you as well, now wasn't he? And look where that got you."

While Beryl gloated, Jesse gathered his wits. "Sam is a better being than you. You're nothing but a *witch!* I'd say bitch, but it would be an insult to Sam's mother."

"Ah yes. Sam. Bothersome Sam. Well, Sam's not with you now, is he? He can't save you this time, and if you're not careful, I'll just slip back when he's off amusing himself in the woods and grab one of the others. Maybe *all* the others. Then what a party we could have." Her laughter grated like fingernails on a chalk board.

Jesse spun around, fists clenched, trying without success to get an eye on Beryl. His head was splitting, and his stomach felt like he'd swallowed battery acid, but his anger made him forget both.

Beryl continued, "Don't get testy, Jesse dear. You need me just as much as I need you. Let's see if we can work out a deal."

"A deal with you? Get serious."

"It's quite simple, really. I know you're trying to find the entrance to the mountain and the secrets inside it. I want that, too, but for different reasons. We can help each other. You've got a few contacts that I don't have, but I have certain ... mystical abilities that you don't have. So together, we're a winning combination. Forget the others. They'll fumble around, search for you for awhile, and then they'll trot on home. Come on, Jesse." Her voice became velvety, mesmerizing. "Call on that entity of yours and get the guidance we need. I'll protect you against whatever else we run across."

"You must be out of your freaking mind to think I'd hook up with you! If you have so many gifts, go find the entrance yourself. I'm outta here."

"Ha! Just try it! You'll never find your way back! You can't even find your friends. They'll start hiking any minute now and leave you out here to fend for yourself. And you know what? I can guarantee that you'll die before you ever even get to that mountain!" The wind rose and blew colder still. "Don't underestimate me, Jesse."

"And don't *you* underestimate me." Somehow, his hand found its way into his pocket and curled around the selenite crystal Grandma Julie had given him so many years ago. As a small boy, he'd told her it looked like a leaf made of water. Pulling it out now, he held it in the palm of his hand. "Go back to your cold lonely crystal cave. It suits you. This crystal protects me." It was a total bluff, but he threw everything he had into it.

"Don't! Don't aim that thing at me!"

"Why shouldn't I?" he said, turning in a circle, amazed and thrilled at Beryl's response. "Hurts you, doesn't it? What's the matter, Beryl? Is the warmth and power of something pure a problem for you? Hey, I know. It takes your power away, doesn't it?" The stone was growing hot in his hand and starting to glow.

"You'll be sorry, Jesse. You wait and sss—"

Instantly, the air warmed and Jesse collapsed to the ground, closing his eyes as the nausea and dizziness hit full force. But he opened them quickly when he heard Sam's bark.

The cousins found him only a few yards from the campsite, sitting on the ground; pale, shaky, his arms holding Sam in a crushing hug as the coyote licked his face. "Wow. Well. That was a ... whoa ... an interesting experience," he said as he struggled to stand.

The cousins were all over him.

"Where did you go?"

"What happened?"

"Jess! Are you all right?"

"Outside of scaring the freakin' you-know-what out of us, thank God you're back," said Mike. "So what do we do now?"

"Well first, we put a lot more effort into protecting ourselves. Grandma Julie's crystals? I think they're going to be a major piece of that protection. The Crystal Bitch—sorry, Sam—just made a return appearance. I thought I was done for, but when I pulled out my selenite, she freaked, and her power just fizzled. Poof! I was back here."

Joey went pale. "Beryl? Beryl's back? She got past Sam?"

"It's going to be okay, Joe. Just be sure you always carry your crystals with you. Keep them *really* close. In fact, let's all check them right now."

They walked Jesse back to the sleeping bags and helped him to sit. Mike found his canteen and offered it, and Jesse drank gratefully. Then, they settled into a close circle around the ashes of their campfire.

No one spoke as Angela opened the small medicine bag she wore around her neck and poured several smooth, polished stones into her hand. She held up the amethyst first. "Grandma Julie told me she carried this stone with her the whole time during the EarthShift. It's for purity and balance during transition."

She fingered a small, beautifully marked bloodstone. "For healing," Grandma Julie had told her. "She said I'd always been a healer, right from the moment I was born."

Last, there was red coral which she explained was her "woman's stone—to quiet the emotions and eliminate despair." She didn't tell them about the "encourage passion" part, or that their grandmother had added, "Not that I want you to be using that particular facet of it anytime soon!" The boys didn't need to know that part.

Mike turned out his right-hand jeans pocket and showed them another amethyst which Grandma Julie had told him would "balance your warrior tendencies." There was a black onyx for "grace under pressure," and misty blue angelite in a vague heart shape which he'd picked for himself because it was pretty. He remembered Grandma Julie smiling as she handed it to him.

"She said this one would help me stay in touch with my angels."

Joey pulled a piece of smooth black jet out of his left pocket and then dug deep into his backpack and came up with a glowing yellow teardrop of amber. "Grandma told me these will help me with my healing, and they'll help me get rid of any bad stuff I happen to be carrying around, too." Digging deeper, he pulled out an oval of picture jasper; dusky blue over rich browns, like an evening sky over the desert.

He remembered Grandma Julie studying the stone as she explained that it was a stone of protection, and makes it easier to be in touch with your own power. "She told me that Uncle Jon brought this to her one day when she was feeling lost and sad. And that it worked wonders for her. She said I should keep it for a while. So how about you keep it for a while and see what it does for you, pal?"

Like Joey, Jesse had carried only one of his crystals on his person. Now, he leaned past Sam, grabbed his pack and extracted a small leather pouch. When he raised his head, he was smiling.

"What's the joke, bro?" Mike asked.

Jesse opened the drawstring and dumped the stones into his hand. Another amethyst crystal flashed purple in the sun. "Grandma Julie told me that everyone can use some help against negative stuff," he said. Beside the amethyst, was a smooth blue stone.

"Is that lapis?" Angela inquired.

"Nope. Sodalite. Let's see. She gave me this one when I was having bad dreams and trouble sleeping. 'Cuts down on the mental chatter,' she told me." He broke off, holding up a pale ice-blue crystal which he turned in his hand, watching as the the sun hit its facets.

"Why are you smiling, Jess? This is serious stuff." Joey's patience was running thin.

"Well, Joe, I'm smiling because I just remembered what this one's called ... besides aquamarine."

"Well, don't keep us guessing!"

"Beryl. Another name for this is 'beryl', and it comes in lots of colors, including blue. If it's green, it's an emerald. There are pinks and blues and reds and everything in between. But do you remember the color of that huge crystal, Joey? It doesn't come in that color without something nasty happening to it. Something as *un*natural as all get out. I should've clued in to all this sooner, but it's beginning to make a lot more sense now.

"Beryl—the nasty, evil, witch one—will be back. That's pretty much guaranteed. So there you have it. We've got to be more alert. But I have a feeling that these crystals—some of them Grandma Julie's choices for us, and some of them our own choices—are going to be a big help. This is a break we can't afford to waste. We've got to move faster, look for clues. No more relaxing."

Joey jumped up. "Okay! Gotcha. Agreed. Come on, gang. Pack up and let's go!"

Jesse sat still another minute. Still smiling, he leaned over and rested his head, now clear and pain-free, on Sam's. *Another hurdle cleared. Not fun. In fact, damned scary. But we all came through and we scored big points.*

Giving Sam one more scratch for the road, Jesse returned his crystals to their pouch and carefully put the pouch in his pocket. As he packed his gear, he could almost feel Grandma Julie's arm around his shoulder. And as they headed off down the trail, he was sure he heard Dorado's voice in his head saying, "Job well done, Jesse."

Chapter Forty

"Dave, do you feel anything unusual? I mean, really weird?" Julie and her husband were walking across the meadow, holding hands, picking flowers and appreciating the day.

"I was just about to ask you the same thing, Julie. It's like something deep inside, almost a rumbling, but I don't know if it's good or bad."

"It's a more, ah, *subtle,* vibration, not exactly like anything I've felt before. Is it something to do with this next Shift maybe? Could it have anything to do with Crystal Mountain?" And at that, her voice trembled.

"You're the gal who usually taps into answers, babe. I'm definitely second-string on the psychic team. But if you want a gut feeling, yes, I think energies are ramping up. Probably everywhere and in all dimensions, but I'd bet even more so right here close to the mountain. And good or bad, our grandkids are very much involved in whatever's going on up there. It would make things a whole lot easier if we knew more. If Gabriel could keep us posted, you know?"

"Do I ever! And I think you're right. This shifting stuff has been going on for years now, and everyone we know has done their work. Still, I'm worried. I trust our kids. They've done so much preparation and Dorado has schooled them well. But it's a huge unknown. Just like last time. Maybe even more." Julie had stopped, turned to face Dave, and was gesturing.

Stand by! Dave thought to himself, and smiled as his wife revved.

"It must be incredibly important, this save-mankind mission. I don't mean to make light of it, at all. I mean sure, there are probably others in the world with similar assignments, but as far as I'm concerned, our gang is the one that matters most right now."

"Of course they are," Dave agreed. And in the way of grandparents whose wallets are filled to over-flowing with pictures they're only too happy to share with anyone who might ask, Julie went on. "Think about it, Dave! All the children coming in now ... they're so amazing. No karma. So bright and psychic. They know so much. The Indigos, Goldens, Crystals, the Star Kids. What a learning experience it's been for everyone. And our family has played its part through it all."

"And speaking of family, Julie, I'm sure the others are getting these signs, feeling the vibes, just like we are. It's always been our job to help smooth and soothe. So how about we start in the barn, 'cause you know the animals are way ahead of us with intuition. Then we'll drum up a wonderful dinner for everyone, share some laughs—impossible not to when Joshua's around. Heck, maybe he can even tune in better than we can! Nothing would surprise me where he's concerned."

Dave's adoration for his newest grandson lightened Julie's heart.

"Great idea. Let's head back. Besides, it's getting really chilly. Strange ..."

Cheesy quiche with spinach and onions—or "egg pie" as it was known at Wind Dancer—accompanied the fresh green salad and hot buttered bread served family style on the worn kitchen table.

"It's bizarre," agreed Jerry. "I keep feeling like time is running out, and I can't tell you why."

"Daddy, what's biz ... biz-AHH?"

Jerry smiled as he looked into those big green questioning eyes. "The word is 'bizarre,' Josh. It means that something feels very strange. Different. Do you feel anything bizarre?"

Josh thought about it for a few seconds before hopping out of his chair to perform a little dance. "I feel wiggly. Like this. It's biz ... biz ... it's tickly."

The adults all shared a knowing look. "Yup. It sure is, Josh. But it's okay. Want me to sing a song so you can keep dancing?" Jerry had a beautiful voice that no one had known about until he came back from the Third.

"Yes, yes! Sing, Daddy!"

So young, so carefree, thought Julie. *The little guy has the right idea, so, what the heck!* Jumping up, she grabbed Dave's hand and pulled him out of his seat.

"Faster, Jerry. Pick it up! I feel an old fashioned jitterbug coming on!"

Jeannie joined her son, much to his delight, and jigged around the room. Jerry kept on singing as he reached for his guitar for his impersonation of Elvis. Laughter bounced off the walls and shifted the mood from concern to trust; trust in the universe that all would be right someday soon.

When they sank, exhausted, back in their chairs to share the cake Jeannie had baked earlier in the day, everyone was smiling. Josh's cake took a detour here and there on its way to his mouth, and when his plate was empty, he got a second dessert by licking up what his tongue could reach in the general vicinity. His tummy full, the green eyes drooped as he slumped down in his chair, verging on sleep.

"Wader. Lot's of wader." His voice was slow and soft.

Jeannie leaned toward him. "Do you want a drink, Josh?"

"Wader. Loud. Sammy wet."

"Water? Are you saying 'water'?"

"Wader. Cold. Pretty colors," he mumbled, and with a big sigh, he slipped into a deep sleep.

"Hmm. I wonder what he saw," said Jeannie. "He talks in his sleep sometimes, but just now he seemed to be really seeing something. What do you think, Mom?" She turned to Julie, but Jerry caught her eye.

"Of course, I know he's an amazing child," she smiled at Jerry, "but maybe this is something important."

"All young children are magnetically lighter these days, and so telepathic. We know he connects to his sister easily. Maybe she's dealing with 'wader' right now. If she were in trouble, I don't think he'd be smiling in his sleep. But to be honest, I can't even guess what that was about. He's peaceful and sound asleep now. I'd suggest that Jerry carry him to bed so he can enjoy his dreams." Julie's intuition was seasoned heavily with logic.

"You have a way of making everything okay. Thanks, Mom."

To Mike, the roar sounded like a freight train. They'd been climbing steadily up through rough terrain, and they were still in the forest. Trees towered overhead, blocking the sky. As they took turns leading the way, each member of Jesse's band secretly hoped that there was a spiritual guide pointing them in the right direction. The vibrations were constant now, and they knew the aches and pains they were feeling weren't due to the physical strain or altitude. They'd learned how to deal with that, but the new energies were taking their toll.

Exactly where they were or how much farther the trek would take them, they didn't know. But something was definitely happening. They focused on drinking as much water as they could to stay hydrated, and finding anything edible along the way. They'd all lost a few pounds, and it had been days since Joey had dared to even think about cookies. It just depressed him.

The current leader was Angela. "Do you all hear that?" she asked.

"How could we not?" said Joey. "Please let it *not* be some enormous monster manifested by that evil, crazy woman."

"I'm guessing, but I think it's a waterfall. Since I'm leading, I'm heading that way. Maybe it'll help us get our bearings."

"Lead on, Angie," urged Jesse. "Don't let these clowns distract you."

It took another hour of weaving in and out and up and down—and a few places requiring over and under—before they got their first glimpse.

"Oh, my God! Look at the size of it!" said Angela as she was nearly bowled over by Sam who came barreling up the path.

"Look out! Coming through. Whoa! That is a one big dude," exclaimed Mike. "I can't see much of it, though. Come on! Hurry up! I want to see it all!"

"Take it easy, bud. It's not going anywhere," Jesse smiled.

They broke through the woods at about the half-way mark up the falls. It wasn't Niagara, but when you were standing next to it, it seemed enormous. They stood, watching the water, utterly mesmerized as Sam's howls blended with the thunder of cascading water. The river swirled out of the pool at the falls' base and churned off through a canyon, tumbling over rocks until it went out of sight around a bend. At the top of the cascade, the mists shimmered in the sunlight, creating rainbows resembling an enormous jeweled tiara.

"Wow," whispered Angela. "This is a very special place." She turned to the others, shouting. "Maybe it's just the power of the falls, but I'm shaking a lot right now. I mean, a *lot!*"

Angela could see that she wasn't the only one. The four sat down on the vibrating earth, taking in the beauty, while they tried to steady themselves. Sam wiggled in between them, currently satisfied that the waters were going to stay put and not harm any of his charges. But he, too, was trembling.

Since the spray was cold and wet, they all figured it wasn't an illusion. As such, it stood between them and Crystal Mountain and might well prove to be an impossible barrier keeping them from their goal. They had some decisions to make.

In an unspoken agreement, they closed their eyes and went into a calming meditation, seeking to know more; to understand what this new challenge meant for them and their assignment.

One by one they emerged from the depths of stillness where they were in touch with their higher selves. But no one was jumping up and down with new and profound knowledge.

"So let's share what we got," said Jesse. "I was standing in front of Grandma and Grandpa's barn. It was hard getting the barn door open, but I finally did. Went in, talked to the horses, patted the cat, and walked out again. Absolutely nothing, no messages, no insight. Sorry."

"Well, I was at home sitting on the porch swing," said Mike. "Got hungry and went inside for food. The door was stuck, but I got in, came back out. Got thirsty. Went in again," said Mike. "Nothing exciting."

Joey's meditation had taken him for a visit to Scott and the other kids. "We were playing tag, running around the house and through it. The door kept slamming really loud, and Uncle Jon told us to knock it off. It was good connecting with the family again, but I can't see where it has any bearing on our predicament here."

Angela shook her head as she told the others, "I can't help either. I guess I'm missing my little brother 'cause I could see him in his room playing with his toys. He had a fuzzy bear that he kept throwing out his door, retrieving it and doing it again and again. He was all by himself. He needs me back there to be his playmate." She took a deep breath, struggling to control the longing.

Jesse cleared his throat. "I hate to say it, but our guidance isn't coming through. We all had pretty mundane little experiences. All I'm hearing in common is lots of doors. That's all. We're definitely on our own. So any thoughts on whether we climb up, or down?"

Joey and Mike voted for up, to see if they could figure out their overall position. Angela wanted to go down and didn't feel the need to share that she simply didn't care much for heights. Jesse, sensing the underlying issue, voted with her. Stalemate.

"Well, if I had a coin, I'd flip it. Sam, you're going to have to be the tie-breaker. So, pick it, buddy. What'll it be? Which way do we go now?"

The coyote cocked his head, as though he was thinking it over and weighing his choices.

"Lead us, Sam. Go!"

Sam got to his feet and gave a great shake. He sniffed a little here and there, then suddenly took off down the hill, skidding on the slick pine needles, crisscrossing when the slope became too steep. Checking now and then to make sure they were behind him, he led his pack to the base of the falls with a minimum of cuts and bruises. There, the sniffing continued and Sam's agitation grew. He paced aimlessly around them as the water crashed on rocks worn smooth through the ages, and the river raged over outcroppings. It surged with enough power to sweep away anything or anyone in its path. Once in it, anyone would be lucky to survive.

"Well, gang," said Jesse. "Here we are with no place to go. I'd suggest teleporting to the other side, but unfortunately, we've been told that's not part of this journey. What next? Any ideas?"

Angela stood up, all five and a half feet of her. Moisture from the falls glistened on her blonde curls and her face was smudged with dirt and sweat. She raised her voice to be heard over the roar.

"I know I'm young, but you've always treated me with respect, even when I've had to scold you. So listen up. My feeling is that we wouldn't be in this place at this time if it wasn't meant to be. It's *not* a dead end. We have options. My idea is that we take a deep breath and settle in for the night. We need to eat, we need to rest, and maybe even clean up—just not in the river. If we step back and let all this stuff simmer, in the morning something will pop for one of us. And besides all that, I'm tired and you all look like, well, real mountain men would be a kind way to put it. You could use a break, too. So there."

The bewhiskered cousins with unkempt hair looked at each other ... really looked. And then, Joey's belly laugh burst out, sounding like it came all the way from his toes. He was quickly joined by everyone else, and they all laughed until tears rolled down their cheeks, and they rolled on the ground, clutching their aching sides. Sam went from one to the other, wagging his tail, trying to make sure they were all right. He would have joined in if he'd known how. It was the perfect release at the end of a long and frustrating day.

Much to their surprise, they all enjoyed the best night's sleep in what seemed like forever. When the sun rose, turning the falls to molten gold, they stretched and yawned, brewed some tea, and shared the nuts Angela had been saving.

"Thanks, Angie. Those were really good. Not nearly enough, but really good. Now," began Jesse, "we need to make a plan. I've thought of a few possibilities. Anyone else?"

"Yeah," Joey piped up. "I think we should—"

"Wait!" Angela interrupted. She'd been wandering around the perimeter searching, listening to the guys with half an ear. "Sam is missing. Even if he went exploring or looking for food, he'd be back by now. He always comes when he hears us." *Oh, please don't let it be Beryl.*

After fifteen minutes of searching and calling, Jesse brought them back together. "Okay, we'll have to split up. Joey, you head back up the trail, Mike you head down, and I'll go in-between. Angela, you stay here in case he comes back. If he does, try to let us know, although I doubt we'll be able to hear you. Be careful. If it's a trap, we could be in real trouble. But it's just not like Sam to take off on his own. Pray he didn't fall in the river. Let's go!"

Their calls for Sam were soon lost in the roar of the falls.

Chapter Forty-one

Jon was having more fun with his son and daughter than he'd ever dreamed possible. He and Sara loved being a family—loving, laughing, eating, playing, working and sharing together.

Emily and Walter had the orphanage running smoothly. They were enjoying every moment, able to teach and learn at the same time.

That gave Sara extra family time; time for being a wife and mom. She got such a kick out of making pretty clothes for Mandy, who had adapted beautifully to her new life.

Mandy had quickly become Scott's best friend, and had completely accepted her new mom and dad. Sara had overheard one of her fellow teachers saying that the transition had gone "smooth as silk."

One minor complaint, too minor for Sara to actually mention, was her children's fascination with the screen door. They just couldn't get enough of running through it, letting it slam, running back out—and Jon wasn't any better. *So be it,* she thought. *As long as they're happy, so am I.* When their newly adopted puppy, possibly part beagle, probably part monkey, did the same thing, all she could do was shake her head.

Jon made up stories for the kids—all the kids—and they were insistent that he stick with the same characters each time, having them go on exciting adventures. "Mandy the Muppet" was the first, then "Scott and His Magic Scooter." Now, "Buster the Bouncy Beagle" had joined the cast, and the trouble the three got into produced giggles that were like music to the ears.

My husband is amazingly creative, Sara decided. The listeners weren't consciously aware of the wonderful morals and lessons that every story presented, but they took in the messages all the same. Life was good.

It was story time again, and Jon's imagination was flying.

> *"Scott and Mandy made a special basket for Buster to ride in on Scott's magic scooter. Buster loved it because when he rode there, the wind made his ears flop around. It was a pretty day, and the three pals were zipping through a forest—sometimes over it, because, remember, it's a magic scooter—seeing beautiful, brightly-colored birds and even a majestic bald eagle. Then they swooped down to the forest and stopped to talk to a moose and a beaver. Up they flew again. And then right below them, they saw a huge, raging waterfall. It was loud and beautiful. They flew down and landed in an open spot right next to it."*

Jon described it in great detail and had the kids' rapt attention. But when Buster ran away and couldn't be found, they became very concerned. As a tear trickled down Mandy's cheek, Sara cleared her throat and gave Jon a 'knock it off' look. He shook himself out of the half trance he'd gone into, realizing what he'd just said. Buster quickly reappeared, none the worse for wear, and smiles returned to the young faces around him. The story ended on a happy note and everyone went off to bed with a kiss.

"So what was that about, Jon?" Sara asked. "You were in a different place."

"Whew. I guess I was. You know I never want to scare the kids, but that story started telling itself. It was way too real. And it's not over yet. Something's going on somewhere, Sara, and I don't know what."

"You don't think anything's going to happen to our Buster, do you? Even if he chews everything in sight, I still love him. And the kids adore him! I don't want to lose him."

"No ... no. He's okay. I'll just see what comes through tonight." Jon brightened and smiled at his wife, "Just think positive thoughts, and see Buster—and your shoes—safe in your prayers."

Chapter Forty-two

Angela's nerves were strung taut. She'd been waiting for hours—okay, so it was minutes, but it felt like hours—and her voice was hoarse from yelling. She wanted desperately to ditch her post at the campsite and strike off to do some investigating of her own. Alone, distressed and mightily depressed, she dropped down on her sleeping bag, and laid her head on her arms. When a cold wet nose snuffled in her ear, her shriek could have broken glass.

"Sam!" She threw her arms around his neck. "Oh, my dear, sweet Sammy. Where have you been? Look at you. You're soaking wet. Everyone is out looking for you and—darn it, Sam! You shouldn't have scared us that way!" Happy and ticked off at the same time, she tried to fix a stern look on her face to give a proper scolding, but as Sam sat gazing adoringly into her eyes, she quickly wound down and went back to hugging him.

"Now we've got to see if we can get the guys back here. You could howl. They might hear that." She tested out her own howl and Sam quickly joined in. It was an old game, one Sam enjoyed because it always brought him lots of attention, and generally, it didn't take long for people to come seeking the source of the racket. As Angela had hoped, the boys soon came crashing into the campsite for a joyous reunion.

"I'd sure like to know where he went," said Jesse. "We covered the whole area. If he fell in the river and managed to get out ... well, I don't think he could have, or Mike would have seen him. Look at him. He still wants to get in that water. He's quivering."

"And whimpering." Angela leaned close to Sam. "It's like he's trying to talk to us." Wanting to reassure, she patted Sam's head. "What is it, Sam? Show us. Are you hungry? Does something hurt?"

Angela could have sworn he rolled his eyes. Giving a sniff of abject disgust, Sam stalked off to the edge of the river and looked back at them over his shoulder. When they didn't move, he walked back, woofed once, and headed back to the river a second time.

Angela turned to the boys. "He wants us to follow him. Dad described this kind of behavior back in the Third when Sam brought him to the militia camp where I was being held. Come on, guys. Let's see where he wants to take us."

Leading his pack down the trail along the water's edge, Sam eventually stopped at the base of the falls. The roar was deafening, and the spray soaked them to the skin in seconds.

"Now what, Sam? Did you get caught in the waterfall here?" shouted Angela. "We're with you. Show us what to do, where to go."

It was like something out of an old movie. As they watched, the coyote walked toward the pounding falls. He paused, looked back at Angela, then leapt into the mist and disappeared.

"Sam!" they all shouted.

In less than 15 seconds, Sam reappeared, shook himself off vigorously, turned around and trotted back in.

"Okay," said Jesse. "I'm going after him. Keep an eye out in case I don't make it. You can catch me downriver somewhere," he added with a half smile.

"Wait!" yelled Mike.

"No." And with more determination than grace, Jesse jumped into the falls exactly where Sam had. The seconds ticked by. The cousins watched the foam, occasionally glancing downstream, just in case. After two long minutes, Mike pressed the panic button.

"That's it. I'm going in after him," he shouted. "That's my brother!"

But Angela grabbed his arm. "No! Sam is with him. Give them a little more time!"

Just then, Sam re-emerged with Jesse right behind him, both dripping wet. Jesse was barely able to speak as he fought to catch his breath and control his excitement.

"It's there! Behind the waterfall. There's a ledge barely wide enough to walk on, and an opening. I didn't go in very far, but we have to explore it. I think it might be the entrance we've been looking for!"

His excitement was contagious. "Let's go!" rang as a single voice.

With Jesse in the lead and Sam bringing up the rear, they made their way through the torrent. As Jesse had reported, the ledge was narrow, slick, and more than a little scary. The thought of slipping into the turbulence and be trapped by the hydraulic force below the falls made Angela's knees weak. But she wasn't going to let it stop her, or slow Jesse's team down.

A short distance along was a slight bend which took them further back behind the falling water. There, they discovered an entrance, well camouflaged by falling waters and mist. They stepped through, shook off what moisture they could, paused for a few deep breaths, and checked out their surroundings. It appeared to be a simple tunnel with stone walls and dirt deposits here and there on the floor. Although it wasn't very wide, from where they stood, it looked endless.

A powerful jolt of *déjà vu* slammed Joey and Jesse as they looked around nervously, half expecting Beryl to pop out of somewhere. But the soft light illuminating this passageway wasn't cold blue, but a rich gold, and they heard no laughter, evil or otherwise.

"Okay, let's go in a ways. See what we can see," said Jesse. "Maybe this is just the entrance to an old mine or something." He paused, then said what they all were thinking. "Man! I sure hope not!"

The tunnel wound through the rock, twisting and turning, always slanting upwards. It didn't appear to have been used as any kind of major walkway. There was little in the way of debris, trash or animal remains, but it wasn't festooned with cobwebs or crawling with critters either. It was quite cold and a little damp, which made sense, and there was enough light to see where they were going, which made no sense whatsoever.

Jesse wasn't sure if the vibrations they'd been experiencing had revved up, or if he was still chilled and shivering. "Uh oh. Look at this," he said, stopping so quickly they all plowed into each other like a clown show routine. Leaning around each other, they saw that the passageway had now widened by a few feet, but a big metal slab blocked their way.

Dead end.

"Great. This is just great. What the heck do we do now?" Jesse stepped forward. "Looks really solid." He rubbed his hands over the slab. "Hey! Feel this! It's warm. That's really strange. It feels like ... yeah, I think there's a current going through it. It makes my hands tingle. Try it."

"Yeah, you're right," said Mike after he'd stepped up to press his palm beside Jesse's. "This has got to be a door. I wonder how it opens. That is, *if* it opens. Maybe there's a code or something."

Joey leaned in to test, too—a little tentatively since he was still remembering where a simple touch of his finger on Beryl's blue crystal had gotten him. "I think ... I hope ... this is the way into the mountain and the entrance to the pyramid. It could be. Man! This feels totally awesome!"

Not to be left out, Angela stepped forward. "Wow! I can feel the vibrations in it. I'm pretty sure it's the door, not me." Then she gasped and turned to look at the others, mouth open, eyes wide. "A door! Remember? We all got *doors* when we meditated! There's an energy going on here that's really wild. I don't know what's on the other side, but we've *got* to get in there somehow. Come on, guys. Check closely, touch different areas and don't forget to feel around the edges. Think of words. Something like ... 'Open Sesame!'" She paused expectantly. "Okay, so those aren't the right words." Unperturbed, she dropped to her knees and began a search of the door's lower left quarter.

"I wonder if anybody's in there," said Joey. "You know, like from outer space. And if they are, if they speak English or just use mental telepathy—or speak in weird languages. I mean, this could be anything."

"Work, Joey, work, for heaven's sake!"

"I *am,* Angie. But I can work *and* speculate."

"Well, speculate less and work more."

Joey grunted.

They could find nothing that resembled a handle or hinges, keyhole or keypad. They scraped, stroked, poked, pushed, thumped, and bumped, but the slab remained solid, unmoving—yet somehow alive.

"Well, damn," Jesse sighed, sliding down against the slab. "Someone or something put this here. And this *is* Crystal Mountain. I know what Grandma and I saw at the big bonfire after the first Shift happened. This has got to be where we need to be. Think, guys."

Angela sat beside him, looking pensive as she spoke. "Maybe we *shouldn't* think. Maybe we just need to open our minds and see what comes in on its own. I'll tell you what I'm going to put into my heart, and you can do the same if you want." She closed her eyes and began the meditation. "I'm visualizing a glorious sun shining a ray down onto this mountain, and from my heart and my soul, I'm sending love to the world, to the universe. We're here because of Gabriel, but also because of our unconditional love of nature, our family and everyone in the world. I see the sun lighting up everyone and everything. It's a ... a golden awakening?

And I'm—" Sam growled softly, and Angela stopped, mid-sentence. "Did you feel that?"

Jesse's eyes flew open. "Yeah. It's moving."

Angela and Jesse scrambled up to stand with Mike and Joey against the far wall. They all watched as the door slowly slid upward, revealing a huge, stunningly golden room.

"Wow," breathed Angela. "It's even more brilliant than I saw in my head." They entered cautiously. Slowly. Because it's hard to move fast when you're awestruck.

The room was the inside of a massive pyramid, squared off at the top where a horizontal plane of light shimmered like sunshine on water. They could see now that the sides were gold, including the door which had closed noiselessly behind them. And the space had a sacrosanct quality, demanding reverence and, at the same time, exuding a sense of serenity and grace.

After a tentative hello or two, Jesse began a slow walk around. Angela grabbed Joey's hand and hurried to catch up while Mike took his time, bringing up the rear, checking in all directions for any signs of danger. They moved along the walls, quietly, barely breathing, searching for anything that could take them to the next step.

Her right hand firmly gripping Joey's and her left holding the medicine bag around her neck, Angela opened herself to her surroundings. As they moved along the walls, she heard a soft, gentle whisper, quickly gone. A few feet further, it came again.

"What is it, Angie," Joey asked. They'd been closely linked ever since she was an infant, and now, he was tuned in to even her slightest hesitation.

"I don't know. If I had to describe it, I'd say, 'ghost whispers.' It's there, and then it's gone." She cocked her head, listening intently, then raised both hands, palms up, in the universal *darned-if-I-know* sign.

Jesse tuned in, "What are you talking about, Angie? I don't hear anything. Is someone telling us what we're supposed to do now?" He smiled. "That would be really helpful."

"I'm not sure, Jesse. Maybe I'm desperate and just hearing what's going on inside my own head. And I'm not hearing anything right now." But as her left hand found its way to her medicine bag containing her crystals, she stiffened, stopping dead in her tracks. "No ... listen. I'm sure I heard '*Trust.*'" A pause. "And now I'm hearing '*Love.*'"

It was part of his job to be skeptical at times, so Jesse asked, "And you're sure you're not making it up? Wishful thinking?"

There were times when Angela could be thick-skinned. But when someone questioned her psychic abilities wasn't one of them. Struggling a bit to keep her temper in check, she stuffed her hands into her pockets and stalked off across the wide room.

"Well. Damn." In a mirror image of Angela's frustration, Jesse stuck his hands in his own pockets, where they wrapped around Grandma Julie's crystals. "Wait, Angie. Hey, I'm sorry. We'll listen. Stay with us—"

Believe.

"What? What did you say? Hey, how about if we all get as near the middle as we can, under the peak. Maybe the energy will be stronger—"

SUPPORT!!

"—there."

As the word echoed in his head, Jesse suddenly understood. Grinning now, he motioned for Mike and Joey and Sam to join Angela in the center of the room.

"Let's sit." And when Angela hesitated, Jesse quickly wrapped an arm around her and pressed a kiss to her temple. "I'm sorry, Angela. You were right. I get it now. And you're going to need your pencil, and we're all going to need our crystals."

"Of course!" Angela was too pleased to have the puzzle solved to stay mad at Jesse. She gave him a light punch on the arm, "Turkey." And they all sat down, facing each other with Sam in the middle, and pulled out their crystals.

It started slowly, but as the vibrations increased, so, too, did the words, both in volume and number.

Believe.

Love.

Friendship.

Support. Trust. The whispers continued, as the crystals warmed and started to glow; all positive, beautiful words.

Share. Respect.

Awaken. Harmony. Love. Soon phrases were coming through.

Energy Body. Live as one.

"These are great thoughts to live by, but what are we supposed to do with them?" Joey asked, not really expecting an answer.

But the answer came, echoing off the walls of the hallowed space. *"Find the golden tablets. They are the steps to a higher level."*

"Whoa! Where did that come from?" asked Joey. "So where are these tablets? How do we do it?" He looked around expectantly, but this time, there was only silence.

Jesse wasn't about to be discouraged. After all, they'd already conquered so many obstacles to get this far. And there was so much positive energy in the room. "All right, guys. We've got to find these things, whatever and wherever they are."

"Steps? Like stairs? Wish I'd paid more attention when Dad was putting on the new porch." Joey was up and scuffing around the floor. "And a stairway to what? That's what I'd like to know."

"Guess we'll know when we get there," sighed Mike. "Start looking."

Sam felt a short recess coming on. He stayed where he was, curled up in a ball and tucked his nose under his hind legs, his power nap position. Several minutes later, Sam's golden eyes blinked open just as Angela quietly announced, "Hey, guys, I found one! Look. It says *Peace.*"

"Where? I don't see anything," said Jesse.

"You know when you're reading someone's aura? You look over the top of their head and unfocus your eyes? Try it."

"Hey! Way to go, Angie! She's right! Right there. Wait a sec. I lost it. It was ... Yes! It's there. Fantastic! The word is carved into it, and it looks like it's made of gold." Jesse sounded so excited—and relieved. But Mike, who was always called upon when muscle was needed, pricked up his ears.

"Gold? That's going to weigh a ton!"

Jesse rolled on, "So now we take it—this plate ... slab ... tablet—and make it the first step. Somehow."

Soon, all four cousins were able to recognize and locate the tablets, and had done so. There they stood, each positioned by their finds, without a clue about what to do next. That's when Sam got up, gave himself a little shake, stalked over to Mike, and pounced. Striking the tablet with his forepaws, he sent it gliding smoothly across the floor. It came to rest in the center of the room.

"Huh," said Mike. "It said *Clarity.* Probably should've said *Simplicity.*" And off he went in search of another tablet while his cousins shoved theirs into place beside the first.

Angela, always the organizer, was full of good advice. Common sense, she called it. "First of all, you trust. Remember that word? And look! There's another. Above where the last one was. Joey, you get that one. *Sun.* Let's not worry about making steps right now. Just keep looking."

Look, they did. Sometimes they found duplicates. Several tablets were engraved with *Love.*

"Figures," said Mike. "Doesn't get much more important than that."

They found two that said *See the Light*, and decided to put one at the start, saving the other for last when they couldn't find any more.

Even Sam began to search, discovering *Animal Intuition*, for which Angela gave him a big hug.

There were certainly themes. *Laughter* was followed by *Humor* and *Joy*. Joey found *Abundance* and *Blessings*. Nodding, he said, "Yup. Our family's certainly got a bunch of those!"

They worked steadily, finding words which ranged from *Affection* to *Responsibility* and *Passion* to *Loyalty*. *Honesty* came up several times. *Creativity, Originality, Character* and *Equality* added to the growing golden trail. *Unity* seemed important, and so did *Forgiveness. Oneness* resonated with all of them as they continued their search. *Cheer, Smile, Charity,* and *Compassion* were close together. The cousins' adrenaline pumped as more and more tablets were pushed to the center.

Angela found *Courage* and got a lump in her throat thinking about Emily and Walter and her family, how they helped others, often putting themselves in jeopardy. *Freedom, Peace, Patience* and *Acceptance* joined the rest. *Truth* was doubled as were *Angels, Teach, Learn* and *Knowledge. Pray* and *Spirit* were seen often. Sam pointed to *Gratitude,* his tail wagging, and when he discovered *Enthusiasm*, it made its way to the center bearing a wet nose print, Sam's personal seal of approval.

Humility and *Tolerance* were followed by *Wisdom*. When Jesse found *Rest,* he declared it was time for the group to take a break and do just that.

"This is nothing short of awesome," he said, collapsing on the cool stone floor with his cousins. "I feel ... saturated in the thoughts and beliefs written on these tablets. If the world could function by these words instead of greed, war, hate and fear, what a vital, positive, peaceful place it would be. There are still so many people struggling with Third-dimensional mind sets.

"You know, I thought we—the whole family—were already doing so well living these principles. But the reminders are for everyone, including us."

Seated on either side of him, Mike and Joey reached out and gave Jesse's arms a light punch, the universally accepted sign of male agreement.

Jesse's heart opened fully as he studied his team. It was easy to see they were all affected. All of them were shivering, from excitement or the increasing vibrations, it was hard to tell, but energy was definitely building.

Angela was openly crying; her soul deeply touched. She blinked furiously as another message appeared right by her feet. It was in big capital letters, and said simply, *NOW*. She reached for the boys' hands.

"Remember how we used to draw in the energy when we played the chair game? And we could lift heavy people with just our fingers? I think we should do that now. Draw in that power." Angela looked at Jesse, who smiled and nodded in agreement.

"Each of you put your hand over mine in turn. Don't make contact. Stack the hands. Focus the energy. Just like when we were kids. Concentrate. We need to go into that silence again. Whatever the next step is, I think it's going to happen ... now."

Their concentration was so profound, they didn't notice what was happening with the tablets until Sam, sitting between Angela and Joey, began to whine and nudge. As the tingling in their hands subsided, they withdrew each hand in the correct order from the top down.

"Look," whispered Jesse. "Look at the tablets."

Slowly, beautifully, like a ballet of mathematics and engineering, the golden tablets were tipping and sliding; forming a graceful curve extending up and up until it reached the shimmering ceiling at the pyramid's top. A golden staircase hanging in the air with no sign of support.

Drawing a deep breath, Jesse stood. "All those *words to live by* will take us to the next level, the next step for mankind. We're going to climb to the mountaintop for everyone, and take these messages with us. This is the next part of the Shift. *Our* part of the Shift."

He helped Angela to her feet, then cupped her face and wiped his thumbs under her eyes to dry her tears. Grabbing Joey's hand, Jesse hauled him up and locked him close in a one-armed man-hug. Turning to Mike, who was standing beside Angela, he found himself locked in a bear hug, rocking back and forth for long seconds.

Clearing his throat, Jesse continued, "Let's move, people! The *NOW* is glowing. There's a time thing going on here, and we need to move up. I'll go first. Be careful. Think about each word and its meaning as you step on it. Bring it into your body. Feel it. Know you'll always live it. You too, Sam. You represent the animal spirit world." Jesse looked at each teammate. "Trust. Let's go."

Their first steps were cautious. The lack of railings was more than a little disconcerting. But with each stair, they became more aware of filling themselves—their hearts and minds—with the messages, like a meditation. They began to move more swiftly, any trepidation they were feeling melting away. *Trust* appeared often on the stairs, and Jesse and his cousins were trusting with all their hearts.

It was a very long staircase.

Chapter Forty-three

Julie had enjoyed the beautiful spring day with its bright blue sky, slight breeze, warm sun, the perfume of newly awakened flowers, and the thrill of an all-out gallop across the meadow. Afterward, Misty had been free with her nudges and velvet-lipped kisses, and Julie had been free with the carrots.

As evening descended, her need to meditate dictated that Julie put aside her chores and escape into her special world. Settling into her favorite spot on the deck, she drew in the comfort of the familiar, the comfort of home. Something was going on in the ethers—no doubt about that. But instead of fear, she felt expectation.

After three deep breaths which brought her down into the silence, she went deeper, then deeper still, until she was able to see intense colors which defied description. Her skin tingled as she visualized white light forming a hazy cocoon of protection around her. Shades of purple and hues of deep blue filled her third eye.

A voice came to her, soft but intense:

"Dearest Daughter, it's been a long journey and you've done well. But now, your world is nearly out of time. Call your family together. Bring them home to you. To Wind Dancer. Prepare a bonfire. And trust. Always trust. Offer prayers that your grandchildren will accomplish their goal in time. Their safety and the souls of so many beings in the Third, Fourth and Fifth Dimensions hang in the balance. Listen to your heart. You must hurry."

When the voice faded, Julie swam up through brilliant hues of indigo and magenta and slowly became aware of her body as she returned from the depths of her trance. She blinked, rubbed her eyes, then shivered.

"Wow," she whispered. "Just ... wow. I've got to find Dave! This is big." Her first few steps were wobbly as she ran for the barn.

"Dave! Where are you? Are you in here?"

"Hey, hon. Yeah, I'm here. In the hen house. You know, we've got some really good layers now." The door creaked as he swung it open. "What's up? Whoa, babe. You're white as a sheet. Come on. Come sit down." He led her out and sat her down on a bail of hay. "What's happened, Julie?"

"Oh, Dave ... I just had the most amazing ... message? Visitation? I'm pretty sure it was Gabriel speaking, and now, I'm more concerned about the kids than ever." As her eyes spilled over and her breath hitched, Dave held her close. She recited the message for him, word for word.

When she finished, Dave lifted her chin and looked deeply into her eyes. His voice was gentle. "It'll be okay, babe. Remember all the love and faith and trust we have for each other? For the whole family? Well, concentrate on that. First thing is to gather everyone here. We're all powerful people, but together, we're a force to be reckoned with. And we've done this stuff before, right? Jerry and I will start gathering wood out in the meadow. You alert the troops."

"But why? Why do we need to send group prayers? Why do we have to do it all so fast? What's wrong? And why do we need a bonfire?" She knew she sounded like one of the grandkids when they were badly in need of a nap, but dammit, it had been such a nice day. And now ... this.

As usual, Dave provided the perfect balance. "If I knew the answers to those questions, we wouldn't need guidance from angels," he smiled. "Let's just get busy. You and Jeannie do your thing, and Jerry and I will do ours. Josh can help us. But let's make it an adventure. We don't want to create any fear in him. Deal?"

Struggling to center herself, Julie wiped her watery eyes and met Dave's calm, loving ones. "Yes. It's a deal. What would I do without you?"

"You don't have to worry about that, love, 'cause I'm yours for the duration. Now get going!"

"On my way!" And giving him a quick kiss, she ran back up the path to the house.

As they'd planned, the topmost golden step said *See the Light.* Standing there, looking at it, Jesse saw lots of light, but felt only frustration when he pushed his hand against the shimmering, but very solid, ceiling above his head.

"Any ideas, guys? This whole place is trembling, but it looks like we've hit another dead end."

Angela, enthusiastic as a cheerleader and stubborn as a mule, stepped up to scold her men again. "Come on, guys. We're here. We found the entrance. We opened the door. We found the tablets. We've built the staircase. This is just one more test. But we do need to figure it out fast 'cause I can hear banging on that door down there, and I think your witch pal is right behind us."

"We can't let that kind of evil energy get in here!" said Mike. "It would be a disaster. Come on. Think. There has to be a way through this ceiling."

"Hey guys ..." Joey, who had been quietly turning on his step, examining everything, taking everything in, was pointing. "Something's happening! Hey! Whoa! Look at the steps. That top one you're on, Jess, is getting wider. It's growing!"

"Look at that," said Angela. "It's big enough to hold all of us, even Sam. There must be a reason. Come on, gang, move. Let's get up there."

They didn't question her—it felt too right to question—but after they'd all moved up and were standing close together, it was hard not to be disappointed when nothing else happened.

They shuffled a bit, not really looking each other in the eye, afraid they might see their own fears reflected there. The vibrations were still increasing as the banging from below grew louder.

Sam looked from one to the other, then looked up at the ceiling, then looked down at the engraved gold tablet they were perched on. He scratched at the engraved words with his paw. Angela glanced down and absentmindedly scratched his neck. Sam scratched at the words again, several times.

"Sam." Angela's tone carried a warning.

Sam attacked the words, his front paws digging like pistons.

"Sam! Don't do that. You'll make marks on it."

Sam kept right on digging, giving Angela a look which screamed, "COME ON! PAY ATTENTION HERE!"

The pounding on the door grew louder still, and blue smoke began to creep in around the edges.

Angela dropped to her knees and grabbed at Sam's paws in an effort to stop him from digging. As she did, her fingers touched the engraved letters. "Oh dear God! That's it! Well, I think it's it! Possibly ... anyway."

"Well, spill it," said Joey.

"Clue us in," ordered Mike.

"And please make it fast," Jesse added.

"We're standing, all of us, on a profound saying. *See the Light*. And Sam is working his paws to the bone to get us to pay attention to that. Just that. What if, all together, we chant it—like a mantra?"

"Nothing to lose. Come on. Sam's in the middle," directed Jesse. "Here we go. On the count of three. One, two, three! *See the Light! See the Light! See the Light!"*

The chant resounded, echoing through the golden space. When Sam began howling along with his pack, the banging ceased and the smoke dissolved. They repeated the words over and over again until the chant filled them, and then, the Light ramped up. It came from everywhere, surrounding them in brilliant powerful energy.

"See the Light! See the Light!"

"Look! We did it!" Angela dropped to her knees, thrilled to feel solid floor beneath her. "We're in a different pyramid. We got through the ceiling!"

"Good going, Angie. You called it," said Jesse.

"With Sam's help. Spirit guide—animal guide. Sometimes they're the same thing." She buried her face in Sam's neck as he happily washed her ear.

"All right. Now what?" asked Jesse. "Where are we? What do we do next? I feel like a clock's ticking in my head. Maybe it's the vibrations, but I don't think we have a lot of time." He looked around. "So now we're in a smaller pyramid. Gold, like the first one. Do you see any more tiles to make more stairs?"

Running his fingers through his hair, he closed his eyes. "I remember seeing three pyramids with Grandma, but I couldn't see details. Heck, we were both in shock, and the vision was just a flash. But I think there's something up there, up above us, and we have to *get* to it."

He started pacing, back and forth, rubbing his head as the tension built. "Where the heck is Dorado? If we're supposedly helping to save mankind, it sure would be great to have a little more information."

At the end of his rope and wondering if mankind was, too, Jesse dropped to his knees. "Please, God. Send us your angels. We've made it this far, but now, we could really use some guidance!"

* * *

The family began gathering when they received Julie's summons. And it was just that. No calm invitation this time, not that they hadn't expected it. Most of them were already experiencing a sense of great urgency with glimpses of impending change.

It was the kind of premonition that makes you feel "antsy" as Jon so succinctly put it. For hours, he hadn't been able to sit still, couldn't concentrate on his magical stories for Mandy and Scott, couldn't settle enough to manage a contact with Ekor—and he was getting on Sara's nerves.

When his mother's message reached him, he quickly gathered up Sara and the kids, then scooped up Walter and Emily for good measure. Explaining what Julie had shared, Jon readied them for the emergency meeting. They left the orphanage in the capable hands of the well-trained and loving staff and arrived moments later at Wind Dancer Ranch.

Joshua was thrilled to have his young cousins back again and danced around, singing "shift, shift, shift." Within minutes, they were all hard at work gathering wood for the bonfire.

The tension kept on building as the rest of the family arrived. Chris and Ellen pitched in with preparing food in the kitchen and making sure the youngsters had occasional rest breaks. It was obvious that Bill and Kathy, concerned about Joey, were doing their best to hold it together. Erica was sticking close, being strong for her parents and keeping her energies positive for her brother.

It was touch and go when Steve and Megan arrived. Julie and Dave were mightily impressed to see Jeannie and Jerry greet the other two sets of parents, all of them with tears in their eyes as they shared a few words, then got right back to business.

Long hours later, Dave cornered his wife as he came back for more water and a few more snacks. "Have you gotten any more information,

Julie? Do we know what to do next? We've got enough ammunition to have one heck of a fire, but when should we light it? Do you think we need to do a ritual or prayer or something first?"

"I wish I knew, Dave. Everyone's so on edge. It's too dark to find more wood, but no one wants to quit working. I'm thinking it's time to gather everyone in the meadow. We'll do a meditation. Send out some prayers for the world, and for our grandkids. And then we'll light it. Beyond that, only God knows."

"It's a plan. I'll get everyone. I love you, babe. See you in the meadow."

"Love you, too, honey. Hurry!"

Angela was close to tears. Again. They'd gone through so much, tried so hard to do the right thing; to complete their assigned mission. The mission that would change so many lives, and make a positive change in three dimensions. But they simply couldn't find a single, solitary clue for the next step.

They were trapped in a big golden room—a pyramid without any visible doors or windows. Her buddies were pacing, working their way out to the edges, as Sam sniffed for something that they couldn't find—if it was there to be found. Discouraged, they re-assembled in the middle.

"I'm just plain exhausted right now," said Jesse, stretching out on his back. "These vibrations are so strong they really hurt, and I'm feeling dizzy." Using his arms for a pillow, he sighed and started to close his eyes, but before he could blink, he jumped up, pointing and exclaiming, "Hey! Look up there. Right above us. Is that some kind of clock?"

"It's huge!" said Angela. "I didn't even see it before. And look. It's ticking in time to the vibrations."

"Is this an illusion?" asked Mike. "Because if it is, the illusion reads 11:50. You think maybe we're supposed to do something when the clock strikes twelve? And I'm really hoping that we're all about New Years and new beginnings, and not turning into a pumpkin!"

"New Years or pumpkins, it's all about the next step. Gabriel's depending on us and—"

Jesse stopped when the rumbling started. A low rumble at first, growing louder as the whole pyramid began to tremble. "What the heck? Do you all feel that? Do you hear it?"

"The time has come, young friends. You've been very brave and accomplished a great deal. You must not give up."

"Who is that? Is it Gabriel? It is. I know it is." Jesse was frantic. "Can you help us?" Whether in their heads or their hearts, each of the cousins heard Gabriel's voice.

"Yes, Jesse, you are quite correct. Listen carefully. The final pyramid is actually a very large capstone. It's pure crystal energy and holds unimaginable power. It must be awakened, and you four have been chosen to awaken it. There are others around your world, chosen to awaken other crystals simultaneously. Coordinating this has been a challenge for all Spirit Beings. Dorado has served as my assistant, teaching and training you for many years. He's with your family now, guiding them so they may help you accomplish your goal."

"But what are we supposed to do? How do we awaken a huge and powerful crystal?" asked Angela.

"Dear child, you've managed all the steps which brought you to this place at this time. Your bodies have changed. Your minds have changed. See the Light and embrace the final change. See the Light, then ..."

"Be the Light!" They shouted in one voice.

The rumbling grew louder, tremors increasing in intensity until they were sure the whole structure would simply shake apart and possibly the whole world with it. The clock ticked away the final seconds as Jesse grasped his crystals and reached out to Mike. Mike closed his hand over Jesse's crystals and held his own out to Angela. She laid her hand over them and offered hers to Joey, who, in turn, completed the circle, extending his to Jesse. When Jesse's hand completed the connection, all four cousins, and Sam in his usual spot in the middle, began to glow with brilliant light.

"It's time! Do it now! *BE THE LIGHT!*"

The bonfire was enormous. As they had during the EarthShift, the vibrations had intensified until it was nearly impossible to stand against them. The movement was violent. Everyone was struggling to stay positive; to control their fears so the energies they sent would all be positive.

When Dorado appeared, their gratitude was immeasurable, but it still didn't measure up to the family's concern for the kids. E.T. or not, questions flew from all directions.

"Where are the kids?"

"Are they all right?"

"What's happening right now?"

"What's going to happen?"

"Is this an earthquake?"

"What can we do to help?"

"Please, please, my dear friends, and you, too, little ones. I can't give you answers, quite simply because I don't know them. I will tell you that the young people on this mission did an admirable job up to the point when I could no longer follow them. Be proud of them and of yourselves."

"We are proud, but why did you have to stop being with them?" Julie demanded.

"What might or might not happen is in other hands. You've all been experiencing symptoms of the on-going Shifts for years. You have no idea how far you've come already. But now, we're going to be dealing with the enormous changes that will accompany the next big one if, indeed, it's successful. There's nothing to be done right now except to send prayers. Prayers for your children. Prayers for mankind. We, in our realm, are doing all we can to help. Major adjustments to life are on the way. One way or another, good or bad.

"I'm not sure whether anything I've said has been helpful or more distressing, but I do love you all. And yes, it certainly is rumbling and rocking in your dimension! I must go now. Keep that fire burning bright!"

The energy Jesse and his team were expending was enormous. Eyes closed, holding hands, they *Became the Light* and filled the pyramid with the brilliance of the sun. Deep reverberating sound rolled up through the golden walls, and the floor beneath them shook violently.

But Jesse, his cousins and Sam were experiencing a sense of consummate peace as the light poured out of them and flowed up into the crystal pyramid where it spread and grew until it achieved critical mass, flashing out in all directions to combine with the energies of other crystals at points across the globe.

The darkness in the meadow deepened to pitch-black, relieved only by the fire. It didn't matter. The family was deep in prayer. But as the minutes ticked down toward midnight, the fire rose up, hotter, brighter, and brighter still, until Dave became aware of it on a conscious level. When he opened his eyes to make sure it was still under control, his gaze was immediately drawn to the peak of Crystal Mountain.

"Oh, my God!" he yelled, horrified. "Look at the mountain! Oh, God, the kids are up there!"

What Dave had thought was an explosive volcano was altogether different when his eyes adjusted. In reality, the top of the mountain had simply peeled away. Disintegrated totally. And the glow from within illuminated the night sky.

"It's magnificent," breathed Julie as she squeezed his hand. "It's the vision Jesse and I had years ago—the golden pyramids. We thought there were three, but now I can see that the top one is like a capstone. And, yes, I think it's a crystal, an enormous, radiant, dazzling crystal. Look. Something is bursting out of the top! What is it?"

Jon spoke quietly. "I keep hearing words. Listen, everyone. Listen."

"Daddy, I hear *Love*." said Scott.

"And I hear *Peace*,'" sighed Mandy.

Josh was not to be outdone. "I hear *Laugh*," he announced, and proceeded to do just that.

Erica had been keeping herself strictly controlled, but now she turned and addressed the group. "That crystal is sending us—sending everyone—*Light*. It's *Light* filled with words to live by in the new dimension. *Light* to expand our consciousness and realign our souls. Hey! That means they did it! The kids did it!"

Soon everyone was jumping up and down with joy and happiness. "I can't believe it!" said Julie. "No, wait. I just heard *Believe*. Of course, I believe it! Wow! This is going to change the world, maybe the universe! But ... where are the kids?"

As her voice rose and quavered, Dave realized that between stress and emotions, Julie was balanced on the tipping point of hysteria. As he had in other places, other situations, in so many other lifetimes, he took the situation in hand. Taking her shoulders, he pulled his wife back against his body, and cradled her head against his chest. Then he wrapped his arms around her and began to hum in her ear.

Safe, secure, Julie's system leveled and she relaxed, closing her eyes and smiling as she recognized the song Dave was singing, and immediately she picked up the melody. Music coursed like an electrical charge around the fire, scattering any residual negativity and bringing everyone into harmony.

This little light o'mine, I'm gonna let it shine.
This little light o'mine, I'm gonna let it shine.
This little light o'mine, I'm gonna let it shine.
Let it shine, let it shine, let it shine.

Jess stirred first. Rolled over. Groaned. "Oh, man ... What happened? Guys? Hey ... is everyone okay?"

Slowly, they began to move and stretch, and eventually everyone managed to struggle into a sitting position. Angela found her voice,.

"Look ... look up there. We did it in time! We became the *Light* and we are *Light*. I'll bet we always will be!"

Joey stared in wonder. "That's some crystal up there."

Gabriel's voice boomed through the pyramid.

"I commend your success, my children. The full scope of what you have accomplished is not yet comprehensible to you, but you'll feel the effects in wondrous ways. Know this—the evil which threatened the balance of this world has been banished. People who were ready to make the transition to the Fifth Dimension have now done so. Many are finding their lost children even now. You will never again face the darkness of the Third Dimension. You've all enjoyed many gifts from the first big Shift when you were young. Now you will have many more. The wisdom which brought you here has been released throughout your world in the Shift of the Ages. The door has been opened. You awakened the Crystal of Light, and Earth will flourish under its influence. Go in peace and love, dear

ones. I leave you now."

For a few minutes they sat in absolute silence.

Until Joey just couldn't stand it any longer. "Okay," he said, running his hands through his hair. "I'm pretty much speechless. And, man, am I ever hungry!"

Mike burst out laughing. "That's our Joey, an honest comment, straight from the heart—and the stomach."

"It's time for us to go," smiled Angela. "How about it, Jesse? One more step to guide us through. Let's go home."

Jesse's smile lit the room for a second time. He cleared his throat and took a deep breath. "Join hands. All set, Sam? Good boy. Right where you belong, right in the middle."

"It's true, you know. Just like we were told. Something's shifted inside us. I can feel it in my soul," smiled Angela.

Surrounded by Light, much of it their own, the cousins began the journey home.

"We're going to visualize. Close your eyes. We'll see the light again, only this time, it's a big bonfire. I have a feeling that's what will bring us home." He looked around his circle and gave thanks for the strength and love of his family. "A bonfire of celebration. And love."

And it did.

We shall find peace.
We shall hear the angels,
We shall see the sky sparkling with diamonds.

Anton Chekhov (1860-1904)

FINIS

About the Author

Judith Horky has had a passion for the written word since grade school. After raising her family, Judy returned to the University of Nevada-Reno to pursue a degree in journalism. Her last class—TV production—resulted in a teaching position at the university, which turned her life around, opening the door to freelance work as a producer, associate director and stage manager.

At the same time, a friend introduced her to the metaphysical world, another life altering experience which launched her search for understanding. Her spiritual journey continues to this day.

In 1987, Judy and her husband, Jim, formed Sweetwater Video Production Services in Los Angeles. After many years of entrepreneurial challenges, Sweetwater was sold, allowing Judy the time to fulfill her lifelong dream. To write.

EarthShift was born in 2001 and is now followed by its sequel, *Soul Shift—2012 and Beyond*.

Judy and Jim live with their pound puppy, Jesse, in Southern Colorado, surrounded by sparkling lakes, majestic pines, colorful aspens, and the magnificent mountains they love.

Made in the USA
Charleston, SC
07 November 2010